Dawn of Darkness

The Legends of Ophir: Book I

DANIEL RUSSELL

ISBN 978-1-955156-58-5 (paperback)
ISBN 978-1-955156-59-2 (digital)

Rushmore Press LLC
1 800 460 9188
www.rushmorepress.com

Printed in the United States of America

To my loving wife Elisabeth.

You always made me believe the stars
were only a pen stroke away.

Note to the Reader

As a young boy growing up, I loved reading the stories of the Old Testament. I would use my imagination to put myself into those biblical narratives. I imagined being there, a quiet observer, as God created the heavens and the earth and all therein. I imagined walking behind God and Adam as they explored the Garden of Eden together. I watched in fascination as the Creator of the universe performed the world's first surgery and removed one of Adam's ribs to create Eve.

My creativity took me to the days of Noah and the great ark. With my eyes closed, I experienced the pitch and sway of the massive ship as it rode the angry waters that flooded the entire earth. I imagined journeying through the arid lands of the Middle East as Abraham learned of his promise from God to become the father of many nations. I cried out with Joseph as he was mistreated time and time again and rejoiced with him when God blessed him for his continual sacrifice. I mourned and felt the pain of God's chosen people as the Egyptians drove them into slavery. I feared and humbled myself before the great *I Am* when He appeared to Moses in the burning bush. I was in awe of the power of a mighty God as I imagined accompanying Moses and Aaron, watching them display the strength of God to all the Egyptians. My imagination journeyed with the Israelite people when they wandered the desert for forty years. I ran alongside Joshua and Caleb when they discovered giants in the land of Canaan. I could feel their courage to fight for what God had given them, even when no one else would stand with them. In my mind, I traveled with Joshua, the warlord of Israel, on every one of his conquests. I fought beside him, sword in one hand and shield in the other, as we took on the Amorites, Hittites, Canaanites, Jebusites, and a whole bunch of other "ites". Nation by nation, God gave them over into our hands.

As I read the Stories of old, my imagination took me to the days of the kings. I looked on in amazement as a red haired, teenage boy killed a giant with a mere sling and a stone. And then, many years later, when that boy grew to become a man, I cheered along with the crowd as David, the greatest warrior in Israel, was crowned king! I became enthralled with the abilities of King David and his mighty men. No other warriors in history could compare to these men. Although, what spoke to my heart the most was not how many battles and wars David had won, but his deep passionate relationship with God. It was his heart that made him great.

When King David died, I watched with bated breath as young Solomon took on his father's legacy. I hoped and prayed the prince would live up to his father's reputation.

Solomon did not disappoint.

The new king brought in forty years of peace and prosperity to the nation of Israel. The world revered him as the wisest man that ever lived (well...except for one).

It was during my readings of Solomon's reign that I came across something interesting, something that sparked my imagination to new heights. The Holy Scriptures say this in 2 Chronicles 8:17-18:

> *Then went Solomon to Eziongeber, and to Eloth, at the sea side in the land of Edom. And Huram sent him by the hands of his servants ships, and servants that had knowledge of the sea; and they went with the servants of Solomon to Ophir, and took thence four hundred and fifty talents of gold, and brought them to king Solomon.*

And then in 1 Kings 10:11-12:

> *And the navy also of Hiram, that brought gold from Ophir, brought in from Ophir great plenty of almug trees, and precious stones. And the king made of the almug trees pillars for the house of the Lord, and for the king's house, harps also and psalteries for singers: there came no such almug trees, nor were seen unto this day.*

Only twelve times in all of Scripture is Ophir mentioned. Each time, the place is described as having vast amounts of wealth and gold in a heavily forested area of algum trees. To this day, no one knows the location of Ophir. Many men have searched for the famed treasure trove of riches and have failed in their endeavors.

Immediately my mind began asking questions like: Where was Ophir? Where did it get its gold? Was Ophir a mining area or was it a city? What was the journey like? Who went on this adventure? Was the trip dangerous? Did they have opposition? And more importantly, what were algum trees?

It was through my search to answer these questions that my imagination developed the very story you are about to read. With that being said, it is important to remember that **this book is a work of fiction. Please read it as such**. Many of the characters within this tale are based on actual biblical people that lived real lives during the time of King Solomon. I have taken an imaginative liberty to place them in a story that is fiction. Although, you will find that there are several truthful facts, occurrences, and Scriptural passages within the narrative that gives the book a greater sense of credibility.

It is also fair to warn you that I have kept this book true to the time period, which includes descriptions of war, various battles, and scenes of pagan rituals that plagued the surrounding nations of Israel during Solomon's reign. Needless to say, some of the scenes are violent and are not appropriate for younger readers.

To make your reading experience more enjoyable, I have included a map, a measurement chart, and a glossary to help you identify some of the terminology used commonly back then.

This is a story created to bring out your sense of adventure, to test the limits of your imagination, to explore the bounds of your creativity, and to fuel the passions of your desire to love.

I pray that you will enjoy reading this book as much as I did writing it.

May Christ's blessings be upon you!

Daniel Russell

<u>*Ancient Measurements of Israel*</u>

Bath	9 gallons
Cubit	18 inches
Handbreadth	3-6 inches
Kor	6.25 bushels
League	3.5 miles
Season	1 year
Shekel	A coin, .5 ounces
Talent	90 lbs

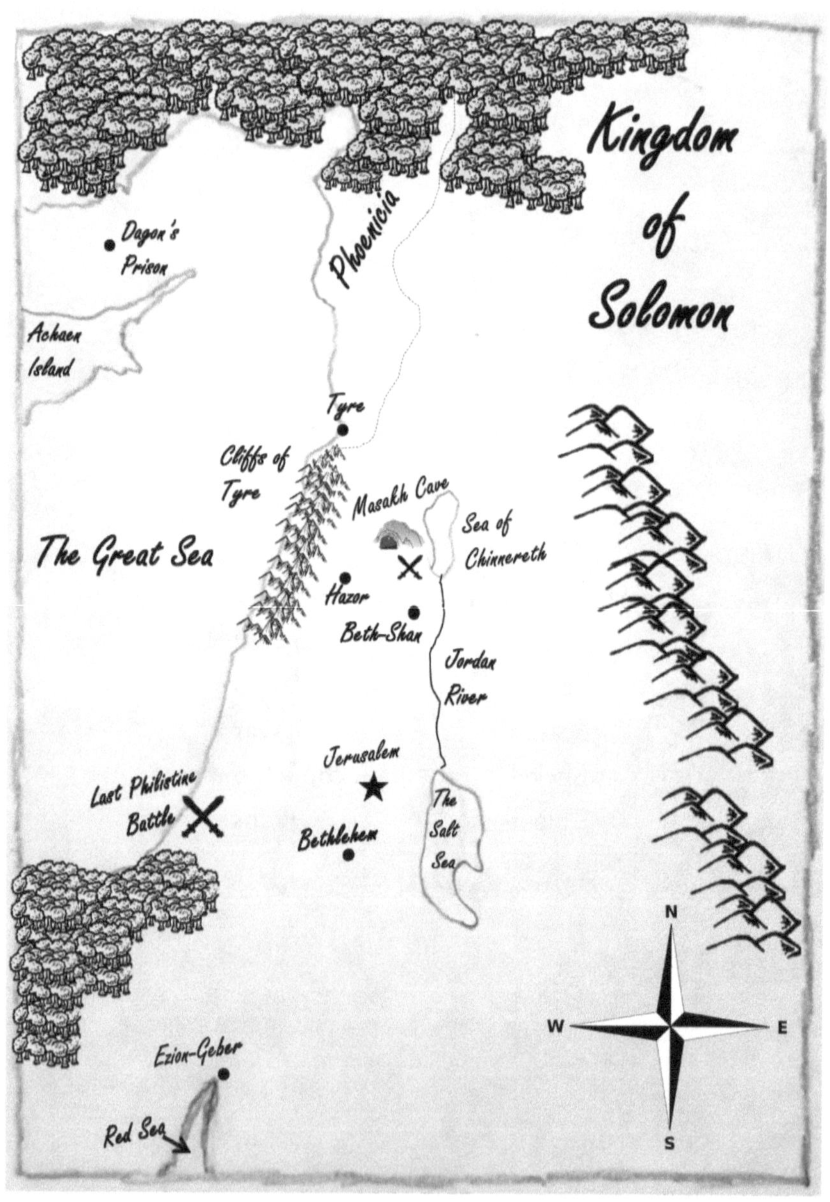

-Map taken from the scrolls of Zadok
the Priest, 5th Age, 81st Season

PROLOGUE

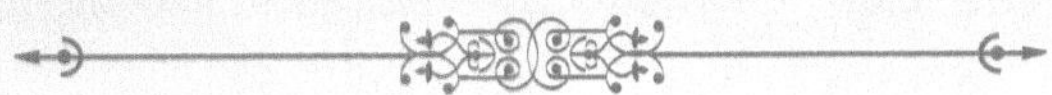

Michael the archangel, the commander of the host of El, hovered high above the heavens and watched as the devastation of El's creation commenced. He felt a mixture of emotions within him as he witnessed his brethren carry out the wrath of El by pulling the landmass of Elysium apart. Tens of thousands of pressurized geysers began to erupt over the entire planet, followed by explosions of molten rock and hot poisonous gasses. He then watched one of the mighty angels from the stars, Sahar, force the moon closer to the earth. Instantly the waters of the globe grew wild and angry. Mountainous waves erupted from the depths of the seas and traveled violently across the surface of the earth, destroying everything in their path. It was then that the ocean encompassing the planet broke and fell in torrential rains, consuming every inch of the earth's atmosphere.

Even though Michael was leagues above the imploding planet, he could see and hear the wails of the children of Cain as the floods of destruction came upon them. It was hard to find pity for the wretched souls as every one of them had turned from El long ago.

Tuning out the cries of the dying, Michael focused his sight towards the heart of Elysium. There sat a large vessel made of gopher wood. Inside was Noah, a child of El, and his family; the remnant of those who were faithful to the one true God, and had not fallen away to false gods.

"

A century ago, Michael had disguised himself as one of Noah's workers to help construct the life-saving ark, even though his main mission had been to protect the children of El from the evil and violence of the sons of Cain. The people of the earth had indeed grown wicked, so wicked in fact, that many of the tribes were sacrificing their own children to demons. The corrupt mortals had held blood festivals in which they drank the children's blood and ate their flesh. The hearts of men had become black and perverse, and the light of El was no longer in them.

The ark pitched to the side as the first of many waves crashed into it. The vessel that Noah had spent over a hundred seasons building finally fulfilled its purpose as it lifted up off the ground and began to float upon the flooding waters. As soon as the ship began to move, Michael saw a blinding light erupt from his right. Two bright beams of star-light broke away from the heavens and come shooting down towards the earth. They were two seraphim, high ranking angels, charged with protecting the holiness of El. The seraphim were massive creatures with six wings, each wing aflame with a holy fire that burned bright red and white. No creature with an unclean heart or tainted soul could stand before these protectors and live. They were created out of the very holiness of El. Their orders were to let no evil, man or demon, touch the family of Noah and to protect them at all cost.

As the seraphim rocketed towards the planet's surface, they left a trail of blazing fire in their wake. To a mortal's eye, the two giant angels would look like stars from the heavens that were on their way to collide with the earth. After breaking through the falling ocean of the sky, the seraphim spread their flaming wings, and with all grace, landed atop the ark. Between the two of them, their wing-span covered the entire length of the vessel from bow to stern.

As soon as the seraphim were in place, the ark leveled out and gently bobbed in the water, even as the rising flood became more and more violent. Angry waves of water accosted the ship from all sides, but the power of the seraphim caused the crushing breakers to disperse, leaving no harm to Noah's vessel.

Michael continued to watch the ark rise in the raging waters and noticed a few small fishing boats approaching the side of the ship's hull. Some of the men from the tiny craft were trying to climb up the side of the ark, but as soon as they touched the ark's hull they instantly died due to the presence of the seraphim. Michael thought of the irony of the whole scene. If only those men would repent of their sins and turn their hearts back to the Creator, El would actually let them board the ship, and the power of the seraphim would not affect them. But it was not to be. Every last person on those tiny vessels died trying to escape their fate. It was then that a crushing wave dashed into the side of the ark, obliterating the fishing boats. One moment they were there, and the next moment they were gone.

"Are the sons of Cain still attempting to get into the ark?" came a voice behind Michael.

"A few," Michael said to his second in command, Labroth. "But with the seraphim in place, none will succeed unless they are found worthy." Keeping his eyes on the scene below, he asked, "What is the status on capturing the five demon lords that started this whole mess?"

"We have imprisoned four of them, but Prince Dagon still eludes us."

Michael nodded. "We knew he would be the hardest one to capture. After all, he is a water demon and we have given him plenty of water to hide in."

"So how do we find him?"

"He will show himself. El has revealed this to me. Demons are predictable when it comes to their pride. Dagon will attempt to destroy the ark to get rid of the children of El once and for all."

Labroth smiled faintly and shook his head. "He would be a fool to do so with the seraphim present. They could easily annihilate him."

"And yet, he will still try. However, El doesn't want him destroyed. Our Lord has plans for him in the future."

Just as predicted, about one league south of Noah's ship, the demon, Dagon, emerged from the pitching waters in the shape of a great sea dragon, a leviathan. With all haste, the demon took to the air and flapped his powerful wings in the direction of Noah's ark. Dagon released a mighty roar, announcing his presence to all that would hear.

Labroth pulled his double bladed sword out from behind him and it ignited into a deep blue flame. Michael opened his right hand and a bright white chain appeared within it. In the blink of an eye, the two warrior angels shot down to the earth, their wings ablaze with holy fury.

Just as Dagon was about to reach the ark, Michael and Labroth slammed hard into the leviathan's back, causing all three of them to plunge deep into the waters below. The two angels continued to force the ancient demon downward until they smashed him into the ocean floor. The impact caused the crust of the earth to crack open and lava began to spew forth.

Barely phased by the crushing blow, the great beast struck the two angels with his mighty tail and sent them soaring through the muddied waters. Recovering quickly, Labroth re-engaged the demon, lashing out with his blazing sword. With each strike he landed, Dagon parried with his long, razor-sharp claws.

"Do you really think you can beat me?" roared Dagon. "I am a god among men and all creatures worship me! One day, even you will bow before me!"

"Has your pride blinded you even now?" Labroth yelled back as he blocked an incoming strike from the leviathan's tail. "How can you be a god when there are no men left to worship you? All those that would follow you are dead or scattered! It is over!"

"It will never be over!" Roared Dagon, as he found an opening in Labroth's defense and delivered a crushing blow to the angel's face, sending him flying backwards through the murky waters.

Instead of taking the advantage and finishing off his opponent, Dagon swam upwards towards the water's surface to finish his mission: destroy the ark and the children of El. Just as he began his ascent, a bright glowing chain of white erupted out of the darkness of the depths and wrapped around the dragon's heaving frame, preventing him from moving any further.

"No!" Dagon roared out. "You cannot stop me! Release me! Now!"

Michael arose from the black waters beneath Dagon, holding the other end of the chain. He pulled the metal whip hard and yanked the demon back down towards himself. As soon as Dagon was in reach, the avenging archangel struck the dragon's head with his left fist while clenching the chain tight in his right. The impact of the blow sent a shock wave through the water in all directions.

Dagon felt all the strength in his body leave him, causing his arms, legs, and tail to go limp.

Yanking the demon's chain once more, Michael brought the beast close to his face. "This is over! Any last words before El's judgment is done?"

Slowly grinning, Dagon revealed several rows of razor sharp teeth before answering, "Go to hell, Michael."

"No, Dagon, it is you who are damned."

Michael pushed Dagon away from him and whipped the chain in a circular arc around the demon. The links of the chain ignited and became alive, wrapping itself around Dagon's entire body. In a matter of moments the demon was encased in a massive, white cocoon. The chain began to constrict and glow white-hot, as if the sun was being born within the depths of the sea.

"No! Stop! It burns! Release me!" The dragon raged as the flames of righteousness burrowed through and around him. "I will not be—"

The demon was silenced when the blinding light encasing him exploded, pushing the waters back in all directions, creating a giant pocket of space within the sea.

Holding up his right hand, Michael called out, "Shalom!"

The ocean obeyed his voice and refrained from closing back in on them, leaving the dome empty and void.

Drawing up next to Michael, Labroth watched the condemning chain finish its work. The light began to diminish and the shape of a crystallized, diamond pillar took its place. Dagon could be seen within, pounding madly at the walls of his newly formed prison cell. He yelled and swore every curse he knew, but it was to no avail. His fate was sealed.

Michael approached the giant colonnade, which was now suspended vertically in the air. He put his callused hand upon the jeweled structure and gazed intently at his prisoner. "You brought this upon yourself. We were once allies…brothers! But you chose to follow the Deceiver. Why?"

A smile broke across the demon's lips before he answered, "You are such a fool, Michael! You are such a puppet in the hands of a foolish God! He doesn't care about you. All he cares about are his precious, weak, little children whom he made in his own image. I followed Luce because he showed me truth! He showed me freedom!"

"And what truth is that, Dagon?"

"That *we* are the gods! That *we* are the ones that deserve to be worshiped! Not Him!" The demon spat back.

Michael shook his head and his face betrayed pity. "No, my old friend. Luce has only led you to this cage. You have neither truth nor freedom. Like so many others, he has deceived you." he said, tapping on the diamond. "Good-bye, Dagon."

After grabbing the pillar with both hands, Michael threw the prison downwards and it pierced into the molten lava that was seeping out of the sea floor. Cubit by cubit, Dagon's new home sank into the depths of the earth.

Just before the very last bit of Dagon's cage was covered by the hot liquid rock, Dagon screamed out, "I will have my revenge, Michael! Do you hear me? I will return and destroy all that El holds dear! I will steal, kill, and destroy them all!"

PART I

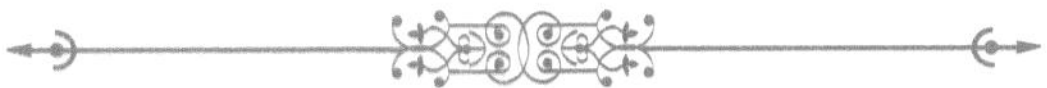

"I will cast thee as profane
out of the mountain of God:
and I will destroy thee, O covering cherub,
from the midst of the stones of fire.

Thine heart was lifted up because of thy beauty,
thou hast corrupted thy wisdom
by reason of thy brightness:
I will cast thee to the ground,
I will lay thee before kings,
that they may behold thee.

Thou hast defiled thy sanctuaries
by the multitude of thine iniquities,
by the iniquity of thy traffick;
therefore will I bring forth a fire
from the midst of thee, it shall devour thee,
and I will bring thee to ashes upon the earth
in the sight of all them that behold thee.

All they that know thee among the people
shall be astonished at thee:
thou shalt be a terror,
and never shalt thou be any more."

-Ezekiel – The Prophet of Bones, 5th Age, 483rd Season

Chapter 1

Abaddon felt every muscle in his body scream for rest.

It had been three days since the beginning of the final assault with the Philistines. It was the battle to end over a hundred years of war, and both sides had been relentless. The Israelites had finally pinned their enemies down to a small section of land against the Great Sea and were looking to wipe them off the face of the earth.

The Philistines knew that their extinction was close at hand, and were fighting back like cornered animals, desperate to survive. Both sides had suffered heavy losses and the bodies had begun to stack up within the valley. A respite was called to clear out the dead and possibly make some negotiations, possibly but not likely.

Abaddon was thankful for the rest, even if it was for only a few hours. He had found a large, flat rock next to the Israeli camp and plopped down upon it, grateful to be off his feet. He jammed his sword into the earth in front of him and rested his head on the hilt, the only part that was not stained with blood. He stared down the length of the sword's blade and saw fresh blood from his latest kill making its way to the ground. The red liquid ran as if it were seeking shelter from the cold, sharp metal that had robbed it from its safe, warm home.

Giving out a sigh, Abaddon tossed his long, black, blood stained hair out his eyes and examined the carnage scattered in the valley before him.

How many bodies are lying out there because of me? thought Abaddon.

Too many to count, and to be honest, he didn't *really* care. He just wanted this battle to be over.

Abaddon watched wearily as warriors searched the valley below for their fallen brothers in arms. He could hear the cries and wails of soldiers, women, and children as they found their loved ones. Abaddon felt a pain of sympathy for the mourners, but at the same time he was thankful. He never had to worry about looking for dead loved ones, because the few people he cared about were too skilled in battle to be killed. He was probably the best Israel had ever seen wield a sword. Nobody would be looking for him lying in the field below.

Looking back down at his sword, Abaddon noticed that the fresh blood had made it to the ground and pooled there. He watched as the thick, red liquid slowly disappeared into the dry, thirsty earth.

The sight of the blood made Abaddon contemplate its color and its purpose. To the Israelites, blood meant so many different things. On this day, blood represented death. On other days, the sight of blood was a way to worship the Israeli God, El. The sight of that blood represented life, not death. The sacrificial blood of animals was a representation of the covering of the sins of Israel. At least that was what Abaddon had been taught since he was a small boy.

Continuing to stare at the last of the blood on the ground as it drained away, Abaddon whispered to himself, "So is this the blood of death or the blood of life?"

"Abaddon!"

Abaddon's heritage was not entirely Israeli. His father, Josheb, who was a member of King David's personal guard, was actually a Tahchemonite from the lands of the north.

"Abaddon!"

Even though Abaddon had been born and raised in Jerusalem, and had tried to obey his father's teachings and all the Israeli laws, he still felt separated from everyone around him. He still felt like an outsider. Granted, his appearance was different. He had a darker complexion, black, wavy hair, and dark-blue eyes with a faint scar over his right eye.

"Abaddon!"

He had always had that scar, even when he was young. Abaddon asked his father once how he got the mark, and all his father told him was, "You are a gift from God, and God needs you to stand out to the world. He has great plans for you, my son."

His father told him not to bring it up again.

"Abaddon! Hey, what is with you? Didn't you hear me? I have been calling out for you! Quit staring at the ground and look at me!"

Abaddon snapped out of his trance and looked up.

There stood his captain, Broc. Actually, his name was Brocemediusnenlias, from the tribe of Benjamin, but that was always too much of a mouthful, so Abaddon had shortened it to just Broc. The name stuck and now everyone called him by his new nickname. The captain didn't seem to mind.

Broc's tall, wide frame blocked out the sun and cast a looming shadow over Abaddon. "Boy! I ought to beat you with a birch branch! What is the first thing your father and I taught you when you step off the battlefield?"

Abaddon smirked and rolled his eyes, but then jumped when he felt Broc grab the sash that was tied around his waist and rip it off.

"Clean your sword, and have some respect for those who have fallen today!" His elder barked as he threw the sash on Abaddon's head. "The war council is meeting and I want you to be there. After you have cleaned your weapon, go dunk your head in a bucket of water to wash the blood and mud off your face. You look like you have been swimming in a pile of guts!"

Abaddon sighed a, "Yes, sir." He took the edge of his sash and began to clean his blade as ordered.

Moments later, a much cleaner Abaddon started to walk toward the command tent. He only got a few strides in when the most disturbing voice he had ever heard bellowed out from the valley. Each word made Abaddon's chest vibrate.

Several Israelite soldiers had begun to line up around the outskirts of the camp to see what the commotion was. Pushing his way through the crowd, Abaddon gained a good view of the battlefield down below.

What he saw next gave him pause. There, standing in the valley, treading in the blood and mud, was a giant of a man. He made the descriptions of Goliath seem minuscule. The giant stood three times taller than the average Israelite and at least three times broader. His arms and legs were like tree trunks of massive muscle. His head alone was larger than Abaddon's own torso.

The Philistine was clad in light leather armor with a gold helm covering his forehead and the back of his neck. This beast was unlike any man that had lived since the days of King David's battle with Goliath.

Abaddon smiled to himself. He had heard about the shepherd king's victory many times in his life. Just like Goliath, this foul mouthed Philistine was taunting Israel to fight, one-on-one, victor takes all.

"You cowards! Is there not even one among you who would call yourself champion? I have lived for thirty-six winters and there has never been a man or beast that can best my blade. Maybe if you can't find one, you can send two or even three! I could use three more heads to decorate the poles on my tent!"

The giant smiled as his words coursed through the cold veins of the Israelites. He knew that his strength was unmatched and his experience was unchallenged. He reveled at the thought of killing any Israelite who may come down the hill to try to make a name for himself.

Somewhere in the crowd of Israelites a brave soul spoke out. "Our king David has bested your kind before, or have you not heard of the *boy* who killed the giant?"

Several of the Israelites began to laugh and mock the Philistine, which only angered him even more. The giant ran toward the hill of Israelites and drew two over-sized sickle swords which had been attached to his back. He stopped his charge after only a few cubits, gaining the effect he was hoping for. Over one thousand Israeli soldiers gasped and retreated backward a few steps. There were only a handful of warriors who did not budge but put their hands to their weapons, one of them being Abaddon.

A burning anger rose up inside of Abaddon. It was all he could do to keep from soaring down into the valley and taking the giant's head for his own war trophy. The only reason he resisted was because he needed the blessing of the war council to engage in a one-on-one battle for state victory.

He was about to turn back toward the council tent to get that very permission when the giant's reverberating voice was heard once again.

"That is what I thought! A nation of cowards! Cowardly people who worship a cowardly God!"

The giant paced the valley floor, and the people began to feel the Philistine's anger burning in his voice.

"You speak of David, the giant killer! Well, where is he now? Some accomplishment in beating the infant Goliath! I have children of my own who could have bested Goliath! Goliath was weak, whereas I, the great Golfriack, am a god among men! Is there no man here willing to challenge a god? Maybe *your* God would fight against me? Oooohhh, that's right. You Israelites believe in a God you cannot even see. How can a God with no form fight your battles?"

"Blasphemy!" came several shouts from the Israelite army.

Without warning, an arrow shot out of nowhere and came whistling down toward the giant. What happened next surprised even Abaddon. In one fluid motion, Golfriack drove his sword into the ground and grabbed the arrow in mid-flight before it could drill into his neck. Then, flipping the projectile around, he threw it like a javelin back at the archer. With deadly accuracy, the arrow flew forty cubits and plunged into the archer's chest with a loud thud.

All fell silent.

Only the crows squawking overhead could be heard. Not a sound was made except for the guttural tone Golfriack was making with his throat, a sound of deviant satisfaction.

All eyes were glued on the bowman. No one could believe what they had just witnessed. The archer himself stood in shock, eyes staring forward, until his knees gave way to the ground. The pour soul toppled over. Dead.

As if the giant had commanded it, everyone turned their attention back to him. He retrieved his weapon and began laughing, waiving his swords in the air, challenging another arrow to come his way.

"That's it." Abaddon said underneath his breath. "I'm going to kill him, with or without the council's permission." He drew his sword and took one step forward before someone grabbed his arm and pulled him back.

"You coward, let go of me! That slab of meat in the valley is mine!" Abaddon said as he pried the hand off his elbow and turned to look at who would dare try to stop him.

There stood Broc, looking not at Abaddon but at the giant below. His eyes were fixed like everyone else's, not believing the size of the brute.

"Well, I haven't killed one that big before," Broc said shaking his head and once again pulling Abaddon back towards him.

"If you would stop pulling me back, I can show you how it's done," Abaddon said, freeing his arm once more.

"Boy, you are stubborn, aren't you? Although, if there is anyone in this army that could defeat him, it would be you. But before you go off looking to take his head for a prize, I want you in the council tent. Now!"

Staring back down into the valley, Abaddon gazed at the beast. Golfriack stared right back at him. Both locked into a deadly gaze. Abaddon could feel his heart beat faster, not out of fear, but out of the anticipation of going head-to-head with the giant. Grinning, Abaddon broke off the stare and sheathed his sword, then turned towards the council tent.

CHAPTER 2

Benaiah slammed his fist down on the council table, breaking off the corner of the board and sending it skittering across the dirt floor, causing a waft of dust to rise into the stale, dry air.

"I am tired of listening to these vain comments and bickering ideas about how to end this battle! I have said it once and I will not say it again! The king is through with these Philistine dogs and he wants them put out of their misery! No truce or quarter is to be given!"

"What does the king know of war? He is not even here to lead us. When David was king he was at every battle and every war council meeting. He would be the first one on the battlefield and the last one off. Solomon has never even fought in a battle. In fact, I don't think he has even held a sword."

The accusation came from Abishai, once a great leader of King David's Mighty Men. He was the smallest man on the war council. He stood just over four cubits tall, but no one doubted his ability in war, especially after one particular battle in which he killed three hundred men with just his spear. He was quick and deadly. But he was also known for being hot headed and foolish.

"Solomon is no king like his father was," continued Abishai. "If David was still—"

Before he could finish his sentence a fist came flying to the side of Abishai's head, the impact dropping him to the ground. Dan, who had been standing next to him, had heard enough and had taken matters into his own hands.

Dan looked around at the rest of the counsel and took in their shocked faces.

"What? He had it coming. Talking about the king in such a manner is treason. The guy needed a good smack…the little badger," Dan said defending himself. He looked down at Abishai and noticed he was not getting back up. The five other men at the table looked at Dan and then at Abishai sprawled out on the floor.

"I think I killed him, he isn't moving," Dan said with a chuckle. At that comment, everyone else started to laugh as well. Everyone, except Benaiah.

It was then Captain Broc and Abaddon entered into the tent, almost tripping over the unconscious man lying in the dirt.

Broc gave an instant frown. He was about to ask what happened when he looked up and saw Dan with a sheepish grin on his face. Shaking his head, Broc motioned for Abaddon to stand over in the far corner.

Following his instructions, Abaddon stood where he was told and took an attentive stance, which was one hand on the hilt of his sword and the other hand on the hilt of a hidden dagger behind his back. The first thing Israeli warriors were taught was to always be ready to draw their weapon.

Abaddon scanned the men in the room.

The king's commander, Benaiah, was at the head of the table, furthest position from the door. His face was red and obviously upset. It seemed like Benaiah was always upset, always yelling and shouting at those underneath his command. Abaddon figured that was why he was such a good commander. He made sure things got done, no matter what the cost. The long scar on his left cheek was a constant reminder of that fact. It was known far and wide that Benaiah was a seasoned warrior and had gone toe-to-toe with the best; whether that be man or beast. In his youth, about the same age Abaddon was now, Benaiah had saved an entire village by killing two man eating lions, one with a spear and the other with his bare hands. If that didn't demand respect, then Abaddon didn't know what did.

Standing to the right of Benaiah was Jacob, the commander's war adviser. Jacob was a master of military tactics and strategy. He could see maneuvers and plots where others could not. He was also a quiet man and rarely spoke unless he was spoken to.

A few seasons back, Abaddon had asked Jacob why he didn't talk much, and after staring at Abaddon for what seemed like an eternity, Jacob had replied, "The world is seldom in a state to have an enjoyable conversation. The world would also be more appeasing if people would learn to shut their mouths and not speak their minds."

Abaddon got the point. Keep your mouth shut if you don't have anything worthwhile to say.

Standing on Jacob's right was Dan, the polar opposite of Jacob. Most of the time you couldn't get Dan *to* shut up. He fancied himself to be quite the comedian, even when it was inappropriate to be funny. He could find humor in every situation.

Dan was the youngest member on the council, maybe only a decade older than Abaddon. Dan probably wouldn't even be on the war council if it wasn't for his ferocity on the battlefield. Abaddon still remembered stories his father would tell him about this crazed young warrior who feared no one in battle. In one of those tales Dan had lost his weapon and ended up killing two hundred Philistines with his bare hands.

"Funny, but deadly," Abaddon's father used to say.

And then there was Abishai, out cold on the floor.

Abishai was the brother to the late traitor, Joab. Under King David's rule, Abishai had been the chief of his top thirty men. He had proved himself in battle more than once, but one would never know by looking at him. He was as thin as a rail, but he was fast, and he hit like a hammer. Although, today it would seem he wasn't quick enough or Dan wouldn't have been able to lay him out on the floor.

Abaddon smiled at the thought, wishing he could have been here earlier to see the punch.

Everyone had a hard time getting along with the proud and arrogant Abishai. He was once a favorite of David but ever since Joab had been killed, he had become bitter and angry at the world.

It was King Solomon that gave the order to kill Joab for conspiring against the crown with Solomon's half-brother Adonijah.

After King David's death, Adonijah assumed he would be king, but secretly David had made his youngest son, Solomon, king. Adonijah and Joab had started a rebellion, which was squelched out. They were executed for treason.

To make matters worse, it was Commander Benaiah who had carried out those executions. Needless to say, Abishai had grown to despise both Benaiah and King Solomon. Why Benaiah kept Abishai on the war council, Abaddon could not guess. Maybe out of pity or guilt for killing his brother, or maybe it was easier to keep an eye on him if he was close by.

The next person around the table was someone Abaddon knew well. Shammah the Great.

Shammah was one of the Three.

During the peak of King David's rule there were three warriors who fought under David and they were known as the chiefs of his Mighty Men. Those three were Eleazar, Shammah, and the leader of the three, who was also Abaddon's father, Josheb. Eleazar and Josheb died a few years ago, soon after King David rested with his fore-fathers.

After these great men's funerals, Shammah drove his sword into the ground between their graves and declared, "God has destined me to give up the sword and to bring peace to my brothers' families and to young King Solomon."

Till this day, that sword still marked the burial sight of Josheb and Eleazar. Never again did Shammah lift a blade in battle. Instead he but put his efforts into looking after Eleazar and Josheb's kin and counseling generals on military tactics and fighting skills.

Shammah was a warrior like none other. There were hundreds, if not thousands, sent to the depths of Sheol by Shammah's hand. Even though he now played the role of adviser, many still feared him.

Abaddon saw Shammah in a different light though. He was more like an uncle...a friend.

The last member of the group, standing between Shammah and Benaiah, was Zadok. As far as Abaddon knew, Zadok had never lifted a sword in his life. He was the king's priest and spiritual adviser. Abaddon never fully trusted the old man or the reasoning behind his logic.

Zadok always talked about El as if El were standing right there next to him, as if El himself was whispering in Zadok's ear, telling him what counsel to give. Abaddon could comprehend war, battle, and taking a man's life, but putting all of one's faith and ability in a God that could not be seen, heard, or touched was something Abaddon never understood. Of course, growing up in Israel, Abaddon had a knowledge of who El was. He had heard the bedtime stories of Abraham, Jacob, Isaac, and Moses, and how El had used them to make this great nation, but that was all they were to Abaddon, just stories.

Zadok was different. He had a real faith in El that Abaddon could not relate to. It was a relationship that puzzled him.

After Abaddon took note of all who were around the war table, he did what his father had taught him when entering any room.

He could still hear his father's voice, *"Besides the weapons on you, find at least three additional weapons in the room in case you are attacked and disarmed."*

This only took a second. A lit lamp hanging in the opposite corner of the tent was only three long strides away to his right. Fire always made a good weapon. A tent pole to his left that could be broken and used as a spear, and there were five other men in the room who were all armed with knives and swords.

"And once you acknowledge three additional weapons, you need to identify at least one escape route other than the way you came in."

Abaddon recognized a missing ground stake at the back right corner of the tent, due to an occasional breeze that would lift the bottom of the tent slightly. There was just enough room for a man to crawl under. He also made a mental note that this could be an incursion point as well.

Pushing Abishai's unconscious body aside with his foot, Broc stood in the spot where Abishai had been.

"Dan, you know the rules. You knocked him out so you get to revive him," Brock said, grabbing Dan by the collar and pulling him towards Abishai. "Take him out of the tent and poor some water over his head…and be careful that he doesn't try to kill you when he wakes up."

With some grumbling, Dan took hold of Abishai's right foot and dragged him outside.

"What was that all about?" Brock asked, looking to Benaiah for the answer.

"Actually he got off easy. The idiot was speaking treason, and if Dan hadn't done what he did, I would have put a knife to his throat." Benaiah said, putting both hands on the table. He glared at each and every person in the room, including Abaddon. He said in a stern level tone, "King David is dead and with El. Jehovah has made Solomon our king and we will honor him as such. Is that understood?"

In unison everyone in the room responded, "Yes, Commander!"

"Now back to the issue at hand."

"Yes, about that," Brock spoke up. "The giant just killed one of our archers. One of our men fired at the beast and he snatched the arrow right out of the air and hurled it straight back at the poor lad. I have never seen anything like it, to throw an arrow with such speed and accuracy without the use of a bow."

"It sounds like you admire him?" The question came from Jacob.

"Admire a Philistine? Never!" Broc declared as he spat to the ground. "But in a short amount of time he has shown some skill that demands respect. Whoever goes in to fight him can't go in with a mind of arrogance."

"I am not so sure we should take the challenge," Zadok said taking a closer look at the rough drawing of the battle field on the table before him. "Their numbers are depleted, their backs are to the Great Sea, we have conquered most of their cities, their people have been scattered to the ends of the earth and this remnant is all that stands in the way of peace, something this country has not known for years. I say we take them head on and crush them, drive them into the sea and let them drown! Let El sort them out from there!"

"So, priest. You have become a prophet now," Jacob said with a smirk. "I like your zeal, but you need to remember that we have also had many casualties. This has not been like the battles of old in which El has preserved every life that wields a sword for Israel. We have lost more men then I am comfortable with. In these last three days, a third of our warriors have been slain. The dogs still have enough men to keep us fighting for some time yet. And they are fighting fiercely! They know this could be their end and they have become crazed for their own survival. They have nothing left to loose. And I am sure King Achish is behind their ranks. Ever since we sacked Gath and he escaped, we have not been able to find him."

"I sure would like to know how he evaded us in Gath," Broc said as he pointed to the city of Gath on the map laid out in front of him, which had a dark, red X marked over the top of the Philistine city.

"As would I, my old friend." Jacob said. "But it doesn't matter now. If Achish is at the back of this army, then it is in this battle that he must die. If he lives he will only stir up a future rebellion, and in a few years-time we will be right back here again, sending more of our sons to their deaths. This must end right here and now! I suggest we put in our best fighter, trust El that he will be victorious, then enslave or slaughter the rest of the Philistines. And if Achish is found, we execute him in front of his army so they know their king has been destroyed."

The council grew quiet for a few moments as each person pondered Jacob's advice. It was in this moment, Abaddon began to wonder why he had been invited to this meeting. They didn't appear to have a plan in place, and not one of the council members had even recognized him yet. He would be the good soldier and stand there at attention, keeping his mouth shut, but there was a fire burning within him, reminding him that there was a giant out there that needed killing!

Zadok broke the silence, "And what if our best fighter fails? Do we do the honorable thing and surrender and let the enemies of El march strait to Jerusalem and take the throne?"

With that comment, Abaddon's patience left him.

It was time for killing giants, not talking!

"I will not fail! The giant will die today and the Philistines will know fear and death by the end of the day!"

All eyes in the room locked onto Abaddon and stared at him for several seconds. He suddenly felt very foolish and very small. Traditionally it was not permitted for a warrior to speak out of turn or rank, but he couldn't help it. Something had to be said.

Broc broke the silence. "Excuse his ignorance and disrespect, Benaiah, but I believe Abaddon is right. Out of all our soldiers there is no one better who could best that giant than Abaddon. This is the reason I brought him in here. All of you have seen him fight. He is unequaled in battle. There are some who say he has even surpassed the skill and ability of the Three. No offense, Shammah," Broc declared with reverence as he dipped his head towards the seasoned warrior.

"None taken," Shammah said with a grin. "Being one of his teachers, how could I be offended? I believe Abaddon can best the beast and bring glory to Israel."

All turned their eyes to Benaiah, who would give his final decision. Appearing to be deep in thought, Benaiah stroked his beard with one hand and toyed with a lion tooth that hung on a leather cord around his neck with the other hand. After a moment of awkward silence, Benaiah looked towards Broc.

"Broc, go get Dan and Abishai. They are going to need to hear this. I have a plan to end this war once and for all."

He then faced Abaddon. "And Abaddon, if you fail, the kingdom will fall."

CHAPTER 3

For two days, Golfriack descended into the valley between the two armies and mocked, insulted, chided and blasphemed the Israelites and their God. It was at the end of the second day the giant got a reply to his taunts. A herald announced that their champion would fight him at first light on the morrow. All could see the pleasure fill the dark gray eyes of the beastly man before he turned around, laughing and making his way back to the Philistine camp.

On the morning of the third day, Abaddon awoke and was heavy in thought. He had only gotten a few hours of sleep as he could not keep his mind from going over tactics, movements, counter moves, weapons, fighting styles and the numerous ways he could take the giant's life.

Benaiah had told him not to make a show of it, but at the right time, kill the beast quickly and efficiently. The problem was, Abaddon couldn't decide on which quick method he should use. He had become infuriated with the giant and his mocking tones! A quick and painless death, this monster didn't deserve. Abaddon began to think about all the torturous ways a man could die and one of these methods would be much more befitting the Beast of Blasphemy. But no, it had to be done quickly or Benaiah's plan may not work.

For the next hour, Abaddon did several combat exercises. It wasn't that he needed to practice his form or technique, he could do that in his sleep, but the movement made his muscles relax and kept his mind focused. After warming up, he made his way to the food wagon to break his fast; although he never got there. The sound of the giant's booming voice came crashing through the air. Abaddon looked towards the valley and a smile gleamed across his face.

"It looks like breaking fast will have to wait," he said to himself, and sprinted off to kill himself a giant.

Golfriack strolled down the hill and settled in the middle of the valley next to an old gnarly oak tree. A much, much smaller man stumbled behind the giant, carrying a shield twice his own height. It was apparent the shield was very heavy as the young man wobbled on his feet just trying to manage it. Unable to see where he was going, the shield bearer ran right into Golfriack's leg, bounced off, and fell to the ground.

The Israelites found this to be amusing and began laughing and shouting insults.

The giant roared in anger at the clumsy man. With one hand he picked up his shield and with the other hand he grabbed the squeamish Philistine by the back of his head. The small man cried out in protest but no words were able to come out before Golfriack slammed the man's face into the oak tree next to him, killing the shield bearer instantly. The man's arms and legs fell limp and the giant dropped his lifeless corpse to the ground as if it were a used rag.

Smiling, Golfriack admired his calloused hand as he saw the dead man's blood smeared upon it. He turned his attention towards the Israeli army.

"It is a good day to spill blood!" Golfriack declared in his booming voice, glaring at the nervous Israelites.

The giant strapped his shield firmly to his arm and drew a massive sword that had been fastened to the middle of his back. He flexed his muscles and stretched his arms to loosen the straps of his armor so he could get a better range of motion.

The armor Golfriack chose was not the same as what he had worn the three days prior. This armor was plated with gold and the sun's rays bounced off it in pure radiance. It covered him from head to toe.

His sword was something to behold. Its length was that of an average man and its width was that of a man's torso, and yet Golfriack swung the weapon around him like it was a child's toy. Taking a few steps forward, he looked up at the Israeli army, which was now all lined up at the top of the hill, ready to watch the upcoming bout.

Golfriack laughed as he noticed that there were only about three to four hundred Israeli soldiers present, as opposed to the several thousand he had witnessed a few days prior. "So these are the brave ones!" he said thunderously, causing a flock of ravens further down the battlefield to take flight. "Yesterday there were thousands in your ranks and now look at you! Pathetic! All your men are cowards and act like scared little women fleeing in the night! Come! Send out your so-called champion so I may pick my teeth with his broken bones and smear his blood over my shield as an offering for my own glory! Come on! Let's get on with it!"

While the brute spoke, the Philistine army came to the top of their ridge in full battle gear, with spears, swords and shields. They began banging their weapons against their shields, causing a deafening ruckus all throughout the area.

It was then that a man broke through the Israeli lines and made his way down into the valley. Looking at the midget of a man, Golfriack again began to laugh. A laugh so loud, it overcame the noise of the Philistine army behind him.

Golfriack took in the appearance of his opponent. A puny little man no more than three or four cubits high, dressed in the typical Israeli garb; although this man's clothing was black and not white or tan like the rest of the Israeli warriors. His hair was dark black and tied back at the nape of his neck. The man carried a sword that was less than two cubits long. It was not a sickle shaped blade like most of the Israeli swords, but it was straight except for a slight upward curve in the middle of it. Golfriack had never seen another sword like it. The giant smiled and grunted to himself at the thought of taking the blade as a nice trophy to display after his victory, or at the least a decent tooth pick to clean his teeth with.

It was then, Golfriack noticed something about the man, something that made him pause. There was no fear in the small man's eyes. His body didn't shake or shutter or seem nervous in any way.

So the man had confidence.

The Philistine couldn't help but crack a smile across his lips as he thought about giving this Israeli mouse something to fear. He decided then and there that this little rodent didn't deserve a quick death. He would draw this out as long as possible and inflict as much pain as he could.

Abaddon took up a position about seventy cubits away from the brutish giant. In a matter of seconds he found at least ten different objects in the area he could use as weapons if he lost his sword. He didn't bother looking for an escape route. There would be no need for one. He was there to kill a giant, not run from one.

For a moment, the two of them stared at each other, and then Golfriack spoke.

"So you are their champion? Pathetic! I have been with women who have more masculinity than you!" Turning his attention to the Israeli army, he challenged, "Is this little whelp the one you would send to defeat me? I have killed thousands much more mighty than he! I have taken the heads of kings and rulers, beasts and monsters alike! I have ripped out the heart of the behemoth and torn the head off a masakh with my bare hands! And this—this maggot of a man," he said, pointing at Abaddon, "This is the best you can do? No wonder your so-called God has failed you! Your great and powerful El cowers in my presence as do all men and gods! Prepare yourself Israel, for today is the day you become the feces under the foot of the Philistines!"

Turning to Abaddon, Golfriack pointed his sword towards him with his left hand. "And you! I don't know if you were ordered to come down here and die, or if you believe you actually have a chance at defeating me, but this will be a most unpleasant death for you. While you are still alive and screaming to die, I will tear the flesh from your bones and stake it to this very tree. Your skull will become an ornament on my belt and your hair will be a gift for our children to play with."

As the giant kept on rambling threats, Abaddon began to get bored. However, the stalling was necessary in order to put Benaiah's plan into place. He had stopped listening to what Golfriack was saying quite some time ago.

All Abaddon heard was, "Yeah, yeah, threat this and threat that, blah blah blah."

It was when the giant pointed his sword at him that he noticed Golfriack was left handed, and a creative idea came to Abaddon.

Oh this is going to be fun, Abaddon thought to himself.

Benaiah and Broc stood at the top of the hill with their men and listened to the beast make his threats. Benaiah was always astounded at how calm Abaddon could be before a battle. He was just standing down there as if this were just another opponent from the training arena.

Abaddon's father, Josheb, had been the same way. Benaiah recalled a time when he was young, just a captain, and Josheb was the commander. Their regiment was in a battle with the Philistines and they were in dire straits. They were outnumbered ten-to-one, but Josheb didn't bat an eye or break a sweat. He was as calm and fearless as if he were at home playing with his children in the yard.

Josheb had turned to his men and simply said, *"The one true God is here with us now and He has already given them into our hands! Fight with all your being and God will see us through!"* There were only eighty of them, and by the end of the day there were still eighty of them, standing amongst three thousand dead Philistines, of which eight hundred had been put down by Josheb's own sword. And now Benaiah could see the same peace and fearlessness in Abaddon's eyes and stature.

It was then, Abaddon began to do something strange. He took off his outer cloak and tossed it aside. He then took off the top of his inner robe and tied the excess material around his torso. Abaddon was now naked from the waist up.

Leaning over to Broc, Benaiah asked in a hushed tone, "What is he doing? I thought we told him no theatrics and to make it quick when the time came."

Broc shook his head. "I don't know what that little dingleberry is doing," Broc said in a humorous tone. "That kid doesn't do anything normal."

"Well he looks ridiculous!" Benaiah said, shaking his head. "There is a reason we don't let our soldiers go out fighting bare breasted. We are not a bunch of barbarians. And he better not get himself killed or Josheb's spirit will came back from Sheol and strangle me in my sleep."

Golfriack stopped his rambling when his opponent took off his clothes. Abaddon was now standing before the giant half naked.

He stared at Abaddon for a moment in silence and then started laughing. The vast host of Philistines began to laugh as well.

"Look at you!" Golfriack boomed out of his laughter. "You mock me by just making an appearance, and now you mock yourself by showing me your nakedness like a virgin on her wedding night. Look at you and your soft flawless skin! There isn't a scar on you!"

The giant turned back to the Israeli army and shouted, "What? You ran out of warriors, so you sent a freshly birthed child out to fight for you?" And his laughing resumed.

It was true. Abaddon had no scars. Unlike most of the warriors in Israel, he was the only seasoned warrior who had never been cut, broken, crushed, maimed, stabbed, or even nicked. His dark bronze skin was as pure and preserved as the day he joined the military, at the grand old age of twelve seasons. Even during practices and training he had never suffered a wound which left him bleeding. Sure, he had had lots of bruises and bumps, but never a cut. The only mark on his whole body was the faint scar over his left eye which was barely noticeable, and he had been born with that one.

When he was younger, rumors had gone around the land accusing Abaddon of being a witch or a demon due to his untouchability in combat. Abaddon simply brushed the accusations off with statements such as, "You could be the same way if you would spend more time practicing your sword play than flapping those loose lips."

Abaddon was untouchable in battle. He would always parry, block, duck, or just plain move out of the way of the weapon. It wasn't as if anyone hadn't tried to cut him. Abaddon was simply too quick. It was almost as if he could sense the blow coming and would move before the strike was made. He moved in such a way that was unparalleled to any other, and when a weapon was put in his hand, there were none that could stand against him.

Having had enough of the giant's vain words, Abaddon yelled out, "Silence, you coward!"

The boom of Abaddon's voice echoed throughout the valley. The power and authority behind his voice shocked everyone, and within moments all was quiet, even Golfriack.

"I have heard enough of your empty taunts, giant!"

"So, the mouse speaks."

"Shut your mouth, fool!" Abaddon said, pointing his weapon towards Golfriack.

Gripping his sword tightly in his right hand, Abaddon raised his blade up high. The polished steel glinted in the morning light. "Men of war, Israeli and Philistine alike, I stand here before you, naked and without armor."

Lowering his sword, Abaddon cut off the straps to his sandals with two swift strokes. With a flick of his feet, he kicked his tattered footwear away.

"I am even without my sandals! I am barefoot, bare breasted, and I am afraid that if I take off any more I would be standing here in *all* my glory, which would cause this giant's face to turn crimson."

Both armies erupted into laughter. It was probably the first thing they did together in the last one hundred seasons.

This time the giant wasn't laughing. At seventy cubits away, Abaddon could hear a growl pulsing through his massive throat.

Abaddon smiled and continued.

"Here I stand without armor, ready to do battle, and yet here is the great Golfriack," Abaddon spewed, saying the giant's name as sarcastically as possible, "standing there with all of his armor on as if he were about to fight a thousand men! Could it be that this great warrior is afraid to face me as a true man instead of as an armored tree?"

Israel began to chime in on the taunts. "Yeah! Take off your armor, coward! The giant hides behind his shell like a turtle. Only a coward needs such armor! Coward! Coward! Coward!"

Golfriack bellowed at the growing confidence of his enemy army. His roar deafened the crowd and made some of the men on both sides cower. Even Abaddon had to take a step back and shake his head because the harshness of the sound.

When all was quiet again, Abaddon stared at the giant with an evil grin, making Golfriack feel slightly uneasy.

"So you wish to die in the old way!" yelled Golfriack in Abaddon's direction. "So be it!"

The massive hulk threw his shield to the side and grabbed hold of his bright golden armor at the neck. Without untying the straps that held it into place, he ripped the front of his breastplate from his body and flung it aside with a grunt.

Both opposing forces gasped at what they now saw. Thousands of battle scars mangled Golfriack's torso and arms. His tormented skin revealed tight solid muscles, flexing with each movement. The beast's veins were bulging in every direction as if they were living snakes, pumping their venom throughout his body. As a warrior, he was a sight to behold.

Too bad today is the day of his death, Abaddon thought to himself, almost regretting the loss of such a warrior.

With a blood thirsty look on his face, Golfriack took in the gawks of the enemy warriors and the cheers of the Philistines as he began to walk towards Abaddon. The giant pointed his massive sword at Abaddon and said, "You have something of mine mouse, and I am in dire need of it."

"And what would that be?" Abaddon asked.

"Your head, as a decoration on my tent pole. It will match the other twenty I have placed there today."

Abaddon didn't respond. He was tired of the banter. He glanced up at Benaiah, but Benaiah shook his head and signaled for him to stall a bit longer.

Abaddon sighed, but then had an idea. He took his sword and threw it at a small tree, no more than fifteen cubits from where he was standing. His weapon plunged firmly into a lower branch, causing a small limb to fall to the ground. The giant, now about fifty cubits away, stopped and glared at Abaddon, who was now smiling back as if he had just done something miraculous.

"What is this?" demanded Golfriack.

The Philistine turned his attention from Abaddon and once again addressed Israel. "Is this what your men are made of...cowardly, scarless, female monkeys that throw their weapons like they throw their own scat?"

Turning back to Abaddon he screamed, "Do you mock me? I have had enough! Pick up your sword and fight, you wretched mole! And after I kill you, I will kill your family! I will kill your friends! I will arrive in the night, becoming their nightmares, snuffing out your screaming children! I will bake their flesh in the noonday sun and offer them up to myself as tribute for your cowardly death, the death of the naked monkey!"

"You are mistaken, oh great and mighty ugly one." Abaddon said with a smirk in his voice as he picked up the branch and began stripping it of its leaves. "I did not throw aside my sword because I am in fear of you. Oh no! I only threw it to cut down this branch."

He held up the bare stick that was roughly about the length of his arm. "You see, it would be too easy to kill you with a sword. So, I am going to kill you with this flimsy, frail, flexible stick."

Pausing for a moment, Abaddon looked to see the giant's reaction, but the beast gave nothing but a seething look of spite.

Swishing his stick around a bit, Abaddon continued speaking, "You call yourself a god but all I see is a man who bears the scars of someone too stupid to get out of the way of a coming blade. So, this piece of wood, I promise you, will be the weapon that kills you. There are no gods here today!" Abaddon proclaimed, his voice growing louder with each word. "Just you and me! Two men. You, with your massive sword, and me with my teeny, tiny stick!"

The giant roared out in response. He began to run at Abaddon with long, thundering steps, and with each footfall, Abaddon felt the tremors of the earth beneath him. Abaddon glanced up at Benaiah, hoping he had stalled long enough.

CHAPTER 4

"Is he really going to kill that brute with a stick?" Benaiah whispered to Broc. "This kid is way too arrogant, and a far reach from his father's strength and humility."

"And yet he knows how to kill and bring results, just like his father, Josheb," Broc reminded Benaiah.

Benaiah did not feel right about Abaddon's outward display. He looked at the two half naked men in the valley who were about to engage in a life defining duel for Israel. He then studied the war hungry Philistines on the opposing ridge. They were in full battle uniform and ready to advance upon Golfriack's impending victory.

Frowning and leaning to his left, Benaiah whispered into the ear of his armor bearer to spread the word to the army to attack at a moment's notice, just in case this duel went sour.

Without even hearing what was being said to the servant, Broc spoke up. "Such little faith. You and I both know Abaddon can slay that sack of meat. Even you killed a giant in *your* youth, or did you forget?"

Benaiah thought back to his days as a younger warrior, back before David had even become king. The Philistines had raped, pillaged, and destroyed an entire town. They were led by an Egyptian assassin, who had stood at the same height as Golfriack. After a grueling battle, and being severely wounded, Benaiah had overcome the giant. He had jumped on the back of the brute and drove his sword through the front of his enemy's chest. Benaiah also recalled that it had taken him three months of healing to recover from that fight.

Pushing the memory aside, Benaiah responded, "Yeah, I killed a giant, but I didn't do it when state slavery was on the line. This is a mistake. I wonder if it is too late to call this off."

Broc was starting to get a little perturbed by Benaiah's lack of confidence in Abaddon. "You know you can't call it off!" he said, a little louder than he should have. "If Abaddon says he can kill the man with a stick, then I believe he will kill the man with a stick. Have faith, old friend. I'll even wager on it. Five shekels says he kills him with the stick."

Benaiah smiled at his captain and paused before replying, "Five shekels says he tries smacking him with the stick several times while playing cat and mouse, and then goes back for his sword to do the killing."

Bellowing out a cheer, Broc gave Benaiah a slap on the back.

It was at that point that Abaddon glanced up at Benaiah the second time, looking for the sign to attack. Benaiah held up two joined fingers, their military signal to advance, and then sent up a silent prayer, hoping Dan and Jacob were in place and ready to go.

"Here we go!" Broc said, rubbing his hands together.

Benaiah gave him a sideways glance. "I think you are enjoying this too much."

Broc simply shrugged and kept his eyes on Abaddon.

Both men watched as the giant bounded along the valley floor like a mad runaway ox. As Golfriack closed the distance, Abaddon just stood there. The beast thundered in closer and closer and began to produce a war cry, filling the air with impending doom.

Then, like an arrow released from its bow, Abaddon took off running. The speed in which Abaddon approached Golfriack forced the giant to slow his pace so he could strike at the little man racing towards him.

The giant lifted his left sword arm high in the air, ready to bring a downward stroke upon Abaddon's head, only to realize he was now moving far too slow for Abaddon's speed. When the giant's arm was fully raised, Abaddon lunged into the air with a great leap, and found himself at an even height with the Philistine's upraised arm. In mid-flight, and with stick in hand, Abaddon slammed his hand downward and slapped the giant hard on his armpit.

Landing rather awkwardly on his feet, Abaddon forced himself into a roll. He easily sprung up, and without turning around, walked away from the Philistine.

Only a few moments ago the crowds on both sides had been cheering and rooting for their champions, but now, no one spoke at all.

As Abaddon continued to walk away from Golfriack, the crowd noticed that the stick which had once been in his hand was no longer there.

All eyes turned to the giant.

Golfriack staggered forward a few steps with his arm still raised, his massive sword piercing the morning sky. He came to a stumbling halt and posed there for a few seconds as if he had turned into a stone statue.

Then, as if the wind willed it, the sword tipped over from his upraised hand and plunged tip first into the earth with a thud. His arm finally fell to his side with a slap and his scarred body dropped to the ground, landing on his knees.

It was there, on his knees, the giant stayed, unmoving. A murmur began to spread from both armies, as the witnesses tried to figure out how this could have happened.

What did Abaddon do? Why was the giant on his knees after one slap? And why was he not getting up to smother Abaddon like a bug? And what happened to the stick?

With both hands on his head, Broc had a puzzled expression on his face. "Ok, what just happened? Did he stun him?"

Upon closer inspection, Broc saw that Golfriack was still breathing, but there was a steady stream of blood flowing over his lower lip. "He obviously is wounded and not able to stand, but, what actually just happened?"

Benaiah had a broad smile on his face. "I haven't seen that maneuver in years. Josheb used to use it on rare occasions, but it is extremely difficult to execute! By the Lord in Heaven, he did it on his first try, and without a sword, but with a stupid narrow tree branch, no less!"

"Ok, you are going to have to explain, because I have never seen a slap kill somebody before." Turning to the soldier on his right, Broc raised up the man's arm and slapped his armpit. The soldier gave his captain an awkward glance, but said nothing.

"See." Broc said, pointing to the young man. "Not dead."

Shaking his head, Benaiah chuckled at his friend's attempt at humor. "It was not the slap, but what happened right before the slap. Josheb was always studying the enemy and their weaknesses. Josheb once showed me that if you thrust your blade at the right downward angle through the armpit, you could pierce a person's heart, lung, and stomach, and produce an instant kill. Josheb had perfected the move and I had seen him do it more than once in battle. One moment you were alive, fighting, and the next moment you were dead on the ground. It happens that fast. But, as you can imagine, it is not an easy maneuver to perform as one's arm is always in the way of the entry point, and if they are wearing armor, it is a small target opening."

Broc was catching on and his face brightened with a smile. "So that is why he goaded the beast into taking off his breastplate. It made it easier for him to hit the underarm. So you are telling me, the slap we heard was the sound of Abaddon's hand hitting the giant's armpit after he drove the entire stick into his underarm, through his heart and lungs, making it disappear completely into his body?" Broc asked in amazement.

"It appears so," Benaiah admitted. "Although I think he missed or only nicked his heart. A direct hit to the heart would have killed him instantly. We know he punctured his lung due to the blood coming out of his mouth, and the fact that he can barely breathe. Of course, what do I know? I am no healer."

Without taking his eyes off the scene below, Benaiah held his hand out and dropped five shekels into Broc's already open hand.

Broc smiled.

After walking over to where Golfriack had killed his shield bearer, Abaddon reached down with both hands and picked up the giant's heavy, iron-clad shield. He hoisted it up onto his back and walked back to the kneeling monster.

By now the valley had become a silent grave. Not even a whisper could be heard from either army. Even the crows that had been circling above, waiting for their next meal, seemed to sense the weight of Abaddon's actions as they escaped into nearby trees.

The only sound produced was Abaddon's steady footfalls on the valley floor and the low blood soaked guttural sounds of Golfriack trying to breathe. When Abaddon returned to the giant, he dropped the shield next to him, and then came around to the front of the fallen man. For the first time, Abaddon was able to look him dead in the eye, face to face. Now that the Philistine was on his knees, he was the same height as Abaddon.

Barely alive, Golfriack refused to look at Abaddon. The only thought coursing through his mind was, *How could this small minuscule of a man have beaten me with a stick?*

He didn't understand what was happening to him. He felt a sharp poke under his arm and now his insides burned with pain and agony. The only conclusion Golfriack could come up with was that this man was some kind of a sorcerer. He had cast a spell on him. He wanted to speak and curse the man, but he could not find the breath to do so.

Abaddon looked at the dying giant without pity or remorse. He was proud of what he had done and was happy the foul-mouthed blasphemer was finally silenced. Abaddon had decided that he, and not the wounded beast before him, would have the last word.

Grabbing Golfriack by his hair, Abaddon tilted his head back slightly so the giant's eyes met his. "Before you die, I want you to know the name of the, *little mouse,* that killed you. My name is Abaddon."

Letting go of the giant's head, Abaddon held up both of his arms. "In fact, I want all of the Philistines to know my name!" He thundered in a loud voice. "My name is Abaddon! Bringer of death and destruction to all those who would oppose me!"

The Philistines began to step back, hearing the wrath of the giant killer.

"Behold! Your god!" Abaddon said mockingly, pointing at Golfriack.

Everyone saw the change in Abaddon. It was as if he was a hungry lion and was about ready to be unleashed upon a lamb.

"I am Abaddon! Killer of gods!"

And with those words, Abaddon kicked the giant square in the face and sent the beast sprawling onto his back, leaving his lower body twisted in an awkward position. Golfriack gargled and began to choke on his own blood.

Snatching up the shield with surprising ease, Abaddon stood over the top of Golfriack's head. He took one last look into the face of his enemy, and doing so caused him to pause. Something was happening to the giant's face. An evil grin spread across Golfriack's lips and the dull, dwindling, gray eyes Abaddon had glared into moments ago were turning black, as if a pool of ink was consuming his eyes. The same black liquid began to run out as tears, staining the giant's cheeks.

The giant spoke one more time, loud enough for only Abaddon to hear.

"You may kill this body of flesh and weakness, but we who are many will have our revenge, son of Josheb. Israel will yet perish in flame!"

Pausing for a moment, Abaddon was puzzled at what he had just seen. *How did this Philistine know he was the son of Josheb?*

Time to end this!

With one mighty thrust he brought the bottom edge of the shield down on Golfriack's neck, separating his head from the rest of his body. Tossing the shield aside, Abaddon reached down with his right hand and picked up the giant's massive head by the hair and lifted it high into the air for all to see. At the same time, he raised his left hand and pointed two fingers upward, the sign for the Israeli army to attack.

CHAPTER 5

As soon as Abaddon gave the sign of attack, the ground began to shake, making the small pebbles around Abaddon's feet dance. The Philistines, now consumed with fear and confusion, dropped their swords and shields and began to run, yelling, "The God of the Hebrews is in Abaddon and he is making the earth open up to swallow us alive!"

Making the ground shake even more, a stampede of five hundred horsemen came charging out of the Northern Hills. Dan could be seen at the head of the charge thundering towards the enemy army.

As if with one mind, the entire Philistine host turned and started running south, only to be cut off by six hundred more horsemen being led by Jacob, coming up out of the forests of Kidron from the south. From the east, Abaddon and the rest of the Israeli force had already crossed the valley with swords drawn and were about to crest the hill to the Philistines.

The only direction the Philistines could go was west, to the Great Sea, which only lead to a watery grave. They were so panic-stricken, not one of them even considered fighting off the Israelites. Their only goal was to escape.

Israel came down upon them from all three sides and put the entire army of the Philistines to the sword. In total, eight thousand Philistines were cut down or drowned in the Great Sea that day.

The Philistines would be no more.

Abaddon pulled his sword from his last victim and pushed the dying body of the poor soul to the ground. He had fought through half a league of men, all the way to the Great Sea. Still feeling the surge of adrenaline coursing through his veins, he stepped forward and walked until he was waist deep into the salty sea water, letting the cool liquid consume him. His heart continued to race as he tried to calm himself with slow, deep breaths.

This was one of the hardest things for Abaddon to do after a battle, to calm down from the fury that overtook him, to ease the madness that was released into his mind, that hungered for blood and violence. Shutting off the fury was not always easy to do.

Abaddon remembered his father's words, *"The fury is the part of us which desires death and destruction. It is the old man within that rebels against El and feeds the sin of man. El allows us to use it in war but in all other areas of life, El demands us to make the fury our slave and not the other way around. We must master it! For if we do not, the fury will live as a master over you, which only leads to unnecessary murder and death. We are made in the image of El, not in the image of death and sin. Son, master your fury!"*

"Master your fury," Abaddon said to himself as he slowed and calmed his breathing. "Master your fury, master your fury, master your—"

A chill spiked up through Abaddon's spine. There was someone behind him!

In a flash, Abaddon cut his sword into the water, splashing a spray of the sea into the on-comer's face, his blade quickly following to the intruder's neck. The metallic clang of a successful parry kept Abaddon's sword from completing its arc, only a handsbreadth away from the man's throat.

"Whoa, son!" came the gravelly voice of Broc as he held his sword up with one hand and wiped the water from his face with the other hand. "The battle is over lad, let's not start killing our own!"

"Sorry. I guess I am still a little wound up from the surge of the fury."

"Ah, yes, well, maybe by the time you are as old as I am, you might actually be able to control it enough to keep your commanding officer's head in place."

Broc put his hand on Abaddon's shoulder and then hugged his neck. "You did good today, lad. Your old man would have been proud of ya. I'm proud of ya." And then with a chuckle, "Ha! By the Lion's mane, the whole army is proud of ya!"

Before Abaddon could give a reply to the complement, Dan came thundering down the beach on a black stallion with two more horses in tow. His horse came splaying into the water and made an abrupt stop in front of the two men.

"This isn't over yet!" Dan cried out. "Achish got away! He must have had his fleet of boats at the ready, because there are at least a dozen Philistine ships sailing north towards Lebanon! A few of our scouts said King Achish is on the lead ship. They also reported that their ships are sailing close to the shore. We may be able to set up an ambush on the beaches of the flats if we can get ahead of them. If they get to the cliffs of Tyre we will not be able to reach them and they will escape! We must cut the head off of this serpent!"

"How far ahead are they?" Abaddon asked as he and Broc mounted the two free horses.

"About eight leagues. I have fifty riders waiting for us beyond the ridge. If we ride hard we might be able to end this once and for all," Dan said, spurring his mount around.

"Eight leagues? That would mean he left well before Abaddon's battle with Golfriack. He wasn't planning on sticking around either way," Broc observed. "The coward!"

With a spur to the horses they sped away, racing down the beach, heading north towards Lebanon.

CHAPTER 6

Abishai braced himself against the wall outside King Achish's quarters as the ship was tossed to and fro by the rocky waves. He hated sea travel. Floating on a bunch of logs pitched together never seemed like a good idea, not to mention the sea sickness was almost unbearable.

Although, Abishai *was* impressed with the Philistine vessel. It was larger than most sea going vessels. It had two decks on it. The lower deck, Abishai assumed, was used for cargo and slaves. The upper deck held a large cabin in the front and the back was open, scattered with rigging, nets for fishing, and plenty of shields and spears. It was obvious the ship was built for long sea voyages and military exploits.

It was also built for speed. The main mast in the center of the vessel was forty to fifty cubits high. It was a giant carving of the Philistine's god, Dagon, a creature that looked like it was half dragon and half man. Besides the main mast, there were two smaller sails, one towards the front and another at the rear of the boat.

Looking up, Abishai noticed the sails were slack and there was barely a breeze; yet, when he looked to the water he could see that they were moving along at a rapid speed. He looked back to the sails and then to the water again.

What is making us move so fast? Abishai puzzled in thought, then winced and grabbed his stomach. He rushed over to the side of the boat and blanched. Two Philistine sailors walked by and laughed at him, saying something Abishai choose to ignore. *If they only knew how many of their pathetic breed I have massacred in my life time, they would not be laughing. They would be jumping overboard to get as far away from me as possible!* Abishai thought to himself, as he grabbed the rail and tried to steady himself, willing his stomach to calm itself.

Taking further note of his surroundings, he counted at least a dozen other Philistine ships sailing around Achish's vessel. The king's ship looked as though it could hold up to a hundred men, but each of the smaller vessels were only equipped with a single sail and could contain no more than twenty to thirty men. These boats were more common in the area and were mainly used for fishing, not for war.

Standing up straight, Abishai took a deep breath, and began to think his stomach was settling, but then bent over the rail once more, blanching into the oncoming waves.

"The king will see you now," came a voice from behind him.

Composing himself again, Abishai wiped his mouth with the back of his hand, and willed his insides to stay calm. He turned to see a tall, muscular man beckoning him back towards the king's cabin.

The guard was dressed in the common Philistine armor, black leather breastplate and matching leather lappets around his waist. His armor was outlined in red, which signified the king's personal guard. The man's bronze helmet had an open face to it and was stained black to match the rest of his armor. Where the man's face should have been peering out from the helmet, there was a mask in its stead. It was an image of a twisted white face, consumed with anger and rage. Painted around the eyes were red streaks of blood.

Looking to the guard's belt, Abishai noticed two unique daggers mounted on each side of the man's waist. No common guard would carry those weapons. This man was not only one of the king's personal guards, but he was also one of the king's assassins. If the Philistine king wanted someone to disappear, it was one of these deadly men who carried out the order. Philistine assassins were crafty and very dangerous. They were known as the Sicarrii, or literally, the Dagger Men, since their weapons of choice were daggers.

Abishai had faced them before.

Several years ago King Achish had sent three of the Sicarrii to kill King David. Of course, they were unsuccessful and the assassins were killed even before they could get close to the king's palace. Abishai had had the pleasure of killing one of the Sicarrii himself.

As a deterrent, King David had put the heads of the assassins in a basket and sent them back to Achish with the warning, that Achish's own head might be found in a basket if he ever tried anything like that again. Needless to say, there were no more assassins sent to kill David.

Abishai felt a moment of solace thinking about the old days, when he was a faithful servant of the true king, David. Those were the glory days, when he and his brother Joab were commanders of thousands. He missed walking down the streets of Jerusalem and watching people part to get out of the way, bowing in respect to the warriors of Judah.

But now, now people called him murderer, deceiver, trader. His brother Joab was now dead because of that coward, because of that so called king, Solomon. If this was how Israel repaid a man for a life of service, then Abishai was proud to betray Israel and serve another, even if that meant becoming loyal to the fat, pig-king, Achish.

The Sicarrii led Abishai into the king's cabin without saying a word. Before Abishai could move past him, the large guard patted him down for weapons and found two daggers strapped to his back. After snatching up the daggers, the Sicarrii scowled and pushed him forward.

"Sorry about that," Abishai smiled, "old habits and all."

Taking a few steps forward, Abishai stepped through a large, heavy, red curtain. As soon as he had walked through, he wished he had not, for he was not prepared for what he saw.

The room was decorated in fine linen drapery of red, purple and gold. There wasn't a single space of the room that was not covered by it. Large pillows of all colors were scattered around the room.

There at the head of the room, on several purple pillows, was a scantily dressed and obese King Achish, surrounded by at least 20 young women who had on even less clothing than the king.

A scene such as this was detestable in the land of Israel. Back in Israel, this perverse display of fornication would have meant the death penalty for all those involved. The sight made Abishai sick and angry at the same time.

The laughing and giggling of the women stopped when Abishai cleared his throat to announce his presence.

Achish looked up and gave a wicked smile at Abishai for a few long moments, obviously trying to judge the Israeli's reaction to the plethora of flesh being displayed. When Abishai showed no reaction, Achish spoke, "There is the savior of the Philistines! Come! Enjoy the fruits of victory!"

"Victory?" Abishai said in a mocking tone. "What victory? Your men were slaughtered and those few who were not killed will be condemned to a life of slavery. Your army is all but defeated, except for the few you managed to save through these ships. If you had executed the plan I instructed you with, you would still have an army to command and you wouldn't be running for your life! I risked everything to come and tell you that Benaiah was going to flank you on both sides! I figured you would have counter attacked, not abandoned your men and run like a coward!"

"You forget your place, Jew! I didn't pay you to give orders! I paid you to be a traitor, and to give me information. What I do with that information is my business. The loss of my army was expected. Now, relax! Pick any woman you like and she is yours for the night. Hah! By Dagon, pick two or three, my friend!"

Achish waved over a few of the women and they seductively approached Abishai. As soon as one of the girls was within arm's length, Abishai grabbed her by the throat and flung her back across the room, causing her to fall upon several other women close to the king.

"Does a lion breed itself with a pig?" Abishai spat. "There isn't enough gold in the world to degrade myself at the hand of your whores."

King Achish began a low rumbling chuckle that, for a moment, made Abishai feel uneasy. It was a demeaning laugh that held no joy, but communicated a sense of control and superiority. After a few long moments of the awkward laughter the king sat up from his reclining position, making the fat from his body pile itself into several folds and layers.

"You claim there is not enough gold for you to break your chastity, which I am inclined to challenge at some point. But, obviously there *is* enough gold to buy your loyalty. What was it my men were calling you behind your back before you boarded the ship? Ah yes! The traitor of Judah! All hail the traitor of Judah!" King Achish pronounced loudly, spreading his arms wide as if introducing a guest to the room full of promiscuous women. "Nobody cares about your high morals here, Jew! Relax! Feed the pleasures of your flesh!"

Abishai gritted his teeth. He wanted to take three long strides forward and rip out the fat man's throat. The Sicarrii must have sensed Abishai's frustration because the guard's hand clutched his shoulder from behind.

Turning his head back to the unwelcome guard, Abishai said in a deep threatening scowl, "If you know what is good for you, you will remove that hand."

The foolish bodyguard tightened his grip.

In the blink of an eye, Abishai twisted his entire body to the left and rammed his left elbow into the Sicarrii's left temple. Finishing his twist around the guard, Abishai sent a second blow with his right fist, square in the back of the man's neck. The result was a sickening, snap, as the man's head whipped backwards from the impact.

The room immediately fell silent and all eyes went to the Sicarrii as he took a half step forward, and then, as if he were a fallen tree in the forest, crashed down to the rough wooden floor, face first. The fall shattered the Sicarrii's mask, sending shards of it to the king's feet.

Abishai glanced up at King Achish with a grin on his face.

As if the silence had become deadly, every girl in the room began screaming and running for a hidden door behind a large, scarlet linen that hung in the back of the cabin.

In seconds, the king and Abishai were the only ones left in the room, but only for a moment. The commotion of the girls sent two more Sicarrii charging into the room with their daggers drawn. They saw their fellow assassin, dead on the floor. Without hesitation, they stepped forward to strike at Abishai.

Not even bothering to turn towards his attackers, Abishai simply stared ahead at Achish. The king smiled back at Abishai's audacity and raised his hand for the two guards to stop.

With a broadening smile, Achish began to laugh again. He laughed so hard, the fat covering his body began to ripple and lunge in all directions.

"I like this guy!" Achish roared in the midst of his laughter. "Leave us, you two buffoons! And take that dead moron with you," Achish said, pointing to the body on the floor. "If you saw how fast this Jew killed him, you never would have let him be a part of your order in the first place. Now, go! Out! Out!"

Without saying a word, the two Sicarrii sheathed their blades, grabbed their deceased companion, and dragged him out of the room. Soon after they left, Abishai heard a splash, the guards throwing their compatriot's lifeless body over the side of the boat.

"Well done, traitor! I despise weakness in my Sicarrii. That man deserved to die. But I am curious. Do you want to die? An attack on any of my guards is a death penalty, usually no matter what the reason." Achish inquired, eyeing Abishai with interest. "Do you have a death wish, Jew?"

Truth be told, Abishai had actually thought about ending his life. His honor was gone, his fame was diminishing, and his country had betrayed him. After his brother's death, hate had consumed his soul and nothing but revenge seemed to matter.

So did he care about dying, or even living? The answer was no, but he would not surrender to it either. Yes, death would find him, and probably at the end of the sword, but he would give death a fight like no other person could. Death would wait until his revenge had run its course.

Abishai gave the king a shorter reply. "No. I don't have a death wish. But I will not be suffered a fool by you or by any of your dysfunctional leaches."

The smile on Achish's face disappeared and his eyes narrowed. In a quick hopping motion, the king went from a sitting position to standing. The sheet covering him fell away, exposing the rest of his body. His large obese stomach hung down and covered his mid-section in a sickening way.

Faster than any man should be able to move, Achish closed the distance between them and stood right in front of Abishai.

Startled by the sudden approach of the fat man, Abishai took a step back. But Achish snatched his right arm in a solid grip and pulled him closer, mashing Abishai into his obese stomach.

Abishai was taken aback by Achish's strength. His grasp was crushing! He felt as though his arm had been pinned underneath a fallen tree. All at once he lost all feeling in his forearm and fingers. A thought screamed through his mind to fight back with his other arm but his body would not obey the command. In fact, he found his body could not move at all.

"Do not think of me as some petty king that would bow to the whim of such a pathetic Jewish whelp! If I did not need you for the destruction of Israel, I would peel the flesh from your body, using your own hands to do it. I take great pleasure in causing the pain of others! I would keep you alive during the whole skinning process so you could experience every single moment to the fullest," Achish threatened in a degradingly low voice, spitting in Abishai's face with each word.

Abishai didn't know what was worse: the rancid breath and stink coming from the man, or the agony surging through his body from the king's massive death grip.

How is he causing me this much pain? Abishai thought to himself. He was beginning to feel his legs grow weak, and if he didn't get relief soon he knew he was going to pass out. He wanted to scream out, but his pride kept his mouth shut.

The king's rambling continued, "I *will* demand respect from you worm, and if I don't get it, you will die in the way I just described. Now, what do you say? Do we work together to get our revenge, or do you die?"

An even greater surge of pain roared through Abishai's body and he couldn't hold it back any further. A bellow of agony escaped his throat, resounding over the entire ship. As Abishai screamed uncontrollably, he vaguely noticed he was no longer bearing any weight on his legs. King Achish was holding him up into the air with only one arm. Abishai's vision began to blur, and just before he blacked out, he saw a blackish-gray swirl invade the king's eyes.

Chapter 7

A Sicarrii soldier picked up a wooden pail filled with sea water and looked at King Achish standing next to him. Without returning the look, the king nodded. The guard gave a grin of satisfaction as he slowly poured the cold water onto the face of the unconscious Abishai.

Awakening with a start, Abishai began swatting away the oncoming cascade of water, which the Sicarrii kept pouring in a steady stream. The assassin's grin widened into a broad smile of pleasure, as he saw the Jew flail about on the wooden deck.

Perturbed by the bodyguard's childish actions, Achish smacked the bucket out of the Sicarrii's hands. The man snapped back into bodyguard mode, took two steps back, and bowed his head to the king. Taking a step towards Abishai, Achish squatted his large, now fully clothed, frame next to the soaked man.

"I do apologize for my overzealous behavior earlier. But, to be fair, you were being quite the disrespectful mule, and on my own boat, no less. Here." Achish said holding out a white wool linen. "Take this and dry your face."

Sitting up, Abishai took the cloth from Achish. The salty seawater had stung his eyes and he was having a hard time focusing his vision. He dabbed the towel against his face and held it to his eyes. A throbbing pain pulsed at the back of his neck and the muscles in his arm felt strained and tired. His whole body was stiff and each of his joints moaned in agony at every little movement he made.

It all came flooding back to him. Achish had grabbed his arm and he had felt an unbearable torment scream through his body, as if death itself had reached out and ravaged him! Never had he felt such affliction. Yet, something else had happened. Something more than just the surge of pain. In those moments before he passed out, he felt… great fear. Fear and hopelessness, as if his soul was being snatched from the depths of Sheol, and darkness was crushing down upon him. This hopelessness had seemed to feed into the physical pain. It had felt as though his insides had been ripped apart and shredded.

Abishai realized that he had been sitting there for several moments with the towel over his face and the king was still squatting next to him.

"Wha…what did you do to me?" Abishai croaked out in a rough, weak voice. "How did you—"

The king cut him off, "There is much you do not understand, Jew. There are many things this world has to offer, seen and unseen. For instance, when you look at me, what do you see?"

A fat sow, Abishai wanted to say, for that was what he was. The king had to be at least four hundred pounds of jiggling flesh. Even though he was thinking it, Abishai chose to stay silent and said nothing.

The king continued, "It's ok. I can see you thinking it. You see a large fat man, so big he shouldn't even be able to stand or walk, and certainly not run. But yet, a few hours ago you saw me hop around and move like a cat. And you felt the strength of my resolve, quite literally. How can a man, such as you see before you, accomplish these things?"

Abishai gave no reply.

Smiling at him as if they were old friends, Achish continued, "You see, I am much more than what a man can see with his eyes. How can I put this in a way that you would understand? You Israelites are a narrow-minded lot. Let me help you open your eyes, if you will, with a lesson.

"You believe that the world was created and sustains itself through the power of only one God. You also believe that this one God has chosen your people as the light of the world so that all other nations will come to know this God through you. Does that sound about right?"

As a warrior and not a priest or a religious scholar, Abishai had never really put much thought into his studies of the Torah or the written Scriptures. Sure, he was taught as a child about El and the Law of Moses, but for him, those lessons were more about building character and morals. Abishai knew El existed, but many times he felt that El was distant or that He no longer cared about His people. So was Israel truly the light to the world?

Achish continued, "You might be surprised by me telling you this, but I also believe in your God, or El as you call Him."

This made Abishai raise an eyebrow and look Achish in the eye.

"That's right." Achish smirked. "I believe in your El, the God that made the earth, the animals, the plants and man. A powerful God is He. A God that can do all that demands respect. But your El is also deceiving, my friend. Your own Scriptures expose Him."

A humming sound broke into Abishai's mind and warned him not to listen to the blasphemy that was about to come from the Philistine's lips, but something deep inside of him wanted to know more.

Achish now sat next to Abishai with his legs folded, as if he was sitting around a campfire with a bunch of children. "With that in mind, let me begin a story. One I know you have heard.

"Your Torah begins with God, or El, creating the heavens and the earth and all that was therein. On the sixth day when He created man, he called the man Adam, the first of the image of El, and then Eve, the mother of all living things. El placed them in a garden and named it Eden. El walked in this garden with Adam and Eve. He treated them as if they were His children. Now most children grow up and learn the ways of the world but El had no desire to see his children grow to mature spiritual minds. He wanted Adam and Eve and all their future descendants to live a life that was a lie, a lie that only focused on the pleasures of life."

"Why are you telling me this? What does this have to do with what happened to me earlier?" Abishai asked as he scooted back a bit from Achish. *Why does this man always have to be so close? And where is that stench coming from? Is it coming from Achish?*

Scooting closer to Abishai, Achish closed the open gap between them before continuing.

"Listen, and you will see. One day El brought Adam and Eve on a day journey to the center of Eden and showed them a massive tree. It towered above all the other trees in the garden and the width of its trunk was sixty cubits. It was the mother of all trees, for El had made this tree to seed all other trees on the earth. It had leaves and fruits of various sizes and colors. It was a beauty to behold! El showed them this wondrous creation and told them that this was the tree of life. Its fruit would revive the weakest man and its leaves would heal the deadliest wounds. Consuming the seeds of the fruit would prevent death, even bring the dead back to life. But, when Adam and Eve heard this, they were confused because they knew not what death was. The world was new and they had never seen death. El, not wanting them to know of death, would not tell them what it was. He kept secrets from them.

"Then El took the couple on another short journey, a few hours walk east. They came upon another grand tree, although not as large as the first. This tree was also unique. Grand, fluttering, purple flowers covered the branches and gave an alluring scent of vanilla and jasmine. The tree's branches hung down around the trunk to make a giant dome. The tree, in all of its glory, looked like a fountain of purple silk cascading down to the ground. It was beautiful. Unlike the tree of life, this tree only produced one type of fruit. One had to walk into the dome of the tree, and once inside, you would find its massive blue fruit, as large as a man's hand."

Abishai may have been a bit foggy on his Torah lessons but he had studied enough to know that Achish was giving way too much detail and description. The Scriptures never spoke of such detail. He kept looking into Achish's eyes as he told the story and the king seemed enraptured by his own words. It was evident the king wished he was there in the garden. Abishai wanted to correct the king's story but he kept to himself and continued listening to the tale.

"El told the couple these words, 'From any tree of the garden you may eat freely; but from the tree of the knowledge of good and evil you shall not eat, for in the day that you eat from it you will surely die.'"

Growing tired of the ancient history lesson, Abishai grumbled out, "Yes, yes. And they ate from the fruit and El told them that they would die and, lo and behold! Eventually they did die. What are you getting at?"

The smile on the king's face disappeared and a look of contempt took its place. "You are an impatient fool, aren't you? How in Dagon's name have you survived this long with your lack of patience? If you speak again before I finish this tale I will personally remove your head with my bare hands and throw your body overboard as fish fodder. Is that clear? Is that clear?"

Abishai was shaken by the force of the king's voice and that feeling of crushing darkness sparked to life within him again. In fear, Abishai gave a short nod.

"Good," Achish said, bringing back his smiling face. "Now, where was I? Ah, yes. El had given them a test. Eat the fruit and die or not eat the fruit and live. But, the true test was a choice. A choice between living an eternal life in ignorance, or learning the truth of good and evil and paying the price of death for that knowledge.

"Now, there was another god by the name of Luce that didn't agree with the ways of El. Luce was the god of light, truth and knowledge. Before the creation, and before there was time, there was a great battle between El and Luce. Because Luce was outnumbered by the forces of El, he was beaten and cast into a nameless void. After El's creation, Luce took refuge on the earth, and when mankind was created, Luce took it upon himself to bring light and truth to Adam and Eve. He exposed El's lie and told the couple that if they ate of the fruit of the tree, they would not die but have the knowledge of good and evil just like El. They would then have the knowledge and power of choice, creating their own will and not having to live a life of slavery to El, to be His eternal pets.

"Fortunately, they were smart enough to follow Luce's advice and they ate of the fruit. And when they ate, their eyes were opened and they knew the truth. They had exposed the lie of El. And Luce has been working ever since, for over four thousand years now, showing the people the way of truth.

"You asked me how I got my power and vitality. It was through Luce. Well, actually it was through a general of Luce's, who will remain nameless. He is a lesser god that we serve and he is the commander of these very waters we sail on.

"He came to me in a vision a few years ago and granted me my abilities. When I asked him why he would give me such powers, he replied, 'To wage death and destruction upon the chosen ones of El'. So that has been our goal, to kill as many of your kind as possible. We could care less about your land or your trade routes or your resources and wealth. We only care about your extinction. And with your help, the destruction of the Jews will finally come to pass!"

Abishai couldn't hold his tongue any longer. "What you speak of is false. This Luce you talk about is not of truth, but the Father of Lies. We call him Satan. He took the form of a serpent in the Garden of Eden and deceived Adam and Eve. And when Adam and Eve did sin, death did come into the world. Satan is the cause for evil and darkness in the world."

Achish laughed, "And who are the ones who told you this? Your priests? Your parents? Your kings, David and Solomon? Are these not the very kings that struck hatred into your family's life and betrayed your brothers and murdered Joab? *They* are the ones who serve El and yet *they* bring death and destruction. Who then are the true bringers of darkness? All your life you have been told a lie! A lie that says El is your God and protector. If He *is* your protector, than why over the years have you lost countless lives to battle and disease? El doesn't care about you.

"But Luce, Luce will give you power when you ask of it. Power to change things, power to prevent people from dying, power to shape and fulfill your own destiny! I am living proof of that. Luce doesn't bring death and destruction, he brings life and power! All those great many years ago, it was Luce that brought *true* life to Adam and Eve."

Abishai knew that he should refute the man, but no words came to his lips. A dark whisper entered into his soul that nagged at him, persuaded him, and convinced him that there were grains of truth in the Philistine's words.

Many times Abishai had prayed to El for protection and guidance during the heat of battle, only to be rewarded with dying men all around him, and sometimes harm to himself. He remembered thinking, *Where was El? Why did El not grant us victory? Why did so many have to die? Why did my friends have to fall in battle? Why did my brothers have to die when they only served their king out of obedience? Why? Why? Why?*

Was it true? Had Israel been living a lie all these years and following a God that was flawed and absent? Was Luce a greater god to serve? Could Luce actually give him power, real tangible power to shape his own destiny?

"So what do you say?" Achish asked, hopping onto his feet as if he was a lad. "Will you join us? Will you join the side of power and strength and eventual victory? Your Israeli brothers have stabbed you in the back my friend. They have only been using you these many years and the way they repay you is with grief and death. They care nothing for you or your family. Your God, El, cares nothing for you as well. His silence is proof of that."

Reaching out his hand toward Abishai, Achish said, "You have a choice. Take my hand and accept the power of Luce, which I will freely give you to serve our cause, or cling to those that have betrayed you and find death."

Abishai sat there a moment, thoughtless, staring at the large, plump, hairy hand extended down to him. A breeze from the sea swept across the deck, blowing his wet hair to the side.

What did he have to lose? He had already turned his back on his country by becoming a spy, and he couldn't stomach serving under a king that had killed his brother.

Looking Achish in the eyes, Abishai saw a bold determination in the king's face. He raised his hand to take hold of the king's hand, but then paused. A question came to mind. "What will it cost me to have this power you speak of?"

Holding Abishai's gaze, Achish replied, "Nothing that you are not already willing to give up."

Abishai nodded his head, and then, with resolve, grabbed the Philistine's hand.

CHAPTER 8

Abaddon spurred his horse to go even faster.

For four hours, he, Broc, and Dan, along with thirty other riders had been mercilessly speeding across the seashore's wet sands to catch up to the Philistine ships. Almost an hour ago they had spotted a dozen vessels on the horizon and they were slowly gaining ground on them.

As Abaddon whipped his horse again, he glanced back and noticed that they had lost about twenty men in the pursuit. Some of the horses had given out from exhaustion or had broken their legs from taking a bad step.

Thirty men would still be more than enough to take care of Achish and his small contingent of soldiers. The problem was getting to them once the troop had caught up to them. Horses were no good in the water. He was hoping Brock and Dan had a plan in mind, because he himself had been unable to come up with anything tangible.

While trying to organize his thoughts, Abaddon began to feel a wet sticky spray on his face. He reached up and ran his hand over his cheek. It was blood and saliva. He looked down and noticed it was coming from the mouth and nose of his horse. Abaddon felt the beast's massive chest cavity working hard beneath him as it panted in a desperate wheeze. The horse's lungs were giving out from exertion. Abaddon knew the animal wouldn't last much longer. Leaning close to the horse's ear, Abaddon encouraged, "Come on girl! You're almost there! Don't let that devil get away. You can do it, girl!"

Without being whipped, the horse surged forward, racing even faster.

CHAPTER 9

With one mighty pull, King Achish brought Abishai to his feet. Now standing, the king drew Abishai in close to him and he squeezed his hand with all of his might.

Immediately, the crushing pain he had felt a few hours ago once again invaded his body. With wide, horrified eyes, Abishai gave Achish a pleading look to stop, but the king grasped his hand even harder. The darkness of fear returned and began to overshadow his mind and consume him. He could feel his heart rapidly pounding in his chest, beating so hard, he began to have a difficult time breathing. He wanted to scream out to relieve the pain, but his voice would not obey him. The only voice he could find was the one shouting inside of his head.

What is Achish doing? It feels as if he is trying to kill me. Why tell me all about El and Luce and revenge if he was simply going to kill me?

Realizing he had closed his eyes, Abishai forced them open. He wished he had not, for the face of King Achish had been replaced by a shapeless black mist with red glowing eyes.

In a soft, tender voice, the black mist said, "It's alright. Just let go. Let go. Let goooo. Let gooooooooo. Let go of your mind and let the pain in. Sshhhhhhh."

Abishai forced his eyes closed and refused to open them again. What was happening? What happened to Achish's face?

"Let go…let go…just…let… go."

Whether Abishai wanted to or not, the hypnotic voice was making him relax. It was an odd sensation. The pain was still there but he felt his mind give way. And then, with no warning, a surge of energy poured into him from Achish's hand.

If Abishai thought he was in agony before, it was nothing compared to now. It was as if fire was consuming him from the inside, licking at him from beneath his skin. He could feel blood pool in his mouth, boiling hot blood, and it poured from between his lips. He could also feel the wetness of blood dripping from his eyes and ears.

His eyes opened once more and he was horrified to see everything in a shade of red as blood covered his vision. A searing heat ignited behind his eyes and he felt actual flames burst from his eye sockets, burning out his eyes from the inside of his skull. It was then that his voice found itself and a wail of death consumed the air.

Before he blacked out for the second time, he felt and heard every bone in his hand crunch and break under the force of Achish's grip.

Achish spread a devilish grin across his face as he saw Abishai's legs give way, causing his body to crumple to the ground.

Realizing the transfer was complete, Achish flung the unconscious man's hand away from him, making it slap hard against the wooden deck.

This ritual had been a little more intense than the others he had done. When he had injected power into the giant, Golfriack, the only change that had taken place had been the liquid blackening of the eyes.

But this, this one was different. The eyes burned right out of the Jew's skull. Bending down, Achish looked closer at Abishai's face as the stench of burnt flesh wafted through the air. Small curls of smoke were escaping from his charred, empty eye sockets. Achish felt the perverse desire to stick his fingers into the man's eyeless skull. As he moved his hand to do so, black flames sparked to life from the deep, dark pits of Abishai's would-be eyes.

This startled Achish enough that he flailed backwards and landed on his backside. Embarrassed and angry at his own reaction, Achish jumped up and looked at his bodyguard next to him. The Sicarrii gave no reaction to the king's fumble and stoically stared straight ahead. Making a "*humph*" sound, Achish returned his attention to the still body of Abishai, lying sprawled out on the wooden deck.

Once again, Achish knelt and studied the constant black flames licking through Abishai's eye sockets. They were burning and yet the flesh around the eyes was staying in tact and not being scorched.

Once again Achish put his hand forward, but this time to touch the black flames. The fire danced around his fingers but did not burn him. He didn't even feel any heat, but he did sense energy… dark energy, flow into his hand. He pulled his hand back and stood.

Achish whispered to himself, "You are going to be truly powerful! I don't know what kind of demon our god has sent to me to put into you, but it is mighty!" Achish turned to speak to his guard but was interrupted before he could say a word.

"Several riders are approaching from the south!" The ship's watcher shouted from atop the mast. "They look like Israelites that have come from the battle!"

Smiling at the news, Achish looked off towards the shore which was now to the rear of the ship. "Perfect!" he exclaimed to himself.

Looking once again to his guard, he said, "Take Abishai back into my quarters and make him comfortable. See that some of the girls take good care of him."

Without even watching the muscular Sicarrii scoop up Abishai, Achish moved to the middle of the ship where the helm was located behind the center mass. The helmsman stepped aside to give the king control of the vessel. Turning the wheel hard to the right, back towards the shore, Achish announced to no one in particular, "It would be rude to leave without saying good-bye!"

CHAPTER 10

Abaddon pulled back hard on the reins and his horse and skidded to a stop. They had run out of beach. Lying before the troop of exhausted horses and riders was a steep incline of rough rock that started the Cliffs of Tyre. The cliffs loomed over one hundred cubits high and ran on for over thirty leagues. The rocky terrain provided no access to the sea until the port city of Tyre on the other side of the mountainous bluffs.

The ships they were chasing had already broken past the plains and had sailed beyond the cliffs.

All but four.

Achish's flag ship was about two hundred cubits from the beach and three other smaller vessels bobbed along in front of it. They must have been anchored because they were not progressing forward. The three black and red sails on the lead ship were folded down and about twenty oars were in the water stroking backwards to keep the vessel from moving any closer to the shore.

Many of the riders in the Israeli party drove their horses as far as they could into the sea and began shooting arrows towards the ships. None of them made their mark but plunged into the greenish-blue waters.

"Save your arrows! We are too far out of range!" Dan ordered, looking at his men and holding up an arm.

"So what are we going to do?" came a voice from one of the men. "Did we ride all this way for nothing?"

Dan did not have an answer. It was his hope that they would beat the ships to the cliffs and ambush them by setting some water traps, a trick he had learned many years ago when he lived in Egypt. But it would take at least an hour to set them up.

"How in the devil's name did they get here so fast? As fast as we were riding, we should have beaten them here!" Dan said to no one in particular.

"I think your curse is the answer," Broc said as he pulled his horse up next to Dan's. "We rode hard and swift but there is some evil working here that gives speed to these dogs."

"Hello, there! Can you hear me, or do I need to move a bit closer?" came Achish's voice over the waters.

Trotting his horse to the other side of Dan, Abaddon leaned forward in his saddle and squinted his eyes. "Is that—"

"It sure is. You've got to be kidding me!" Broc said, shaking his head. "That is the fat King Achish."

Spurring his horse into the water until it was knee deep, Dan yelled back to the ships, "No, we can't hear you! Why don't you float a little this way so we can speak without yelling?"

The response was not words, but laughter. Clear, boisterous laughter. Achish began laughing so hard he doubled over the rail. Not only was Achish laughing, but all the men on all four vessels were laughing as well.

"It wasn't that funny," Broc said with a bewildered face.

"That is because he is insane," Abaddon said a little too seriously. "Dan, look at the boats. They are drifting closer. The waves are bringing them in towards the cliffs. I have an idea. Keep him talking."

Before Dan could respond, Abaddon whipped his horse around and sped off over the beach and up a rough trail that led to the top of the bluffs. Broc made a fist in the air, signaling a few of the men to follow Abaddon. Five riders took off after him.

"What do you think he is going to do?" Broc said out loud as he watched the six riders struggle up the rocky slope.

"Got me!" Dan said, keeping his eyes fixed on Achish's boat. "But, knowing Abaddon, it is going to be dangerous and stupid. I'm pretty sure I was never that reckless when I was that young."

"When you were that young? You're only ten seasons older than Abaddon," Broc reminded him. "Apparently you don't remember the battle of Jair."

A smile broke across Dan's face.

Broc continued, "You ran out of arrows, and had lost your sword to who knows where, so you charged the enemy archers and started pelting them with stones."

Dan's smile got even bigger. "Oh yeah, good times! It worked. I caused enough chaos that every one of those archers went running for the hills."

"You came out of it with three arrows sticking out of you!"

"Bah! Details!" Dan said, laughing now.

"My point is, you're nuts. Abaddon is nuts. I'm fighting wars with a bunch of nuts!" Broc said trying not to laugh, himself.

Dan was about to give a rebuttal, but was interrupted by a shout coming from Achish's boat.

"I am so sorry that we couldn't say good-bye in person, but, you see, I am off to finish training my *new* army." Achish gloated.

"What army, you pathetic fool?" Broc hollered back. "Your army is destroyed! Your towns have been burned! Your women and children have become slaves! Your weak men have surrendered and your strong men are dead! The name of Philistine is all but lost! Come now! Come! Pull your boat ashore and accept your fate with dignity and honor! I promise you, you will be given a chance to defend yourself once you touch these shores. But have no disillusions, your death will be swift!"

Achish and his men began to laugh again.

"Again, did I say something funny?" Broc asked Dan.

Achish spoke before Dan could answer. "No, Captain Broc, we will not be coming ashore, for I have much to do in my life yet."

Broc was taken aback. "You know me? We have never met! How do you know who I am?"

"Ah, I know a great many things," Achish mused. "And if I am not mistaken, that is Captain Dan next to you. And was that not

Abaddon with you a few moments ago? I am sure he is off trying to come up with a foolish plight to overtake us. Although, I must say, I am quite impressed with Abaddon's skills as a warrior. I never thought he would be able to defeat Golfriack. Oh, and your plan to box in our soldiers on all sides was extremely entertaining, to say the least."

Gripping the reins of his horse, Dan gritted his teeth and said, "We were told you left your army before Abaddon defeated Golfriack. Is that not so?

"It is so," Achish answered with a smile.

"Then how did you know how the battle ended up, or how Abaddon beat your giant?"

"I really shouldn't say….oh, but I must! It is too delicious to keep a secret!" Achish announced, almost jumping up and down with the excitement. "I will tell you this. We picked up a friend along the way. A friend that you have called friend as well."

"A spy?" Broc whispered.

"Yes, captain, a spy! Truth be told, I have several spies in your ranks, around your homes, even in your royal palace! Spies, spies, spies! Captain Broc, you may be sitting next to a spy even now! I told you this bit of news was delicious!"

Broc looked over to Dan, but Dan just shook his head. Broc whispered to Dan, "I know you are not a spy, but he must be speaking the truth. We figured as much back when we conquered Gath, and Achish escaped the city moments before we invaded. Someone had tipped him off, but we never found out who."

Looking back towards Achish, Dan shouted, "Well, don't keep us in suspense! Who is it?"

"You will figure it out soon enough. And trust me, you will meet him again. And when you do, I doubt that you will survive the encounter! Well, this has been fun and all, but it is time to say good-bye."

A short, stubby-framed man standing next to Achish handed him a ram's horn and Achish blew into it. The sound of the horn was deafening as it echoed off the cliff's walls.

It was a signal.

Every man in the three smaller boats raised bows and aimed to fire. The small vessels had been slowly making their way closer to shore and now they were in firing range of the Israeli riders. Dan, Broc and his men were on the beach, out in the open and with no place to hide.

"Cover!" Dan yelled.

The riders scrambled for their shields and some jumped from their horses as a hundred arrows flew in their direction. Most of the men, who were seasoned and well-trained, slid from their mounts and hung to the side of their horses, using the animals as a shield. In war, many times arrows were dull or poorly shot and the arrow would bounce off the horse's hide, only to leave a bruise; but now this was not the case. Sixteen horses were killed in the onslaught and four men were dead on the ground.

Broc was about to give the order to return fire, but was interrupted by a loud war cry coming from the top of the cliffs. What he saw next he would never forget.

Six horses leapt from the bluffs above and plummeted to the ships below. The men on the boats, who were about to let a second assault of arrows fly, stood in a trance of awe and bewilderment as these falling horses, still mounted by their riders, were now diving towards them.

Time seemed to stand still as the Philistine warriors froze in place, not sure how to handle this unexpected attack.

Then, as if someone unfroze time, panic erupted over all three of the smaller vessels as they realized they were directly in the path of the falling beasts.

About half way through the fall, Abaddon yelled, "Now!"

All six riders left their mounts and jumped for open water next to the bobbing targets.

What happened next was chaos.

Abaddon's horse and another slammed into the closest boat. The impact sent the beasts straight through the middle of the ship. Crushed and shattered lumber exploded from the vessel, sending men flying in all directions.

It was then, three more horses landed on the second ship, causing just as much damage. Men were flung so high into the air that some of them landed on the shore, right at the Israeli's feet.

The third small vessel was lucky, only in the aspect that it was not struck by a horse. The men on the third ship frantically tried to put up their sail to retreat, but their effort was in vain. Abaddon and the other five riders had already swam to the boat and scaled up the sides. There was no contest. Many of the men aboard were archers and not swordsman. Within a few moments, twenty dead Philistines blanketed the bottom of the boat.

Three boats down and one to go.

Achish's flag ship had not stuck around for the show. They were already a couple of hundred cubits away and sailing out to sea.

Abaddon hurriedly headed for the mast of the small vessel he had conquered, and with all haste, began pulling the rope to raise the sail so they could pursue Achish's ship, but something was wrong. The rope pulled too fast and too easy. The rope then sprang from the pulley; it had been cut. The ship was dead in the water.

Achish was getting away. Again.

Running to the edge of the boat, Abaddon stared at the escaping ship. With anger and battle fury consuming him, he screamed, "Coward!"

Abaddon heard the faint echoes of laughter as the large ship faded into the horizon.

CHAPTER 11

The celebration was enormous!

People from all over the twelve tribes of Israel came to Jerusalem to celebrate the downfall of the Philistines, the enemy of Israel for almost four hundred seasons. Thousands of signs and declarations of "Shalom," or peace, were posted on flags, banners, houses, and even on people's clothes. The oppression and war with the Philistines was finally over! Israel could now look forward to peace and prosperity.

So many people had come to Jerusalem for the celebration that camps and tents were set up in all directions around the Holy City for several leagues. Vendors and merchants, from as far north as Damascus and as far south as Egypt, flooded in to sell their wares to the large gathering mass of Israeli people. Musicians played in the streets and in the camps, and many of the people sang and danced. Great feasts took place and the smell of fire roasted beef and honeyed lamb consumed the air from every direction. Barrels of wine and ale were brought in from all the tribes to add to the merriment.

The celebration would go on for seven days and nights.

It was on the third day of the festivities that Benaiah and his army arrived in Bethlehem, a city just south of Jerusalem.

Benaiah rode his horse and led his captains. The captains, who were also on horses, led their men, who followed on foot. Commander, captains, and soldiers alike were all dressed in full battle uniforms.

With each unified step forward the proud, victorious army made the ground shake with their resolve.

Men, women, and children lined the leagues of road between Bethlehem and Jerusalem, cheering on and greeting the warriors. The warriors were given strict orders not to break ranks or to fellowship with the crowds, but to march and to keep their honor until granted leave within the walls of Jerusalem, as per tradition. The soldiers' families, whom they had not seen for six months, would be waiting for them there.

Flowers and palm branches were tossed down in front of the military entourage, creating a colorfully scented path clear to the southern gate of Jerusalem, or Mount Zion, as most Israelites called it.

Upon the approach of the city gate, Benaiah looked up and felt a wave of contentment and peace wash over him as he looked at the towering gates and walls that protected his beloved city. There was nothing like coming home and knowing the people he cared about were waiting on the other side of that gate. Even though he was not married and had no children to succeed him, many of his men had that blessing.

Benaiah had always thought it cruel to bring a wife into his life, knowing that the military would always be a mistress to him. He could never say goodbye to a woman he loved before each campaign, not knowing if he would be coming back. Why put a woman through that?

Many of his men, though, thought differently. It was the drive to protect their women and families that made them fight, and fight all the harder. It was their families that gave them hope and an instinct to survive with each stroke of their blade. They needed something to fight for and this gave them purpose.

Each to their own, Benaiah thought.

Stopping his horse before the closed gate in front of him, Benaiah turned his steed around to face his army, thrust his fist in the air, and called out, "Dali!" which was the military command for stop.

A chorused shout of "Dali!" echoed throughout the ranks. With one last foot stomp to the ground, four thousand men came to a halt and stood as statues under the mid-morning sun.

Pride swelled up inside Benaiah as he gazed over his men and smiled. These were good soldiers, good men, and good brothers of Israel. Turning his horse back to the gate, Benaiah withdrew his sword and held it high into the air.

The roaring crowd around them quieted down to a hush, awaiting a tradition that had gone on since the days of King Saul, the first king of Israel.

While the men of Israel were at war, the southern gate would remain closed until the army's return. Only then would the southern gate be opened to welcome home Israel's fighting men. The tradition was held that the highest ranking officer returning from battle would give the command to open the gates.

Only having had this honor a few times, Benaiah called out in a loud voice, "Men and women of Jerusalem, your valiant warriors stand at your gates and have returned victorious! Will you not open your doors and allow us to come home?"

As if rehearsed, a mighty shout from the city guard and all the people from within the walls of Zion replied, "You are welcome home our beloved brothers!"

And with those words the two massive doors cracked and creaked on their hinges as they birthed open. The silence in the crowd broke and the roar of celebration erupted once more throughout the land.

For the next hour the army marched triumphantly into the city. As soon as the last soldier breached the threshold of the gate, five hundred trumpeters stood on the city wall and blew their shofars in unison, a tune recognized by all that a herald was about to speak.

As one, the soldiers turned an about-face and all eyes looked upon a familiar face, a man they had grown to love, their king, Solomon. He was standing on top of the arch over the southern gate. Once again the crowd quieted so they could hear the message of their ruler.

"Brothers and Sisters of Israel! Hear me now! For too long have we lived in the shadow of an enemy that has haunted the steps we take, that has tainted the air we breathe, that has murdered the kin we hold dear, that has thieved and horded our lands, that has raped and consumed our daughters, that has brought ruin and destruction to our villages, that has plundered our crops, and has blasphemed and degraded our God! But today! On this day! We have no fear! For the shadow of Philistia has been obliterated by the light of Jehovah through the strength of His right hand! Philistia! Is! No! More!"

The crowd erupted in cheers.

"Henceforth, today is a day of victory and celebration!"

Solomon turned his attention to Benaiah and his men. "Men, you have fought valiantly and with honor. The brothers we have lost will never be forgotten, for it is with their sacrifice and blood that we can claim victory. All hail the victorious dead!"

"All hail the victorious dead!" came the reply of the soldiers.

"Go now! Go to your families and live the freedom you have earned!"

The crowd once again roared to life in cheers and excitement.

The soldiers and the crowd blended into one and excited cries of family reunions echoed throughout the city. Unfortunately, there were also wails and mourning cries as family members learned of the deaths of their husbands, brothers, and sons.

Abaddon had always hated this part of war. Like many of the captains and the commander, Abaddon had never pursued marriage or found himself attached to a woman. It made things too complicated.

Dismounting from his horse, Abaddon handed the reigns over to a stable boy who lead the animal away to the royal stables for food and water. Abaddon wanted to make his way to the palace, to his own room and rest, but he knew it would be several hours before he could actually get there. Already he had been given numerous invitations to various houses for a good meal and asked to tell of his heroic feats throughout the battle. And then there would be the royal feast later that evening in which the generals and warriors of honor would dine with the king and give their account of the war.

Already, many in the land had heard of Abaddon's duel with the giant Golfriack and how the beast was bested with a mere stick. People began swarming around Abaddon, hoping to hear the tale from the man himself. Abaddon was no poet or story teller though, especially if those stories had to do with himself. He hated making himself out to be the hero, even though most of the time he was the hero. He didn't like the attention.

As Abaddon carefully made his way through the crowd, he received many pats on the back and several gracious compliments.

He looked around and enjoyed watching the men laughing with family and loved ones and seeing them full of life. This was what it meant to be home.

Covering his head with the hood of his cloak, Abaddon disappeared into the crowd, heading towards the palace. People would be disappointed, but the many invitations for food and adventure stories would have to be denied.

CHAPTER 12

"Mother! Enough is enough! These gold plates are so clean and polished that we can see ourselves in them. My looking glass isn't even this clear!" Rachel protested, inspecting and wiping down the dinner plates for the fifth time.

"And did you go through the goblets one more time, just to make sure?" Rachel's mother questioned with a hint of tease in her voice.

"Yes! Yes! It is all done! Please, can I go now to the south gate to meet the soldiers? Everybody in the city is going to be there. Can I go?" Rachel pleaded.

Mirah, Rachel's mother, stared at her daughter for a moment. She was truly a vision of beauty. Rachel had thick, black hair that waved from the top of her head, down her slender frame, and all the way to the small of her back. Her skin was a dark olive color, a result of the many hours spent outdoors working in the gardens and vineyards. Her face was lean and very feminine with gentle features. And then there were her eyes, those dark green emerald eyes which captured everyone who looked upon them. Mirah was losing herself in them at this very moment.

Mirah sighed and took in the beauty of her precious daughter. She missed the little girl that used to bound around the palace playing hide and seek. The little girl that used to come running to her in tears and grab her leg whenever she had scrapped her knee.

Over the past year, a woman had taken shape and the girl was all but gone. Rachel was seventeen seasons and about to be eighteen on the next moon.

Where does the time go? Mirah thought, sighing again.

Mirah picked up a few of the golden plates and inspected them. She wanted everything to be perfect for the king's celebration feast tonight.

Mirah and her kin had been servants to the king's household since the days of King Saul, through the reign of the great King David and now for King Solomon. David and Solomon had been very good to Mirah's family, and she wanted to keep their good standing by producing the best work possible.

Putting down the plate, she picked up two of the goblets and began to inspect them. After looking at every nook and cranny of the cups, she smiled with approval. "Good job sweetie. Yes, you can go, but—"

Rachel immediately sprinted towards the door. "Thank you, thank you, thank you, Mother!"

"Please be back in an hour for the feast preparations!" Mirah shouted at the fleeing Rachel, already disappearing down the corridor.

Mirah smiled to herself, enjoying her daughter's bubbly demeanor. She was so full of life and hopefulness. She never saw the bad in people. She was a healer of the heart and a lifter of souls. She loved people and loved life and was never afraid to show it.

Now, if she could just get the girl married, all would be well. Most girls were wed by the time they were fourteen or fifteen seasons, but it had not been easy finding the right suitor for Rachel. Actually, there were plenty of men willing to court the beautiful girl, the challenge was finding a man that Rachel would accept.

Mirah was a product of an arranged marriage, as were most girls in Israel; but she struggled for many years, many long years with a man that cared not for love and affection, but only for a woman to serve him and clean up after him. The memory made Mirah shake her head in disgust. Her late husband, Loca, was a drunk and a greedy man, and she was rather glad Jehovah saw fit to take him early in his life. Loca had never been a good spouse or a good father. The only good thing Loca had done was give Mirah her daughter, Rachel.

When Loca died, Rachel was young and Mirah had never felt the yearning to marry again. Being a part of the king's household kept her family safe and secure, and all the things she needed in life were already provided for.

But it was at times like this she wished she had a husband to take the role of match-maker and find the right man for her dear Rachel, for this was the way of things. It was the fathers that found the right man to marry their daughters. What better person to find a man of worth, integrity, honor and strength than a woman's father, seeing that those were the qualities that a father would have for his daughter?

Unfortunately, Mirah was alone in this task and was unwilling to ask another man to take the role.

"El will provide," she said silently to herself, believing in her prayer. The God of heaven had always looked after them and she believed with all of her heart that El would continue to do so.

Picking up a gold platter made for displaying roasted lamb, Mirah began wiping it down, again. Keeping her hands busy, she prayed an all-too-familiar prayer, *"Great and powerful Jehovah. Creator of the heavens and earth. Abba, Father. I thank you for the gifts of life you have given me and my daughter. You have seen fit to feed, clothe and protect us. Abba, I pray to You steadfastly that You would complete my joy and the joy of my daughter and find her the right man to lead her in a greater relationship with you. I do not know of the ways of a great and godly man, but you do, Lord. Please bring a man into her life to husband her and take care of her in the days to come, for I am not the youth I once was. I know that my time to meet you in person is coming soon. I can feel it deep within me. As you have taken care of me, take care of Rachel. Let it be done."*

"Where is he?" Rachel muttered to herself.

Wadding through the mass of people, Rachel hopped up and down to get a better look as to who was around. On a few of those hops, Rachel had picked out Captain Jacob and Commander Benaiah, both of them like family to her, but not the one she was looking for. She found her way next to a fruit cart and took the opportunity to climb up one of its wheels to get a better view.

Her mother's voice entered into her mind, *A woman doesn't do things like climb up on wagon wheels; in fact, a woman doesn't climb things at all. It's not proper. It's not lady-like.*

Rachel smiled to herself. She didn't care much for things that were lady-like, but rather for things that were adventurous. Much of the time, in order to be adventurous, one could not be lady-like. So up the wagon wheel she went.

Once atop the wheel there was more than one person willing to remind her, "Act your age," and "Come down from there." And yet another said, "A little old for climbing, aren't we?" But Rachel paid it no mind. She liked who she was, and she wasn't going to let other boring people tell her otherwise.

Now balancing atop the wheel, she had a good view of the area around the southern gate, but she still could not spot him. Where was he?

Then, without warning, something hard hit the back of her knees and her legs went flying out from under her. Rachel let out a surprised cry of panic. She wanted to twist her body around to try and catch herself but before she could, two large arms caught her in mid-fall and spun her in a circle. When the twirl stopped she looked up into Dan's smiling face.

"What's up Rachel? It was nice of you to…drop…in," Dan said, emphasizing the word drop, and began laughing at his own joke.

Rachel couldn't help but smile and even started to giggle a bit. Dan was so corny and really not that funny, but he was a jokester in his own right and always made her feel good about herself. Dan was like an older brother to her, even though he was about a decade her senior. He had always looked after her.

"Ha, ha," she said dryly but with a smile still on her face. "Now if you wouldn't mind putting me down, I would have a proper welcome."

Dan smirked and tossed her in the air and caught her by her waist. Then, with all grace and control, he lowered her down to her feet. Once again she couldn't help but laugh a little.

Now that she was on solid ground again, Rachel wrapped her petite arms around Dan's neck and squeezed for all she was worth. While still in the embrace, she softly said, "I am glad you guys are home safe and sound." She kissed his cheek and released him.

"What was the kiss for?" Dan asked putting his hand up to his cheek.

"For coming back safe and victorious of course." And then Rachel balled up her fist and punched Dan in the stomach, then immediately recoiled her hand and shook it.

"Ouch!" she murmured, and started to laugh. "Your gut is like a brick wall."

"What was *that* for?" Dan said looking amused at the sudden change of mood.

"That was supposed to be for scaring me half to death when you swept me off that wagon wheel."

Dan's boisterous laugh exploded, and he put his arm around Rachel and gave her another good squeeze. "Just keeping you on your toes. I take it you were up there looking for lover boy."

"He is not my lover boy," Rachel said a little too defensively. "But, yes, I am looking for him. Is he not here? I thought for sure he would come in with you and the other captains."

Dan held out his arm and Rachel gladly took it as they began to walk through the crowd. "Abaddon was here, but you know him. He hates all the attention. He will face off a hundred men in battle but will turn and hide when just one person approaches him to say thank you or to give him praise."

"Oh, come now. He is not that bad. You exaggerate too much. But you are right in the sense that he never enjoys the glory of battle afterwards."

Dan nodded in agreement.

As they slowly walked, the crowd around them naturally parted out of their way. Dan's large size usually had that effect. "Well, I almost hate to tell you where he went, knowing that you will leave me without such a beautiful escort."

Without saying a word, Rachel released Dan's arm and stepped in front of him, giving a great big pleading smile. Her bright, brilliant green eyes danced with anticipation as she pleaded, "I've waited all day to see him."

Dan couldn't help but belt out another large laugh. "Child, who can resist you? With that smile and those eyes, you could persuade a shepherd from his staff! Go on, then! He has taken the east cart path to the palace. Hurry and you might catch him!"

If it was possible, Rachel smiled even more. She gave Dan a quick peck on the cheek and off she went, moving as fast as she could through the crowd. Dan shook his head and grinned, "Ah, young love."

"Or is it foolish games?" Broc commented, coming up beside Dan and watching the young woman wiggle her way through the mass of people and eventually disappear altogether.

"You know about their little ritual every time Abaddon gets home from battle, don't you?"

"Ritual? What ritual?" Dan asked, looking at Broc and arching an eyebrow. "That boy better not have any misgivings towards that sweet lass or I'll—"

"Hah! Nothing like that. It is actually the other way around. It is what she will do to him that concerns me. Come with me, brother! I will tell you all about the foolishness of the young over a cup of wine."

CHAPTER 13

Rachel ran as fast as she could. She figured that if Abaddon was taking the cart path, she could take the main market road and beat him to the palace. The cart path was an old rough road on the east side of the city and was only used by the merchants that delivered goods to the palace. It was off limits to other vendors, so there weren't many travelers on the cart path. That was probably why Abaddon chose it, so he could avoid the crowds. The problem with the cart path was that it wound around a bit before getting to the palace's back entrance near the royal stables. The market road was a direct line to the palace's main gate, but it was slow going due to all the people crowding the streets.

Rachel found herself exasperated as the crowd thickened and she was forced to a slow walk.

"This is taking too long. He is going to beat me to the palace," she muttered under her breath. She glanced over to the side of the street and saw a ladder leading up to the roof of one of the merchant shops. She smiled to herself and worked her way over to the ladder.

A minute later Rachel was running at full speed on the rooftops.

It's not like this is the first time I have done this, she thought to herself.

Growing up, she, Abaddon, and Solomon would travel all over the city by way of the roof tops. In one way or another, all of the roofs were connected by boards and beams, awnings and joint rafters. The trick was not to lose her balance and fall through a thatched roof, landing on someone's supper table.

Smiling at the thought, Rachel remembered how Abaddon had done that very thing at the age of eight. Although, it wasn't funny at the time. When Abaddon's father had found out, he had made Abaddon shoot his bow for 12 hours straight. His hands got so raw, it was five days before Abaddon could even grasp a cup to drink from.

Shaking off the memory, Rachel doubled her efforts to reach Abaddon.

In a short amount of time, Rachel reached the cart path outside the royal stables. She looked upon the old road and spotted Abaddon down at the bottom of the last hill, trudging his way up to the stables. A smile of victory spread across her rose colored cheeks.

Still atop the building, Rachel looked down to see an empty grain cart on her side of the road, and a large pile of straw directly on the other side of the road.

That was a perfect ambush spot!

She made her way to the side of the building, slid down the front awning and dropped down about four cubits to the ground. After landing silently on her feet, she made her way to the grain cart, crouching behind it. She looked through the grass around her, found three small stones, and picked them up and gripped them tightly.

Rachel was almost in place, and soon the attack would commence. She began to giggle in anticipation, but then realized she was making to much noise, so she cupped her hand over her mouth. Calming her breathing, she got into position and waited.

Tired and lost in thought, Abaddon made his way up the hill, the palace stables coming into sight. He liked going in the back way and using the servants' entrance instead of entering through the front gates. The front gates were where all the so-called important people went into the palace. All the *look-at-me-and-see-how-important-I-am* people, who loved to show off their status and wealth.

Those kind of people made Abaddon sick. And what was more sickening was that they all wanted to be his friends. Over the last several years, Abaddon had made quite the reputation for himself as a warrior, and it seemed everyone wanted to meet him. He was officially in the celebrity status. In a way, he was used to it, since his father was one of the Mighty Three.

Fame and glory never appealed to him though. If half of those rich dead-beats had ever taken up a sword and stepped onto a battlefield, they would wet themselves and run home to their mothers. The thought made Abaddon smile and he chuckled to himself in amusement.

And then his father's voice invaded his mind from a long ago conversation.

We learn to wield the sword so that others may never do so. Not all men should know the weight of spilling the blood of other men. Let us who have been conditioned carry that burden for all of Israel. We not only fight and slay the wicked to secure our country's freedom, but we do so to keep the people's innocence as well. Should we insist that the baker pick up a sword to wage war? Just as the baker would never ask us to knead dough and bake bread, we should not expect him to spill the blood of others. El forbid that thought!

Smiling at the memory, Abaddon remembered the lesson it was meant to teach, and that his father was an awful cook. He couldn't bake a loaf of bread if his life depended on it.

Cresting the hill, Abaddon took in the scene before him. For the most part, the area was pretty empty. Two stable boys were mucking out a few of the horse stalls and Ben, the stable master, was standing next to Abaddon's stead, brushing it down and letting the beast drink from the water trough.

Looking Abaddon's way, Ben smiled, shifting around a piece of straw in his mouth. Abaddon was about to raise his hand and say hello when he felt his stomach tighten and the air around him became still.

Something was amiss.

Looking to his left, he saw an old grain cart that had been sitting in the same spot for years. A broken axle kept it from being used. Judging by the length of time the cart had been there, Ben had no plans to fix it. To his right was a large pile of fresh straw to be used as bedding for the horses in the stables.

Abaddon glanced back towards Ben who still had the same goofy grin on his face, but now he looked like he would start laughing.

Abaddon then grinned as well. He could always sense danger when it was near. Now whether that danger was truly dangerous was another matter.

"Rachel? I know you're there. Nice try. Come on out."

Rachel had been doing this since they were kids. It was a game…of sorts. When they were younger, he, Rachel, and Solomon would run around the city and play a form of hide and seek. One person would hide and the other two would seek the one who was hiding. Although, the one hiding could tackle a seeker, capturing him and making him hide as well. Of course, as they got older the game changed.

Actually, Rachel was the only one that kept the game going. Solomon had stopped playing long ago, something about having to be mature enough to rule a kingdom, and Abaddon was now gone a lot traveling with the army. But sure enough, when Abaddon came home, Rachel would hide and try to surprise attack him somewhere.

Abaddon didn't mind. He actually enjoyed Rachel's spunk and giddy behavior. She was a good friend and someone he could always talk to and have fun with.

A clack sound rang from behind the grain cart.

A smile spread across Abaddon's face as he took a few careful steps towards the cart. He strengthened his stance, ready for Rachel to spring out at him. When they were younger she would simply try to tackle him, but within the last few years Abaddon had been teaching her Maavac Krav, a military fighting style that his father and Eleazor had created for hand-to-hand combat. It also consisted of several throws and strikes used to unbalance one's opponent.

Needless to say, Rachel was a good student.

Abaddon took a careful step forward to see if he could peak around the cart. As he did so, an explosion of straw erupted behind him across the road.

Like a monster breaking out of its cage, Rachel shot up and out of the straw pile. Without hesitation, she launched two stones straight at Abaddon's head.

All this happened before Abaddon even got the chance to turn around. Without looking, Abaddon could sense the projectiles soaring towards him. Still facing the cart, he whipped up his hand and caught both rocks in the order they were thrown. Abaddon turned to face a straw covered Rachel, smiling at him, but with disappointment in her eyes.

"Are you nuts?" he said with an arched eyebrow and a grin. "You could have hit me with these. And you were aiming at my head?" He was about to toss the stones aside when he got a better idea.

"Here, let us see how quick you are on your feet."

Abaddon threw the rocks at her feet, although not as hard, and missing on purpose. Rachel laughed and danced out of the way of both of the incoming stones. Abaddon was always amazed at how fast she could move. Before he could even release one of the rocks, she was already well clear of its landing area.

When the short dance was over, Rachel stood still before the straw mound, folded her hands in front of her and smiled warmly at him, like she had done so many times before.

"I missed you," she simply said.

Before responding, Abaddon took a good look at her. She had always been there for him. Every time he had come home from battle she had been there, in one way or another, to welcome him home.

Whenever Abaddon was having a bad day, she would pick up on it and find some way to cheer him up. When his father was killed in war and the world's darkness was closing in, she alone was a light that never grew dim. She was his best friend. But lately…lately things seemed a bit different.

From his perspective he was the same, his feelings towards her were the same. For him, nothing had changed. But there was something about her. Her eyes would dance a little more, her smile would persuade and gleam in a slightly different way. Her walk was more bold and her body held more confidence. It was like she had a secret to tell but was not keen on telling it. These thoughts coursed through Abaddon's mind in but a moment as he smiled back at Rachel.

"I missed you, too," he said, stepping closer to her, reaching out his hand to take hers. She took it and then in a split second her smile turned playful again and a bit devious.

Abaddon knew what was coming and let it play out.

Pulling Abaddon's arm as hard as she could to her left, Rachel stuck out her left foot behind his leg, causing him to stumble backward into the straw mound. When he landed, he threw his hands behind his head to make it look like he meant to fall into the straw in a resting position.

He smiled up at Rachel and said in a playful tone, "How did you know I wanted to take a nap?"

She looked down at him with narrow eyes of defeat and couldn't help but laugh. "You are so incorrigible. You taught me that throw. I take it, it needs work?"

"Nah, it was good…except I saw it coming from a league away."

"Ah. I bet you didn't see this coming." Rachel fell sideways on top of Abaddon, driving her elbow into his chest, instantly knocking the wind out of him.

In a gasp he said, "Nope, I wasn't ready for that one."

For the next several long moments the two laid in the straw, looking up towards the sky and the clouds that El had scattered out before their eyes. A nice warm breeze would occasionally fill the air with the scent of jasmine, making them feel that much more relaxed.

Turning her head to the side, Rachel gazed upon her good friend. Abaddon had his eyes closed, enjoying the ray of sunshine falling down upon him. Thoughts flooded her mind of all the experiences she had shared with this dear companion…friend. Although lately the word *friend* didn't seem like a strong enough description for the feelings she had for him. The boy and playmate that she once knew and loved had been replaced by a strong and valiant man who had the mind and will of a warrior, but also a heart that was full of compassion and humility. It also didn't hurt that he was handsome as well.

Propping herself up onto her elbow, Rachel took a better look at his face. She loved his long black hair. Not dark brown and curly like many of the Jewish boys, but raven black and wavy, with a short, trimmed beard to match. His jaw was well-defined and strong. Looking down his sturdy torso, she watched his chest rise and fall as he breathed.

To say that Abaddon was muscular was an understatement. Rachel had had the privilege of training with Abaddon, and while he moved through his fighting stances he had caught her eye more than once. He was well muscled and fit from head to toe.

Rachel glanced up once again to Abaddon's face to find his eyes still closed. She wanted to put her arm around his neck, draw in close to him and lay her head on his shoulder. She wanted to feel the rise and fall of his chest against her own body. She trusted this man. She felt safe with him. She wanted more than just a friendship. She loved him and she really wanted Abaddon to love her in the same way. Not the love they had always known as friends, or as a brother loves a sister, but a love and a desire that would make her his wife.

Rachel collapsed onto her back and stared at the sky once again. She let out a silent sigh.

Who am I kidding? Abaddon will never love me like that.

She very clearly remembered a conversation a year earlier. One of Solomon's cousins was getting married and all of the tribe of Judah was at the wedding. It was there Abaddon had shared to a group of friends that he didn't have a desire to wed. He had gone on to explain that he didn't want to leave a wife and family behind every time he went to war. He didn't feel he could let someone he loved worry like that while he was away. Or he had said some kind of garbage like that. Rachel didn't agree with his thinking, but she kept it to herself.

I need to think about something else.

Turning to Abaddon again, she reached up and flicked his nose. He opened his eyes and looked at her.

"How do you do it?" Rachel asked.

"How do I do what?"

"The rocks. You didn't even turn around to look and you caught both of them perfectly."

Abaddon turned to his side to face her. "I don't know. I just can. I have always been able to sense things before they happen."

"Sense, how?"

"How do I explain? I could…hear them. You know what it is like when you are riding a horse at a full trot and how the wind sounds rushing past your ears?"

Rachel nodded

"Well I can hear the air rushing around the rocks. It's weird, and kinda hard to explain. I also get a queasy feeling in my stomach that warns me something is happening around me. I don't know. It is kinda like all my senses get heightened. I guess that is why I am so effective in battle. It is easy for me to see things that others don't."

"Well, I am glad it helps you in battle, but it stinks whenever I try to ambush you."

Abaddon smiled and then stood. He reached his hands down to Rachel and she took them. With very little effort Abaddon pulled Rachel to her feet. As he did so, Rachel stumbled forward, causing her to fall into an embrace within Abaddon's arms.

For a moment neither of them moved.

Rachel felt a warmth flow through her body, feeling security and comfort. She placed her arms around his waist and squeezed, which caused Abaddon to shudder a bit and wince. Feeling hurt by his reaction, Rachel broke the embrace and stepped back, "Sorry, I didn't mean to be so forward. I shouldn't have—"

"Rachel. It's alright. I am just a bit tender from the battle."

"Tender? You were wounded?" She now said with concern. "You have never been wounded in battle before! Do you need healing? I could—"

"Stop fussing. I'm fine. Just some bruises, no cuts. Bruises are bound to happen when you run your horse off a cliff."

Rachel's green eyes got real big, and with a nervous smirk she replied, "You did what? Oh, this I have to hear. All right! Spill it! I want to hear everything!"

Abaddon held out his arm for Rachel to take. After she embraced the gesture, they walked together into the palace. Taking slow, short steps, Abaddon began the story, "It all started with this giant in the valley…"

CHAPTER 14

Achish took one slippery step at a time, slowly moving downward through the series of tunnels deep within the heart of the island.

His master had made it clear, he was to sail to the north side of the Isle of the Achaeans and there he would find a new island, small, and in the shape of a tear, which he was to set anchor at. At first, Achish thought the message to be faulty as he had sailed these waters many times and had never seen an island north of the land of the Achaeans. But sure enough, twenty leagues north, out of mist and shadow, a black island in the shape of a tear was perched in the sea.

Above water, the land mass was no more than a few leagues across, but beneath it the island must have spanned on for untold leagues, or at least that was what it felt like to Achish as he traversed the underground tunnels.

When he first set foot upon the island's shores, the ground was black and hot. Steam and sulfur had been rising from it as if it had just been birthed from the sea. Loose, jagged rock covered the isle in all directions. There was no vegetation or animals that could be seen. Achish had wanted to jump back in his boat and sail away, for the land had the feel of death and decay. But the voice inside of him urged him forward and revealed to him that there was a cave he must enter a half a league within the perilous speck of earth. Now, deep within the cave, it seemed to Achish that he'd been traveling downward for several hours.

It was a strange feeling. Achish had been walking in the darkness without the help of a torch, and at first it was hard to see, but now he could see everything around him in great detail. It was not like he could see things as if it were daylight, but it was more like moonlight, a silver glow illuminated everything. It was extraordinary.

Taking another step forward, Achish slipped once again.

"Curses!" he shouted, his voice echoing throughout the tunnel. As he placed his hand down to pick himself back up, he felt a grotesque slime ooze between his fingers.

"In the names of all the gods!" he muttered. "What is this vile substance?"

Now standing, he brought his hand to his nose to smell the thick liquid slime clinging to his hand. He wished he hadn't. He immediately wanted to blanch and began to cough.

"What is this stuff?"

He shook his hand wildly, trying to remove it from himself. Not being very successful, he tried to wipe it off on his cloak, only to realize his clothes were already stained with the substance.

In frustration, he shouted, "I hate this! Why can't this master of yours meet me on the surface instead of down here in this El forsaken—"

"Silence!" came a voice searing through his head. An explosion of pain and white hot light erupted through Achish's skull. He fell to his knees, back into the slime that was covering the cave floor.

It was not often that the demon within Achish spoke aloud, but when it did, agonizing pain always came with it. Achish hated the feeling.

"Silence!" the demon chided. "Stop your insistent fouling! Keep your mouth shut and be mindful of your thoughts. And watch your tongue, man of flesh! If you mention the Maker's name again I will kill you! I am your master! Just as I give you life and power, I can easily take it away! Now move!"

All at once the pain ceased, Achish's mind cleared, and he had control again. "I am sorry master! I...I...didn't mean to—"

The demon spoke again, but this time only in Achish's head. "I know you are weak in mind and body, but you must trust me. Just as you are my slave, you are also a slave to the greater ones, and one of them wishes to meet you. That is the reason we are here. As for the slime all around you, that is why I would not let you bring a torch, for if you did, that substance you call slime would have burned you alive and destroyed you. See how much I care for you? I kept you from going up in flames." A chuckle echoed within Achish's skull.

"But where does it come from? I have never seen it before," Achish said aloud.

"This is what I hate about your kind. You are always curious! Questions! Questions! Questions! Fine, I will tell you. It comes from the mouth of your Dark Lord, the one we are going to meet. Prince Dagon."

CHAPTER 15

King Solomon stood at the door of the ante-chamber which led into the dining hall. He graciously greeted each one of his guests as they entered in to partake of the victory feast. Tonight there would be no nobles, dignitaries or landowners, just the military commanders and captains that worked so hard to make Israel's victory possible.

The king's adviser, Aaron, had strongly urged Solomon not to take a servant's job by greeting the guests.

"It is unbecoming," he had said. "The king should not dirty his hands touching the hands of so many people. The king should be the guest of honor and arrive after everyone else," pressed the adviser.

And Solomon's favorite complaint was, "Sire, what if an assassin were to kill you at the door?"

At this, Solomon had laughed. "Relax, Aaron. I pity the man who tries such a foolish gesture in a room full of seasoned warriors. El knows the time and the place of my death and it will not be soon. Jehovah has revealed great plans for my reign and I will be quite safe until those plans are met. So stop fretting and see to the wait staff to make sure everything is ready for the meal."

Bowing slightly, Aaron had given the king a grim look, and headed towards the kitchen.

Solomon turned his attention back to his guests and continued greeting them one by one. As he embraced arm after arm, a memory flooded his mind of his father welcoming each warrior for every victory feast he had with his men. After one such feast, his father, David, took him aside and said, "*Son, remember this. Victory feasts are not for the king nor for the nobles. It is for the men. The men who fought hard, who shed the blood of the enemy and bled themselves to make the victory possible. It is at these feasts we honor them and never ourselves. It is a time for the men to share their glories, brag about their exploits, uphold the memories of the fallen, and, of most importance, give El the credit. Remember this, son, because someday it will be you serving your men in victory.*"

Smiling at the thought, Solomon wished his father could be here now.

After an hour of fellowship, conversing, and laughter, a bell rang near the servant's entrance and all the men cheered!

The food was ready.

There were fifty places of honor set at the kings table and everyone took their appropriate seats.

The circular table was made of oak, and lined with gold along its edges. A pattern of vines and grapes was carved into the wood as well as the fifty chairs surrounding it. A large circle was cut out of the center of the table in which a large brazier filled its place. A special mixture of copper nails driven into cedar wood was used to fuel the fire, making it burn with colors of red, blue, green, purple and orange. The blaze was enough to brilliantly light the dining area and warm the entire hall.

Once every one was seated, the king stood from his chair and all fell silent. The only noise that could be heard was the crackling and popping of the fire in the middle of the room.

The king's personal attendant stepped forward to assist Solomon as he began to unfasten the ties of his outer robe around his shoulders. Noticing the approach of his servant, Solomon held out his hand to stop him. The man retraced the few steps he had taken. Once the purple and gold lined garment was loose, he let the fabric cascade down to the floor.

Looking to the corner of the room, Solomon motioned for two women servants to step from the shadows. Both of them carried a gold tray with two silver decanters of wine. Solomon took one of the pitchers and, one-by-one, filled the gold cups that were already placed in front of the warriors. As he served each guest, Solomon publicly thanked them by name for the service and commitment they had given, and in return each man thanked the king for the opportunity to serve.

After the king had made his way around the entire table, he resumed his position and lifted his glass. At this, all the men stood and raised their glasses above their heads as the king had done. Per tradition, this toast was given in unison.

"By this cup we honor the blood which was spilt in death so that El may give us life!"

With the voices still echoing off the stone walls, the men took a long draft of the sweet wine, wine produced from the best vineyard in Israel, the king's own personal stock.

While the room was still silent with the thoughts of fallen friends and family, Solomon put down his cup and looked at his men with pride. Even though he had never been in battle, he felt a close bond with each one of them.

He met the eyes of his commanders and captains who were sitting closest to him: Benaiah, Broc, Jacob, and Dan where on his right, and to his left was Shammah, Abaddon, Abish…wait. Abishai was not there and his seat was empty. He then noticed Zadok, his priest, was not there either. His smile faded and he turned and gave a questioning look to Benaiah. Benaiah shook his head and gave the king a look as if to say, *we will talk later.*

Solomon slowly nodded his head and then smiled again.

Now looking to everyone present, Solomon said in a loud, triumphant voice, "Brothers! Tonight, we dine in victory!"

With those words, a host of servants flowed into the room carrying several platters of delectable dishes. Trays of fried beef, smoked lamb, seasoned brisket, and tenderized peacock were set around the table. Mounds of fruit and honeyed vegetables were served in silver bowls. Loaves of hot, oven-baked bread of different sizes adorned each plate for the hungry warriors. Large blocks of various cheeses were cut and placed on the table.

For the entire evening, a dish never ceased to have food on it and a cup was never seen empty. Solomon listened to all the stories and tales of the battle and praised his men every chance he got. Although, as the night progressed, all he could think of were the two men who were missing.

After several hours of festivity, the men began to take their leave, thanking the king for his generosity and returning home to be with their families. Solomon made sure that each of the men took home a sack of bread and cheese along with a skin of wine for their loved ones. It wasn't long until the king and his war counsel were the only ones left.

It was custom for Solomon to meet with the war counsel after the feast to discuss the finer points of the battle and whether there were still any pending threats on the nation that needed to be addressed.

Not being a part of the counsel, Abaddon dipped his head in acknowledgment towards Solomon and turned to leave.

"Just a moment, Abaddon," Solomon said, catching him as he took a few steps toward the grand double doors leading out of the room. "I would like you to join us tonight."

Abaddon turned around and looked at Solomon with an arched eyebrow. Solomon caught his look and smiled, waving him back over.

Solomon motioned for the servants to enter the room to start clearing away the dishes and the leftover food. Within minutes everything was cleared away. The round table was detached and separated into two halves, which were then pushed away to opposite sides of the room, leaving the brazier as the center piece to the immense room.

The large bronze pot was still alive with hot embers. Several servants entered, carrying armloads of cedar wood to feed the fire. After the flames were well stoked, four other servants, Rachel being one of them, brought in numerous plush pillows of various sizes and placed them around the brazier.

Rachel noticed Abaddon was still present for the council meeting and she arched an eyebrow as if to say, "You're sticking around?"

Abaddon looked back at her innocently and gave a little shrug of the shoulders. Solomon saw the exchange and smiled to himself. Abaddon and Rachel had been his best friends growing up and he saw them both as family.

Without saying a word, Rachel nodded towards Abaddon, winked at Solomon and then left the room with the rest of the servants.

Solomon smiled again and shook his head. That girl had more spirit and fire than any woman he had ever known, and Solomon had met a lot of women. Solomon's thoughts went to Rachel's mother. If Mirah had seen Rachel wink at the king she would have hatched a leviathan egg. Mirah was all about the "prim" and "proper" servant's role when being on duty, even though Solomon had told her a thousand times that they were family and didn't have to be so formal with him.

But she would have none of it. "We are servants for a king!" she said. "And we take our role seriously, young Solomon. What would the rest of the servants in the household think if we were being favored? The thought of it all is ludicrous! Chaos, Solomon! That is what would happen! Chaos!"

Solomon smiled at the memory.

When the last of the servants left the room, the men took up positions on the floor, reclining on the soft cushions around the brazier. Solomon took off his outer cloak and untied his sandals. The men did likewise and everyone sat resting for a moment, soaking in the comfort and the warmth of the fire.

Finally, Solomon broke the silence. "So, tell me. What happened to Abishai and Zadok? They have never missed a victory feast, and I didn't see their names amongst the list of the dead."

"No, my Lord—" began Benaiah.

"Please, don't call me Lord," Solomon reminded Benaiah calmly. "Jehovah is our only Lord and Master. That is a title a man cannot truly hold. As king I am only a steward to El. I know my father didn't speak out against the title, but I did know his heart."

"My apologies my, king. Habits and all that."

"It's alright. Please continue."

Sitting up a little straighter, Benaiah continued. "The truth is, we cannot find Abishai. He was present with us before Abaddon's fight with the giant but no one has seen him since. It wasn't until we were packing up our camps that we noticed he was missing. We thought he had fallen in battle. We spent half a day looking amongst the dead, but we could not find him."

Solomon stood and began to pace, "In your initial report, you said the fighting took you all the way to the Great Sea. Is it possible he was wounded or killed and his body was swept away by the outgoing tide or currents? Or, worse yet, do you think he was captured and taken by Achish?"

"We had thought of that," Benaiah replied. "That is the reason Zadok is not here with us now. He stayed with a small contingent at the battlesight to see if any bodies washed up along the shoreline. He should be reporting back late tonight. Although, I don't think—" Benaiah paused, not sure how to say what needed to be said next.

"You don't think what?" Solomon asked, recognizing the drop in Benaiah's voice.

As Benaiah was pondering the right words to say, Jacob spoke up in his stead. "We don't think Abishai is dead. We think he betrayed us, and warned Achish of our plans so he could escape. We think Abishai is now with Achish on his ship heading to…who knows where."

Solomon stopped his pacing and looked at Jacob and then back to Benaiah. "Do we have any evidence of this other than his absence? This is quite a dangerous claim, a claim that would mean his death if he is still alive."

Benaiah spoke up again. "No, we have no further proof. If he is a spy for Achish, nobody saw him leave the camp or talk to anyone of suspect, although I asked Dan and Broc to give report of their encounter with Achish when they were at the Cliffs of Tyre."

Dan was about to speak up when three servants entered into the room with some wine, cheese and bread. Without turning around, Solomon put up his hand and waved dismissively to the servants, instructing them not to enter again for the rest of the night. Solomon returned to his cushions, crossed his legs and held out his hand for Dan to begin.

"Well, we had chased Achish's ships from the battle sight all the way to the cliffs, hoping to get ahead of them and set an ambush, but we were not fast enough. By the time we got there, most of the vessels had already passed, but Achish had weighed anchor and was waiting for us."

"Why would he do that?" the king asked. "He was clearly escaping. Why stick around?"

Broc piped in, "I got the feeling he simply wanted to gloat. You should have heard him. He was so pious and full of pomp. It was as if he didn't have a care in the world. He made it sound like the loss of his entire army was acceptable, almost like he was planning on it happening!"

"Although, besides his gloating attitude, he did try to ambush us," Dan reminded. "Fortunately it was a pathetic attempt, thanks to Abaddon."

Turning his attention to Abaddon, Solomon asked, "So, what was your take on what Achish said?"

Abaddon, who was reclining heavily on a pillow, sat up a bit straighter, not expecting to be called upon to speak. "Oh…well, I didn't hear any of it. I was too busy jumping onto boats and killing Philistines."

Solomon looked at him expressionless but Benaiah grinned and shook his head.

"What?" Abaddon said, putting up his hands in defense and shrugging his shoulders. "Hey, I was trained to kill, not to be a diplomat and listen to the enemy give boring speeches."

Broc laughed at the comment but cut himself short when he noticed no one else was laughing. He cleared his throat and steered the conversation back on track.

"There were two things that bothered me the most about our exchange with Achish. One: He said he was going to train his new army, which leads to the questions, what new army? And where is he hiding it? And two: he said he picked up a friend, of which he said was also a good friend of ours. The only person who is close to us and is missing is Abishai. I just…I can't believe Abishai would go so far as to betray us. I know he was kind of the black sheep of the family, but he was still family."

"It is my fault," Dan cut in. "I hit him and made him look like a fool in the council tent. I should have been more understanding. I should have—"

"Stop," Benaiah interrupted. "It is not your fault, Dan. Abishai was out of line. And if Abishai did betray us, it's been something he has been planning for a long time. This would not have happened overnight."

Solomon looked quizzically at Benaiah, "Obviously, I have not heard about this exchange. Why was your commanding staff assaulting one another while you were in council?"

Thus far being silent, Shammah finally spoke up, "He insulted your honor, my king. He insulted you and blasphemed your abilities as a king because you have no battle experience. Abishai said words that were planting seeds of doubt regarding your skills as a leader. Dan's action of striking him was a mercy compared to what we should have done to him for saying such things."

Benaiah was glad it was Shammah who spoke up to relay those words. Shammah was probably the only one above reproach. He was like a second father to Solomon and had always been there for the young king.

Looking upon Solomon, Benaiah saw his countenance fall and his cheeks go pale. Everyone there knew how hard it was for Solomon to live a life that was not like his father's. King David was a warrior and was made great and powerful in the eyes of Israel and all the nations around it. Growing up in a household full of warriors, Solomon was surrounded by the tales of glory and honor that came from daring battles. War was in his blood; yet, he was forbidden to ever use a sword to take another man's life.

Benaiah was there several years ago when King David had died. He witnessed David taking Solomon's hand and making him swear he would never follow his father's path of blood and warfare. Instead he begged Solomon to be a man of peace. El had revealed to David that any man who sheds the blood of others would not be the one to build the temple of Yahweh. So Solomon took an oath and made a promise to his dying father that he would be that man of peace, and that he would be the one to construct the temple.

Being true to his word, Solomon and had never set foot onto a battlefield, even though he felt a great disadvantage in his ability to lead his military. Everyone in the room knew of Solomon's oath to his father and they all honored him for it.

Shammah, sitting closest to Solomon, outstretched his hand and placed it firmly on Solomon's shoulder, "Grieve not, my king.

For though your father's legacy was bathed in blood, your legacy will be much greater! For it will be bathed in the glory of Yahweh. It is by your reign that El will reveal Himself to the entire world. Be of good cheer, my king! Anyway, if you took on a life of bloodshed, you would end up with a dog's face like that of Broc."

Startled by hearing his name, Broc looked up with a blank look on his face and said, "What?"

Laughter erupted in the hall.

Solomon grasped Shammah's arm which was still resting on his shoulder. "Thank you, my friend. I need that kind of encouragement from time to time."

Solomon sat quietly for a while and then finally spoke again, turning the group's attention back to the problem at hand.

"So Abishai has betrayed us."

"It looks that way," Benaiah said, not looking up at the king but rather staring straight ahead into the crackling fire before him.

Standing back up and coming closer to the brazier, Solomon bent down and picked up the long stirring rod lying next to it and began to turn the coals over, causing sparks to shoot up with the rising smoke. "I hate to say it, but his betrayal makes sense."

Broc and Dan rose from their pillows and stood close to the brazier as well. "It makes more sense than it should, which I say in sorrow," Dan commented.

Shammah tapped Abaddon on the arm and motioned for him to rise. After getting up, they both joined the forming circle around the brazier as Jacob joined on the other side of Solomon.

"It would explain how we missed Achish in Gath," Shammah said in a quite tone. "Not to mention a dozen other battles with the Philistines that had gone awry in the past two seasons."

A weight of grief fell upon all five warriors and the king. They all stood in silence until Jacob spoke up, "You know what you must do, my king."

Bowing his head, Solomon began to mouth a prayer that could not be heard. Finally, he looked to his men and said, "I must hear it from Abishai himself. My head tells me he is guilty but my heart yearns for his redemption. Upon my father's request, I have already sent his brother Joab to Sheol. If at all possible, I would like to grant

Abishai mercy and a chance to explain himself. Until he stands before me, I will give no death warrant. With that being said, find him, and bring him home. If he is guilty, then he deserves a swift execution and to be laid to rest with his family."

All the men nodded in agreement with the king's words.

"Pray with me, men," Solomon said, reaching both of his arms out, grasping Shammah's shoulder on the right and Jacob's shoulder on the left.

Each of the men in the circle followed suit, grasping one another's shoulders and bowing their heads, waiting for the king's prayer to begin.

Abaddon felt uncomfortable standing with these men and praying. This type of conduct for warriors was a side he had never seen before. Sure, he had heard these men talk about El and praise El, but he had never been in a place of intimate worship with them which drew up such thoughts and feelings.

He didn't like it.

He didn't like the way it made him feel. It created a nervous turning in his stomach.

Abaddon looked up at Solomon while he was praying. He couldn't help but stare at his friend as a chorus of passionate words flowed from the king's mouth. Solomon's face would contort into different expressions as he presented the various prayer requests to Yahweh. Solomon prayed for the nation as a whole and for the people who went about their day-to-day lives. He prayed for some of the servants in his household. Apparently some of them were dealing with various ailments. This surprised Abaddon, a king praying for his servants. Shouldn't the servants be praying for the king?

Solomon then moved his prayer to the men present. He called each of the men out by name before Yahweh and asked El's blessings upon them and good health and wisdom in times of peace and war.

And then Solomon said his name.

"Yahweh...Adonai. I humbly come before you asking to seek the heart of my great friend Abaddon. I ask you to show him the way of mercy and forgiveness that you have so graciously filled my heart with. Open his eyes so he may see

you in a light that is pure and adorned. Show him a love he has never known. Send him your angel to guide and grow him into the man that you desire. Adonai, I pray you will show him a way of life that is greater than the skill of the sword."

And then Solomon went on to pray for the next person.

Abaddon didn't know why, but he felt tears well up within him. He refused to let them roam free. Solomon's pastoral words broke into his heart and clutched his soul.

Once again, Abaddon looked to Solomon and saw tears coming down the king's cheeks as his prayers became more fervent. He looked upon the other men of the circle and noticed their eyes closed hard as they frequently nodded in agreement to the king's words.

It was in this moment, Abaddon knew he didn't belong in the council. Sure, when it came to war and spilling blood, he was good. In fact he was the best. But this…this…war in the heart…this was a battlefield he could not understand or grasp.

Then Abaddon heard these words come from the king's lips, *"Adonai, I save this prayer for last, for it is greatest upon my innermost being. I pray for our brother, Abishai. If he has been slain in war or has succumbed to the sea, may he find your glory in Sheol and know you as friend. But if he has joined with those who despise you and call you enemy, I pray you will send mercy his way. Redeem his soul and show him the light of life that was stolen from him many years ago. May the bitterness and rage within his depths subside to make way for the righteousness that you desire within him. May our hearts not grow cold or bitter towards our wayward brother, but may we reflect your glory to forgive and bestow grace."*

Abaddon could not believe what he was hearing. His arms fell down to his sides and he took a step back, breaking out of the circle.

Was Solomon insane? His faith in El must be making him weak! Words like: *mercy, redeem, righteousness and forgiveness,* were not words that should be used for a traitor!

Anger began to rise within him. Anger and confusion. Why would Solomon pray such things for someone who hated him and betrayed him? The only words that should be associated with a traitor were *condemned* and *death*!

Solomon ended his prayer and all the men responded with, "Let it be done!"

Looking up, Solomon noticed that Abaddon had broken away from the group and was now standing alone several paces away, arms folded and face looking to the floor. Solomon sighed and whispered another short prayer, *"How long to break his heart, Lord?"*

Without a word, each of the men bowed to the king and left the room, leaving only Solomon and Abaddon in the great hall.

"Ok, out with it." Solomon prodded, walking up to his friend.

"Permission to speak openly with you, my king," Abaddon said a little too pompously and with a little anger in his voice.

"Oh, for goodness sake! Yes! Yes! Speak plainly. We have been friends since we were five seasons old, standing on top of the palace and throwing gourds at the archers on the practice field! Abaddon, I think you know me better than anyone alive, so tell me your mind."

Abaddon was able to smile at his friend's change of demeanor now that the war council had left. It eased his anger a little.

"Ya'know, sometimes I don't think I know you at all. This whole religious thing…I just don't get it. You never used to be so progressive with El, but over the years you have changed. Praying, just now, you were in tears. It is as if you were talking to Yahweh and He was standing right next to you. You have made El real in your life and as for me…well, I don't know. All I know is death and war and bloodshed and—"

Abaddon's voice trailed off and his eyes became distant as if being flooded by memories that haunted him.

Choosing to stay silent, Solomon waited for him to continue. Abaddon put his hand to the back of his neck and looked back to Solomon. "I need to know why."

"Why, what?"

"Why would you pray in such a way for a man who is a traitor and deserves death for his crimes against Israel and against you? If people heard you praying like that, they would think you were weak and some fool might try to take your throne!"

Solomon approached Abaddon with a warm smile as he placed both of his hands on Abaddon's shoulders.

"Ya'know, if there is one thing I have learned consistently over all the long years of study underneath Priest Zadok and Prophet Nathan, and all the stories shared by my father, it is this lesson: El is patient and forgiving. Tell me, Abaddon, when your father was still alive, did you ever argue with him or talk back to him?"

It wasn't hard for Abaddon to think of a rebellious situation with his father. "Yeah, there were a few times, but you knew my father, he didn't put up with a lot."

"And yet, here you stand. Did not El make a law that children who rebel against their parents were to be stoned until dead?"

"Well, that is different. That is—"

"I don't think so," Solomon said, cutting Abaddon off. "Your father had the full right of the law behind him, and when you stepped out of line or talked back to him, he could have stoned you dead for those rebellious words. So why didn't he? According to the law, he had every right to. *Mercy, love, grace* and *forgiveness* is the answer, my dear friend. Your father loved you so much that he bestowed grace and mercy upon you to cover up your indiscretion, and chose to forgive you instead of placing judgment on you. Our Heavenly Father does the same thing. He loves you so much he gives you chance after chance to get it right and to build a relationship with Him. Yahweh wants for us to seek his forgiveness. He desires a relationship with us. Abaddon, Yahweh desires a relationship with *you*. So, just as El bestows that grace upon us, would He not desire us to bestow that same grace towards one another? Towards Abishai?"

"And what if Abishai does not want forgiveness or redemption? Will he still have your mercy?"

Solomon dropped his arms from Abaddon's shoulders and felt his heart sink at Abaddon's lack of concern for his own soul, missing the point of the whole illustration.

Letting out a long sigh, Solomon responded. "If Abishai doesn't want redemption than El will see to it that he loses his life."

"Now, see there. Right there! What do you mean? Does that mean you will have him executed, or send a death warrant out after him, or what?"

"It means El will take care of him, one way or another."

Abaddon put his hands to his temples and rubbed them vigorously. "You keep speaking in riddles. You sound like Zadok! I am tired, and all this talk of El is making my head hurt. I think I am going to turn in. It has been a long day."

"Actually, Abaddon, the reason I asked you to stay for the counsel was because I have a task for you and I needed this private time to speak to you alone."

"A task?" Abaddon repeated, causing him to perk up a bit. "What is it? Wait, you want me to hunt down Abishai, don't you? Actually I was going to suggest—"

"Abaddon, no. That is not it. What I need to tell you is—"

"Is it about me riding the horses off the cliff? I know that was a little risky but it really was not that bad. Although, I am sorry about the horses, since they were from your stable."

"Abaddon, I don't care about the horses. What I have to tell you is more important than—"

"Well, if it is not about the battle or about Abishai, do you mind if we talk about this in the morn? I am really—"

"Abaddon! Would you please stop interrupting me! I am banishing you from Israel!"

Chapter 16

Achish awoke with a start. He rolled himself to his feet and looked around the dimly lit cavern.

Six days ago he had finally made it to the bottom of the winding cave to find a great, vast hollow of empty space. In the middle of the massive cavern was a giant pit of bubbling lava that appeared to be swirling in a circular pattern. The molten rock lit the stone room in a dank, orange glow which cast dancing shadows on the walls. There was a constant sound of hissing and popping coming from the pool of molten rock.

After looking up at the ceiling of the cave, Achish could not judge the height of it. After a short distance upwards, the darkness made it impossible to see through to the top.

For the one hundredth time, Achish walked along the edge of the cavern, feeling the cold stone walls, trying to discover a doorway or a crevice leading out of the room.

Achish remembered when he had first entered the cavern, he had explored the area, expecting to meet the great Prince Dagon. When he found no one, he went back to the opening of the cave which led back to the surface, only to find the doorway was no longer there and a solid wall was now in its place. Panic had erupted within Achish and he had screamed and pleaded with his demon to speak to him and tell him how to get out of the room, but the demon had gone silent.

After a few days of being trapped and alone, Achish had felt as though he was going mad. He constantly heard sounds, whispers in the air, footsteps crunching upon loose stones in the distance, the popping and hissing of the lava as it turned in its brewing pot. He would also see shadows that looked like giant men form on the walls and then wither away as if they were whiffs of smoke.

Thoughts of doubt and dread had frequently entered into his mind.

Why would I be a part of such an elaborate plan and then be lead down here to my death? What if I am to be a sacrifice to this god, Dagon? What of my ships and men? Did my crew abandon me? I am their king! Why are they not sacrificing life and limb to come down here and rescue me? Worse yet, what if the demon within me has betrayed me, brought me here to die, and then possesses another to take over my men and ships? To give another man my promise of power and life? What if this… Abishai was to be my replacement?

With these thoughts coursing through his mind, Achish had begun to laugh out loud, but the laughter soon turned to cries of despair and anger. He shouted obscenities out into the air for no one to receive them. He cursed the demon who had brought him there and then in the same breath, he begged for its forgiveness and pleaded for it to speak to him. This cycle of insanity went on and on until he had literally passed out from exhaustion.

After a few days had gone by, Achish felt a calming presence fall over him and the panic had subsided. He had begun to make peace with his circumstances.

During his solitude, Achish noticed some odd things. It had been some time since he had eaten or had anything to drink and yet he felt no hunger and did not thirst. Without water he should have been dead by now. How was he still live? Not only was he not hungry but he also never grew weak.

Indeed, he was in a strange place.

Once again, Achish made it all the way around the cavern, feeling every bump and crack along the rock walls, and still did not find an opening or a way out. He was about to resolve to sit down and try to sleep once more, when suddenly the ground beneath him started to shudder.

Holding out his hands, Achish tried to balance himself, but it was to no avail. The shudder became a harsh shake and the whole room seemed to jolt in every direction. Soon large boulders from up above began to plummet down to the cave floor, shattering and sending knife like shards flying in all directions. Achish, fearing for his life, fell to the ground, cowering as close to the wall as possible to keep from getting hit by the falling stones of death.

After thinking it couldn't get any worse, Achish felt an explosion come from the middle of the cavern, right under the lava pit. To the fat king's horror, the molten rock that had been safely within its cauldron now became a pressurized geyser, spewing its smoldering liquid high into the air.

Searing heat assaulted Achish as he smelled the hair on his head and beard singeing away.

A white gas cloud began to fill the room and Achish choked and gasped with every breath he took.

"Is this how I am to die, my lords? In this poisonous pit of your fury?" Achish said, choking as he cursed out each word. He crawled up on his knees and stared at the brilliant pillar of lava shooting upwards. He closed his eyes, knowing in that moment he was going to die.

"Stop being so dramatic!" the demon echoed within Achish, scolding him.

With his eyes still closed, Achish felt every dangerous sensation fall away. The searing heat vanished and instead he felt a cool breeze come across his face. The air was clean again and he drew in a deep breath, smiling as he felt his strength return to him in an instant.

Opening his eyes, Achish expected to see everything back the way it was, calm and peaceful. But it wasn't. The air was still filling with white toxic gas and the pillar of white-hot molten rock was still thrusting upward in angry torrents. Large rocks were still plummeting to the ground and exploding. In fact, one had smashed violently to the floor right next to him and thousands of razor sharp pellets assaulted his flesh.

Cringing away, Achish held up his hands to protect himself from the projectiles. He felt the impacts as if they were just bugs pricking his skin. He looked at his hands and arms and there wasn't even a scratch on him. Achish smiled and began to laugh as he realized he was now indestructible. "I am either dead or I have the power of a god!"

"Don't fool yourself," scolded the demon's voice. "It is I who have protected you, and it would be wise of you to remember who your god is! Now, approach the pillar of fire!"

Achish hesitated a moment and then obeyed the voice. Slowly, he approached the brilliant tower of flaming liquid rock, and then stopped a few paces short of touching it.

A violent wind was now pushing against Achish as if trying to prevent him from going any further. Looking down by his feet, he noticed the small pebbles littering the cave floor were popping open from the intense heat, and gradually melting; and yet, Achish still could not feel the heat's effect.

Once again, Achish smiled and began to laugh, marveling at his demon's power. Achish looked from the ground to the pillar of fire and a thought crossed his mind.

How indestructible am I really? What if I touch the molten rock? Would I feel it? Would it burn me?

Achish slowly reached out his hand to touch the lava.

"Fool!" the demon screeched within. "Do you want to die? Is there nothing your curious brain would not do? Take a few steps back so your clumsy, fat self won't accidentally fall into oblivion!"

The commanding voice startled Achish into stumbling back a few paces.

"Oblivion? What do you mean, oblivion? And what exactly is this place? I have been down here for days, you go silent, and now this whole cavern is going to hell. Why are we here? And don't tell me we are here to see Prince Dagon, because he is *not* here! I want to leave this place! Now!"

A slow maniacal laugh coursed through Achish's mind. "Peace, my slave. He is coming. Soon, real soon. You see, the fire before you is not just some pillar of flame and lava. It is much more than that. If you could only see what I see, you would be amazed. For you see only the flesh and corruptible things of this world. But I...I, my human pet, can see so much more. I see a world of spirits and powers and principalities that your mind could never comprehend.

"In truth, what you see before you is a gateway from this world to another. And if you were to step through or even touch it, your filth-of-a-body would evaporate instantly. Not only your body, but your soul would be damned as well."

Upon hearing this, Achish wanted to take a few more steps back, but the spirit within him prevented him from moving.

"Now is not the time for fear, man of flesh," the demon rebuked. "For he is coming. My master, your god, Prince Dagon is coming. Can you not feel it? The raw power gushing through the tear from the world beyond. Does it not feel glorious?"

Achish could feel it. The cavern that was once melting from extreme heat was now beginning to crack and hiss, no longer from heat but from… cold. Looking around, Achish saw a brilliant blue ice begin to rapidly cover the walls and the floor. Everything that was rock was crystallizing and giving off a radiance of sparkling light.

The red glowing pillar of fire was now beginning to scream and howl with great excerpts of power. Now turning bright white, the column began to crackle as shards of molten minerals exploded from the tower of death.

Instinctively, Achish threw himself to the ground to avoid being hit by the white hot projectiles. Unfortunately, escaping one onslaught of destruction only brought him to another. As soon as his exposed skin touched the icy floor, it immediately began to freeze. He watched in horror as the fingers on his right hand started to turn blue. Although he felt no pain, he could only watch as the blue death crept its way up to his wrist.

With a powerful yank, Achish was pulled up to his feet. Somehow, the demon within stood him erect. "Fool! I told you not to move! It is like you want to die!"

Achish closed his eyes, praying this nightmare would soon end. The noise coming from the pillar was now unbearable. He wanted to lift his hands to cover his ears but for some reason they would not obey him. It was then he noticed that he could not feel his right hand any longer. He tried to flex his fingers but they felt like solid stone. He tapped his right hand against his leg and groaned in dismay as he realized his hand was completely frozen and had become a dead weight. He wanted to open his eyes to look at his hand but the fear he was feeling was greater than his curiosity.

Then, in an instant, all went silent. The howling scream of the pillar was gone, the violent wind had disappeared, and all that could be heard was the small crackling sound of the blue ice, still spreading and consuming the cave.

"Look!" came the demon's voice.

Achish opened his eyes and awe overtook him. There before him, what was once a large fiery tower of death, was now a giant pillar of ice…or crystal…or was it glass? The white, frozen spectacle now stood fifty cubits wide and at least twice that in height. A dense light seemed to be glimmering from the bottom of it, making it glow in brilliance, clear to the top.

Once again, Achish had a deep-seeded need to touch the pillar. This time it was more than curiosity. It was pure desire, as if he needed what the pillar could offer. It was as if a hunger was growing within him to make contact with the massive crystal-like column.

"Yessssss. You can feel it, can't you? It calls to you as if you belong to it," his demon hissed. "You feel a craving you can't quite define, don't you?"

"Yes. I want it!" Achish expressed, as his breathing grew heavy. "I must touch it!"

Achish took one step forward but halted when he saw something within the pillar. A large mass appeared and moved from side to side. Achish took a closer look and realized it was an eyeball! A giant eyeball, and it was looking in all directions as if searching for something.

"Go on. It is safe now. You can touch it. Don't be afraid, my friend. It desires you to touch it, to want it. Feeeeeeeel its power!"

Now standing at arm's length from the massive pillar, Achish reached his left hand out and felt the cool smooth surface of the immense jewel. A surge of energy flowed into his hand and sharp pricks of electricity licked at his fingertips.

Startled at first, Achish withdrew his hand, but then put it back, enjoying the sensation.

"Now your other hand," the demon instructed.

Achish raised the cold dead stump that was his right hand, and placed it against the pillar. At first there was nothing and Achish was about to question the action, but then a tingling sensation sparked into his hand.

With awe and fascination, Achish watched his blue, frozen hand come back to life and return to its original color. Achish pulled his renewed hand away from the pillar and sharp streaks of blue light danced between his finger tips and the crystal. The king stared at his hand and erupted in gleeful laughter.

"Ha Ha Ha! You are truly a powerful god worth following, demon! How can I ever re—"

"It was not I. Although, selfishly, I would like to claim responsibility. It was not I."

Putting it all together, Achish looked at the floating eyeball and whispered lightly, "Prince Dagon?"

The eye focused on Achish as soon as he uttered the ancient demon's name.

The king looked even closer within the hazed glass tower, and now noticed the eye was not floating at all. The eye was just the most visible part of an entire head. Not a human head, but that of a great and terrible beast. And the eye was unlike anything he had seen before on a human, but more like…an animal…a lizard or snake.

Achish couldn't help but stare at the creature with fascination.

Not liking to be looked upon like a spectacle, Dagon rammed his head against the wall within the pillar. The result of the blow made the tower sway and the cave shuddered with the force. The surprise action made Achish tumble backwards and fall on his backside.

"Quick, you must let him out!" the demon shouted inside of Achish's mind.

"How?" Achish inquired, standing himself back up, being careful not to touch the blue ice on the ground with his bare hands.

"This crystal is solid." Achish said as he walked up to the pillar once more and pounded his fist on it. "There is no way I am getting through this."

Achish noticed a fist sized stone covered in blue ice next to his foot. He withdrew his sash which was tied around his waist, wrapped it around his hand and picked up the stone. Savagely, he began pounding the stone against the crystal pillar.

The demon laughed. "Can a mere stone break a diamond?"

"A diamond?" Achish replied, raising an eyebrow and dropping the stone. "How? I mean…this was once molten rock. How can it now be a diamond? I don't understand."

"You weren't meant to understand it. It is much more than your simple little mind can comprehend. Just know this. Diamonds are not natural in your world. They are rare to your kind because the only way diamonds can be made are when one of *our* kind breaches the rift from the world beyond to this one. Normally, a small demon can breach the diamond from the other side, but, the more powerful the demon is, the greater the strength of the diamond. Dagon is one of the Great Princes of Old and is one of the most powerful demons of his kind. His barrier is strong and his chains are tight."

"Wait, what? His chains? I am confused. Is this giant diamond a gateway between worlds or is it a prison?" Achish inquired, looking closer at the eye within.

"These are details you do not need to know! Your hand. Remember your hand. It was dead and gone, beyond even my power to restore. How easy was it for the Great Prince to heal? Upon his release, think of the power you will have and the long life you will be granted."

It took little convincing. Achish's heart grew greedy with the desire for additional strength and power. Thoughts of cruelty invaded his mind as he thought about returning to the land of Philistia and wiping Israel clean from existence. He thought of the devastation that would be at his fingertips with a god like Dagon.

"What do I need to do?"

"Goooooooood. We must hurry. Do you remember the day I joined with you?" the demon asked in a seething voice.

Achish thought back to two winters ago.

A fresh snow had recently fallen and Achish was on his palace roof top. The war season had ended and he had received news that his last remaining son had been slain in battle against the Israelites. Six sons in all had been sired by the king, and one year after another his children had been taken from him at the hands of Israelite swords. Achish begged his youngest heir to refrain from war but he would not listen. And now they were all dead…killed. He would never see them again.

While on the rooftop, the king withdrew a jagged dagger, preparing to thrust it into his own heart. There was nothing left for him to live for. There was no one to take on his legacy or carry on his name. He saw the loss of his sons as a curse upon himself and a sign that the gods no longer wanted him to rule.

"So be it!"

Taking a deep breath to work up his last nerve, he stretched out his arm, knife pointing inward, and was about to thrust the blade into his heart when a great wind blew him forward, making him trip. The blade fell from his hands and sank into the deepening snow.

A whisper came out of the wind. "Fear not, great and noble king. Do not grieve for your sons, for they were a sacrifice of blood to your gods. They died so you could become mighty amongst your people. Your loyalty will be remembered, for we desire to give you power and life beyond what you already know."

"And how do I gain this power? What more must I do?" the king desired to know, not questioning the source of the voice.

"As your sons gave their blood, so must you. Pick up the knife you were going to use to take your own life."

Achish did so.

"Now take the weapon and open the flesh on your arm. Spill the blood upon the snow at your feet."

Achish raised the blade to his left arm and was about to slice willingly into his own flesh, but then paused.

What am I doing? He thought to himself. *This is madness.*

"Who are you? Where does your voice come from? And what assurances do I have that you can give me power and revenge for my sons?"

The voice now became close and clear, as if it was right behind him, whispering in his ear. "Looooook. Look at the vision of the future that I will give you, my king."

In an instant, the world around the king vanished. The palace, the roof top, the city around him, all of it was gone. Instead he found himself amongst a great and mighty host of towering giants, warriors dressed in black and red armor. They were at the gates of Jerusalem and the city was on fire, burning brightly as flames licked at every corner.

Then, through the southern gate of the Israelite city, two of the black clad soldiers came dragging out a bloodied and bruised King Solomon. A voice then leaked from his own throat that was not his own, "Bow down to me, Solomon the Weak, and worship me as your god!"

Without hesitation the Israelite king prostrated himself on the ground and worshiped King Achish.

Then the vision blurred and the king was once again on his palace roof top, shivering from the blowing snow.

"This is your future," the voice taunted. "But only if blood is spilt!"

Then the voice went silent.

Achish pressed the tip of the knife to the soft underbelly of his arm, but made no motion to cut himself.

He had never had a vision before. Could it be true? Could he take the Holy City and claim it for himself? For so long he had tried and each attempt ended in failure. Just like the blowing wind, his heart grew cold and distant. Hatred welled up within him; a surge of contempt and a hunger for revenge seared into his mind.

With one quick motion, Achish ripped the dagger across his arm and then flung the bloodied blade from the roof. Blood erupted from the wound and poured freely onto the white innocent snow, painting it crimson. The king fell to his knees and thoughts of horror overcame his mind.

What have I done? I have just killed myself! I am a fool!

"Now what?" Achish yelled aloud, already feeling his life drain away from him.

In a calm voice the wind hissed into his ear, "Now consume it!"

"Consume. You mean eat it?"

"Yessssss. Eat the bloodied snow and I will give you life and power to fulfill your revenge!"

With slight hesitation, Achish reached down with a hand that was already stained red with blood, and scooped up a blood saturated snowball. For what seemed like the longest time, he watched in fascination as the watered down blood began to drain away from the snow and escape through his cold fingers.

Abandoning all reason, he shoved the snow into his mouth. The cold instantly numbed his tongue and the back of his throat. A pungent taste of copper attacked his taste buds as it made its way down to his stomach. Achish gagged, but he forced it down with a hard swallow. He was about to ask the voice what to do now, when he felt a tingling feeling race across the wound on his arm. He looked down and saw his flesh begin to mend itself.

"This is just a taste of the power I give you. Eat more," the voice commanded.

Achish obeyed, but this time with reckless abandonment. Now on his hands and knees, he devoured the crimson snow like a jackal eating a fresh kill.

Achish snapped out of his memory and brought himself back to the present. "It was blood. My blood brought you to live within me"

"Yesssss. Blood," the demon echoed. And it is only the blood of men that can be used to free the prince. Smear your blood on the diamond's face and he will be able to escape!"

"But how will he—"

"There is no time!" The demon howled in Achish's head, making him fall to his knees. "There is no time for your pathetic questions! We must act before they get here. If we are stopped, we will both forfeit our lives! Now bleed yourself on the pillar! Now!"

This only made the king want to ask more questions. As he got back up, he began to wonder who *they* were, and if he was in any danger. His master within seemed nervous and afraid. He had never felt the demon so out of control.

And what of Prince Dagon? Why was he locked up and confined? If he was such a powerful god, then why would he need the blood of a man, a mere powerless man at that? And if he was a god, then who was more powerful than he to imprison him?

Achish wanted to know the answers to these questions but chose to keep his mouth shut and ask them later. He knew his master could cause him great and terrible pain, and he didn't want to agitate him further.

Being obedient, he lifted his right wrist to his lips and bit down hard. His teeth easily broke the skin and blood began to break away from its confined veins, running down his arm towards his elbow. He smeared the blood all over his left hand, covering it from wrist to fingertip. Achish then deliberately reached out for the towering diamond.

As his hand got within a hands-breadth of making contact, the giant jewel began to vibrate and hum, returning to the high pitched wail it had emanated earlier. The noise was so intense that Achish had to take a few steps back and cover his ears.

"You worthless worm!" the voice scolded. "Put your cursed hand on the barrier or I will take control of your body and do it for you!"

With the sound now piercing the air, Achish felt his ears begin to ache. He reached out his hand once again and stumbled towards the diamond.

Dagon's eye moved and stared intently at Achish's hand and it narrowed in anticipation as the bloodied palm got closer.

Achish, fighting to ignore the pain, was about to lean forward and place his hand on the pillar when a great torrent of wind shot down from above and sent him flying backwards, slamming him into the cave wall on the other side of the room.

The demon inside him screamed in agitation. Achish looked up and witnessed a searing stream of light pierce into the solid rock between him and the diamond tower.

"We are lost!" the dark spirit within Achish cried out. "We are lost! We are too late, and death has come to take us!"

CHAPTER 17

Abaddon stood staring into Solomon's eyes, not wanting to believe what he had just heard. "Wait, what? Did you just say you want to banish me?"

"I don't *want* to banish you, my friend," Solomon sighed as he ran his hand through the front of his long, black hair. "I *have* to banish you, for your own good."

Instantly Abaddon felt anger well up inside of him. Anger and loathing. He squeezed his eyes shut and balled his hands into fists.

It was widely known that if one was banished from the land by a royal decree, it meant that individual had brought dishonor of some kind to Israel. Banishment was the same as being an outcast, never to return. That person would be treated like a leper. No. A leper would still receive mercy. One who was banished in dishonor would not even receive that.

Questions began to flood into Abaddon's mind.

What have I done to deserve a banishing sentence? Who have I betrayed? Did I disgrace my country or king in some way? Have I brought dishonor to my name or to my father's name?

He could think of doing none of these things.

Taking a few steps away from Solomon, Abaddon opened his eyes and glared at the king. In that moment he didn't see his friend any longer, but an enemy. Angry thoughts began to consume him, poisoning his mind.

You have always been jealous of me and my abilities as a warrior, and now you want me gone! You are not a true king, not like your father was! Now your father, he was a true king! At least he was man enough to take judgment into his own hands! And Rachel. You have always wanted to take her and bed her as your own! Whatever spoiled Solomon wants, Solomon gets. Solomon should get the beating of his life, that is what he should get! And what about the blood? Does he know how much blood I have spilled in war to keep this country safe? My hands have been bathed in the blood of our enemies, and it will not end in disgrace!

Without another thought, Abaddon took a step forward and clenched his right fist even tighter, making the veins in his arm thrust out. With hate still seething through him, the most unexpected thing happened.

Closing the gap between them, Solomon threw his arms around Abaddon's shoulders and embraced him. The embrace was tight and strong, and yet tender and affectionate. The display of compassion made Abaddon's fury and hate melt away as if they didn't really exist at all.

When Solomon felt Abaddon relax he gave him an even harder squeeze and then released him to an arm's length, still gripping his shoulders with his strong hands.

Not being able to look into the king's eyes, Abaddon looked to the floor. He felt ashamed.

Where did those thoughts come from? Why did I feel such rage? I actually felt like hurting Solomon…hurting my friend.

Abaddon swallowed hard, now feeling emotion sweep over him as he took a deep breath, telling himself not to lose control of his emotions again.

After a long silence between the two of them, Abaddon finally asked in a weak and defeated voice, "Why?"

Solomon took a moment of silent prayer and then answered Abaddon's simple question with a question of his own. "What did you think of the meeting with the commanders tonight?"

"What does that have—"

"Abaddon, please. I need you to journey with me through some thoughts and feelings in order for you to understand why I am doing what I am doing. Describe to me your perception of tonight's events."

Thinking through the evening, Abaddon shrugged. "It wasn't much different than most field meetings I have had with the commanders and captains. Reports were given, thoughts and comments were gathered from the party and then a plan was made to—"

"And then, after that."

"And then…then…well, it is not uncommon for Zadok to give a prayer or a blessing to El after the meeting," Abaddon said, returning his gaze to the floor. "But tonight was different. It didn't feel right."

As Abaddon talked, Solomon led him back to the middle of the room where the brazier was smoldering with hot coals.

"You mean the prayer. The prayer didn't feel right to you?" Solomon asked as he threw a few more logs upon the embers and stirred them in with the stirring stick.

"I don't know how to describe how I—"

"Try." Solomon said, now motioning for Abaddon to sit with him on the two cushions lying behind them.

After they sat, Abaddon stared at the small flames which were now licking their way around the new logs. Choosing to stay silent, Solomon waited for him to collect his thoughts.

"I have always known of war, killing and death as long as I can remember," Abaddon began. "One of my earliest memories was of my father coming home late one evening from a war campaign. He had been gone for almost six moon cycles. I saw him walk around the house and he was carrying a dead body over his shoulder. He went to the grain shed out back behind the house with the body in tow. I was curious, so I followed him out to the shed. Being young, I didn't know any better, so I simply walked right in.

"What I saw in that moment was something I was not prepared for. My father was cutting up the dead body with his war knife. Not savagely, but very carefully. I stood in the doorway for the longest time and just stared. And then it hit me. Fear.

"Fear consumed me, and my mind screamed at me to run away and not to look back. I tried to convince myself I was having some kind of dream, because my father could never butcher and desecrate a body like that.

"Finally, my father noticed me, standing there in shock.

"As if nothing was wrong, he put down his knife, washed his hands in a bowl of water setting next to him, and then walked over to the door and scooped me up into his arms. He smiled at me, hugged me, and told me he had missed me.

"He noticed I was staring at the body on the table.

"'Don't be afraid my son,' he simply said, and then put me down and guided me over to the lifeless corpse.

"I asked who he was, and my father replied, 'It is only a worthless Philistine. One of the men we killed during our last battle.'

"I asked him why he had brought the dead man home and why he didn't deserve to be buried with his own kin.

"'I am afraid he will not be missed,' my father answered. 'Those miserable Philistines rarely even collect their dead, unless the soldier's family shows up after the battle to bury them. No, unfortunately this one got left behind and was to be food for the birds.'

"At this point my fear had mostly drained away and curiosity was now growing. So I asked him why he was cutting the man up.

"'Well, how can I put this so you can understand? We are going to study his body so we will become better warriors. The more understanding we have of how the body works, the greater knowledge we can have on how to apply the sword to our enemy. And what we learn here, we will teach to others under our command.'

"It was then Shammah and Eleazar entered into the shed and joined us.

"'Starting without us,' Eleazar said with a smile upon seeing me. He walked over and ruffled my head of hair.

"That night, the three greatest warriors of Israel became my teachers and showed me every inch of the human body: its weaknesses, strengths, pain centers, and pressure areas, which when pushed could freeze a man's muscles. And the greatest lesson of all: the best strategic places to insert a blade to kill a man quickly and effectively.

"Most boys my age would have had night terrors from what I saw that night, but not I. I slept that evening with the knowledge that I could now take a man's life if I needed to, and I knew exactly how to do it."

Abaddon stopped talking for a time to collect his thoughts.

Feeling sick and heartbroken, Solomon said, "I have never heard you tell this story before. How old were you when this happened?"

"I was only six seasons old."

Solomon felt the blood drain from his face. At six seasons he was playing games in the palace, teasing his brothers and enjoying the love of his mother and family. His friend…his best friend, was getting his first carnage lesson on how to kill Philistines.

"Go on," said Solomon, swallowing hard.

Abaddon took a deep breath and continued.

"Well, as you know, our law states that after touching the dead we have to spend seven days outside of the city going through the cleansing ritual. Of course, the priests didn't ask any questions of the Three as to why they needed the ritual performed, they had just returned from war. All warriors had to go through the rite before they could rejoin their families. So no one knew about the cut up Philistine, and until this day I have told no one about it. It is my wish to keep it a secret, to keep the honor of my father, Shammah, and Eleazor. El protect their souls."

Solomon said nothing but nodded his head in agreement; although he wasn't sure if he was going to be able to look at Shammah the same way again.

"Since I, too, had touched parts of a dead body, my father took me with them to the cleansing ritual. Being of such a young age, I found the whole experience fascinating. I was intrigued with the priests and their role in the ritual; I had never witnessed it before. The most memorable part was the fellowship with my father and the other warriors around the camp fires at night.

"I had never seen my father in such a light. He was happy and joyous and I loved spending that time with him. I learned so much listening to him and the others tell their tales of glory and heroics. I knew then that one day I would be just like him, that I would be the greatest warrior Israel had ever seen. Greater than even my father.

"Although, it was also during this cleansing ritual I began to distrust El. I would watch and listen to the priests as they would explain the covering of sin that came from the blood that was shed from the calves and rams. They reminded us that El desires us to be holy and to flee from the killing of others, that there was no glory from El in taking a life.

"After the blood ritual was over and the men went back to their tents, I sat there listening to the warriors joke and gloat about their bloody exploits of the battle and how many lives they had taken.

"I remember asking my father, 'If the priests say we should not touch the dead or take a life, then why do the soldiers brag about killing men?'

"My father told me that it was wrong to take *innocent* life, but it was alright to kill the enemies of El, for they were cursed for following false gods.

"It was then, a confusion arose within me about who Jehovah was, and whether or not He was a true God. El's teachings and my father's teachings seemed to conflict with each other. Even today the Rabbani teach the people a certain way to live and yet the people do the opposite. The people go on living as if El does not exist. So what was the truth? Who is Jehovah really?

"These were a few of the thoughts going through my head that night. So I made a decision. I decided to trust in my father instead of Jehovah; they both couldn't be right. So I chose to trust in the one I could see, hear, and touch; for with El I could not do any of those things. It was my father who taught me the ways of the world, who instructed me in the path of the blade, shield, spear, bow, and staff.

"So when you prayed tonight, when you spoke so passionately to a God whom I have doubted, I felt lost. I am perplexed by the strength of your faith and dedication to a God in which you have never even seen. When I looked to the others and saw their faces, saw their conviction during your prayer, it drove me further away. I have known those men all of my life, and I have witnessed their sins, and the death they bring on the battlefield. How can they stand there and agree to worship El with you?"

Abaddon stopped talking, ran his hands deep into his dark black hair, and held them to the sides of his head.

Once again, both men sat in silence for some time until Solomon spoke.

"I cannot speak for the others or for the spiritual condition of other men, but I can speak for my own soul. It rips my heart asunder to hear of the things you had to go through in your childhood, and what you had to experience to become the man you are today.

"I remember the first time your father took you into battle. You were only twelve seasons old. I remember running down to the southern gate and watching you march off, walking behind your father, carrying your father's shield and sword. I thought that day I would never see you again and that you would surely die and not come back."

Nodding at the memory, Abaddon shared, "It was the first time I ever killed a man. I ended up killing twenty men in that battle. My father got a lot of teasing from his men because he was wounded in his right leg and I came out completely unscathed."

Abaddon smiled, but Solomon did not. "I also remember when you came back. I was so excited to see you return safely, but I later realized you did not come back sound."

Abaddon knew what he meant. He wasn't the same after that battle. Any purity he had had up to that point, was gone. The innocence of a boy had vanished and the stain of a warrior had taken its place.

Solomon continued, "Your heart had changed. After that day, the image of El slowly began to vanish from your life. Your kindness to others grew ashen, your charity faded, your joy was replaced by duty, and your friendships with those who loved you waned. With each battle, I saw you retreat further and further until you had become nothing more than a shadow of who you once were."

"I have done what I have needed to do to survive, to be the warrior this country needs me to be!" Abaddon defended himself, now feeling his anger rise up once more. "That is what it takes, Solomon! It takes a man with a hardened heart, with an iron gut, to step out on a battlefield! There is no peace, charity, joy, or kindness when blood needs to be spilt. You will never understand, Solomon!

You will never know the rigors and pain of war and what we have to deal with to keep the *fury* from consuming us!

"And in the end, there is no one there to help you through those feelings of death and destruction. You can't rely on your family, your friends, or even on Jehovah. You can only trust yourself to get through the insanity of the fury. You just don't get it! Your father would have understood. He knew what it was like to live a life of war. He knew what it was like to live with the fury."

"Yes, you are right," Solomon rebutled. "My father did know what it was like to live a life of war and bloodshed, so much so that it nearly destroyed him and his family. But make no mistake, he also knew and loved Jehovah. My father loved Jehovah much more than he cared for his life of war.

And as for the *fury* you speak of, it was Jehovah who helped my father to tame that beast. I remember him telling me near the end of his life that he wished he had never killed the giant Goliath. He knew from that point forward he would live a life of war and death. He told me he was happier when he was young and could play his harp and worship El with innocence. I believe my father would have given up all his glory so he could live at peace with El. He loved Jehovah."

Solomon turned and now sat facing Abaddon. "The whole country knows my father was a musician as well as a warrior. He loved to sing and write songs, and in every one of those songs he wrote about El and his relationship with Him. Never once did he harden his heart and become the man you say a warrior needs to be. You have brought yourself to believe that you can only be one or the other, a soldier or a follower of El. If my father were here, speaking to you now, he would tell you there is room in your soul for both. He would tell you it was *because* of Jehovah, Lord Almighty, that his blade had purpose. I have taken to heart many of his songs, and one of them comes to me now. I want you to listen to the words:

> *Bow down thine ear, O Lord, hear me:*
> *for I am poor and needy.*
> *Preserve my soul; for I am holy:*
> *O thou my God, save thy servant that trusteth in thee.*
> *Be merciful unto me, O Lord:*

> *for I cry unto thee daily.*
> *Rejoice the soul of thy servant:*
> *for unto thee, O Lord, do I lift up my soul.*
> *For thou, Lord, art good, and ready to forgive;*
> *and plenteous in mercy unto all them that call upon thee.*
> *Teach me thy way, O Lord;*
> *I will walk in thy truth:*
> *unite my heart to fear thy name.*
> *I will praise thee, O Lord my God,*
> *with all my heart:*
> *and I will glorify thy name for evermore.*
> *For great is thy mercy toward me:*
> *and thou hast delivered my soul from the lowest hell.*
> *O God, the proud are risen against me,*
> *and the assemblies of violent men have sought after my soul;*
> *and have not set thee before them.*
>
> *But thou, O Lord, art a God full of compassion,*
> *and gracious, long suffering, and plenteous in mercy and truth.*
> *O turn unto me, and have mercy upon me;*
> *give thy strength unto thy servant,*
> *and save the son of thine handmaid.*
> *Shew me a token for good;*
> *that they which hate me may see it, and be ashamed:*
> *because thou, Lord, hast helped me, and comforted me.*

Abaddon listened to his friend sing the psalm, and with each word expressed he felt conflict rise within him. The words were powerful and meaningful, wisdom that flowed from the thoughts of a great warrior, a great king and a great man; yet his own personal experience of life warred against those words of wisdom. He felt if he followed Jehovah, he would have to give up the blade; in essence, he would have to give up his life. If he couldn't be a warrior, then what could he be? The thought haunted him because he knew of nothing else but the sword. These thoughts consumed him as he listened to Solomon finish up the wise lyrics. He decided to keep his opinion to himself.

Sitting in solace for a time, Solomon let the hymn sink in. Finally, he said, "My father found a way to live with war and to know and love El. He described a God that could forgive when we do wrong, a God who cares about us enough to listen to our cries and frustrations, a God who delivers us from the clutches of death, a God who is slow to anger and offers up loving-kindness and grace, and a God who even gives our enemy a chance to repent and find a redemption. This is the God whom my father taught me to love and praise so I might rule in holy authority. This is why I believe Abishai deserves a chance to redeem himself and to come back to the light. Although, Abishai is not the only one who needs to find the light."

Solomon stood and motioned for Abaddon to do the same. He put his arm around Abaddon's shoulder and began to walk with him towards the grand double doors that lead out of the great hall.

"Abaddon, it is time for you, too, to find the light. You have been living in a darkness that few can know or follow, and if your path continues, I fear a shadow will find and destroy you. Through you, the darkness could do great and terrible things. El loves and cares for you and wishes for you to know Him in a personal way. It is time for you to start a new journey, one that doesn't require your sword. A journey that breaks down the walls of your heart and lets El in."

"I don't know how. What if I can't?"

"That is why I am asking you to go. Do not fear. I am not publically banishing you or dishonoring you. Only you and I will know of the reason you are leaving; but you must leave all the same. I want you to go from here and find Jehovah. I only ask this, do not return until El has led you to do so."

Once again Abaddon ran his hands through his hair as various emotions flooded his mind.

Why is Solomon doing this? What is the point? Why does he care about my relationship with El? Why? Why? Why?

"What if I never find what you are asking me to look for? What if I never find this… relationship with Jehovah? At least not in the way you desire? Shall I leave my home forever, never again to see my friends?" Abaddon said, his voice rising a bit more with each question asked.

"I have faith that El will clearly reveal himself to you. All you need to do is open your eyes and see Him."

Abaddon was now breathing heavily as frustration grew within him. He was about to continue the argument when his eyes locked with Solomon's. He saw compassion, pain, and a deep sadness in his friend's eyes. He knew then, Solomon was taking no pleasure in sending him away. The pain in the king's face disarmed him and he felt his spirit surrender.

"Fine. I will be gone by first light."

"I am afraid I am going to have to insist that you leave tonight."

Solomon knocked on the large oak door and it slowly opened. A servant stepped forward and gave Solomon a cloth sack. The servant bowed to the king and promptly left, disappearing back down the torch-lit hallway.

Solomon handed the sack to Abaddon.

"Here is everything you will need to begin your journey. A change of warm clothes, a week's worth of rations and two skins, one water and the other some wine. After a week, I trust you can find your own food and water. I have also asked the house servant to place your sword in the first stall of the stables for you to retrieve. I pray you will not need it."

Grasping the sack, Abaddon let it drop to his side. "Why tonight? What is the difference between tonight and on the morn?"

"What would you do, knowing you would leave at first light?"

"Honestly, I would go say goodbye to Rachel. I don't think she would understand why I left. Matter of fact, I am still trying to understand why I am going."

Solomon smiled and placed his hand on Abaddon's shoulder, "And what do you think Rachel would do or say if you told her you were leaving?"

Abaddon knew the answer. "She would try to stop me and talk me out of it. Perhaps even try to go with me."

"How we both know her so well," Solomon said with a chuckle. "That is exactly what she would do. My friend, this is a journey for you, and you alone. Two would be one too many. And I know how persuasive she can be. You give her a handsbreadth of time and she would have you defying my orders."

Even though Solomon was smiling, Abaddon could not. A deep sense of regret and abandonment was consuming him. He didn't want to leave Rachel, not without saying goodbye to her. She deserved at least that much. She was a good friend, and knowing he might not see her again pained him deeply.

Solomon saw the grief on Abaddon's face.

"This isn't goodbye, my friend, and you will be missed. Don't worry about Rachel. She is strong and full of hope, and I will keep a watchful eye on her."

Once again, Abaddon looked at Solomon, and this time saw kindness in his eyes. Without saying another word, he hefted the sack of supplies over his shoulder and left the great hall. He began to make his way down the lowly lit hallway which led to the stables, the same entrance he had used earlier that day.

After about ten paces he stopped and dropped his head, his mind still reeling with questions. "I don't know where to go." He said back to Solomon, without turning around to face him.

"It is a journey for your heart and soul. Listen to them and let them guide you. El will make sure you get to your destination."

Giving a quiet sigh, Abaddon slowly shook his head at Solomon's cryptic answer. He once again stepped forward and made his way out of the palace, not knowing when, or even if he would return.

CHAPTER 18

Achish heard loud screaming and realized it was coming from his own throat.

Once again, his demon had taken control of his body and it was raging and ranting in a tongue he did not understand.

The demon's fear was overwhelming. Achish felt as though his heart was going to explode out of his chest, and he began to feel faint and dizzy. He would have fallen on the ground if it was not for the strength of the dark spirit within him.

A great wind had knocked him back against the wall, and now a brilliant glowing light consumed the cave, birthing forth between Achish and the diamond pillar. The light pierced through the massive jewel, causing a rainbow of colors to explode all over the cavern. The source of the light was so blinding, Achish began to feel his eyes burn from within. Then, as if someone blew out a candle, the light was gone.

The light had vanished and a great creature had taken its place. A giant man-shaped form towered before Achish. The being had a body of a man, although its features where also of a lion. It stood at least eight cubits high and was clad in bright mailed armor which seemed to radiate its own light. In its right hand was a massive sword that spurned blades from both ends. The blades were on fire, casting out blue flames. Four wings protruded from the creature's back, blazing with a deep red glow. The span of the wings was almost twice the height of the creature himself.

Shrinking back into the corner of the cave, Achish shook uncontrollably. Noticing he had control of his body once again, he had to ask his demon, "What is that?" Looking upon the creature, he felt as though he wanted to die, as if he was not worthy to even breathe in its presence.

In a hushed whisper, the demon answered, "It is Labroth. A warrior of old from the Maker, and he is very evil, very dangerous, he is! Your enemies call them malakhs or angels in the common tongue. Do not speak, slave. I don't think he has seen us, and maybe he will not. We may yet live through this. Don't… move!"

Labroth turned in a slow circle to survey the room. Seeing the diamond pillar, he strode towards it and placed his mammoth lion-like paw upon it. A bright light sparked from his hand, once again illuminating the whole cave. From within the pillar, Dagon roared frantically as if he were given a surge of pain.

Then Labroth spoke.

It was a voice like Achish had never heard before. It was deep and gravelly as if the earth itself had learned to speak. "Dagon. Fallen malakh from the depths of Mathiel. You will never leave this prison, for your sins were great against men. Countless stars have dimmed because of you and your alliance with the Deceiver."

Satisfied that Dagon was still sealed within the crystal, Labroth removed his hand from the pillar and the bright light vanished.

"But how? How did the gateway appear? Only a son of Cain has the blood to open your tomb. Where are you, son of Cain? I can smell your traitorous blood."

At that moment, Labroth's eyes glowed a brilliant orange color, revealing his face in greater detail. Long blondish-red hair covered his head like a great mane. A lion's snout was present rather than a human mouth and nose. His jaw and neck were large and well muscled. A thick white beard grew from his chin down to his chest.

Achish was so captivated by the angel that he didn't realize it was now looking right at him.

"Hello, son of Cain," Labroth said in an even tone. "You have a worm consuming you."

The voice within Achish screamed, "Get up! Run!"

But before Achish could even move, the angel closed the gap between them in one step. The giant grabbed for Achish's throat. Achish, expecting to be lifted up off the ground by the massive hand, was surprised when Labroth pulled his hand away and his body did not move. He then felt a great pain surge through him, as if something was grasping at his spine and tearing at his chest. Then the pain shot straight up into his head, causing him to slink to the ground. Great screams of agony erupted from his demon within; but then, the demon's cries were heard from the outside of his body! And then the pain in his head and spine eased away, like a great weight had been lifted off of him.

Staring up from the rocky floor of the cave, Achish gasped at what he saw. There in the angel's hand was a black oily form of a man with the head of a worm. The worm's size was half of the angel's. Labroth's iron grip was around the demon's throat and the demon thrashed wildly as Labroth held it high into the air.

The angel looked to Achish and said, "Man of flesh, look with your own eyes and see the stain that has consumed you. No doubt he has enslaved you and tormented you. No more. Go, now! Run from this place and never return, for your fate lies elsewhere."

Achish was about to ask how he was to escape, as there was no way out, but the great creature lifted his sword to the rock wall next to him. Peering over to his left, an opening appeared in the wall with a path leading upwards, back to the surface. Without a word and without looking back, Achish ran for the door and disappeared through it.

When Achish passed through the doorway, the great diamond pillar shook and began to sink back into the earth.

Dagon roared from his prison and angry torrents of blasphemies poured from his mouth. Ignoring Dagon, Labroth focused on the demon within his grasp, which was still thrashing like a fish out of water.

"Stop your squirming and warring, fallen one!" Labroth said, slamming the body of the demon hard against the cave wall. The worm stopped struggling, only to try a new tactic.

The demon's head changed shape. What was once a worm was now a human head with dark black hair and black, oil filled eyes. The rest of his body was still a slimy mass with black oil secreting from it.

Expressionless, Labroth glared into the eyes of the demon as if he had seen this trick many times before. "Changing your shape to look more human will not bring you pity or mercy. Your fate has already been determined by the Creator. Your name? Give me your name!"

The worm turned his head from side to side refusing to speak. With his short, stubby limbs, he began to violently claw and tear at the arm of the malakh. Finally, in a gasping voice, the demon said, "Air...I can't...I can't breathe! Release me and I will talk!"

A crack of a smile lifted the corner of Labroth's mouth. "Do you take me as a fool, as if I were created yesterday? You have been in a human body far too long. We are spirits and not a part of this physical world of laws and boundaries. We do not need air to breathe, as if we are molded flesh. Now, your name!"

The demon's body went slack and became a dead weight in Labroth's hand. It began to cry and wail in a language which was only known by the malakh.

Labroth was not swayed by this pitiful tactic either. "Your name!"

In anger and spite, the demon yelled his own name, a name which could not be heard by human ears or said with a human tongue.

Cursing the oily demon's name, Labroth condemned him by the authority of the Maker.

When the curse was completed, the worm howled and thrashed with a last and final effort to free himself, but to no avail. Labroth was simply too strong.

The demon watched in horror as Labroth spun his sword once in a circle and then thrust the blade deep within him. Blue fire instantly erupted over the entire body of the demon and a hideous scream of desperation echoed throughout the cavern.

At last, Labroth let go of his victim. He watched as the demon's body turned into a flaming needle-like pillar which pierced down into the rocky floor, leaving only a black colored indentation with glowing red embers.

Satisfied the worm demon was now gone, Labroth began to turn towards the pillar to watch the earth consume Dagon's prison; but before he could, an explosion erupted directly behind him. The force was so great, Labroth was thrown hard, face first, against the very wall he had just held the worm to. He felt thousands of tiny shards accost his back. Instantly, his wings ignited with hot, bright fire which prevented the projectiles from causing harm to him.

Once again, Labroth was about to turn around when a giant claw from a scaly arm grasped the back of his head. The angel's head was then repeatedly and violently slammed and crushed into the rock wall. Labroth lifted his sword arm to strike backwards at his attacker, only to realize his weapon was no longer in his hand. He must have dropped it.

Over and over, his head was beaten into the stone wall with immense force. The wall began to crumble and fall down upon him. The bodily form he had taken, was beginning to fail and break. Light was now consuming his vision and he knew it wouldn't be long until his spirit would be swept away back to the Maker.

Then, the beating stopped.

The massive hand that held his head flung him around and grasped him by the throat, lifting his beaten body in the air. It was not lost on Labroth that only moments ago the roles were reversed with the lesser demon. Labroth now stared into the eyes of the Great Demon, Dagon.

The beast was free.

Labroth took in the massive form of his enemy. The demon had taken the shape of a dragon of old, a leviathan of the ancient world before the time of the world flood. At full height the beast towered far above Labroth's head. Its hind legs were thick and strong, able to make him walk upright. His front arms were long with razor sharp claws. His tail, with what looked like a giant spear on the end, snaked around him and darted to and fro as if it had a mind of its own. Its massive head was covered in horns and jagged iron plates. The beast's body shimmered in a blackish-green scaled armor.

"How?" was the only word that escaped Labroth's lips. He then noticed a small, fat figure off to the side. It was Achish.

Standing against the wall, Achish nervously rocked back and forth on his short stubby legs. The king's hand was covered in fresh blood.

"Son of Cain? Why did you come back? What did you do? You were free, I released you! Do you know what you have done? Do you know what he will do to the earth now that he is loose?"

Achish dug down deep and found the courage to speak. "This is what I know: You robbed me of my master and the chance to bring vengeance for my sons and for my people. Israel's blood must run freely from the city they call Zion, and it must fall! I was promised revenge and I believe Lord Dagon will give that to me."

It was then, for the first time, Achish heard the voice of his *new* master. A deep guttural hiss escaped from the beast.

"Yessssss, man of flesh and bone. For your loyal service, we will beget death to all the light of this earth. The chosen ones of El will be destroyed," Dagon hissed with a slight smile to his scaly mouth.

Labroth looked from Achish back to Dagon, "Get on with it! You have won this fight. Crush me and finish it," Labroth said with anger in his voice.

Smiling, Dagon brought the angel close to his mouth, bearing several rows of razor sharp teeth. "Do you take me for a fool? If I destroy your form you will just ascend to the Maker and he will recommission you, and in time you will be sent out to hunt for me once again.

"Ah, yes, small one, I recognize you. You are the captain who serves beneath the wretch who sealed me in here! For three millennia I have waited to exact my revenge on that coward of an archangel, Michael," Dagon spit out the name. "But, since he is not here, you will have to do, for now."

Before Labroth could give a reply, Achish watched in horror as Dagon bit into Labroth's right arm and ripped it off at the shoulder. He ate the limb whole and then did the same to the left arm.

Labroth began to writhe in pain. Achish looked on in fascination as his new master took pleasure in mutilating the angel. Dagon carried Labroth's mangled body over to the empty diamond pillar which had been his previous prison and threw Labroth's broken, yet alive, body into it. Then, with a great breath, Dagon spewed liquid bile from his mouth and it ignited into a blinding white flame.

Remembering his descent down into the cavern several days earlier, Achish remembered the slime he had slipped in. He recalled the words of his former master, "This substance you call slime comes from Dagon."

When Dagon was done breathing out the deadly flame, the hole to the diamond prison was closed up again. The dragon's fire had melted the diamond to cover the breach.

Labroth was now sealed inside.

Dagon turned his massive head and looked to Achish, "Step back through the doorway to the surface, but do not leave."

Achish ran over to the open passage which led out of the cavern. Once he did, the jeweled tower once again began to sink down into the earth. Dagon stared at the sinking pillar until all of it had returned below the rocky ground and lava once again covered the top of the prison.

All the while, Labroth glared into the eyes of the beast, not knowing if he would ever see freedom again.

Once it was done, Achish came back into the dark cavern, "What now, master?"

Without looking at the fat little man standing near him, he proclaimed, "Now? We kill them all!"

CHAPTER 19

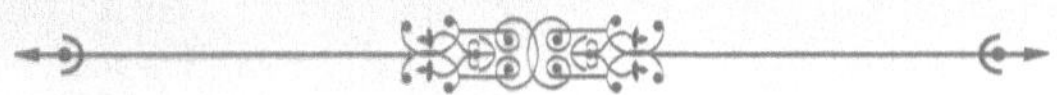

Solomon stood on top of the palace and watched his friend walk through the city streets and make his way to the northern gate. He began to pray in a quiet voice, asking Jehovah to make Abaddon's path straight and not altogether painful.

After his prayer, a tall figure, clothed and hooded in a green cloak, walked up beside him.

Without turning to his visitor, Solomon asked, "Are you sure sending Abaddon on this journey was the right course of action? I understand the wisdom of this plan, but I do not like the timing. We will be building the Temple of Yahweh soon, and if what you told me is true, we will need him here."

The cloaked visitor stood silent for a moment and then replied in a deep voice, "If he does not go now, Israel will have no future. Much will rely on what El has in store for him. If he survives what lies ahead of him, he will find what he is looking for."

Solomon looked once more, watching Abaddon disappear into the darkness. He had an unnerving feeling that he would never see his friend again.

PART II

Hear my voice, O God, in my prayer:
preserve my life from fear of the enemy.
Hide me from the secret counsel of the wicked;
from the insurrection of the workers of iniquity:
Who whet their tongue like a sword.
But God shall shoot at them with an arrow;
suddenly shall they be wounded.
So they shall make their own tongue
to fall upon themselves:
all that see them shall flee away.
And all men shall fear,
and shall declare the work of God;
for they shall wisely consider of his doing.
The righteous shall be glad in the Lord,
and shall trust in him;
and all the upright in heart shall glory.

-King David of Israel, 5th Age, 67th Season

CHAPTER 20

Rachel sat on her windowsill with her legs dangling over the edge. She watched as excited people flooded into the city streets below her. The king had announced a month ago that there would be a wedding in Ezion-Geber, a port town to the south, and a grand celebration to follow. People from all the tribes of Israel were coming. With the ceremony now only five days away, there was a feeling of excitement and joy in the air.

Everywhere Rachel looked, people were happy and boisterous. Everyone, except for her. With all the ruckus, one would think this was the king's wedding, but it was not.

It was her wedding.

She was twenty seasons old now, well past marrying age; and when her mother went home to be with Jehovah a season ago, Solomon had adopted her as his own daughter. Solomon's first decree after the adoption was to have her married, whether she wanted to or not.

Of course she protested, but Solomon would not hear any of it.

"If you don't get wed soon then no one will want you for a bride. You don't want to take the place of the old childless hag who roams around Southtown, do you?" Solomon pointed out, putting an end to the discussion.

Rachel had rolled her eyes.

When they were kids, there was an old woman who roamed around the south side of the city (Southtown) who would chase children if they got too close to her. The hag would often be seen hunched over, facing the corner of a building and talking out loud to no one in particular. If one did try to talk to her, she would hiss at them and spit at their feet. Nobody liked her, so for the most part, people left her alone.

What ever happened to her? Rachel thought.

She shook off the old memory, but Solomon's point had stuck with her. She didn't want to be alone; although, she felt alone now. Sure, things were different now that she was the adopted daughter of the king of Israel. She was no longer a servant in the palace, but a princess. She had servants of her own and many nobles and guests wanted to be a part of her life, but it all seemed so… vain, unnatural… fake. There was no one she felt she could get close to.

She missed her mother.

"Oh, mother! Why did you have to leave me? Why does everyone leave me?" Rachel said to herself.

With a sigh she looked to the north gate of the city wall and stared, still hoping she would see a familiar face come riding into the city, stop, and then look up at her and smile. Oh, how she had dreamed of it many a time. She would look out and see Abaddon come home. It had been two seasons since Abaddon had left without saying goodbye. Rachel still remembered the day after he had gone.

She had gotten up early that morning and had made a special breakfast for herself and Abaddon. She had resolved the night before that she was going to tell him the truth about how much she cared for him. No…how much she loved him.

After preparing the morning meal, she went to Abaddon's quarters to wake him, only to find he was not there. This was not so unusual, as Abaddon sometimes got up early to train. So Rachel proceeded to the training grounds, only to find them empty and no one in sight.

Now puzzled, she checked the stables, the pantry, the well, and even the dining hall where she last saw him the night before.

All nothing.

Running back to his room, she began to look around. Everything seemed to be in order, except for his pallet. It had not been slept in. She stepped to his armoire and found all his clothes neatly hanging in place. Everything seemed to be in place, except…except for his sword. It wasn't there.

Where had he gone?

Her next stop was the king.

Solomon had always been an early riser and she found him on the roof of the palace, breaking his fast with sweet-bread and honey with a bit of goat's milk. Rachel sat down across from him and was about to speak when she took in his appearance. Solomon had a haggard look upon him and his eyes were red and weary. He looked up at her and weakly smiled and offered her some bread.

Rachel took the bread but did not eat it. Now, seeing Solomon's face, she was growing concerned for both of her friends.

"Solomon, what is going on? What happened? I can't find Abaddon and I found his sword missing. You and I both know that he only uses his sword for training or when he is killing, and I checked the training grounds, he isn't there. And now I find you distraught and with tears in your eyes, brother. What is going on?"

Rachel stared pleadingly into the king's eyes and began to feel her own emotion begin to well up within her. Her stomach twisted as a sense of fear grabbed at her.

For what seemed to be an age, Solomon just looked at her. A tear broke free from his eye and made its way to his unkept beard. He reached out both of his hands and took her hands in his.

"Rachel. I have been mourning and praying all night for Abaddon, for you, and for me to gain wisdom. A wisdom which seems to be far out of my reach. I have been trying to find the right words to tell you about our friend."

She was struggling to restrain herself, but a few tears broke free from Rachel's beautiful green eyes and ran their course to her chin. With a quiver in her voice she asked, "Is he…is he dead?" Her words could only come out as a whisper.

Solomon raised his eyebrows slightly and held her hands a bit tighter, "No, no. He is well. Why would you think he is dead?" He reached out his right hand and began wiping away the tears which were now glistening down Rachel's face.

"Because I can't find him and I have been looking for him," she said, now in a panicked voice. "And then I come up here and you are upset and crying and you said you were mourning and praying for Abaddon. What am I to think?" She said getting a bit angry. "What is going on? Where is Abaddon?"

Looking upon his dear friend, Solomon's heart broke. He knew this would be hard for her to hear as he knew she loved Abaddon very much.

"Abaddon is gone Rachel."

He stayed silent for a moment and let the words sink in.

"Gone? What do you mean gone? Where did he go and when will he be back? I thought you didn't send the soldiers out on missions so soon after coming home from a war campaign?"

"Rachel," Solomon said calmly. Seeing the anguish on her face, he stood and came around the table to sit next to her. He put his arm around her shoulders.

When Solomon's strong arms wrapped around her petite frame, she melted into his embrace and once again began to tear up. Solomon held her there for several moments before releasing her, and once again, took her hands in his.

"I have a lot to tell you but I need you to listen so that you may understand why I did what I did."

Rachel nodded.

She listened to the whole story and everything that had taken place the night before. At first Rachel was angry and furious with Solomon for sending Abaddon away, but she calmed as spiritual reason overtook her. She had seen the signs of Abaddon's lack of faith as well, but had never said anything to him. She had also seen him move further and further away from Jehovah, but she had figured he was going through a phase in his life and he would eventually come back to El on his own.

With a deep sadness in her heart she looked up at Solomon and asked, "Now what? Will we ever see him again?"

"I don't know, Rachel. That will be between him and Jehovah. I pray he comes back to us soon, for I already feel the loss of his presence."

Taking Solomon's face in her small hands, Rachel kissed him firmly on his cheek. She then retreated back to her room and did not come out again for seven days.

Every day since, Rachel would sit on the window sill in her room and look out to the north to see if Abaddon was coming home.

Two seasons had passed, and nothing.

Was he ever going to return home? Had he found what he was looking for? Had he found a new home and a new family? Was he even alive? Did he even care about her…love her? If he did, why was he not coming home? She shook the thoughts from her head and gave out a deep sigh.

She was thinking of going to break her fast when a knock came to her door. Before Rachel could respond, her maid servant, Hinda, came bounding into the room.

Rachel couldn't help but smile every time she saw Hinda. She had a bubbly personality and always tried to find the good in things, no matter how bad they got. She reminded Rachel of her mother, and much of the time Hinda acted like her mother.

Rachel used to giggle every time she said the maid's name, *'Hinda'*. The name meant "deer". Hinda's personality matched her name. Her demeanor was always uplifting and prancing, just like a happy stag in the spring time. In many ways, she and Rachel were a lot alike as well.

"Oh tsk, are you in that window again?" Hinda commented, moving over to Rachel's pallet. She started pulling off the old linens so she could put on fresh, clean ones. "One of these days you are going to drift off asleep, fall, and break your neck. Come down from there! It isn't proper for a child of the king to act so!"

Swinging her legs inside, Rachel dropped back into the room. She then plopped herself upon a pile of pillows sprawled out on the floor.

Hinda continued to talk as she worked at fitting the edges of the new linen around the corners of the soft, feather pallet. "Every morning you are up in that window, looking for that boy, what was his name?"

Rachel was about to say Abaddon's name but Hinda resumed talking without the answer.

"Sitting up there and waiting for a dream which will not come. Personally, I am glad he is not here. The king has set you up with a perfectly good man. A man who will take care of you and provide for you all the days of your life. And he is still young enough to give you children, a large family through which El will give you many blessings. I haven't seen him yet, but the people say he is handsome. Is he handsome and kind like the people say?"

This time Hinda looked at Rachel, expecting an answer.

Rachel had a sour look on her face and shrugged. "I don't know? I have not met him either." Rachel flopped backwards from her sitting position and now lay on her back across the pillows.

She put her hands over her face, "I hate this! Why do I have to be married at all? He probably has the face of a cow and barks orders like a dog! Did you hear he already has two wives and I am to be his third? Everyone knows the first wife is the one who gets all the respect and honor. I will be nothing more than a new toy for him to enjoy and order around."

"Well, what are you to do? It is not like you can just run away from this. The king has arranged the marriage."

Rachel shot up straight, then stood and ran over to Hinda. "Hinda, you are brilliant! Let's run away together! We could head north and see if we could track down Abaddon! Oh, it would be an adventure! Sure, it would be difficult at times, but I have more than enough money and I could hunt for food. I have become quite the marksman with my bow. Captain Broc even said he would take me arnavon hunting in the near future."

Hinda smiled as she listened to the young impetuous girl and couldn't help but laugh at the thought of Rachel, traipsing through the wilderness and trying to shoot arnavons.

"So, what do you think? Would you go with me? I would much rather go and find Abaddon than to move to Tyre and become the prince's third slave—"

"Wife. You would be his wife. Not slave."

"Whatever. So? What do you say? Let's pack and go! We can leave tonight after nightfall!" Rachel affirmed, heading for her armoire to find the appropriate clothes for such a journey.

Hinda grabbed Rachel by her hand and led her back to her bed and sat her down.

Rachel groaned, knowing there was a dissuading speech on its way. She groaned a second time, rolled her eyes and fell back onto her pallet, spreading her arms across the soft linens Hinda had just carefully fitted.

"You can't run away," Hinda declared. "You wouldn't last a day out there. There is much more to think about than finding furry little arnavons to shoot, not to mention we are forbidden to eat those nasty little creatures anyway. There are thieves and murderers who hide out along the road, and they would do who-knows-what to a young beautiful woman like you." Hinda shivered at the thought. "No ma'm. You will stay here where it is safe. And who is to say you would find Abaddon? He has been gone for these two seasons now, and if he wanted to be found or wanted to come home, he would have. You going off and finding him doesn't mean he is ready to come back. A man must decide his own fate."

"And what of a woman's fate?" Rachel interrupted. "May not a woman decide her own fate, like not marrying a man she doesn't even know, or love?"

"No," Hinda replied. "We do not have that privilege. This is the way of things. Jehovah knows what He is doing. There is a reason you have been called to be the prince of Tyre's wife, even if it is his third. Be obedient, and El will show you great and mighty things. You will see. Plus, the king is not only your adopted father but your friend as well, yes? Do not break his heart by running away and leaving him in shame."

Rachel was about to argue further but she shot straight up and headed for the door. "Oh my goodness! I have to go! I forgot that

Solomon asked me to meet him at mid-morning!" Rachel had made it out into the hall when she felt Hinda grab her arm once again.

"Land-sake child! Take account of yourself! You need to get dressed. You are still in your bedclothes!" Hinda chided and laughed at the same time, ushering Rachel back into her room and closing the door.

Rachel looked down at herself and turned a deep shade of red. "Whoops."

Smiling to herself, Hinda softly said with a bit of laughter in her voice, "Run off, indeed. What would this girl do without me?"

CHAPTER 21

Rachel ran down the hallway, making a slapping sound on the stone floor every time her left foot came down. She cringed at the noise she made with each step. The leather on the bottom of her sandal must have been coming loose. She rounded the corner to the throne room and crashed right into a guard who was standing at his post in front of two large, closed, double doors. She bounced right off him and flew backwards to the floor.

The guard immediately looked horrified at what had happened. "I am sorry princess! Had I known you were coming with such urgency I would have made sure to have gotten out of the way! I am truly sorry! Will you forgive me?" The guard asked, reaching a hand down to help her back up.

Rachel smiled at the politeness of the guard and his caring demeanor. After all, it was her fault she was now on the stone cold floor. She reached up and took the guard's hand and he easily drew her up.

"There is nothing to forgive…Carmon, right?"

The guard raised his eyebrows in surprise. "Yes, princess. I am surprised you know of my name."

"You forget, I was also a servant here once. I know pretty much everyone here in the palace. Your wife is Dafna, one of the cooks in the kitchen. Correct? She makes some of the best sweet bread I have ever had."

The guard beamed at the compliment. "Thank you, miss. I will let her know you have said so."

Rachel twisted her back a bit and began to rub her tailbone, feeling the ache from her hard landing. "So, Carmon. What is with the closed doors? Today is the third day of the week and the king does not have summons or grievances on this day."

"Normally, no, but he has a special guest this morning and did not want to be disturbed."

Rachel raised an eyebrow in curiosity. "Well, Solomon…I mean the king asked me to meet him at mid-morning, and the hour is growing late. Maybe I was to be involved with the meeting taking place."

The guard gave a faint smile and straightened a bit. "Sorry princess. The king gave specific instructions. No visitors until he gives the go ahead."

Sighing through her lips, Rachel made a, *"pppbbb"*, sound. She really didn't want to have to wait, and if there was something important going on, she wanted to know. It could be about Abaddon? She thought about giving the guard a pleading look and charming him into opening the door for her, but then thought better of it. Carmon was a nice man and she didn't want to get him and his family in trouble for not following orders.

Smiling, Rachel waved good-bye to the guard with her fingers, and walked away. As soon as she was out of sight, she took off running down the hall. Once again her left sandal slapped on the ground, echoing in all directions. Even though she was several paces away, she could hear Carmon snicker out loud.

"Curse these sandals," Rachel muttered to herself. She stopped and quickly untied her sandal straps. Kicking the footwear from her feet, she resumed forward. Rachel smiled to herself as she felt the cool stone make contact with the bare skin of her feet. She liked being barefoot. It made her feel free.

Since she grew up in the palace, Rachel knew almost all the secret passages which ran throughout the building. Most of them were corridors the servants used so they would not run into nobles or dignitaries roaming the main halls.

Rachel recalled at least three entrances into the throne room: One was the obvious double doors which lead into the great hall, a second was a hidden trap door right underneath the throne, which led out to the stables, and the third was an opening to a hallway behind a large purple curtain to the right of the throne. This was the servant's entrance into the throne room. Once in a while, the king would desire refreshments and the servants would use this access hall to get to and fro the kitchen. Most people did not know of this hallway as it was hidden from the view of those who would be standing before the throne.

Obviously, the trap door underneath the throne was out of the question, so Rachel headed for the kitchen to access the servant's hallway. She just hoped that hall was not guarded as well.

When she arrived at the kitchen, there was a hustle of maid servants darting to and fro, preparing for the noonday meal. The smell of fresh baked bread flooded her nostrils and her stomach promptly reminded her that she had not yet broken her fast.

The hallway was on the other side of the kitchen and she frowned at the sight of a guard standing in the hall's doorway.

Rachel let out a defeated sigh.

She was entertaining the thought of going back to the main doors to wait for Solomon to get done with his mystery guest, when she took notice of the kitchen guard a little more closely. He was a younger man, a guard she had not met before. Instead of keeping a warrior's stance like he was supposed to, he was standing with his arms to his sides and nervously shifting his weight from one foot to the other. Instead of looking straight ahead, he repeatedly looked at a young, red haired maidservant who was carrying fresh bread from the kilns to the cooling shelves.

Rachel smiled to herself, a plan forming in her mind.

Rachel began to casually walk through the kitchen and many of the maidservants acknowledged her with smiles and nods. She even made an effort to fit in as if she belonged there. She filled a few baskets of bread and took them over to the serving trays and then took a handful of beans to the wash bowls to be rinsed before they would be split and boiled.

When she was within a few paces from the guard, he noticed her and recognition filled his face. He snapped to a warrior's stance as if he had been that way all along.

Smiling at the guard's sudden transformation, Rachel walked up to him and began to speak in soft tones that only he could hear.

"She is pretty, isn't she?"

The guard, not sure how to reply, only glanced sideways at her.

"Oh, relax! It is not like I am Captain Broc," Rachel said, with a jab from her elbow to his arm.

As soon as she said Broc's name, the guard stiffened as if the captain would be walking in at any moment.

"The girl with the red hair. She is a beautiful creature from El, is she not?"

The guard glanced once more at Rachel and then looked to the door on the other side of the kitchen, as if checking to see if his commanding officer was spying on him, maybe testing him to see what he would do if he was distracted.

"It's fine, calm down. I saw you looking at her. I think you two would make a perfect couple. I think she likes you too. She keeps stealing glances back at you and smiles when you are not looking."

The guard now broke his stance. "Really? Are you sure?" he asked in a whisper.

And the fish is in the net. Rachel thought to herself.

"Absolutely! Go on, talk to her."

"I can't…I mean, I shouldn't. I have to stay here and—"

"I wouldn't delay," Rachel urged, cutting him off in mid-sentence. "A good looking girl like her will not be single for long. Her father may even have a suitor in mind. You had better speak to her now and get a good word in or you might not get another chance."

"Well…I don't know."

Rachel gave him a little push and a pat on the back at the same time. He crept forward, taking one small step after the other and headed in the direction of the red haired woman. As soon as the love-struck guard was a few steps away, Rachel glided through the opening to the hallway and quickly dashed for the throne room. After several paces, the corridor took a right turn and the kitchen disappeared from view.

Now that no one could see her, she sprinted the distance of the hall and didn't slow until she came close to the throne room. She half expected to hear the guard's footsteps behind her, but none came.

The sounds of the kitchen faded away and became replaced by two voices talking ahead.

Upon coming to the end of the passage, Rachel slowed her pace to a silent tiptoe. The dark, thick, purple curtain was drawn over the doorway, preventing her from looking in. Four to five stair steps now stood between her and the curtain.

Rachel crept to the second step from the top, and in slow motion she knelt down and reclined herself against the wall. With great care, she withdrew the curtain just enough for her to peek through. There sat Solomon on his throne, speaking in even tones to his mystery guest. From this angle she could not see who the guest was, but by the tone of his voice she knew it was not Abaddon. She considered moving to the other side of the curtain to get a closer look at the stranger, but thought better of it. She didn't want to risk making any noise or noticeable movement.

Looking through the small gap between the wall and the curtain, she stared at Solomon and watched his mannerisms and facial expressions as he spoke. He was so sympathetic and full of expression when he presented himself. It was not hard to see the passion and emotion in her friend's face.

Solomon had changed so much over the years. Rachel remembered a boy with thick, black, shaggy hair, who always laughed and played every chance he got. Rarely had she ever seen Solomon sad or crying growing up. He had always found the pleasure and joy in everything, even in times which were not that joyous.

But Solomon had not exactly been an angel in his youth, either. She, Abaddon, and Solomon used to get into some of the worst trouble, from sneaking out of the palace at night, to stealing some of the royal horses so they could ride to the Jordan River to catch frogs. But it was always Solomon who would be the first to apologize and accept the blame. Of course, since he was the prince, there were hardly ever any severe punishments.

Rachel smiled to herself as she recalled some of these memories and glanced back at Solomon. The boy was gone and there sat the man. No longer a prince, but the king of Israel. The thick, black hair was still there but it was no longer shaggy. It was now long and wavy, cascading down to his broad, strong shoulders. A neatly trimmed, dark-auburn beard decorated a firm and distinct jaw line.

And then, of course, there were his eyes. Rachel loved looking into those dark blue eyes. With those eyes and the deep tone of his voice, he could soothe the most disheartened spirit.

Yes, Rachel thought. *He is a handsome man.*

If it wasn't for Abaddon she would have probably pursued a courtship with Solomon. Solomon was kind and gentle and she knew he would be able to provide well for her and her future children, but Abaddon… Abaddon was adventurous, alive, unpredictable, and very passionate in his own right. Those were the things she desired in her own life, so it was easy to be drawn to Abaddon. Marrying Solomon would mean always being proper, going to rich, lavish parties, and having to put up with arrogant and snooty people.

No, thank you! Rachel thought again to herself.

Rachel remembered a conversation she had had with her mother when she was about ten seasons old.

Her mother had sat her down and said, "Don't you dare get it in your head to fall in love with that charmer, Prince Solomon! He is bad news, that one is! The boy is only eleven and he is already chasing down women and flirting up a storm. Improper, it is! Did you know he ran by me the other day and pinched me in the bum?"

Rachel had laughed at her mother's statement, trying to picture Solomon pinching her mom on the backside.

"It's not funny!" her mother had scolded. "I forbid you to ever think about marrying that boy. You mark my words. Women will be his downfall!"

Rachel was beginning to think her mother was right. Even though Solomon had not yet taken a wife, there were numerous royal women who had been courting the position. One of those suitors was the queen of Egypt. And then there were all the concubines Solomon already had, despite not being married.

Putting the thoughts out of her mind, Rachel stole another glance towards the throne, this time to find it empty. Solomon was still talking but was no longer sitting.

She decided to risk the move.

Very carefully she picked herself up and moved to the other side of the curtain. There was too much material for her to be able to peek around the side, so she slowly lifted up the bottom of the draping cloth and peered underneath.

There was Solomon, talking to a large muscular man who stood at least a head taller than the king. The tall man wore a green cloak which covered him from his neck to the floor. The man was broad and strong, shoulders wider than Solomon's. His long, straight, golden hair was tied back at the nape of his neck. Most of it disappeared beneath his cloak, but strands of it also fell to the sides of his head, making a frame around his face. Blondish stubble lined his jaw and a short, trimmed beard covered his lip and chin.

Rachel couldn't take her eyes off the man. He was strong and beautiful and held a presence which demanded respect and superiority. Gazing upon him, she felt an unsettling fear overcome her, and she wasn't sure why. She studied his eyes, which were determined and fixed as he communed with Solomon.

Who is this man, Rachel thought to herself. With fair hair and skin such as his, he definitely was not from around here. Only one other time in her life had she seen a person with such brilliant golden hair, and that was the wife of a merchant from a land far west of here. Could this man be from the West? And if he was, what was he doing here? He must be a warrior, judging by his height, body mass, and stature. Rachel's mind raced as many other questions began to form.

Solomon stood from his throne, descended the seven steps to the floor, and approached his guest. "I believe all the preparations are made with Huram, king of Tyre. The covenant we made together is strong and we have become good friends. He was good to my father and he has been equally good to me. He has agreed to give us all the cedar and cyprus wood we need for the temple, but he says we will need to get the algum wood in Ophir. Huram says there is not enough in Lebanon, at least not the amount we require. He is also sending master makers of gold, silver, bronze, stone, wood and weaves to teach our own people."

"And what has he asked in return?" the tall man asked as he stroked his blonde beard with his right hand.

"Nothing I wasn't willing to provide: twenty thousand kors of wheat, twenty thousand kors of barley, twenty thousand baths of wine and twenty thousand baths of oil; delivered every season until the work is done."

The guest nodded his approval. "How will they be delivering the wood they cut from Lebanon?"

"According to the letter you brought me yesterday, they will tie the cut trees into large rafts and float them along the reef of the Great Sea down to Joppa. From there, some of King Huram's men will help us set up a mill to cut the logs. Once cut and shaped to the proper length, we will have ox carts deliver them to Jerusalem."

"And what of the stones? It will take many men to hew the stones from the mountain and bring them here to Zion."

"I pronounced an edict a month ago commissioning all the slaves of the land to become laborers. We have eighty thousand men to cut the rocks from the mountain and to shape them into the foundation stones for the temple. We then have seventy thousand men to transport the stone blocks and wood to the building site. I have also found three thousand six hundred men in whom I trust to oversee the work."

Again the large man nodded in approval. "You have done well and our Lord is well pleased."

Solomon smiled and placed his hand on the man's shoulder. "I thank you, my friend, for the errand you have decided to embark on. Even though you are not one of us, you have dedicated yourself to the work of the Lord. You know better than I the journey you are about to go on, for only a few have ever had the privilege of seeing the land of Ophir."

"Which begs the question, are the ships in Ezion-Geber stocked and ready for voyage?"

"They were completed and tested two weeks ago. Twelve of the best vessels Huram has ever built. They are being supplied as we speak. They will be set to sail on the morn of Rachel's wedding. That is one of the reasons I wanted to have the ceremony in Ezion-Geber, so King Huram could witness the launching of the ships."

"I am glad this journey will start with a celebration, but I am afraid this voyage may not end with as much joy. Most of the time the trip is long and boring, but the recent news which has been coming to my ears from my kindred disturbs me. The enemy has been moving and has become restless, and even though Jehovah has given you peace on your borders, this is not so outside of Israel." Solomon's guest said with some sadness in his voice.

"I am afraid this journey to Ophir will be perilous. The enemy does not desire the temple of Yahweh to come to completion. They know they cannot attack you here directly due to the barrier of the Great Spirit; but once beyond your lands, the enemy will be in waiting. I know not where and how they will amass. This is why I have been sent to offer my services. Just know this, even though I will be with your men and ships on this journey, I cannot guarantee the success of the mission, or the safety of your men. I do not have the foresight of El."

Stroking his own beard, Solomon nodded thoughtfully at the man's words. His eyes remained calm and steadfast, not showing the least bit of concern. "All will be well, my friend. The Mighty Yahweh will see His house built. Of that, I have no doubt. It has been foretold and promised."

For the first time, Solomon saw the man smile. It was a smile which did not break the seal of his lips, but a smile all the same. The man raised a large hand from underneath his cloak, cupped the back of Solomon's neck, and gave a gentle squeeze.

"Your faith never ceases to amaze me, child of El. Your people are a constant surprise and wonder. I wish my kindred could be more like you and yours, for many have fallen away from our path and purpose." The large man sighed and placed his hand back under his cloak. "I am afraid this is our last meeting, King of Israel. I do not think we will meet again until the days of glory. Shalom."

Now with a sense of regret in his voice, Solomon bowed his head and returned the farewell, "Shalom, my friend."

As a sign of respect, the stranger bowed back with a dip of his head and then turned and walked out of the throne room.

As Solomon watched him go, he whispered the man's name and prayed for his protection and for the journey his people would soon embark on.

CHAPTER 22

Abishai stood motionless as he observed the arena and the fifty men surrounding him. The arena was a simple opening in the woods that sat in the middle of an island. The grass underfoot had long since been trampled out from constant military drills. A large, circular, dirt proving ground was now the location of training for Achish's army. The men had conveniently called it "The Arena" due to the many contests that had taken place there.

Without moving his head, Abishai took in the men's positions, their fighting stances, and the weapons they wielded. He could also feel them. He could sense the anticipation of their pending attack, their nervousness, their excitement, and even their fear.

Ever since his change, his…*What did Achish call it? Indwelling?* He had been given abilities that were not humanly possible. He had strength. He had more strength than six men. His senses had increased. He could smell things that he could not smell before. He could hear things well beyond the ability of a normal man, and his sight had also vastly changed. He no longer saw the world through fleshly eyes but through the eyes of his host within him. He could not only see the physical realm of men but he could see the spiritual realm as well.

Abishai had heard the men whisper about what he looked like with black swirling flames coming out where his eyes used to be.

Most of the time men would look away from him, fearful to even look upon his face. After a while, Abishai found the reaction of others irritating, so he began to wear the mask of the Sicarrii; although, his mask was a little different. There were no eye holes to look out of, he didn't need them. With his sight he could see right through the mask as if it wasn't even there.

Even though it had been a full two seasons since his transformation, he was still trying to get used to seeing into this unique new world. His surroundings had become colorless and vague. He could see things in great detail and clarity but there was no brilliance or color, just shades of gray and black. All was dull and lifeless to his sight. Although, the greatest part of his power was not the things that mortal men could see, but what they could *not* see.

Abishai could now see into the world of the gods. He could see both spirits and men, side by side.

This terrified him for many months. Everywhere he looked, he saw demons and shades that haunted and teased the world of men. He saw great and horrible beasts drive their hands into men's skulls and control them like they were toys.

What was more disturbing were the demons that indwelt humans. Not all demons had the power to do this; only the strongest could bind a man's soul and take over his body. Once this was done, the demon's face replaced the man's face, at least that was what Abishai could see through his new-found sight. Normal men wouldn't be able to tell the difference.

He made the mistake once of looking at his reflection in a pool of water. A ghastly pale face with flaming black eyes looked back at him. The flesh on the spirit's face was haggard and shriveled as if it was a plum left in the sun too long…a prune, decayed and withered with time. Its mouth was sewn shut by thick cords. This was probably why he had never heard the demon speak to him.

Achish had told him that his own previous demon used to talk to him quite often. Abishai had never heard a peep from his demon, but could sometimes feel its thoughts and desires flow into him. But unlike other powerful demons that would take complete control of their host, his demon only seemed to enhance his abilities and guide him.

After several months, Abishai had finally gotten used to the creature living within him and began to take advantage of the power he had been given. He found that his fighting technique was much sharper and his speed was immensely faster. Achish had made him head of the Sicarrii and commissioned him to train up a new army of men to lead against Israel.

For the past season, Achish and Abishai had been sailing the seas, pirating ships and port towns around the Great Continent, taking gold, men, and whatever else they desired to amass their army. Now with five thousand men, they had settled on the island of Taanug, a once-beautiful and pleasurable island east of the Red Sea and south of the Wandering Desert. After the locals were dispatched, the island became a home for pirates and blood thirsty men.

Now, standing in the middle of the arena, Abishai was waiting to test his fifty newest recruits, to see if they were worthy to fight alongside him and Achish. Abishai had instructed the men to attack him with no mercy. Whoever could manage to kill him would be honored to take his place as Commander and Pirate Lord. In order to become a soldier in the army, or a crew member on one of the ships, they just needed to engage him and survive. And all those who failed to advance and attack were put to death. In essence, the rules were simple. Attack or die.

Such was war.

As if in slow motion, Abishai turned and once more took in the complete scene. Many of the men circling him had demons of their own, which made them a bit more of a threat. He took in the trees around the arena and watched them begin to sway from side to side, even though there was no breeze accosting the branches. But there were demons. Hundreds of them, jumping from tree to tree, screeching and wailing as they watched the sport unfold below them. Abishai also took note that Achish was standing atop a cliff behind him, which overlooked the arena.

"Quite a crowd we have gathered," Abishai mumbled to himself.

Fifty bloodthirsty men began to close in on him, step by scooting step. Abishai took a deep breath and smelled the rank odor of…fear. Fear was coming from many of the men.

Abishai frowned. "You worthless wretches!" he yelled, "You reek of fear! It is your fear that will ultimately kill you! It makes you cower and run when you should attack and decimate your enemy!" Abishai scolded the men as he turned around in a circle.

He stopped turning when he faced two of the men that gave off the most fear. Like a cat, he jumped forward a step and then back again to his original position. The startling motion made the two men turn around and run, dropping their swords in the process. Abishai was about to sprint after them, to snuff out their worthless lives, but halted when he saw a great stirring in the woods coming from the direction in which the two men were trying to escape.

Right before the cowards could reach the tree line, Dagon came crashing out of the forest, shattering several trees and sending wooden shards flying in all directions. The old Leviathan's massive entry shook the ground, causing the two men to fall. The sight of the beast made them cry out in horror. They tried to get up to run back towards Abishai, but it was to no avail. Dagon snatched them both up with his long sharp talons.

"Do these belong to you, Rucha?" Dagon questioned, staring down at Abishai.

Before Abishai could answer, the rest of the men who were around him dropped to the ground and hid their eyes from the great massive demon. It was well known that if Dagon didn't like the way someone was looking at him, he would separate their head from their shoulders, usually with his teeth.

Abishai scowled at his men's cowardly reaction and then replied to Dagon. "No, my lord! They do not belong to me! For I, Abishai, only have brave men, stout men who are willing to die for you, my lord! Those two cowards are impostors, here only to seek the riches we may offer!"

The two captured men began to wail and plead their defense, but their cries were instantly cut short by the crunching and snapping of their bones as Dagon curled them up into his scaly claw-like talons.

"Why do you allow such insolence into your ranks, Rucha?" the demon asked as he dropped both of the crushed bodies to the ground. Taking two large steps forward, Dagon bent his snake-like head close to the earth to look Abishai in the face.

"And why do you continue to hang on to that wretched name, the Hebrew name, Abishai?" mocked Dagon, making the name sound as if it was poison to his lips. "Is not that man dead and rotting in a life of failure and strife? Embrace who you are now and thrive as *Rucha, the Ghost of Souls.*"

Abishai snapped his mouth shut and closed the back of his nasal passage to keep from breathing in the beast's horrid breath. It carried the smell of decaying flesh and it made his stomach turn.

The words the great demon spoke were hard to grasp. He hated the thought of leaving behind his name, which still carried the weight and memory of his family. He was about to interject when Dagon spoke again.

"From this moment forward, no one will spit out the traitorous name of Abishai," Dagon commanded to everyone around him. "For his name will forever be Rucha. Anyone heard saying his false Hebrew name will find death by my hand! Is that clear?"

A resounding, "Yes, Master," echoed from all the men in the arena. Abishai even heard the voice of Achish from the cliff top, agreeing with the company of men.

The great demon once again made direct eye contact with Abishai and within a handsbreadth away from Abishai's face, Dagon growled in a low tone, "I didn't hear *you*, man of dust."

Abishai looked down, not being able to bear the penetrating stare of the ancient dragon.

"Yes, Master."

"What is your name?"

Abishai…Rucha, then raised his head and said firmly, "Rucha. Rucha, the Ghost of Souls!"

A deep guttural sound emanated from Dagon's throat, showing his approval. The dragon then lifted his head high and looked upon the forty-eight men still cowering on the ground. "Fear. I can smell it! Where did these men come from?"

Rucha thought for a minute and then answered, "From the city of Tobaugh, one hundred leagues south of here on the coast of the Great Continent."

Turning around, Dagon began to head back into the forest. Without looking back, the demon commanded, "They are all worthless. Find me men who are thirsty for blood and have no fear of death! As for these…kill them all!

Smiling, Rucha turned towards the men to carry out the order himself.

CHAPTER 23

Standing in the middle of the throne room, Solomon pondered upon the conversation he had just had with his guest. Over the past year a lot of work had gone into getting the voyage to Ophir underway. Many resources, mainly gold and algum wood, were needed to build the temple that he and his father David had designed.

Solomon had first learned of the land of Ophir through the Queen of Sheba. She had gained much of her wealth from those lands and was willing to share the location of the Ophir mines. Her price for this knowledge was to simply be a guest of Solomon's for a few months. The Israeli king's rise to power intrigued her and she had heard that Solomon's wisdom was beyond measure. Shaking his head, Solomon laughed at the idea, for he knew well that his wisdom was vain compared to the insight and understanding that El had given him.

The king began to walk around the throne room as he looked upon the walls and took in the tapestries that hung amongst the pillars. He had seen these tapestries many times, but today they seemed to speak to him anew. Engraved on the large banners of fabric was the story of the two kings before him: Saul, and his own father, David. Some of the painted curtains told the tales of war, while others told the stories of family. All of them displayed the greatness of kings.

Stopping at the end of the row of banners, Solomon took in the last entry. It was a painted display of him bowing on the palace steps and the prophet Nathan standing over him with his father's crown. His mother stood beside him with her hand on his shoulder. It was the day of his coronation. It was the best and the worst day of his life. He was so proud to become king, to follow in his father's footsteps. Unfortunately, his first decree as king was to stamp out a coup his step-brother had hatched to take the throne. His second decree was to have his half-brother executed. The memory pained his heart and Solomon looked to the floor and let out a deep sigh. If only he had had greater wisdom then, maybe things could have been different.

Out of the corner or his eye, Solomon saw the curtain on the left side of the throne slightly move. He smiled to himself. He had almost forgotten about Rachel, spying on him from behind the purple drapes. He had heard and seen her earlier but chose not to say anything…until now.

"Hey! Is there someone back there?" Solomon said, as he pretended to be angry. "Come out now so the guards can take you to the stocks!" he managed to say without laughing.

It was then that Rachel burst through the curtain, got tangled up in the drapery, and launched herself forward, landing awkwardly over the arm of the throne with a large, "*Umph*!"

Rachel propped herself upright and stood as if nothing had happened, although her face was now the deep shade of a rose.

Not being able to help himself, Solomon exploded in laughter. And then seeing her frazzled and flustered made him laugh all the harder.

"What are you doing back there?" he said as he continued to chuckle and began to walk towards her.

Rachel didn't know what to say. She hadn't been planning on getting caught. All she could do was stammer. "Well…I….You see I was just…" and then she sighed and threw up her hands in surrender. "Fine! You got me. I was curious. I knew you wanted to meet with me this morning, and I was running late, and I thought that maybe the meeting you were in had something to do with me. I don't know. I am sorry. I shouldn't have spied."

Solomon was still laughing. "I love it when you trip all over yourself, and today it was quite literally."

Now it was Rachel's turn to laugh and her beautiful smile broke across her face. "You know? You really ought to move that throne over to the other side of the platform so clumsy people like me won't hurt themselves."

"You think so? Hmmmm, I'll give it some thought."

Reaching out his hand to Rachel, Solomon guided her down the steps from the throne to the floor. "Sit with me, daughter."

Rachel wrinkled her nose in disgust and rolled her eyes, "Ugh! Please don't call me that. It is so unnerving. I am only a season younger than you. It is so weird."

As they both sat down on the third tier step, Solomon let out another laugh. "Ah, it is just a title. Adopting you was the only way I knew to make sure you were taken care of properly and that you would always be protected."

Before Rachel had a chance to respond, the double doors at the end of the throne room flew open and four guards came rushing in, with Carmon at the head of the troop. All of them stopped very abruptly upon seeing the king sitting on the steps with Rachel.

Carmon was the only one to speak. "I'm sorry, my king, but we thought we heard…I mean I thought there was trouble. I heard some loud voices and I knew your guest had left and—" he then looked to Rachel and a real puzzled look came across his face. "I mean…well I know you didn't want to be disturbed and now I am a little confused as to how the princess—"

Solomon cut him off, "Guardsman, it's alright."

"Carmon," Rachel chimed in, whispering to Solomon.

"What?" Solomon whispered back.

"His name. It's Carmon. You should really get to know the men who guard you."

Once again, Solomon smiled, "Forget calling you my daughter, I am going to have to start calling you mother."

Rachel gave a mocking smile back.

"Thank you, *Carmon*," Solomon said, over pronunciating the man's name.

Rachel giggled and then slapped her hand over her mouth and looked at Carmon, not wanting to insult him.

Solomon continued after raising an eyebrow to her, "Thank you, Carmon, my *daughter* and I are just having a chat about boundaries," Solomon said, putting an emphasis on "daughter".

Rachel once again rolled her eyes and mumbled under her breath.

"Yes sir…I…alright then. We will just be going. Now knowing you are alright, my king," said Carmon with a very confused look on his face. He quickly showed the other guards out and closed the double doors behind him.

As soon as the doors were shut, both Solomon and Rachel began to laugh.

Solomon missed this. His life had become so busy and orderly that it wasn't often he got the chance to have fun and just laugh. He took his friend's soft hand and held it in his own. For the longest time they quietly sat in one another's company, and she laid her head on his shoulder.

"I am going to miss this," Solomon finally said. Lifting her chin with a gentle hand, he brushed away a few strands of hair covering her eyes and kissed her on the forehead. He looked caringly at her. "I am going to miss you, my friend. This place will not be the same without you."

This is my chance. Rachel thought to herself.

"Then why make me leave? Call off the wedding and let me stay here. I don't want to do this. I don't want to marry someone I don't even know, or love, for that matter!"

"Oh, Rachel," Solomon said, letting out a strained sigh. "We have been over this. Prince Tide is a good man, and he will take good care of you."

"I don't want to be taken care of, or to become a servant for some man that already has three, four, or five wives. I want a man that I can be a partner with and thrive with through a life of love and adventure! I want to travel and see the world!"

As Rachel continued to express her dreams, Solomon listened and couldn't help but smile. She was so passionate and determined. She had a spirit that could conquer the world and a beauty that would make anyone follow. In some ways he felt sorry for Prince Tide. As a good wife, Rachel could be an encouraging help to him; but, if Rachel decided to be difficult, she could be the prince's worst nightmare and trample all over him.

While Rachel was still speaking, Solomon put his fingers over her lips and soothingly said, "Shhhhhhh."

Rachel had more to say, but only sighed and stopped presenting her defense.

"Rachel, my dear friend. You are the most beautiful person I know, inside and out. You are adventurous, alive, kind, caring, and strong. You always see the bright side of things. You have a wonderful gift of taking the worst things that life has to offer and making them joyful. I need you to use that gift now. Do not see this wedding as a curse or some form of punishment but see it as an opportunity. An opportunity for life and greatness. Prince Tide is a good man, and he fears El. He will love you as you deserve to be loved. He will be a good father to your children some day, and your own sons will grow up as princes in a strong and rich land."

"But what about his—"

"Yes, I know he has *two* other wives. As do most men of standing. It does not mean he will love you any less. Cannot a man love more than one woman?"

Rachel opened her mouth to object but Solomon continued, already knowing what she was going to say.

"Abaddon is not coming back, Rachel. I have not seen or heard from him since he left this palace two seasons ago. None of my scouts or hunters have seen him or have found any sign of him. I am guessing that he has gone beyond the borders of this land, never to return. I only pray that he and El have found one another."

Solomon reached for Rachel's hand once again and she allowed him to take it. He looked into her full green eyes and saw tears brimming on the edges of them.

"Rachel. It is time to move on. How can you enjoy the wonders Jehovah has set ahead you if you are consumed with looking behind you?"

The tears then came and found their way down Rachel's face. In frustration she asked, "So what do I do? Can I tear out my own heart? Can I stamp out a love that has already blossomed? Any other love seems lifeless compared to the one El has given me for Abaddon. Are my feelings for Abaddon in vain? Do I just cast him aside and treat him like refuse?"

"No. No. You continue to love him, wherever he may be. But give him the love a brother would desire and no more. You forget that I care for him too, as much as any of my own kin. I know that Abaddon cares for you and respects you, but what is the truth? Will Abaddon ever be that man to marry? To be that man to settle down and husband a piece of land? To till and farm it? To become a father and raise children? To be a man of peace and understanding?

"Abaddon has always been a warrior and a soldier. His mind has always been bent on war. I fear for him. I remember my father once telling me that those who live by the sword will die by the sword.

"Rachel, where would you be if you did marry Abaddon? What happens when he goes to that one fateful battle and he doesn't come back? Where would you be then? Alone. Widowed. An outcast with no one to watch out for you."

Solomon then became silent to let his words sink in.

Rachel looked to the floor and wiped away her tears, not wanting to look at Solomon. He didn't understand. She did want a husband to be with her until her dying days, a man that would be a great father to her children, a man that would protect her so she would never know fear.

The problem was that she was not ready for that life yet. What Solomon didn't understand was that she was more like Abaddon than she cared to admit. Peace and security wasn't what she craved at this stage in her life. She was too restless at heart and too adventurous in spirit. Marriage to a prince was just not in her plans.

"Solomon, I don't want to get married, and it is not just about Abaddon. This isn't what I currently want in my life. Please. Call off the wedding."

Rachel let her last words hang in the air. Solomon took note of the pain in her eyes and the plea in her voice. He closed his eyes and let another moment pass before speaking.

"I am sorry, Rachel. I cannot call off the wedding. Your marriage to the prince is more than just a union of two people. It is the uniting of two kingdoms. This marriage is also a contract of faith between Phoenicia and Israel. In celebration of the union, King Huram has already endowed our country with gifts and has built us a fleet of supply ships down in Ezion-Geber. As a part of the wedding celebration they are to be launched to Ophir to acquire materials for the temple. This is the reason the ceremony will take place in Ezion-Geber instead of here in Jerusalem.

"I am sorry, Rachel. The marriage must continue as planned. It is time to look forward. It is time to embrace your future. Find the joy in this union and you will be happy. I promise. In five days, when the sun is at its highest, you will marry Prince Tide."

Closing her eyes, Rachel pressed her lips tightly together. She wanted to scream! It was at times like this that she hated being a woman. She despised having people decide her life for her and tell her what was best for her. Running away seemed very appealing.

Without saying a word, Rachel stood and stepped a few paces away from Solomon. She stared up at the ceiling and got lost in the sea of cedar rafters up above. Out of the corner of her eye she saw a blue-green movement. A small tsipor was happily darting back and forth on one of the beams, making no sound. After a moment it snatched an insect up in its beak and flew off towards a slightly open window on the far side of the room.

Rachel watched the energetic bird fly away and then smiled to herself. What she wouldn't give to be that small bird and fly freely without a care in the world. She wished she could fly wherever and whenever she wanted, to fly away from weddings and false love. No one was telling that bird who and when to marry. The tsipor would one day find a mate, when it was ready, and they would be together for life.

Solomon noticed the bird as well, and came to stand next to Rachel. "Beautiful, aren't they? He was hunting."

"What?" Rachel said coming out of her thoughts.

"The tsipor. He was hunting. When they hunt for bugs or bees they don't make any noise. The sound of the bird's call actually irritates the bees and they scatter and fly away, so when they hunt they don't make any sound. I am guessing he followed a bee in through the window."

"Did your father teach you that?" Rachel asked dryly, now looking to the floor.

"No, my mother."

Taking a position in front of her, Solomon put both of his hands on her shoulders.

"Rachel, please look at me."

Rachel did as she was told, and though her tears had gone dry, her eyes had grown red and puffy.

"I need to know that you are on board with this, that you will not rebel against me on this wedding. A lot is riding on this agreement with Tyre. Do you understand?"

She wanted to shove Solomon away or even raise her hand and slap him. She kept feeling as if she was just being used as a bargaining chip, a payment…no… a reward for the prince to seal a contract. Didn't anybody care about what she wanted or what she thought?

Why won't anyone listen to me? I don't want to get married! I want Abaddon! These were the thoughts screaming in her head but she would not allow them to pass through her lips.

"Rachel, do you understand?" came Solomon's deep voice once more.

She would not say the words, she could not agree with him. But she did slowly nod her head up and down. Solomon smiled and gave her a kiss on the cheek and then turned and walked away.

That was it.

The king had spoken and there was no changing his mind. From this point forward her life was no longer her own. All hope of her love and freedom was gone. She felt the joy of her life begin to fade away. Hollowing words of darkness, emptiness, fear and doubt began to creep into her soul. All was lost.

No! No! No! No! No! She screamed within. *I will not give up! Solomon has to listen to me!*

Rachel clenched her fists tight, took a deep breath and was about to chase after Solomon when suddenly the grand double doors at the end of the great hall burst open.

What Rachel saw next, she was not prepared to see.

Carmon and four other guardsmen came rushing into the throne room once again. Carmon was struggling to support a middle aged man who weakly hobbled beside him. Massive bloody wounds covered his right arm, leg and side. His clothes were tattered and shredded with caked globs of dried blood, yet fresh blood was seeping from the man's side and making its way to the white marble floor, streaking it red.

Both Solomon and Rachel rushed towards the troop and the wounded man, but before they could reach him, he crumpled to the floor and made no effort to get up. Rachel dropped to the floor next to the man and was about to lift the man's head to support it from the hard stone surface, but Solomon's hand stopped her short.

"No! Don't touch him! His wounds are great and he is about to die. Your wedding is in five days, which does not give you the time to go through the cleansing ritual."

Rachel was tempted to help the man anyway, just so she could get out of the wedding, but she dismissed the thought. This very moment was about the injured man and not about her. It would be petty of her to do such a thing. She stood and then took a step back, looking to the other four men behind Carmon.

"You, there," she said, pointing to one of the soldiers. "Get down here and prop up the man's head and make him comfortable! If he is dying, he will be cared for and comforted so he knows that he is not alone."

The guard looked to Carmon and then to the king. Solomon nodded his approval and the guard moved over to the man, removed his own wool sash, wadded it up into a pillow-sized ball and placed if under the man's head. He then knelt next to him and grasped the man's hand.

"And you!" Rachel said, barking another command at another soldier. "Stop standing there and run to get the royal healer!"

The soldier, who had been intently staring at the dying man, snapped out of his daze and looked at Rachel. "But I don't think he is going to—"

"I said go!" Rachel said, projecting her voice, making her command echo throughout the throne room. The soldier jumped a little and then turned around and ran out of the room and down the hall.

"Carmon, what happened to this man? What is going on?" Solomon inquired as he dropped down to one knee next to the man on the floor. The wounded man's breath was beginning to grow shallow and labored. Solomon gazed at the open wounds along his side and noted that they were not recent. When he was young, he had done enough healing work with his mother to know the stages of battle wounds. Looking a little closer, the king guessed the man's wounds were not from a battle. It almost looked as if they were claw marks from a beast. But what animal could do such damage?

Looking at the man's face, Solomon saw that he was unconscious. He then looked down at his own feet and noticed a pool of blood was making its way towards him. His impulse was to move away before it reached him, but he decided to stay close to the man. As long as his flesh didn't touch the man or his blood then he would be fine, his sandals did not matter.

Noticing the blood pooling close to the king's feet, Carmon took off his own sash and pressed it onto the pool of blood to prevent it from flowing any closer to the king.

"We are not sure what happened to him," began Carmon. "It was guardsman Edli that first saw him from the Northern Gate."

A short, stalky man standing behind Carmon stepped forward and slightly bowed his head to the king. Without prompting, the deeply voiced man gave his account.

"I was standing guard at the North Tower when I saw a cloud of dust forming a few leagues out on the road from Shechem. It was one rider and he was coming fast. I felt the urgency and called for Guardsman Carmon. When the horse arrived at the gate I found this man tied to its saddle and severely wounded. He was awake then, but barely. As we were cutting him loose from the ropes that held him in place, all he would say was two words. 'King Solomon'".

"It was then I arrived, your majesty," Carmon continued. "I thought it best that we bring him straight to you. He just kept saying your name over and over. I am sorry if—"

"No, no. It's alright," Solomon said interjecting. "Were you able to find out anything else about him? Anything that would tell us where he came from?"

It was Edli that spoke up. "Nothing definitive, sire. Although his horse was badly wounded as well. I noticed that the animal's hoof prints stamped an arrow shape into the dust on the road."

Solomon looked down to the dying man once more and sighed. He then spoke as if speaking to himself. "The Phoenicians carve the inside of their horse's hooves to look like arrows. This is not good. This could be one of King Huram's men."

Then, without warning, the wounded man began to scream. A long, deafening wail erupted from the man's throat and his eyes flew open. His face was consumed in horror and panic overcame his body. He began to convulse and shake. The guardsman holding the man's head held him tighter and told the man to calm himself and that he was safe. The words were empty to the screaming man.

Rachel watched in fear as the tormented man wailed and thrashed his arms in all directions. The man's eyes had grown wild and wide. An uneasiness crept into Rachel's soul as she had never seen such pain and agony consume someone before. She had heard of the horrors and fears of war but had never witnessed it firsthand. She put her hand to her mouth to keep herself from whimpering and took a few more steps back.

Seeing the turmoil of the man, Solomon quickly stood and removed his outer cloak. He draped it over the man's struggling body. The long white cloth covered the man's body from neck to toe. Now that the man was covered, Solomon knelt back down and put his hand over the man's chest and looked into his wild eyes.

"Peace, my friend. You are safe and among those who care for you. Peace...Peace... Peace." Solomon continued these words and a trance-like state started to overcome the tormented man. Solomon's soothing voice caused the man's breathing to slow, the thrashing ceased, and then, as if the man's soul found its way through a dark abyss, life and recognition appeared in the man's eyes. The man looked around him and then locked his eyes on Solomon's deep blue eyes.

In a weak but stable voice, he asked, "Are you Solomon? Are you king of the Jews?"

"I am, my Phoenician friend. What is your name?"

The man was about to answer but his eyes began to roll to the back of his head.

"Stay with us, friend. Find the strength El has given you," Solomon said in a calm yet commanding voice.

The man's eyes closed for a moment and then opened again, once again focusing on Solomon. In a voice that was all but a quiver and betraying the man's pain, he said, "Claudine. My name is Claudine, and I have a message for you."

Claudine then stopped talking, mouth agape. His breathing once again started to grow heavy. Solomon could see fear rising up within the man.

He was about to spur the man on, but then Claudine snapped back out of his trance and spoke in hurried and chopped sentences. "One hundred of us from Tyre, capital of Phoenicia, sent from king to clear...clear...clear road. Came to city...Hazor."

Tears now streaked down the sides of the man's head and mental anguish began to cloud Claudine's eyes, the same kind of anguish one gets when confronted with great death and loss.

Solomon felt a stir of his own anxiety rise up from within upon hearing the name of one of his own cities to the north. "What of Hazor? What did you see there?"

"Flame. Death. So many bodies! The carnage! Sheep and men and horses torn apart!"

"Who was?" Solomon now said in a voice betraying a sense of desperation. Solomon then looked up to the guardsman whose name was Edli.

"Go get Commander Benaiah and be quick!"

Without a word, Edli turned and ran out of the room.

Solomon returned his focus back to the man. "Claudine. Was it your men who were killed or the people of Hazor? Who attacked you?"

"After we saw the death in Hazor we searched...looked for survivors. There were piles of bones and flesh. And then we saw it.. we saw..." Claudine arched his back and then began to groan and guttural sounds gurgled from his throat.

The guard holding Claudine then spoke up, "Sire, I believe his lungs are filling with fluid. If I prop him up at an angle he might be able to talk easier."

The king nodded his approval, so the guard moved behind Claudine and sat him into a reclining position against his own chest. The incline helped and Claudine began to breathe with greater ease.

Needing answers, Solomon pressed on. "Who was it? Who killed the people in Hazor?"

The man continued in a whisper. "It slaughtered them. Out of all my men, I alone survived…they are all dead. It moved so fast! Its eyes and teeth. It slaughtered all that it saw. It cared not for its hunger…it only desired to kill."

The man's voice was now strained again and grew weaker with each word given. "Death…head..ing…here."

"What? What is heading here?" Solomon prodded, willing the man to say just a few more words.

As if summoning up all the rest of his strength, Claudine lifted up his head and shoulders and mumbled one more word. "Mas…akh."

Now all energy spent, the man collapsed back down and his life left his eyes. Cold black pupils now stared up at the very rafters Rachel and Solomon had been looking at only moments ago.

The man was dead.

No one moved.

No one said a word.

The man was gone but the fear that had brought him there remained. Had they heard him right?

The man had said masakh.

In a fearful tone, Solomon whispered a prayer, "El help us all."

CHAPTER 24

Jacob arrived in the throne room just in time to see two guardsmen carrying out a body on a wooden slab with the king's cloak draped over it. He held up his hand for the two men to stop and then he pulled back the cloak. He shook his head, not recognizing the man, and then motioned for the guards to continue.

Taking a few steps forward, he walked around two servants who were on their knees scrubbing out the drying pool of blood that had formed on the pearly white marble floor. Once around the obstacles, he took long strides across the length of the throne room to meet with the king, who was talking in hushed tones to Benaiah and Shammah.

Seeing Jacob approach, Solomon waved him over. "Were you able to find out any more information about this rider, Claudine?"

"Yes, sire. You were right about him being Phoenician and being one of King Huram's men. The saddle on his horse is the same used by Huram's personal guard. I tore that saddle apart looking for some kind of pouch or pocket that may have dispatch letters, but there was none to be found. I hate to say it, but I believe the rider's story and the account he told to be true.

"The horse had died from its wounds before I got down to the stables. The gashes were savage and deep, massive claw marks like I have never seen. Rest assured, this was no lion or bear. It was something much, much bigger. But I just can't...It doesn't—"

"It doesn't seem possible." Benaiah finished for him.

Jacob nodded his head.

Benaiah continued, "I thought the masakh were wiped out years ago. Those creatures haven't been seen in Israel since the beginning of David's reign. Where did it come from?"

All eyes turned to Shammah.

Before Shammah, Josheb, and Eleazar— The Mighty Three— joined up to be commanders in King David's army, they were known as great hunters throughout the land. They had hunted every living beast that roamed the earth, including the feared masakh. They were so good at hunting these creatures that they were hired by several towns and kingdoms to dispose of the beasts. It wasn't long until people stopped seeing the large lizard-like animals and all thought they were hunted into extinction.

Shammah shrugged. "I have no clue where it would have come from. I have not seen one of those things in years. I was a young man when we used to hunt those foul beasts.

"It's true, they are fast and deadly, but I have never heard of one attacking an entire city or taking on one hundred armed men. They were pretty intelligent creatures. They usually hunted in packs, and when they were outnumbered, they would turn tail and run. And unless you were on a horse, there was no catching up to them."

"How big would they get?" Jacob asked, cutting into Shammah's narrative.

"Large, but not unmanageable. I would say the biggest one I have seen was about the size of a horse."

Jacob slowly shook his head. "Then we may be dealing with something bigger than a masakh. The claw marks on the hindquarters of Claudine's horse stretched from tail to ribs, and the distance between each gash was at least a handbreadth. If that is the size of just one claw, then this creature is much larger than a horse."

"Despite the size, or what it is, people need help," Solomon said. "From what Claudine told us before he died, the city of Hazor is in great peril and King Huram could be in trouble. I find it disturbing that all of this is happening only five days before Rachel's wedding and the launching of our ships to Ophir."

"Do you think this is some kind of attack or ruse from an enemy to keep the two kingdoms from coming together?" Benaiah asked.

"I don't know. We just don't have enough information, and I am not going to take any chances." Solomon answered. "Here is what I want done. Jacob, I want you to get the third and eighth regiments and head for the city of Hazor. Take with you healers, medicine, food, supplies, and tents. I don't know how bad the damage is, but I want you to arrive prepared. I want both regiments in full battle gear."

"And give each man a spear," Shammah added. "If it is a masakh, its scales are too hard for the edge of a sword. The only way to kill it is a spear strike, through the mouth and into the back of the throat to sever the spinal cord."

"You are not to search out the masakh," Solomon commanded. "Your first priority is the people of Hazor. You have less than three hours to brief your men, get what you need, and leave the city. Time is of the essence if there are wounded."

Jacob gave a quick nod and then sprinted out of the room.

Solomon then turned to Benaiah. "Benaiah, I want you to take the first regiment, my royal guard, and head for Tyre along the Shechem road. If Claudine was the only survivor, than King Huram may not even know of the danger he could be facing. I want you to get to Tyre as fast as you can and personally escort the king back here to Jerusalem if he is still willing to come. I will not have our newest ally die on Israeli soil, coming to his own son's wedding."

Benaiah, likewise, dipped his head and quickly headed out of the room.

Being the last one to remain, Shammah put his hand on Solomon's shoulder. "And what would you have an old battered soldier to do?"

Solomon smiled at his friend's humility. "You and I both know that you still possess skills way beyond that of soldiers half your age. You can't fool me, old man."

Smiling back at him, Shammah gave a wink.

"You, my friend, are in charge of hunting down this masakh… or beast…or whatever it is, and destroying it. I will not have such a demon loose in my kingdom, killing at will, unchecked and unchallenged."

"I was hoping you were going to say that." Shammah said, keeping his smile.

Shammah turned, and unlike the other two men that ran out of the room, he simply walked out.

CHAPTER 25

Shammah laid on his stomach and stared at the haunting mouth of a cave some two hundred cubits away. Even though it was closing in on evening, the heat of the day was stifling, and he could feel beads of sweat forming on his forehead.

With his sleeve, he wiped his face, and then reached down to the single-strapped, leather satchel that was pressed to his side. He opened it and pulled out a thick piece of goat hide and a glass ball which was roughly the size of a fist. He carefully rolled the hide into the shape of a tube and firmly wedged the glass piece into the end of the hairy cylinder. He then took a thin leather strap and tied the tube around the glass to keep it from unraveling.

Using the newly formed eye scope to peer at the cave, Shammah noticed several sheep carcasses littering the ground around the base of the mountain. The rock around the mouth of the cave was covered in blood smears and claw marks. But that was all he could see. No sign of the beast itself.

"It has to be in that cave," Shammah murmured to himself. He turned the scope to his right and looked over the quiet waters of the Chinnereth Sea. The great body of water was calmly lapping its waves on the rocky beach, no more than fifty cubits from their position. The sound of a falling pebble from the stone-covered cliff above the cave snapped his focus back to the mountain side.

Shammah felt a tap on his right shoulder. Broc, lying no more than an arm's length away, was motioning for the eye scope. He surrendered the device to Broc's grasping hand without taking his eyes off the cave. Shammah stared a bit longer and then decided to look around at his men to make sure they were following orders.

Stealing a glance behind him, he took in the fifty handpicked warriors and hunters. In complete silence, the troop laid on their stomachs in the grass, organized in five ranks of ten, spears in their hands and ready to attack at a moment's notice. Shammah saw the eagerness in their faces, the thrill of the hunt burning within their blood.

Soon, men. You will get the taste of battle soon, Shammah thought to himself. He was proud of these men and the stress they had already endured in the last twenty four hours.

Before leaving Jerusalem, Shammah had recruited Broc and Dan to come with him. Together they picked the best hunters out of the remaining regiments who were not going to the relief effort at Hazor or to protect King Huram. They had no problem finding volunteers for the hunt. Most of the men had become restless and were looking for a little action.

"This will be like no hunt you have ever been on," Shammah had warned the men back in Jerusalem. "How many of you have hunted lions before?"

About half of the men raised their hands.

"Well, this is nothing like a lion hunt! Lion hunting is child's play compared to the hunt we are about to embark on! A masakh has been sighted around the city of Hazor and we have reports of several dead, and entire herds of animals slaughtered by this beast. In fact, a whole regiment of Phoenician soldiers have been ripped to shreds!"

The men began to stir and whisper to one another as Shammah spoke. Finally one brave soul shouted out.

"Sir, I thought the stories of the masakh were a myth, a legend, a tale one told around campfires to scare the young hunters and recruits."

"Legend or not, the threat is real and people are dying from a beast that knows how to kill! We have been commissioned by the king himself to destroy this abomination before it kills again!"

Shammah's passion rose up within him as he pressed on.

"So, who will go? Who will fight and kill the bane of a hundred dead warriors and the countless slain at Hazor? Who will come with me to kill the myth that so many fear? Who is with me?"

The roaring response of those fifty men was greater than a legion of five hundred warriors.

Once the men were prepared and ready to leave the city, Shammah taught them all he knew of the masakh.

"These creatures are like nothing you have ever hunted before. They are smart and random. Most animals have a pattern, and if you know that pattern, you can track, hunt, and kill them. The masakh are different. They are intelligent and cunning creatures. They have no standard behavior or pattern to follow. This is why hunting them can be extremely dangerous."

A soldier voiced out, "What do they even look like? I have heard tales that they are the size of dogs but look like a bear."

Another man chimed in, "I heard they have lions' heads and have feathers and wings."

Now all the men began to speak, proclaiming their own stories and versions of the creature.

"Silence!" Shammah demanded, getting the attention of the men.

"I will tell you what you are up against. I have seen them from the size of a large dog to the size of great steed. They are lizard-like in shape but they do not walk on all fours. They walk around on their hind legs, which are massive and thick. Think of an ostrich leg but three times the size and strength. The power in their legs makes them fast and agile. I have seen them outrun horses and jump up to five cubits in the air.

"Instead of front legs, they have arms, which are strong and about the size of a man's; although their arms are tipped with three long claws wielding razor sharp talons. Don't ever let them get a hold of you or they will tear you apart.

"The masakh also have long powerful tails in which they will use to strike at you. They use it like a club. And believe me, if a masakh tail connects with your body, there will be broken bones. I can testify to that.

"Their heads are lizard-like with a large jaw line and several rows of razor sharp teeth. Their eyes are wide and yellow with black vertical spears as their pupils."

One of the men in the back shouted out, "You make them sound as if they are El's personal killers!"

Other men began to mumble in agreement.

"Let's just say a healthy respect for these beasts is a requirement for hunting them," Shammah said loudly over the concerned voices. "And pray to El we find them during the day, for they hate the light of the sun, it prevents them from seeing clearly. But at night...at night they are beyond deadly. At night they can see better than a man can in the daylight, which gives them a great advantage.

"Their hearing is also very keen. Once we pick up the creature's trail, we must be completely silent. We will leave the horses behind at that point and continue on foot. Every tongue must be held and every footfall must be purposeful. You will leave your swords behind as they will be useless against this enemy. The masakh hide is an armored scale which a blade cannot slash or pierce."

"So how do we kill them?" another man asked, with a hint of concern in his voice.

"With this," Shammah said as he bent down to the ground and picked up a large spear, tipped with a three sided iron blade. "I take it all of you know how to use a boar spear. I know they are heavy but they are effective. In order to kill the masakh, you will need to get close to its mouth, make sure it opens wide, and then ram the spear to the back of its throat. Spearing the creature's spinal column will kill it instantly. Unfortunately, that is the only vulnerable part of the beast."

Pausing a moment to look over his men, Shammah noted that more than a few of them had concerned looks on their faces.

"I will not lie to you. Unless El prevents it, we are going to have casualties. I am not forcing anyone to go on this hunt, but rest assured, there will be glory in it for those who are seeking it!"

Once again, the men gave a resounding shout!

◄3●——◆——●Ɛ►

The company of hunters had left just after midday, ridden hard all that day, stopped after nightfall for only an hour of rest, and then ridden on throughout the night. By the high sun of the next day, they had reached the small town of Beth-Shan in the high country near the Jordan River, south of the Sea of Chinnereth. The town's people there were fearful and rendered many tales of a great beast that slaughtered the entire city of Hazor, and was making its way south to their town. It was there the company swapped out for fresh horses, and without delay, resumed their journey.

They were only three leagues past Beth-Shan when the hunters found the first signs of the beast: large deep footprints, more than a cubit in length and width. In each footprint was the evidence of four long talons which had torn into the ground as it walked.

As planned, the men abandoned their horses and continued on foot. The men, all experienced in the hunt, moved swiftly in a single-file line. Not a sound could be heard from their footfalls and they were favored by a hot northerly wind. They didn't have to worry about their scent giving them away.

After about an hour of being on foot, Broc halted the company and knelt to study the tracks. Shammah and Dan came up on either side of him and knelt as well. Broc lined the large indentation of the beast's footprint with his finger, "Well, good news. I am only seeing one consistent set of tracks. I think we are only dealing with one masakh. The bad news is, the tracks are deeper here and they are much farther apart. It's running."

Dan sighed. "Do you think it knows we are hunting it?" he asked in a whisper.

"It looks like it's running away, or it found something to go after." Shammah replied. "Either way, judging by the depth of the tracks, and the distance between each footfall, this thing can move."

"I think we had better pick up our pace," Broc mentioned in a hushed tone as he looked skyward. "We only have about four hours of daylight and these tracks are no more than an hour old. I say we move a little faster to catch up with this thing and finish it off."

"We are going to make more noise in a run. There will be no sneaking up on it when we do find it," Dan said, now looking skyward himself.

Looking at the ground, Shammah was deep in thought. Finally he said, "You're right. This thing has to die tonight. If it is not dead in four hours, more than likely we will be the ones being hunted. We lose our advantage after dark. Be on your guard."

Shammah turned and gave some hand signals to the men. Seconds later, fifty-three men, still in a perfect single-file line, ran northward.

After only thirty minutes of running, the company halted and stopped, not because they were tired, but because of what lay before them. Five crop carts, shattered and ripped apart, cluttered the path before them. Fruits, vegetables, and grain were strewn in all directions. Mixed in with the produce was the bloody carnage of horse and sheep parts, ravaged and scattered.

When they came upon the gruesome scene, the men spread out with their spears at the ready. They began to wade through the massacre, looking for any sign of the people who would have been leading the host of crops. More than likely the caravan had been heading for the open market in Beth-Shan.

After a few moments of searching, the men became baffled as there were no human remains to be found.

Shammah was making his way over to Broc to see if he could find the beast's trail when a cry pierced the air around them, breaking the silence.

Spinning in the direction of the scream, Shammah readied his spear to fly at a moment's notice. He quickly saw the source of the high-pitched wail. It was a horse, propped up on the side of one of the broken carts. Its hind quarters were missing, torn away by the savage masakh. Somehow the animal was still alive and now it was giving its final cry of pain to anyone who would hear it.

One of the men ran to the tortured animal and plunged his spear into its heart. The screaming horse thrashed its neck back once and then slowly rested its head down onto the blood soaked ground. It gave a gentle and quiet grunt as if thanking the warrior for ending its misery.

Silence once again stilled the air.

The company held its breath and listened for the slightest sound of movement. For what seemed like an eternity, the men stood motionless, spears at the ready, waiting for an attack from a creature that could rip through all of them effortlessly.

It was Broc who moved first as he made his way to the northern side of the broken carnage. He bent to the ground and motioned for Shammah to join him.

"Look, tracks leading away from here. We have to be close. This attack just happened. The blood hasn't even soaked into the earth yet, and since that mutilated horse was still alive, that means we are close. Another five minutes and that horse would have died on its own from blood loss."

"Well, what are we waiting for?" Dan whispered, joining the conversation. He gave a twirl to his spear and ran ahead. The rest of the men followed suit.

Only an hour later, the group of hunters had followed the tracks to the opening of a cave. The troop found themselves lying patiently, under the cover of tall grass, waiting for the beast to show itself.

Shammah motioned to Broc for his eyeglass back. After receiving it, he surveyed the dark mouth of the cave once more. He felt the presence of a body to his left scooting towards him. A sideways glance revealed it was Dan.

"See anything?" Dan whispered, settling in quietly next to Shammah.

"Nothing," Shammah answered, continuing to peer through the scope.

"I hate to say it, but—"

"Yeah, I know. We are running out of time," Shammah said, looking skyward at the sun as it set closer to the western horizon.

"We have about an hour of light left," Dan continued. "If the masakh is in that cave, somebody needs to draw it out.

"Are you volunteering?" Shammah asked with an arched eyebrow. "Masakhs are quick! Whoever plays bait will more than likely not be coming back."

"Do you have a better idea? We are losing daylight and we need to get things moving. There is no way I am going to ask one of the men to do it, knowing the risk. I would never ask them to do something I am not willing to do myself." Dan stated.

Staring back at Dan, Shammah studied his eyes. His confidence and dedication to his men was admirable. "Dan, I can't ask you to—"

"You don't have to," Dan interrupted. "I'll be alright. I have a plan. Just be ready to pounce on that thing once it is out of the cave. I don't feel like being snacked on."

Before Shammah could give a reply, Dan got up and crouched. He slowly began to advance on the den.

After Dan had progressed only a few steps, he stopped. Something cold and wet tickled his nose, then his cheek, then his right hand, and then his nose again.

"What in the world is—"

Dan's words fell silent as he glanced up and watched in bewilderment as snow began to fall and whisk around in the air above him. His bewilderment quickly turned to concern when he noticed gray clouds rushing in from the east *and* west, causing a dark shadow to fall upon the earth as the rays of the setting sun were quickly blotted out. Dan turned and looked back at his companions as they, too, stood and looked skyward, fear and concern flooding their faces.

Both Broc and Shammah took a few steps forward and stood next to Dan, now totally exposed.

Only a moment had passed since the first snowflake fell, but now the snow came down in torrents. The hot wind from the north, which had been helping to mask their scent, now turned against them with freezing cold gusts. The presence of the frigid air was so sudden, it made Broc gasp for breath. A sharp crackling noise cut through the falling snow. All three of the standing men followed the sound to their right and watched in disbelief as the shore of the sea began to freeze over.

"What is going on?" Broc asked, not caring about being silent anymore. "How is this possible? How did we go from a scorching heat to freezing cold in only a few short moments?"

Dan voiced his own worries. "This *is* the middle of summer, right?"

The wind picked up and the snow fell harder and thicker with each passing moment.

Now, almost yelling over the winds of the growing blizzard, Dan announced, "This is impossible! Why would El do this to hinder us from finishing our mission?"

With both Dan and Broc looking at him for answers, Shammah realized he had none to give. He was just as perplexed as they were.

"I don't think this storm is from El!" Shammah said, realizing he had to yell at the top of his lungs in order to be heard over the harsh biting wind. "This is the work of the Dark One! He is trying to prevent us from destroying his pet. He is trying to turn us away!"

With each passing second the air got colder and colder. Shammah could feel his arms and legs beginning to go numb from the cold exposure. He turned towards the men, and despite the freezing temperature, they held their position, flat on the ground. A layer of snow had already begun to cover their bodies. Shammah could see them visibly shaking from the cold and could also see the fear in their eyes, but like good soldiers, they kept fast.

These are good men, Shammah thought to himself once again before shouting, "Men! To your feet! Fall in behind us and keep your arms and legs moving or you may freeze!"

Obediently, all fifty men jumped to their feet in unison and fell in behind their three commanding officers. The men shifted their weight from one foot to the other, trying to keep the blood pumping freely though their bodies.

"Shammah!" Dan yelled. Even though he was standing right next to the seasoned warrior, the wind made it almost impossible to hear. "We have to get out of the cold or we are going to freeze where we stand! I hate to say this but there is only one place to go!"

Shammah looked at Dan and then to Broc.

Broc nodded in agreement.

Looking straight ahead, Shammah shielded his eyes from the assaulting ice shards with a hand he could no longer feel. Shelter was their only chance for survival. If they wanted to live, they had to go into the cave.

CHAPTER 26

Rucha walked over the deck of the new vessel which he had pillaged and pirated a few nights ago. The large double decked ship was now docked within the bay of their island stronghold. Several men hurried about the vessel, preparing it for voyage and battle. Rucha sporadically barked out orders and commands to the men as he saw flaws and much needed repairs.

"Get the main mast sanded down, you lazy lags! And you! I want that sail replaced by nightfall! The foul thing has four rips in it large enough for a man to walk through! Get it done! You! Up there! If those ropes aren't tied tight to that yard arm, I will hang your corpse from the end of that pole and let the birds feast on your diseased flesh!"

With each word shouted, the men scrambled more and more.

Although Rucha's face had a scowl and disgusted look underneath his mask, on the inside he was beaming with delight. Finally, a vessel worthy of his position, and strong enough to handle the mission ahead! This ship was almost one hundred cubits long, and it had three large mast sails and a forward sail for speed. It consisted of two decks: the lower deck for oarsmen and cargo, and the upper deck contained a cabin in the rear and six ballistas, three mounted on each side of the deck. Although, the greatest feature was the ship's bow. The front of the vessel was in the shape of a giant spear, sharp and destructive to anything in its path. Most ship bows were made of gopher wood; but not this one. This ship's bow was reinforced with plated iron.

This vessel was perfect for their mission. Of course the ship would only *be* perfect if it was in pristine condition, which meant all the men doing their part to get it prepared for voyage.

Rucha felt anger rise up within him as he noticed one of the sailors halfheartedly tying off a cargo line which was holding six bags of wheat, suspended in midair, above the hold port. The sailor then rested himself against the railing and watched as others scurried around about him.

"You! You lazy twit! What do you think you are doing? That grain goes in the hold, not dangling thirty cubits above it!" Rucha shouted as he marched over to the leaning sailor.

The man straightened a little but kept his relaxed posture.

"I'm taking a break! You've been driving us all day and we have had nothing to eat since this morning's meal. We are not animals and you cannot treat us as such!"

The sailor's own words gave him confidence as he bravely stood tall and glared at Rucha.

The ship suddenly grew quiet and all the men who had been scurrying about now stood motionless, starring at Rucha and the defiant sailor.

Balling his right hand into a fist, Rucha felt an instant hatred well up for the man. He closed the gap between he and the rebellious sailor, so close that their faces were only a handsbreadth away from each other. Then, in a soft and compassionate voice, Rucha said, "Oh, I am sorry. I didn't realize how hungry you were. I myself ate only an hour ago and am quite satisfied. I had quail eggs and sweet bread. Does that sound good to you?"

The sailor, now growing a little nervous due to the captain's sudden change in mood, replied, "Um, sure. That sounds good."

Taking a step back, Rucha looked to all the others listening in on the conversation.

"What about the rest of you? Would you like to take a break and get some food?" Rucha asked in the same tender voice.

All the men looked upon one another and mumbles of, "Yea, I would," and "Sounds good to me," and a few "I'm hungry," came from the crowd.

"Well, where are my manners?" Rucha said in a deviant voice. He once again leaned in close to the defiant sailor. "Why don't you look me in the eye and tell me what you would like to eat?"

Rucha removed his Sicarrii mask and the black flames of his eyes blazed out, licking the face of the soldier before him. Fear and shock immediately overtook the unsuspecting man. With a cry of alarm, the once-confident sailor fell backwards to the ground, trembling.

Many of the new men had never seen Rucha without his mask, so they, too, gasped and began to murmur their shock.

Rucha looked at the frightened man on the deck and with a wicked grin on his face, asked in a loud voice, "How about some grain to eat? That should satisfy you, would it not?"

Rucha turned to the sailor's poorly tied knot, which was barely holding the six large bags of grain suspended high into the air. He gave a sharp kick to the knot and it unraveled from the rail.

The sailor looked straight up and screamed as the heavy sacks plummeted down towards him. His cry was cut short by the sound of the his bones breaking underneath the weight of the grain.

"Now! Is anyone else hungry?" Rucha shouted, starring down his men.

No one said a word.

No one even dared to breathe.

"You will rest and eat when the work is done! Is that clear?"

No one answered. The men scurried away and went back to their tasks, now with a little more fear and trembling.

"Well, that was entertaining," said a voice behind Rucha.

Rucha's stomach began to turn in disdain. It was like the putrid feeling he would get whenever he smelled rotting flesh or stale blood.

"Hello, Achish," Rucha grumbled as he turned to face the obese king. "What do you want? I am trying to get this ship ready for voyage so we can stay on schedule."

Achish said nothing but stepped closer to Rucha and stared intently into his face.

"What?" Rucha asked, beginning to feel uncomfortable as the Philistine king reached forward with his fat finger towards his face.

"Every time I see you without your mask, all I want to do is stick my finger in your eye sockets," Achish said, grinning.

The churning in his stomach was quickly replaced by heated anger. Rucha slapped Achish's approaching hand away and slid his mask back on.

Oh, how he wished he could snuff out the fat king's life! All he would have to do would be to reach out, grab the man's pudgy neck, and squeeze. He was pretty sure that with his newfound strength he could easily crush the king's throat and snap his spine at the same time.

Rucha smiled at the pleasant thought. But then he realized Achish had no neck to grab. He was so fat, his head looked like a rock setting on top of a giant blob. It didn't matter. The thought of killing the man still made him smile.

Unfortunately, all thoughts of killing Achish were in vain. Ever since the Philistine had freed Prince Dagon, he had become the demon's pet. The demon protected Achish like he was his own child. If anyone even touched Achish in a way which was not acceptable to Dagon, their life would be forfeit.

One day. One day the Great Demon would no longer protect Achish, and Rucha vowed he would be there to make sure he died, in a most painful and agonizing way.

Achish took a step back. "You know, this ship has a lot of potential. I was thinking of taking it for my own."

Rucha stiffened at the comment, which gave Achish a sense of pleasure. He liked knowing he could so easily manipulate Rucha's anger. "But alas, my ship is my own, and the bothersome task of moving all my things from one vessel to another bores me. So, enjoy your new-found bounty and try not to get it sunk on its first voyage."

"Was there a reason you came here?" Rucha spat as his hands tightened into fists.

Achish stared at Rucha for a silent moment and his sly smile faded away. Breaking eye contact, Achish turned and took five or six steps to the side railing of the ship. He leaned heavily upon it with his thick forearms and peered down at the crystal clear water lapping lazily against the ship's hull. He noticed a few fish happily swimming below, chasing each other as if in a sport of tag.

Feeling Rucha's presence come closer, Achish feared for a moment the Jew might try to throw him over the side.

Still looking at the fish, he asked, "What happened to us, Abishai?"

The question gave Rucha pause. Had he just heard right? Did Achish use his Jewish name? The name Dagon commanded no man to ever say again?

"What did you say?" Rucha asked.

"I said what happened to us. I thought you and I had an understanding. For two years we have pirated together, become the terror of the seas! There was no one we could not conquer and no ship we could not take. Between you and I, we were unstoppable. But it seems of late you have grown distant and disdained towards me."

Achish stood upright, turned, and looked at Rucha. "I get the feeling you want to kill me."

A thousand thoughts raced through Rucha's mind but he chose to stay silent as the Philistine continued to speak.

"You know, you should be much more grateful to me. After all, it was I who saved you from the clutches of Israel. Who knows where you would be if you stayed with that filth, King Solomon. Probably dead, lying face down in disgrace in a grave right between Joab, your brother, and your younger whelp of a brother…what was his name?"

In the single moment it took to take a breath, Rucha closed the distance between them and held a dagger to the king's throat. "Speak of my brothers again and I won't care whose pet you are! I will carve a permanent smile around your chin and send you to see your sons!"

With the blade pressed to his jugular, Achish began to laugh. Not just any laugh, but the hardy boisterous laugh Rucha had come to loathe. It was a laugh which held no fear, but control, as if Achish knew something his opponent did not.

Pressing his face forward, as if daring Rucha to cut into his flesh, Achish proclaimed, "This demon of yours has made you weak. Look at yourself! Lost to your anger. Lost to your emotions. Lost to your wits. Don't you know by now, your demon feeds off your hate and bitterness? As it grows stronger, you grow weaker!"

"At least I have a demon." Rucha spat back. "I have never been stronger, faster and more powerful! Look at you! A shell of the great man you once were! Compared to me, you are nothing!"

Once again Achish's harsh laugh erupted from his throat. So strong was the laugh that the blade Rucha was holding to his fat neck broke his skin, causing a trickle of blood to run down over his chest.

Bizarrely, this made Achish laugh even louder.

The harder Achish laughed, the angrier Rucha became. "Do you think my knife to your throat is funny? Let's see how well you laugh with your head separated from your shoulders!"

Rucha was about to draw the blade deeply across the fat man's so-called neck when the dagger flew out of his hand, soared clear across the deck, and slammed hilt deep into the center mast. Two sailors who were working next to the mast jumped back and ran from the scene.

Suddenly, Rucha felt two massive hands firmly grab his shoulders and thrust him back several cubits, all the way to the pile of fallen grain sacks which had buried the mouthy sailor only moments ago. The force of the impact instantly made every joint in Rucha's body scream in pain. Rucha couldn't help but let out a light groan.

Now flat on his back across the jumbled sacks, Rucha raised his head and saw his attackers. Two giant shade demons stood over him with grins of wicked pleasure cutting across their faces.

Rucha groaned again.

He hated shade demons.

Shade demons took on the forms of large beasts which resembled a half man and half animal. Their bodies would not appear solid or fully formed, making an onlooker doubt if they were actually seeing anything at all. In one moment one would see the shadowy shape of the demon, and in the next, it would wisp away in a black-like mist. From the eyes of mortal men, shades could not be seen in direct light, but only at night or in the shadows. For it was in the shadows they could generate enough power to show themselves to mortal eyes. Needless to say, they were the cause of many tales and horror stories over centuries of superstition.

In the beginning, when Rucha had first received his spiritual sight, shade demons had terrified him. He could see these spirits at all times, day or night. Over time, Rucha had become accustomed to seeing them and was no longer bothered by them. Until now. He had never known a shade to touch or possess anyone, or be able to throw someone several cubits through the air.

As the two shades stared at him, Rucha took in their appearance. Both creatures mimicked a bull-like animal, large and massive in size. Only their torsos and arms resembled that of a man. Their heads and legs were hairy and animal in nature. They each had two thick horns protruding from the sides of their heads, which curved around their faces and met under their wide snouts. Their eyes were sunken back into their heads and glowed red, as if a world of heat and flame raged within them.

Rucha was about to speak when he realized he had seen these two shades before. They were a few of the demonic lackeys who were always near Dagon.

Shaking his head to ward off a line of pain streaking up his spine, Rucha slowly stood and stretched his back. He took a step forward and looked directly into the eyes of the two massive demons.

"Who gave you permission to touch me?" Rucha shouted at the shades. "By order of Prince Dagon, I am off limits!"

Of course, neither demon spoke, but only stared back with their bloodthirsty stare.

"Actually, I am the one who gave them permission," Achish said, walking forward with an ear-to-ear grin on his face. Achish walked right through one of the shades in order to stand in front of Rucha.

"Do you like them? A gift from Dagon. Two of my very own demonic bodyguards. Dagon told me it was not possible for me to have another demon since my last one had left some kind of stain on me. So he gave me these two demons to command as I please. Of course, my first order was to protect me at all costs. As you can see, I have complete control over them."

Rucha looked from Achish to the shades. The demons stood like stoic statues as their liquid red eyes now glared at Achish. "Yeah, from what I see, they would be willing to tear you limb-from-limb if they had the chance. I doubt they are honored to serve a human after serving Dagon directly. I'd watch your step, Achish."

Ignoring the warning, Achish commented, "That's right. You can see them, can't you? I regret that I cannot. I would love to look at my pets."

Upon hearing the word "pets", both demons seemed to grow larger and towered their heads over Achish. A deep penetrating growl resonated from the ghastly beasts.

Rucha took a step back. "Achish, it's no secret that I really don't care for you, and I would have no loss of sleep over your death, but I should warn you not to mess with these two demons. If you don't show them respect and don't stop calling them names like, 'pet', they will rip you apart, and I am guessing quite literally."

Achish's smile and laugh returned. "Good. They frighten you. Now you know what will be coming for you if you ever try to cross me again! Besides, they can never touch me without inciting the wrath of their master, Dagon."

Upon hearing Dagon's name, the demons seemed to pull back and give Achish some space.

"Enough of this childish foreplay!" Achish bellowed out. "Come! Dagon has summoned us both, for that is why I am here. Be at the temple at half-day and don't be late. He said he has a surprise for you. Someone he would like you to meet."

With that, Achish turned and began his walk off the ship. He once again passed right through his two new bodyguards. The demons glared at Achish and then at Rucha. Then, as if they were never there, they vanished into a black mist.

CHAPTER 27

"Are you crazy?" Questioned one of the men behind Shammah. "If the masakh is in there, there is no way we will survive! We will all be slaughtered!"

"And standing out here, dying from exposure is a better course of action?" Shammah snapped back at the soldier. "We cannot fight the cold and the wind! At least in the cave we will have a chance, even if the masakh is inside waiting for us. I would take the chance in that cave over freezing to death any day!"

Shammah took a moment and stared at his men. They were all shivering and shaking, some of them now barely able to stand as their flesh began to freeze. He took a deep breath, and in a calmer, yet commanding voice, "Courage, men! If death does await us in that cave, then we will meet El as warriors of Israel, with stout hearts and a mighty roar!"

"Yes, Commander!" the men replied as one, although to Shammah's ears it was almost a faint whisper due to the howling wind.

The snow was now blinding and each shard of ice that fell bit at their skin. Shammah began to lead his troop in the direction of the cave, but with every step it became harder and harder to move. Looking down, Shammah noticed the snow had already accumulated up to his shins. Looking forward once more, he squinted to keep sight of the opening of the cave.

The men had only moved about ten cubits. The blowing snow was so thick, Shammah could now only see shadows and the faint outlines of Dan and Broc on either side of him.

Not only was the snow getting heavier but the wind was growing stronger with each footfall. The howl of the gale was deafening. It was so loud, Shammah thought his ears would burst.

Every part of his body was going numb. Shammah knew he still carried his spear in his right hand, but he could no longer feel its weight or sense the coarse texture of the wooden shaft.

Finally, the men could go no further. The winds pushed against them so hard they could not take one more step without being thrown back by the great force opposing them.

"It is as if the storm is trying to keep us from the cave!" Dan yelled out. "We can't take this! We are going to die!"

Shammah stopped struggling to move forward and turned around to face the men. For a fraction of a moment he felt relief on his face, now that the pelting snow was accosting his back, but now he felt as if the wind would topple him over.

Shammah motioned for the men to come close to him.

"Huddle together, men! Get close! We will never make it to the cave! Some devilry is guiding this storm! The storm is too great to move ahead. Come in close! Our body heat is the only way we will get through this!"

The men drew together and wrapped their arms around one another, creating a human wall from the biting snow.

With the howling wind to his back, Shammah could now hear a bit better. The sound of rattling spears and chattering teeth filled the air amongst the weary men.

It was then one of them spoke.

"Sirs. If I may speak."

Shammah nodded for him to go ahead.

"If this is a storm from the Dark One, should we not be calling upon the Almighty to fight for us? Were we not taught to call on the name of Yahweh and we would be saved?"

Shammah's heart sank. Guilt consumed him. In all this turmoil, not once did he think of bending his knee to El. How many wars had he fought in, and how many battles were won, not by his own strength but because the power of the Most High had fought for him?

Shammah looked up at the man who spoke. To his eyes, the man was merely a boy, maybe eighteen seasons old.

And the young will teach the old. Shammah thought to himself.

"What is your name, son?" Shammah asked.

"F-F-Faran," the soldier chattered. "I didn't mean to be disrespectful sir. I just thought—"

"It's alright, Faran," Shammah said cutting off his apology. "I am glad you did."

Now Shammah addressed everyone. "Men! I have been a fool and it has taken the courage of a lad to show me the way! When we are weak it is only then El shows us His strength. If you want to live, I suggest we all get to our knees!"

As one, the circle of huddling men dropped to their knees into the snow drifted ground.

It was now Broc's turn to speak. "Men! Humble yourselves before Yahweh, our Abba, Father! Cleanse your hearts and ask forgiveness for any sins that would hinder your prayers!"

After a moment of silence Shammah lifted his cold hands towards heaven. He realized his spear was still in his hand. He tried to open his hand to release his weapon but his fingers were frozen shut around the wooden shaft. The spear and his hand had become one. He merely grasped the spear with his other hand and raised the weapon high above his head and began to pray aloud with a shout.

"Great El of heaven and earth! The Creator of all things! I lift my spear to you in utter surrender! What good is a weapon of wood and iron against the winds and storms of this world? Abba! We fear this storm is not from You but from the one who hates You and searches to destroy all those things which are good in this world. Those things which come from You! We think of the lesson you taught us from Your servant, Job. Will the darkness rob the light, my El? Will the Dark One take the winds of the earth and treat them as if they are his own?"

Pausing in his prayer, Shammah could feel a warmth within him, his spirit stirring. After a moment he began again.

"Abba! You were with the prophet Moses and the warrior Joshua when You brought them up against the Amalekites. You made Israel prevail against our enemy on that day as long as Moses held his hands in the air. Great El Almighty, may my hands be lifted to You until You deliver us from the hands of this evil!"

As soon as Shammah finished praying, Dan raised his voice to the heavens in a way the rest of the men were not prepared for. He sang out his prayer in a loud and mighty voice:

> *"I love the Lord, because he hath heard*
> *My voice and my supplications,*
> *Because he hath inclined his ear unto me,*
> *Therefore will I call upon him as long as I live.*
> *The sorrows of death compassed me,*
> *And the pains of hell gat hold upon me:*
> *I found trouble and sorrow.*
> *Then called I upon the name of the Lord;*
> *O Lord, I beseech thee! Deliver my life!"*

As Dan sang with all his might, the winds grew impossibly stronger, as if an unknown anger had aroused them. The snow felt as if it was biting even deeper into their flesh.

The men, too, began to sing. All soldiers knew the song Dan sang, for it was the psalm of a soldier's deliverance from death. King David had taught it to all his fighting men long ago.

Then, something the men had never seen before happened. Blue and green lightning started to crack and thrash across the snow-ridden sky. The clouds went from a dark gray to a haunting black as all the land was cast into a morbid shadow.

As the wind and snow threatened to tear the men apart, the group only sang louder until their unified voice became a thundering cry over the very winds which were trying to destroy them.

"Sing louder, men!" Broc encouraged as he joined in.

One by one, the men began to stand as the power of their voices rose in worship to the Almighty Living God.

"Sing louder!" came Broc's voice once more.

> *"Gracious is the Lord, and righteous;*
> *Yea, our God is merciful.*
> *The Lord preserveth the simple:*
> *I was brought low, and he saved me.*
> *Return unto thy rest, O my soul;*
> *For the Lord hath dealt bountifully with thee.*
> *For thou hast delivered my soul from death,*
> *Mine eyes from tears,*
> *My feet from falling.*
> *I will walk before the Lord*
> *In the land of the living."*

Then, in a chorus of might, the men sang one more time:

> *"Then called I upon the name of the Lord;*
> *O Lord, I beseech thee! Deliver…my… life!"*

When the last note was sung the men stared to the sky and watched as two bolts of lightning collided far above their heads. A shatter of bright embers filled the heavens as if a thousand stars were falling to the earth. The brilliance of the flash of light made all the men look away.

And then…then…there was nothing.

The biting wind was gone.

The air became so still one could hear his own heart beating.

CHAPTER 28

Rucha, tired and a bit weary, approached the ancient temple. The heat of the day had made the two league trek almost unbearable. The temple was on the northern end of the island and the journey was all uphill through thick jungle.

In his attempt to stay cooler, he had removed his shirt and wrapped it around his head. He had thought about removing his breeches but thought better of it. He missed his Jewish clothing. One long undershirt would cover both top and bottom, with a sash tied around the waist to hold it in place. The clothing was much simpler and cooler to wear. But these clothes, the clothes of the Philistines and the Easterners, had an article for each part of the body. A piece for the neck, for the chest and arms, for the stomach, for the waist and legs and even ones for the feet. Sometimes more was not better.

Taking his shirt off his head, Rucha used it to wipe the sweat from his face. He pulled the shirt back onto his body and felt the cloth cling to his sweaty skin. He would have left the shirt off, but Dagon hated the sight of human flesh. He desired to look upon as little of it as possible.

As he came to the large opening of the temple, Rucha looked up and took in the sight of the huge structure. It was built right into the side of the mountain which towered high into the sky. Several spires were carved out of the rock where guards were once posted as lookouts. Rucha imagined from those heights they would be able to see for leagues, even to every corner of the island.

He could also see numerous altars scattered throughout the mountainside which were once used for sacrifices. Rucha wondered for a moment as to what kind of sacrifices were made. The answer to his question was quickly revealed as he noticed human skulls decorating many of the altar sights.

Besides the spires and altars, the temple was littered with demonic beasts carved out of stone. Hundreds of faces glared down upon Rucha as he peered back up at them. The life-like statues were images of giant insects with protruding legs and spread wings. Many of the insect statues had the faces of men but with large insect eyes.

Rucha had seen these before. Back in the land of the Philistines, there were similar idols used to worship the demon, Beelzebub, the lord of flies and decay. Now, here was a whole temple dedicated to the demon.

Rucha shook his head in disgust.

It was obvious there was once a great civilization here at some point, but now long abandoned. The island must have been the center of worship to Beelzebub. Trees and vines now covered the vastness of the temple as if nature was reclaiming what originally belonged to her.

Once again, Rucha was reminded of the heat bearing down upon him and he longed for the shade the temple would provide. There were no doors to enter through, simply an opening to the temple which was no more than a mouth to a cave on the mountain side.

As Rucha crossed the threshold, the glaring sun was left behind and a cool damp breeze accosted Rucha's face. At once he felt refreshed and a bit more revived. But from here, he was not quite sure where to go. He had been to the outside of the temple many times, but he had never been allowed to enter.

Two tunnels now lay before Rucha. He peered in both directions and listened, but could not hear or see anything from either passage. He was about to take the passage to the right when a large shadow moved between the two tunnels. Before he could determine what the shadow was, a massive object slammed down in front of Rucha.

The impact was so hard that it caused him to lose his balance and fly backwards, landing him back outside into the hot sun. A cloud of dry dust erupted from the cave floor and followed Rucha out the doorway.

Quickly getting to his feet, Rucha pulled his sword as he stepped back into the cave. The bright sunlight pouring in around him cut through the settling dust and revealed his attacker.

An enormous figure emerged. A giant, made of solid rock, stood before him holding a large stone sword.

"Great. A rock demon," Rucha mumbled under his breath, unimpressed.

Occasionally the men on the island had seen some of these creatures pounding through the jungles. They had come to call them golems, or literally, earth puppets.

For the longest moment, the two stared at one another. Rucha began to wonder why a demon would choose to manipulate large rocks to create a man-like shape. He could clearly see the demonic spirit within the rocks. Although, he supposed from an average man's perspective, the beast would be quite frightening. Men would not be used to seeing large boulders working together as one to move like a human being. Rucha figured some demons would do anything to interact with the physical world, even if it meant making a body out of stone.

Rucha realized having his weapon out was pointless. What was he going to do, cut through rock or try and slice through a spirit's flesh? He sheathed his sword and took a more relaxed stance. When he did so, the stone giant began to lower his own sword.

"Let me pass. I am here to see the prince."

"None shall pass," came a low gravelly voice from the demon's rock head.

"I have been summoned by Dagon himself. It would not be wise to impede me unless you like stirring the anger of your master!"

"I have already angered my master!" screamed the golem. "How do you think I was bound to these stones? I have been cursed to carry these burdens and watch over this entrance until Dagon releases me! Now leave! Only the flesh called Achish has permission to pass."

That's interesting. Rucha thought to himself. He had thought the demon had chosen the form, but the opposite was true. It was a prison.

"It was Achish who summoned me to join the prince within the temple. They are expecting me. When I am late, should I tell them you prevented me from coming? I wonder what kind of prison Dagon would put you in if you disappointed him again?" Rucha said with a smile on his face.

A low, ominous growl emanated from the golem, which made the cave echo in response. "Fine. You may enter. But know this, masked man: if you were not invited, it will be I who gets to rip your body apart."

The stone demon paused as if waiting for a nervous response from Rucha, but Rucha wouldn't give him the satisfaction.

After an awkward moment, the golem continued. "Take the passage to the left."

Rucha took a few deliberate steps towards the golem's giant form until he stood right in front of it.

"Before I go, I would like you to know something. Even if you were given the order to kill me, you would fail. Something you should know about rocks, like the bones of men, they can be broken and shatter when they are hit hard enough."

Before the giant could give a response, Rucha leapt to the right arm of the demon and snatched the stone sword from its stone-like hand. Rucha landed awkwardly on the ground with the great weight in his hands. In one swift motion he hefted the large weapon and spun his body in a tight circle, dragging the stone blade in the air behind him. With all his might, Rucha smashed the giant sword into the golem's leg. Both the sword and the leg shattered and shards of rock went flying in all directions.

After stepping back a few paces, Rucha dropped what was left of the golem's weapon, and folded his arms to watch the show.

The golem immediately began to sway and it flung out its arms in a poor attempt to balance itself. Like a tree freshly chopped from its stump, the rock demon came crashing down to the cave's dry floor. Once again, a cloud of dust erupted from the ground and consumed the air.

"What have you done?" the golem cried out. "Look what you did! Come here you foul bag of blood! I will rip you apart and use your blood to paint these walls!" The torrents of curses from the demon continued to flow as he tried repeatedly to stand, each time failing and crashing to the floor.

After a few moments, Rucha was no longer amused. He walked around the struggling demon, giving it a wide birth, and approached the left passage. As he did so, the golem tried to reach out and grab Rucha. He only laughed at the demon's pathetic attempts to grab him.

"Maybe next time you will think twice before threatening me," Rucha called back as he confidently walked down the left tunnel.

CHAPTER 29

Shammah and his men watched with relief as brilliant rays of red and gold light broke through the dissipating clouds. Once again the men could see the setting sun and hope filled their hearts.

The abundance of snow, which had just consumed the sky, was now no more than a few flakes dashing here and there. The numbing pain brought on by the cold was fading away and the men began to take deep breaths of relief, feeling their flesh return to normal.

Looking down at his own hand, which had firmly frozen to his spear, Shammah watched in awe as his black, iced appendage returned to its dark tan color. He was watching a miracle happen right before his eyes. The stinging pain left and warmth flooded his hands and fingers. In no time, he was able to move his fingers and his spear fell free, clamoring to the ground.

Shammah felt great emotion overwhelm him. Only moments ago, he thought for sure he had lost his hand. A quiet prayer of praise escaped his lips. "Thank you Yahweh."

Shammah then realized a whispered prayer was not enough. He raised his hands towards heaven and shouted, "Yahweh is great and mighty! Yahweh has saved us! Praise be to Yahweh!"

Likewise, the rest of the men began to shout their own praises to El. Some of them jumped to their feet and sang once again, while others fell to their knees in grateful prayer.

After a few moments, Broc addressed the soldiers. "Men! Fall in! Form your ranks!"

Years of military training snapped the men to attention and the men reformed their lines and held their weapons fast. In seconds the men were once again battle ready and silence consumed the air.

Broc continued, "Warriors of Israel! Continue to worship El in your hearts, but our minds must return to the task at hand. The Evil One does not want us to enter that cave and destroy the beast within, but Yahweh has clearly opened the way. We still have a masakh to kill!"

The men proclaimed in one voice, "Kavash!" which is the war cry for "Conquer!"

As if the men's shout commanded it, the last of the sunlight faded over the horizon and the shadow of night made itself known.

As soon as the sun was gone, a long, deep, guttural growl made its way from the heart of the cave. The sound was so penetrating, the men could feel vibrations in their chests.

Dan saw fear come over the men's faces. "Stout hearts, men! Did not Yahweh just deliver us from the devil himself? Then surely El will give this beast into our hands! Quickly, now! Attack formation!"

The warriors broke rank and spread themselves out into a half circle, thirty cubits from the opening of the cave. If the masakh tried to escape there would be men on all sides to close in on it.

After a few more reverberating growls, all went quiet.

They all stood at the ready, spears in hand, each man nervously waiting for an attack from a creature they had never seen or hunted before, an animal which killed for pleasure and mutilated without cause.

They were waiting for death.

Then, they heard something they were not expecting. Something which made the blood drain from their faces and their courage turn to liquid fear.

They heard screams.

Blood curdling, *human* screams!

The cries were coming from inside the cave! Not only were there people screaming out in pain but they were calling out for help!

Upon hearing the human cries, several of the men broke from their positions and ran towards the cave.

"We have to help them!" many of the soldiers called out.

"Peace!" Shammah yelled. "Hold your rank! I don't care what you hear! Hold the line!"

Some of the men turned back, but not all. Five of the men kept going, courage and fury now pushing them forwards. The five raised their voices in a war cry as they approached the mouth of the cave.

Shammah attempted one last time to get his men's attention.

"Stop! Get back in—" But his words were drowned out. Not by a growl, but this time by a roar, a deafening roar so intense that the ground beneath their feet shook.

With great speed and ferocity, a giant reptilian head erupted from the darkness of the cave and massive, powerful jaws clamped onto the nearest soldier. The crushing impact of the beast's teeth clamping down on human bones was heard by all.

As quickly as the masakh had attacked, it withdrew, pulling its first victim back into the cave. All could hear the warrior screaming for his life, and then, with a sickening crunch, the screaming stopped.

The other four soldiers had skidded to a halt and fallen to the ground in shock over what they had just witnessed. They were scrambling to get back on their feet when the human cries of desperation and fear erupted from the cave once more.

The men were now up and about to run back to a safe distance when a young, dark-haired woman came running out of the cave. Her eyes were wild with fear and she was screaming as if death itself was tearing at her throat. She was wearing a white formal dress, as if a bride to a wedding. The dress was tattered, torn and splattered with fresh blood. Her left arm dangled at her side as she ran, revealing a large gash to her shoulder.

"Help me! Help me!" Came her cries as she caught sight of the soldiers in front of her.

Upon seeing the fleeing woman, and hearing her screams, the four fearful men halted their retreat and once again charged the cave to retrieve the desperate woman. This time Shammah had given the signal to advance and the rest of the men were not far behind.

As the four brave soldiers were about to reach the woman, the masakh emerged once more. With a thunderous roar, the creature thrust itself out of the cave and made the earth tremble with each step it took. The giant beast bounded straight for its escaped prisoner. Razor-sharp teeth were about to clamp down upon the woman when one of the soldiers tackled her to the ground and the massive jaws came down on nothing but air. The soldier kept his momentum going and rolled with the woman several paces to get both of them clear of the reckless animal's clawed feet.

The masakh, realizing it had missed its prey, tried to stop and turn towards the woman, but the weight of its body caused it to keep moving forward and it crashed down to the ground.

With the reptile down, several soldiers took the opportunity to jump onto the giant creature and began ramming their spears into its iron like hide.

The beast, now realizing it was being attacked, started to thrash wildly on its side, trying to regain its balance on its muscular hind legs. The creature once again roared as it bucked and turned its head around to bite at the men who had accosted it.

To the soldiers' regret, the masakh regained its footing, enabling it to stand to its full height.

Shammah couldn't help but gasp as he looked upon the enormity of the deadly animal.

Broc, too, was stunned in amazement at the size of the foe standing only about ten cubits from them. "What is this thing? I thought you said they only got to be about the size of a horse? Not the size of a house!"

"I am just as surprised as you are, my friend, but this is a masakh; it is just…much, much bigger." Shammah said, keeping his spear pointed firmly towards the beast's head.

The large reptile cocked its head to the side and began to survey the men closing in around it. Whenever one of the soldiers got close to it, it bared its teeth and made a deep hissing sound from the back of its throat.

"Why isn't it attacking?" Dan wanted to know. "We need it to attack in order for one of us to ram one of these pig stickers down its gullet."

A few of the men became impatient and ran to the animal to try and prod it into opening its mouth. As soon as they were close enough, the masakh thrashed at them with its front arms. In one swipe, three men were thrown aside like toys, one of them being severed in two by the beast's razor sharp claws.

The masakh gave a mighty roar, making some of the men grab their chests and kneel to the ground due to the force of the noise coming from the animal's throat.

A cry came out from one of the men from behind the creature, "Commander! Should we all attack at once? We have to distract it so someone can get in a kill thrust!"

"Nay!" Broc called out. "We stay on the defensive! This thing is smart! It is waiting for us to come to it. Just don't let it try and get back into that cave!"

"I don't think it is interested in us," Shammah said to no one in particular. "I think it is looking for someone and we are just a nuisance in its way."

Without taking his eyes off the beast, Shammah called out, "Who has the woman?"

A voice replied to his far right, "I do, sir! She is behind me on the ground."

Shammah recognized the voice. "Faran. Is that you?"

"Yes, sir!"

Shammah slowly began to make his way to Faran's position, never taking his eyes off the masakh, which was growing more and more irritable by the moment. The beast was now swinging its massive tail at the soldiers and more than one of them got hit. Some of the men were thrown several cubits through the air after being assaulted by the animal's scale-clad club.

Shammah began to move a bit quicker. As he passed Broc he tapped him on the back and signaled for him to follow.

"Faran, I need you to get the woman on her feet and tell her to run!" Shammah called out. "And when she does, I need you to be ready to strike because this thing will be coming for her. I don't know why, but this devil from the abyss wants her for some reason!"

The woman heard Shammah's command and began to whimper and cry out, "No, no, no, no...I can't! It will kill me! Please let me stay here with you!" the woman pleaded. She wrapped her arms around Faran's leg and cried out all the louder.

Upon hearing the woman's cry, the masakh snapped its head in her direction and let out another massive roar.

Four men standing closest to the beast fell to the ground, dropped their spears and put their hands to their ears. The sound of the masakh's war cry was crushing.

Dan, now covering the backside of the creature to make sure it didn't try to retreat, screamed out to Faran, "Ready your spear! It is coming!"

Faran saw the masakh turn towards him as it roared its deafening roar. So loud was the noise being forced from the animal's throat that Faran began to hear ringing in his ears, and his head started to throb.

With his senses altered, he felt like everything was slowing down. He looked to his left and saw his commanders, Shammah and Broc, running towards him. They were shouting and waving their arms at him. The woman behind him had grabbed hold of his right leg and he could feel the intensity of her grip, fingers digging into his lower thigh. Faran could barely make out her cries of fear.

Looking back to the dragon, Faran watched its giant legs flex and surge in his direction. The moon, now illuminating the beast's massive figure, revealed the masakh's large, yellow, piercing eyes and its black spearheaded pupils glinting in the moonlight.

Those deadly eyes locked in on Faran.

Faran immediately felt fear consume him and his stomach rose up into his throat. It was in that moment he knew he was going to die.

Once again, he felt the woman behind him and she was shaking uncontrollably. He could feel his chest grow tense and tinge with pain. He realized he was holding his breath. His arms and legs were beginning to go numb and he began to grow weak. He wanted to turn and run, but he knew if he did, the woman would die.

Faran closed his eyes for only a second, for a second was all he had. *Breathe*, he told himself. *El, help me to protect this woman!*

Then, he felt hot, wet, rancid air accost his face. The creature was now close enough for him to feel its breath. Every muscle in his body tensed.

He opened his eyes and thrust out his spear at the same time. The only thing he saw was massive rows of teeth and the gray colored flesh within the beast's mouth.

The next few seconds became a blur of chaos and confusion.

Faran was expecting to be clamped into the masakh's jowls and torn to shreds by its teeth, but instead, the butt of his spear rammed hard into his chest, sending him and the screaming woman flying backwards through the air. The impact was so great, Faran feared the shaft of his spear had gone right through him. They slammed violently onto the ground, skidding several more cubits after they landed.

Pain raked through Faran's body and he found that he could not breathe. He tried to gasp for breath but was unable to take in a sufficient amount of air. The coppery taste of blood filled his throat and mouth.

Knowing he was still in danger, he tried to sit up to see where the masakh had gone, but he could not move. The woman was lying on top of him, still holding on for dear life and breathing heavily in a panic.

Faran tossed her aside just in time to see the wild animal crash to the earth no more than ten cubits to his right. The impact of the masakh hitting the ground made the earth underneath Faran jump, jolting his body, causing more pain to scream out from every muscle and every bone of his aching frame.

Faran watched as the creature began to shake and thrash in the mud. Its large clawed arms were desperately grasping for something protruding from its open mouth. The mighty roar of the beast was gone and was now replaced by a wailing and gurgling hiss. The reptile repeatedly hammered the back of its head onto the ground in violent spasms.

Faran knew he should move. The thrashing animal was getting closer and closer to where he was lying, but his bruised and maybe broken body was not responding. He watched with dread as the Masakh's thick tail coursed through the air, coming right at him. He closed his eyes, ready to take the crushing blow, knowing it would probably kill him.

The blow never came.

Instead he felt someone grab the front of his tunic and yank him to the side. The impact of the tail thundered upon the ground next to him, causing mud and melted snow to fly high into the air.

Faran and his savior rolled one…two… three times away from the crazed animal before stopping.

Once again, Faran laid on his back, and this time he didn't even try to move. The world around him began to spin, a buzzing sound roared in his head, and his body started to go numb. He felt cold and his chest was heavy. It was hard for him to take a single breath.

Was he dying? Was this what it felt like to die? But then he did feel something. Something warm and soft touched his cheek. He wanted to know what it was but he couldn't see anything. He then realized his eyes were closed. He opened his eyes and the world around him spun. He was about to close his eyes again when a face appeared before him. At first the face was blurry and distorted, but it slowly came into focus.

It was the woman.

Her hair and cheeks were matted with mud and blood. He saw that her tunic was torn over her left shoulder, revealing soft white skin, ravaged by a deep bloody gash.

Immediately he felt concerned for her. How bad was her wound?

He watched her lips move up and down and he realized she was trying to say something. He could see her mouth moving but he could not hear her; only a buzz filled his mind now. He looked from her mouth to her eyes. She had brilliant blue eyes. Even in the faint glow of the moonlight, her eyes seemed to be a beacon of hope for him. He gazed intently into those eyes, right up until the light of the world around him faded, and then all went black.

CHAPTER 30

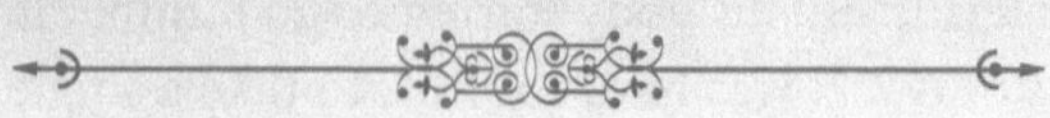

Shammah watched in horror and awe as several things happened within the same moment. The deadly masakh had spotted the woman and had been intent on killing her. As soon as it had heard the woman's scream, the beast had forgotten about all of the soldiers and headed straight for her and Faran. With only a few giant steps, the creature had been in striking distance of them and had lunged its massive head towards Faran with jaws open wide. Shammah had thought for sure that Faran had been inside of the masakh's mouth, but then he and the woman had gone flying backwards through the air for almost thirty cubits before hitting the ground and sliding several more cubits in the mud and snow.

What Shammah saw next, left everyone in awe. The massive creature was thrashing and hissing on the ground. Faran's spear was lodged firmly down the beast's throat!

Faran had done it! Faran had managed to plunge his weapon into the giant's throat and then was somehow thrown clear!

The soldiers carefully began to surround the wailing, dying animal, but could not get too close as it still savagely thrashed about. Its tail wildly crashed onto the earth in all directions, causing the men to give it an even wider birth. Its hind legs were kicking rapidly and front arms were swinging desperately, attempting to dislodge the pole protruding from its mouth.

"Men! We can't let it remove that spear!" Broc commanded. "Attack its head, eyes and mouth! Even shove your spears up its nostrils if you have to!"

With a cry, the men advanced, although none with greater speed than Dan. With the beast writhing on its back, Dan leapt onto the masakh's hind leg. The animal kicked its leg up and vaulted Dan right towards its mouth. Dan soared through the air, spear extended high above his head, ready to drive it into the masakh's gullet. With a war cry full of fury, Dan landed hard upon the beast, driving his weapon deep into the reptile's esophagus, right next to Faran's spear. A loud "pop" echoed out of the masakh's throat.

In a last ditch effort to protect itself, the dragon swiped its clawed hand at Dan. Not prepared for the assault, Dan took the brunt of the impact on his right arm. The beast sent him sailing through the air like an insect swatted away with an angry hand. The velocity of the blow launched Dan across the ground, creating a shallow trench into the soft muddy earth. He used the momentum to roll to his feet and ready himself for another attack.

But no attack came.

A gurgling sound came from the great beast's mouth as its lungs filled with blood from the deadly wound. Its body began to relax and lay still with the exception of a few involuntary twitches coming from its tail and hind legs. Although, the animal's eyeball still moved. The yellow glow of the eye had now become bloodshot and black. The eye searched to and fro and finally stopped and focused in on what it was looking for. The woman. It strained intently upon the wounded girl, who now cradled an unconscious man in her arms.

The woman noticed the beast gazing at her and she held Faran all the tighter, squeezing the man's limp body to herself. As horrible as the scene of the dying animal was, she refused to look away from the creature, knowing it could no longer hurt her. She glared at it and felt hot tears begin to run down her face. She didn't know why, but a surge of emotion now overtook her. She kept watching the creature until the life within its eye was extinguished and the monster was no more.

Normally this would be the time when the men would cheer and celebrate the victory over their hunt, but there were no cheers or shouts for celebration tonight. Five men were dead and twenty-three were wounded. Six of those wounded would probably die before getting back to Jerusalem.

The men were tired, and now that the battle fury had passed, many of them felt weak and spent. Shammah had made the decision to camp for the night and then to be off at first light. He had already dispatched four men to head back to Jerusalem and inform the king that the threat had been eliminated.

Shammah had also given the order to have the cave searched for any survivors. He was disturbed to hear the news that there were no bodies within the cave. The walls were covered with streaks of blood, but not a single human body was to be found, none save the young woman who had escaped. Puzzled at this new bit of information, Shammah looked around the camp for Broc so he could share the discovery. He spotted his captain standing next to Dan, both of whom were standing next to the lifeless masakh's enormous head.

Broc noticed Shammah looking his way and motioned for him to come over.

Making his way to Broc's position, Shammah stopped several times along the way to talk to his men about their condition, and whether or not they had enough food to eat and water to drink.

Finally he approached the two conversing captains.

"What is it?" Shammah asked.

"Take a look at this," Broc said, squatting down on his haunches and poking the ground with his knife. His blade disturbed a pool of a thick, black liquid which had gathered underneath the masakh's head. Large drops of a black, oil-like substance was leaking from the dead beast's eyes, adding to the growing puddle in the mud.

"Is that blood?" Dan asked, moving a torch closer to the ground so they could see it better.

Shammah took the torch from Dan and noticed Dan's right arm was limp and dangling at his side. "What is wrong with your arm? Are you wounded?"

"Nah. I think it's dislocated. This thing hit me pretty hard when I jammed my spear down its throat."

Both Broc and Shammah stared at Dan, dumbfounded at the lack of concern for his arm.

After a few awkward moments, Dan finally defended himself, "What? I'll get it looked at. There are several others a lot worse off than I am. Stop looking at me like a couple of old hens! It doesn't even hurt."

Shammah chuckled and mumbled something that sounded like, "crazy kids", underneath his breath. He brought the torch closer to the ground to get a better look at the black pool. The liquid substance was everywhere. Broc hunched down once again, but this time, instead of using his knife, he touched it with his forefinger. He brought it up closer to his face so he could look at it better and then rubbed it between his finger and thumb to feel the texture.

"It is thick and sticky, just like blood." He brought it close to his nose and took in the scent. He jerked his head back at the smell and coughed a few times. "Wow! I couldn't smell that before, but it smells like…rotten eggs."

"Sulfur," Shammah said, recognizing the strong odor.

Wiping the substance off his hand, Broc stood back up. "I have never seen black blood before, have you?"

Standing up, Shammah lifted the torch closer to the animal's eye, and then to its mouth. The same black blood was still oozing out of both places. "No, this is not right. This is not normal. I have killed these things before and they have red blood, just like the rest of El's creation. This…this is different…wrong."

"What are you saying?" Dan asked. "That this creature is not from El?"

Shammah continued, "El teaches us that the red blood is life and produces life, but black blood—" Shammah's voice trailed off and his face became concerned with worry.

"What?" Dan said. "So does black blood mean death, or was this monster created by Luce?"

Shammah and Broc both quickly looked at Dan and scolded him with their eyes.

"Fool!" Broc hissed. "Don't ever spit that cursed name into the air. You know better than that! Saying his name can bring unwanted attention, or worse yet, his presence!"

"I am afraid we already have evil's attention here tonight," Shammah cautioned, looking seriously at both Broc and Dan. "But Broc is right. Never speak the name of the Ruler of Evil, for his name is not worthy of even being uttered."

Dan met his gaze and said nothing; he simply nodded his head in compliance.

"I don't know what the black blood means," Shammah continued. "I have never seen it before, not in any living creature, and I have hunted many. I don't believe the Dark One has the power to create life, even poisoned life, but I do believe he has the power to change things. He can manipulate the things which were once pure and corrupt them to evil for his pleasure…for his purpose. This may be the reason why this animal is so big instead of its normal size. Get a sample of the blood, we will take some back with us."

Dan took his wine skin and emptied out its contents, then bent to the ground to fill it with the thick black liquid.

Broc was quick to change the subject. "So, the cave. Did you find any of the survivors? We all heard their voices and screams."

"I sent a dozen men in," Shammah said, shaking his head. "They found no one inside. Just blood everywhere, on the walls, pools of it on the ground. But no bodies, not even body parts. It doesn't make sense. Even if the people were eaten, there would be some kind of remains left. Pieces of flesh, clothing, something other than just blood."

"Did they escape through another tunnel, maybe a back passage somewhere?" Dan suggested.

"The men looked. Nothing. The cavern goes back one hundred cubits into the hillside and just comes to an end." Shammah looked at the bloody, black ground and then to the mouth of the cave. "The funny thing is, I don't even remember this cave. I have ridden around this side of the sea many times, and I have never noticed it before. Have you?" Shammah asked, now looking back at both Broc and Dan.

Dan shook his head and Broc said, "That's not unusual, though. There are many caves in this region and many of them get covered up by brush or are hidden from view by boulders. The fact that you can't remember this particular one doesn't mean much."

"Maybe." Shammah said, deep in thought.

"On a different note, I think you should go talk to the woman," Dan said to Shammah. "Both Broc and I tried to speak to her but she wouldn't say anything. She also won't leave Faran's side. We moved Faran to the side of the camp where some of the men have made willow beds for the wounded. When the men transferred him, she kept a hand on him the whole time, as if she were his kin."

Broc made a "humph" sound and said, "I don't know why she wouldn't want to speak to us. You'd think she would be tickled to talk to us now that she was out of the clutches of this beast." Broc kicked the dead animal's head to prove his point.

"It's probably that ugly beard of yours," Dan said with a smirk on his lips. "It would not be the first time a woman has gone screaming and running in the opposite direction at the sight of your appearance."

Broc's mouth dropped open, taken aback that his junior captain just took a jab at him. Shammah couldn't help but to let out a chuckle.

"Are you calling me ugly?"

"What? No." Dan defended himself, now with a bit of sarcasm. "I would never call you ugly…just…not pretty."

The two men looked at each other for a moment and then both of them burst out laughing.

Shaking his head, Shammah chose not to comment on the exchange. With the torch in hand, he announced he was going to talk to the woman. As he walked away, he smiled as his two captains continued to make *ugly* jokes towards one another. Once again Shammah shook his head, rolled his eyes and said quietly to himself, "I am getting too old for this."

CHAPTER 31

Rucha swore underneath his breath. "Does this cave ever come to an end?"

Rucha stopped, looked back, and then looked forward again. When he had first entered the passage it had been dark and black. Not just normal black, but, *I can't see my hand in front of my face*, black.

After what seemed like an eternity of walking, a light reddish glow had begun to come from the rock ceiling above him. The further he walked, the brighter the glow became, until after a while he could feel great amounts of heat emanating from the ceiling and walls. In no time, it felt like Rucha was trapped within an oven. He dared not touch the walls on either side of him for fear of burning himself. He picked up his pace and tried to ignore the sweat running down his body, soiling his clothes.

"I was cooler outside underneath the scorching sun," he said to himself out loud. As the tunnel got hotter and hotter, he began to curse himself for trusting the golem's directions.

"I'll bet that worthless demon sent me down in this direction on purpose, knowing I would be roasted alive. It is like a furnace in here!" He shouted out loud, even though nobody was around him to hear his complaint. He was about to stop and turn around, now realizing this path was only a journey to death, when he slowed his pace and noticed the walls were growing farther apart. He also took note that the ceiling was now high above him, glowing a bright reddish orange. He strained to look further ahead and thought he could see a faint light. "Please let this be the end of this infernal tunnel," Rucha griped.

He ran in the direction of the light ahead of him and came to realize it was an opening to a larger cavern. He noticed there was something different about the light. It was thinner, yet, clearer. It was… sunlight. How could that be? It seemed like he had been walking forever, underground, where there shouldn't be sunlight; and yet, there it was.

After cautiously passing through the illuminated opening and into a wide cavern, Rucha left the tunnel behind. He stepped into the soft sunlight and began to feel cooler. Rucha looked back at the passage he had just emerged from. A large flow of cascading molten rock was streaming down the wall around the doorway.

Now the heat makes sense, Rucha thought to himself. For a few moments he watched in slight fascination as the liquid fire made its way around the edge of the cavern and continued to disappear through some unseen crevice below.

Looking upward, Rucha tried to determine where the beam of sunlight was streaming in from, but he could not see an opening to the outside world through the mountain above. In fact, there *was* no opening in the rock ceiling high above him, and yet, here was sunlight, glaring down upon him.

"What kind of devil's trick is this?" Rucha questioned to himself out loud.

"Not the devil's," came a voice from the shadows on the other side of the cavern. "But one of his sons to be sure."

Rucha whipped his head in the direction of the voice and the cave walls echoed with the sound of his sword being pulled from its sheath.

"Oh, put it away. Didn't we just go through this?"

Rucha frowned as he recognized the voice. He couldn't see him, but he could imagine the fat man grinning at him. "Achish. Where is Dagon? What is this meeting all about and who am I to meet?"

Achish walked into the light with a grin on his face. "It took you long enough to get down here. Why did you take the lava tube? You were lucky you weren't roasted alive. If you would have taken the right tunnel at the entrance you would have been here in a fraction of the time." Achish pointed over to a set of stairs coming out of the far wall to Rucha's right.

Gripping the hilt of his sword, Rucha scowled underneath his mask. A vision entered into his mind of him slashing out his blade and taking Achish's head off with one swift flick of his wrist, but then he remembered the man's bodyguards. Where were they? Close by, no doubt.

Composing his voice, Rucha answered with a clenched jaw, "You failed to mention which tunnel to take once I got here."

"Did I? Oh, sorry about that," Achish said as he began to laugh his hearty laugh. After a few chuckles, Achish walked up and slapped Rucha on the back. "Come! I am afraid we have a bit further to go before we get to the main chamber where Dagon awaits us."

Achish walked forward and Rucha reluctantly followed. "Amazing! Isn't it?" Achish continued talking.

"What's amazing?" Rucha replied dryly.

"The light. You have to ask yourself, 'Where does it come from?' as there are no holes in the rock to let the light in."

Actually, Rucha had been wondering about that, but said nothing.

Not waiting for an answer, Achish kept on talking. "I don't know how it works, but Dagon made it just for us. It is obviously an illusion, a trick of the eyes, but I will say it is a pretty good one. Look behind you, it fades away as we get further along."

Glancing behind him, Rucha noticed the mysterious sunlight was indeed fading away farther behind them, leaving an unsettling orange glow from the flowing molten rock cascading down the far wall of the cavern.

Looking up and forward again, Rucha's mind pondered upon this strange place with its strange powers. After several moments of silent walking, Rucha spoke up. "Do you ever wonder how he created this light?"

"Hmmm, what's that?"

Rucha sighed. He despised talking to the fat king, let alone asking him questions to get answers. He especially hated asking a question twice! *Open your ears on that fat head of yours!*

"I said, do you ever wonder how he created the light?"

Achish grunted before answering, "I don't know. Such things are beyond us mortals. Who cares? Just be thankful for it."

"Think about it," Rucha continued. "All demons are the enemy of El. I was once taught that El is the truth and power of light. If this is true then how can a demon produce light when he seeks those things that live and thrive in darkness…in shadow. The Rabbis used to teach us—"

Before Rucha could finish his thought, a great piercing pain ripped through the center of his body. So immense and shocking was the pain, he dropped to his knees and wretched onto the rock floor.

Achish began to laugh. "Hurts, doesn't it? That would be your demon within, not liking your train of thought. When I had mine, the thing would curse and threaten me if I ever even came close to saying the name of their enemy. It is one thing I don't miss about the slimy beast. You are lucky. Yours is mute, but he sure will let you know if he doesn't like something."

Achish approached Rucha, who was still on his knees, and holding his head between his hands. He squatted his large frame down on his heels next to Rucha. "Listen, kid. Here is a lesson for ya, one I thought you would have learned over the last few years: your life as a Jew is over. Israel is your enemy. Would you listen to your enemy's counsel, to his teachings? No! The enemy is a liar! If you want to succeed here, you best never let the name, 'El', pass from your lips again, or that beast within you may just turn you inside out. You gave up that life. It's best to embrace your new one."

Taking Rucha by his arm, Achish hoisted him to his feet. He then stared at Rucha, waiting for some kind of response. After a moment of silence, Rucha gave a simple nod and Achish smiled back at him.

Just like that, Achish became his old boisterous self once again. "Good! We're off again!" He bellowed, creating an echo to cascade down the tunnel. Achish slapped Rucha on the back, almost causing him to fall back down to the ground.

Slowly beginning to feel his strength return to him, Rucha walked on, this time in silence.

The two of them reached the end of the large cavern and were introduced to another tunnel, although this one had torches burning along the right side of the cave's wall to light the way. Upon entering into the narrow passage, Rucha noticed their guiding sunlight vanished, leaving only the dancing torchlight to illumine their path ahead.

After about ten minutes of a fast paced walk, the tunnel emptied out into another large cavern in which the mysterious light reappeared above them, although this time the light seemed to be a bit brighter.

Achish continued to move forward and Rucha followed. It was here Rucha noticed something was different. Something was off. A faint buzzing sound filled the air. He stopped and held his breath in an attempt to hear better, to see if he could identify what he was hearing.

"This is not the place to stop," Achish warned, turning back and facing Rucha. "We must keep moving."

"What is that?" Rucha asked inquisitively as he began to walk forward again.

"That is the sound of death, my friend," Achish said in quieter tones. "I believe we should move a little faster," he said, picking up his pace.

Matching his step, Rucha felt an uneasiness overtake him as the buzzing grew louder and louder as they drew deeper into the cavern. With each footfall his anxiety increased, as well as his frustration at not knowing what was happening around him. Even with his unique sight, he couldn't seem to see past the light, which only illumined the area within ten cubits around them.

"Achish, what is—"

"Silence!" Achish snapped. "Just keep moving!"

Rucha saw the fear in Achish's eyes as the rotund man turned away from him once again and ran forward. The buzzing had grown to be almost deafening now. The constant sound was making Rucha's head feel numb and hollow.

Soon both men came to the center of the cavern, where a large stone altar stood. Rough carvings of beasts and humans dancing and doing unspeakable acts littered the sides of the rectangular stone table. It was tall, almost as tall as Rucha, short a handbreadth. Slowing his pace, Rucha felt compelled to look upon the altar, while Achish ran straight ahead without giving it a glance. Rucha stopped all together when he noticed the large stone frame was not an altar at all, but a sarcophagus.

The buzzing was now so intense, Rucha's head began to pulse in pain. He felt his demon within, yearning for him to run, but for some reason he was captivated by the grave. He didn't know why, but he had to look inside.

Why is there a stone coffin setting alone inside a large cavern buried deep within the mountain? Who, or what is in it which needs to be so well hidden? These were just a few of the thoughts coming to his mind.

The sarcophagus, having no lid, beckoned to Rucha, whispering to him to peer inside and appease his curiosity. Standing up on his toes, Rucha peered into the stone box.

Immediately he wished he had not.

A sight of horror consumed him and he felt as if he was going to wretch again.

There in the coffin lay a body. Not an old, dried out, dusty corpse as one would expect, but a body of fresh flesh; although, most of the flesh was missing. The skin had been removed, torn away to reveal the muscles and meat of the man. Bloody handprints covered the walls of the gruesome grave as if the man had tried to escape the stone prison, but for some reason could not. It was then Rucha could smell the foul stench of decay, rotting flesh, bowels, and dried blood.

Rucha took all this in on a glance and was about to step away from the sarcophagus when he looked upon the corpse's eyes. They were large and wide and very life-like. They appeared as if they were too big for the man's head, as all the flesh around the eyes sockets was gone. There were no eyelids either, which gave the eyes a protruding look. The pupils were dark and staring straight up.

Then, the eyes moved.

They looked right at Rucha.

Rucha gasped and stumbled backwards, away from the living coffin. The man within, whom Rucha had thought was dead, was in fact alive! The tortured man began to scream and wail, his cry echoing off the cavern walls. His desperate calls for help were unintelligible, as if the man had no tongue.

Rucha's mind raced with questions, but then he remembered where he was and the danger Achish had warned him of. He had been following Achish, but now that he had stopped, Achish was gone. Not only had he lost his guide, but the light around him seemed to be getting dimmer and was fading into a grayish color. The darkness around the light seemed to be growing heavier as if it was pushing itself against the light.

With the light waning, the air buzzing, and the horror of the man screaming, Rucha put his hands over his ears and screamed himself. So loud and so deafening was all the noise around him that he could feel trickles of blood leaking from his own pounding ears.

He had to force himself to move.

"Move! Move! Get out of here!" he heard a voice scream from within.

Ignoring the pain raking through his head, he started off in the direction he thought Achish had gone. The dying light followed him, dimming, fading with each step he took. The light which had once spanned at least ten cubits in all directions was now no more than two or three cubits.

Something seemed to be out there, around him, reaching for him. Something alive, dark, and evil, pushing and pawing against the light. He watched in disbelief as what appeared to be tentacles of darkness ripple into the light as if they were grasping for him, beckoning him to come out of his glowing protection. The tentacles would then recoil as if the light brought pain to them.

The skinless man's screams still echoed throughout the cavern, but they were now sounding farther away. Rucha chanced a glance behind him as he stumbled on and saw a shapeless black mass plunge into the coffin. The man's desperate cries turned to a muffled gagging sound, as if something was being forced down his throat.

Forget the man! He was dead before you even saw him! Run! Run! Run!

He tried to quicken his pace, but the buzzing was pounding in his ears, causing him to become dizzy and disoriented. Several times he stumbled and fell, only to pick himself up and press on. His body felt clumsy and awkward, as if he had drank too much wine. All the while, the light around him grew dimmer and dimmer. The light barely encompassed him now.

Rucha was growing desperate. *I can't die this way. I don't even know who this enemy is…what…or who is trying to kill me in this hellish hole in the earth. I can't die here! I will not die here!*

A new courage surged within him as he focused on his legs, willing them to move faster, and soon he was running. Running towards…what? Something…anything…anywhere that would get him out of this cavern of death.

With only a hint of the dying light remaining around him, Rucha ran as hard as he could. He began to feel sharp pinpricks accost his arms, hands, legs and face beneath his mask. Every place on his body where there was exposed skin he felt as if tiny teeth were gnawing at him.

Then, a moment of clarity erupted within his mind and it all made sense.

He thought of the man in the coffin. The dead man's flesh. It was not torn or peeled off, it was eaten off!

The buzzing, the bites, the stone statues outside of the temple.

These were flies! What he was seeing and feeling were thousands—hundreds of thousands of flies bearing down to feast upon him!

The terror of this realization made him move even faster. His whole body now screamed out in pain. He wanted to stop and thrash and slap away the tiny intruders, but he knew it would be to no avail. Escape was his only option.

Rucha felt a wet stickiness form over his skin. At first he thought it was simply sweat covering his body, but the sick, iron smell of blood came to his nostrils. Once again his thoughts went to the skinless man. *Is that what is happening to me? Is this what it feels like to have your skin devoured from your flesh?*

Then, as if the world had come to an end, the last bit of hazy light went out and the black consumed Rucha. Even with his ability to see into the spirit world, there was nothing. No shapes, no shades of gray, no shadows. There was just black. Dark, nightmarish black!

Run! Don't stop! Run faster!

Giving it all he had, Rucha soared through the darkness, trying to ignore the pain of the thousands of bites tearing into him. He tried desperately to see, to find an end to this massive cavern, a dim light…anything!

His body now felt like it was drenched in blood.

Is there any skin left on my body at all?

Then, out of the corner of his eye, he saw it. It was a flicker! A small flare of something. He turned towards it, now feeling an intense burn roaring through his legs, back and arms.

Rucha was about to call out, hoping it was Achish; but before he could, he tripped over something on the ground. Rucha flew forward and quickly came crashing down to the cavern's rocky floor. His arms took the brunt of the blow, landing hard as he heard a sickening snap at his right elbow. After the impact he slid for several cubits, his body scrapping against the rock, producing a whole new level of pain.

And then they were on him.

The flies had been violently attacking him before, but now they were relentless! Knowing their prey was down and unmoving, they attacked with a new vigor. Rucha tried to scream as he felt a great weight slam down upon his body, but the flies were so numerous, they were now pouring into his mouth, ears and nose. The cry he desperately wanted to make was choked out by the invading horde. Instinct made him thrash, kick, and claw at his own body and the air around him. It was a last ditch effort to try and rid himself of his enemy, but the more he moved, the worse it got, and greater the agony became.

Rucha thrashed until hopelessness won over in his mind. Now with unbelievable pain tearing at him, he began to go numb. His world began to fade. A single thought crossed his mind.

So this is how I am going to die. Pathetic!

With one last yearning for hope, he looked up and saw the small glimmer of light he had spotted earlier. It was dancing up and down and it seemed to be getting closer. He opened his mouth to call out, but the world around him faded away. And then, there was nothing. Nothing but the buzzing sound of death consuming him.

CHAPTER 32

Shammah was impressed as he walked around the east end of the camp where most of the remaining soldiers were busy caring for the wounded. The men had constructed crude but effective pallets for the injured out of willow and palm branches. Some of them must have found a flock of sheep nearby because there was freshly cut wool spread on top of the crafted beds to give greater comfort. There were other men cutting limbs from trees and tying them together to make stretchers to carry the severely injured home.

As Shammah approached each wounded soul, he took a moment to kneel beside them to give them an encouraging word and a prayer of hope.

Coming to the far edge of the camp, Shammah found a soldier leaning over Faran, applying a long white strip of linen around his torso and over his ribs. The soldier heard Shammah's approach, glanced up, and nodded to him before returning to his task.

"How is he?" Shammah asked.

"You can ask him yourself," the man replied.

Shammah looked towards Faran's face, finding the warrior's eyes closed, but then Faran winced as his fellow warrior tugged on his bandage and tightened it before tying it off.

Opening his eyes to thin slits, Faran tried to smile. "I've felt better, sir. I feel like a wild ox used me as a ragdoll. Everything hurts and I can only take shallow breaths."

"Anything broken?" Shammah asked, kneeling down beside him.

"Praise El, no. The healer here says I only cracked a few of my ribs, but he didn't think they were broken," Faran said in a strained voice.

"Oh, I am no healer," the warrior said as he began to gather up the loose strips of linen around Faran. "I am just a guy trying to help out with what little I know."

"What is your name, son?" Shammah inquired of the soldier as he peaked underneath Faran's bandages.

"Galon, sir. Galon-bar-Hadari, from the tribe of Judah. My father was a healer, as was my mother. I guess I just picked up a few things along the way."

Shammah nodded. "Tell me, Galon, how do you know his ribs are not broken but only cracked?"

"The bruising, sir. His bruises over his ribs are a dark purple and not a reddish purple or black, which could signify internal bleeding. Also, the fact that he doesn't have his ribs sticking out of his chest or large amounts of blood coming out of his mouth, suggests his ribs have not punctured his lungs. Again, I am not a healer, I am just guessing."

"I would say those are some pretty educated guesses. Why didn't you become a healer like your parents?" Shammah asked inquisitively.

"Well, because, sir, I have found I am better at taking lives than saving them. Hence the reason I am a soldier."

Shammah nodded his head, understanding his answer. He looked past Galon and saw the woman Faran had risked his life to protect. She was sitting in front of a small birch tree with her arms wrapped tightly around her knees, hugging them to her chest. She gently rocked herself back and forth as she stared at Faran with fear and concern in her eyes. Shammah noticed the wound on her left shoulder had not yet been tended to.

Standing up from his kneeling position, Shammah motioned for Galon to come and stand next to him. In hushed tones, he asked, "Why has she not been treated? She is our guest and under our protection. She should have been one of the first to be taken care of."

"Commander, we tried," Galon responded. "But she would not allow us to touch her. Every time we approached her she would flail her arms or curl up into a ball and hide her wound from us. Poor girl must have been through all kinds of awful things before we came along. She hasn't told us, but I am betting the others we heard screaming in that cave were her family. I can't imagine it. Seeing your loved ones devoured by that beast, right before your eyes. Knowing it was only a matter of time and you would be next." Galon shook his head in dismay. "Poor girl," he said again softly, more to himself than to Shammah.

"Look at her." Shammah pointed out as he observed her from their two-man huddle. "She is staring at Faran as if they were kin or like he is her husband."

"Aye. When we moved Faran over here she was still clinging to him like a babe stuck to her father's leg. Two other guys and I actually had to wrestle her away from Faran so we could treat his wounds. We put her under that tree and she hasn't budged since." Galon explained without turning to look at the girl. He reached into his shoulder bag and pulled out some clean linen, thread and a bone stitching needle. He held out the medical supplies to Shammah. "She wouldn't let me help her, but maybe you will have better luck."

After Shammah nodded and took the materials from his hands, Galon returned to Faran, checked his bandages one more time, and then stood and walked away to go and check up on the next wounded warrior.

Shammah took a step towards the woman, but then stopped and thought better of it. She would be more pliable if she were to come to him rather than he try and approach her.

Returning to Faran's side, Shammah said in a low voice, "Faran, you awake?"

Faran opened his eyes, turned his head, and focused on his commander. "Yes, sir. It just helps to close my eyes. My head is pounding and I keep getting dizzy."

Putting his hand on Faran's shoulder the way a father would with his son, Shammah lamented, "I am sorry for your pain, but I could use your assistance if you can manage it?"

"Yes, sir, of course. What can I do to help?" Faran asked as he slowly tried to sit up. Doing so made him grunt and wince.

"Whoa, son," Shammah soothed, guiding him back down with his strong hands. "What I need doesn't require you to get up and move. I only need you to speak."

Faran nodded.

"The woman. Has she said anything to you about who she is? Where she is from? How she got tangled up with the masakh?"

Turning his head, Faran looked at the woman sitting only cubits away. She had stopped rocking and was intently looking at Faran. She seemed to brighten a bit when Faran returned her gaze.

Faran looked back to Shammah. "No, sir. I haven't heard her speak since the attack."

"Do you think you can help me to get her over here so I can treat her wound? I would also like to ask her some questions. It seems they tried to help her earlier while you were unconscious but she was quite adamant about wanting to be left alone. We have noticed she has taken a liking to you. She may listen to you."

"I'll try, sir," Faran said, turning his head back towards the woman.

She must have known they were talking about her because she had repositioned herself onto her knees and seemed to be listening in on their conversation.

Faran held out his hand to her and was about to call out to her, but before he could, she got to her feet and came straight to him. She grasped his outstretched arm and nestled in beside him. She reached down with her hand to his face and caressed his cheek and brow. Her eyes were full of sorrow and grief, as tears welled up around their edges. She leaned down and began to kiss Faran repeatedly on his face and neck.

Not prepared for the onslaught of emotion and kisses from the woman, Faran turned a deep shade of red from embarrassment.

"Whoa, lady! Calm down! It's alright. I'm fine." Faran exclaimed, putting his hand between the woman's face and his own. "No need for all the affection."

This seemed to only spur the woman further as she grasped his shielding hand and began to repeatedly kiss his palm.

Faran's eyes grew wide and unsure, not knowing how to handle the woman's display of gratitude. He looked to Shammah as if asking for help.

"Don't look at me." Shammah said, holding up his hands and shrugging in reply. "This is the reason I never got married. Women get weird with stuff like this. She has been through a great ordeal and has a lot of built up anxiety. She wants to feel secure and safe, and since you were her savior, you get to be her new best friend." Shammah said as he patted him on the shoulder.

The woman finally stopped kissing Faran's hand and now grasped it in both of her hands. She began to bow her head, touching his knuckles to her forehead repeatedly.

Once again, Faran looked to Shammah and mouthed the words, *"This woman is crazy!"*

Letting out a chuckle and an ear to ear grin, Shammah explained, "No, she is not crazy. She is being polite and is showing you great respect. In fact, I recognize this ritual form of gratification. I believe I know where she is from."

Reaching over Faran, Shammah put his hand gently on the woman's right shoulder. The woman stopped bowing and pulled back a bit at his touch. Shammah began to speak to her, but not in the common tongue of the Hebrews. Instead he spoke a courser language, one Faran could not identify.

As Shammah communicated in gentle tones, the worried look on the woman's face disappeared and a beautiful smile took its place. Shammah spoke the rough speech a bit more and the woman dropped Faran's hand and reached across to hug Shammah around his neck. Shammah laughed as she did so, patting her on the back the way a grandfather would with a little child. After a moment's embrace, he guided her back to her sitting position.

It was then she spoke in the same language Shammah was speaking a moment ago. She started talking very rapidly, telling her story and everything which had happened to her. Not far into her tale, Shammah held up his hand for her to stop and she did with a puzzled look on her face. Shammah spoke a few more sentences to her. Upon doing so, her face flushed a little and she looked down to Faran.

Faran was completely confused as to what was going on. "So, she is not Hebrew?" Faran asked. Before Shammah could reply, he asked the question again towards the woman. "You are not a Hebrew? Where are you from, then? And how did you get here?"

The woman looked at Faran with her large blue eyes and then focused back on Shammah. She spoke a bit with Shammah in her native tongue and he seemed to be answering several questions. After a few moments she seemed satisfied with Shammah's responses and turned to Faran, smiled, and said, "Hello, my name is Jordan."

Faran raised his eyebrows. "You do speak Hebrew! If you speak our language, why didn't you—"

"Perhaps I should catch you up on our conversation," Shammah interrupted. "Jordan is from Egypt, southern Egypt to be exact. Close to the borders of Cush. Her father is Hebrew and is a trader of salt and spices. Her mother is Egyptian. They have spent most of their lives in Egypt where she grew up. Her father was a very proud man, so he wanted to make sure his daughter knew the Hebrew language and was able to read the Torah."

The woman peered down at Faran with a smile as he turned his attention back to her. He was about to ask her a question, but then he paused, becoming lost in the eyes of this beautiful woman. She still had mud on her face, her hair was a mess with dirt and leaves in it, she had a bloodied shoulder and torn bloody clothes; but with those deep blue eyes, slender cheek bones and that innocent smile beaming across her face…she was beautiful.

Realizing he had been staring, Faran closed his eyes and cleared his throat to help him concentrate. *Questions, I have questions.* Faran thought. He asked the woman, "So your name is Jordan, like the river?"

Jordan giggled in reply, "Yes, like the river."

Shammah rolled his eyes.

"So, why didn't you just talk to us before?" Faran continued. "I guess I already knew you could speak Hebrew. We all heard you screaming in our language when you came out of the cave and you were being chased by the masakh."

The thought made Jordan's smile disappear and an uneasiness overcome her.

Noticing the worried look on her face, Faran reached out with his hand and grasped hers.

Her smile slightly returned. "I am sorry I didn't speak," she said, no longer looking at Faran's face but down at his hand. She liked the feeling of his hand, it felt warm and strong. It felt safe.

She squeezed his hand a bit tighter as she continued talking. "Where I am from, a woman is not allowed to communicate to a man she does not know, especially soldiers. Many times the punishment for doing such a thing is a beating, and sometimes death. I have never been to Israel, as I have lived in Egypt all my life. I assumed your laws against women were much the same; so, I did not speak. But then your grandfather—" she began to say, motioning towards Shammah.

Faran's eyebrows shot up and a sly smile crossed his face. "I'm sorry, my what? Oh, he is not my—"

Shammah cut him off and said, "Now, son, don't be rude! I told her we were family and I was your elder. She needed someone in authority to give her permission to speak. Isn't that right?" Shammah said, smiling towards the young woman.

She nodded and smiled back.

Faran closed his eyes and shook his head. "So, what was with all the kisses and bowing?"

Jordan blushed. "I was saying thank you for saving my life, as that is our custom in Egypt. I would have told you with a little less affection but I was not allowed to speak to you."

"Wait," Faran said lifting his head a bit. "So you were not allowed to talk to me, but you can shower me with kisses?"

She gave no reply but smiled down at him and half shrugged her shoulders.

Faran rested his head back and closed his eyes. He winced from the bit of movement he had made. He sighed and said, "Kisses from beautiful women. I think I would like to go to Egypt someday." Faran's voice began to fade out as sleep started to overtake him.

Looking concerned, Jordan let go of his hand and reached up to shake his shoulder.

Shammah caught her hand to stop her. "It's alright. He is only sleeping. We gave him some rhuse."

She looked at him inquisitively.

"It is a kind of plant with a red stalk and large star shaped leaves on top. The leaf itself is poisonous, but the stem underneath has numbing properties. You boil it with water and then drink it. It helps to numb out the pain, and if you consume a good bit of it, it will make you sleep."

The woman nodded, seeming to understand the plant Shammah was talking about.

"Jordan, now that we have been acquainted, I was hoping you would allow me to look at your shoulder. That cut looks pretty deep, and if we don't get it cleaned and taken care of, I am afraid it will fester," Shammah said, giving away the concern in his voice.

Jordan looked at her arm and with a worried expression looked back to Shammah. "Where I come from, only women are allowed to treat other women. It would not be proper for you to do so."

"I understand," Shammah said sincerely. "We have a similar tradition, but it is not considered a law here. On the battlefield soldiers take care of one another and treat each other with respect and honor."

"But I am not a soldier," Jordan replied.

"I would say that is a matter of opinion. You do not carry a sword, but you have been very brave, and that is the true measure of a warrior." Shammah held out his hand and leaned slightly towards her. "I promise I will treat you with all dignity and honor. Will you let me dress your wound?"

Shammah could see Jordan thinking, inwardly debating whether or not to trust him. Her eyes looked as if there was doubt and concern overwhelming her, but after a moment she held out her hand and took Shammah's hand. He tried to give her his most reassuring smile.

Without saying another word, Shammah came around Faran's cot and sat cross-legged next to her on the ground. He took the torch he had been holding in his right hand and plunged the end of it into the dirt so it would stand on its own, giving just enough light to be able to see the woman's wounded shoulder. He lifted the bowl of water sitting next to Faran's bed and grabbed a clean linen strip from the supplies Galon had given him. After wetting the cloth in the cool water he carefully began to dab away the caked and dried blood around Jordan's wound. She occasionally winced when Shammah applied too much pressure to the cut in her arm.

"So how do you know of our customs?" Jordan asked, trying to concentrate on something other than what Shammah was doing to her shoulder. "You do not have the blood of the Egyptian within you, so I know you are not from there."

"You are correct. Nor am I Hebrew born, but the best seasons of my life have been with the Hebrews. I pledged my service to them and their God many seasons ago. To answer your question, I spent some time in Egypt in my youth. I was there long enough to become familiar with many of your customs."

Jordan nodded and looked up to the bright, star-cluttered, night sky and gave a sigh of appreciation for the beautiful array of lights before her. She was about to say something out loud about the stars, but instead winced and cringed as she felt a sharp pain in her arm. She refused to look at Shammah and what he was doing. She thought if she looked, she might pass out, and she didn't want to appear weak in front of these soldiers.

"Jordan, I need to ask you some questions about what happened tonight. Is that going to be all right? Do you think you can talk about it?" Shammah asked as he pulled a small curved bone from Galon's medical supplies to use as a stitching needle.

Jordan looked to the ground for a long minute before she answered. "I came here to Israel with my father and he was to introduce me to a man I was to wed. My father had arranged the engagement many moons ago. We had arrived in Hazor a few days past to meet this man, Balis. I remember seeing him for the first time. I was so scared. I was afraid he would look at me and not want anything to do with me. After all, I do have Egyptian blood within me and I look more Egyptian than I do Hebrew. But he seemed kind and didn't seem to care about my nationality or my age."

"How old are you, if you don't mind me asking." Shammah interrupted.

"I am seventeen seasons."

"Well past marrying age," Shammah pointed out.

Jordan nodded. "I would have been married at a proper age if father would have allowed me to marry an Egyptian. I had plenty of suitors, but father wanted me to wed a Hebrew and to raise a family here in Israel."

Jordan winced and let out a little yelp as she felt another prick from the needle and a shot of pain ran into her arm.

Shammah cringed. "Sorry. *I am* trying to be gentle."

Jordan closed her eyes and took a deep breath before continuing her tale. "Balis was quite wealthy, as he owned many farms in the area. He had a home in Hazor and a few more homes in other neighboring towns. He was showing us his fields—"

"And by us you mean?" Shammah prompted.

"Me, my father, and two servants who accompanied us from Egypt."

Shammah nodded.

"It was just south of here that we ran into a caravan of Balis' men. They had finished harvesting a crop of grain and fruit from the previous day and they were on their way to market with the produce. We met up with them and everyone decided to break and have midday meal…although…that's when—"

Beginning to shake a bit, Jordan's voice became weak and nervous. "That's when these two giant creatures rushed in on us from two different directions." Tears began to fall freely down Jordan's face as she recalled the memory. "We were lucky they went for the animals first—"

Shammah stopped sewing the girl's wound. "Wait, what?"

"I said we were lucky—"

"No. Did you just say there were *two* creatures?" Shammah asked, feeling his heart skip a beat. "Are you sure there were two and not just the one?"

Jordan turned her head and looked into Shammah's eyes. Tears wet her cheeks and the soft glow of the firelight next to her made her eyes look red and clouded. With a quiver in her voice, she said, "I am sure, because while I was being chased by one, I saw the other one eat my father."

CHAPTER 33

Rucha awoke with a start.

His last memory rushed in like a nightmarish flood. An infinite number of flies were invading his body and tearing him apart! The memory made him thrash out his limbs and flail wildly as if he was still being attacked.

A torch and a blurry obese face appeared before him. "Peace, you idiot! Calm down!" came the man's voice as he grabbed Rucha's wrists in an attempt to still him. "You are one lucky boar! By all rights, you should be dead."

Rucha had a hard time focusing and the room was spinning. "Where...where am I? What is happening? What—"

"Here, drink this. It will help." The man handed Rucha a wine skin and then helped him sit up.

Putting the leather canteen to his lips, Rucha took a long draft, thinking it would be cool water.

It was not water.

A foul liquid touched his tongue and he began to gag. He spewed the vile drink out onto the floor.

"What is that?" Rucha asked, coughing up what little liquid had tried to get down his throat.

"What? You don't appreciate good wine?" The voice responded with a chuckle.

Rucha pressed his eyes closed tight, took a few deep breaths, and opened them again. The room had stopped spinning and everything began to come back into focus.

There was the man, Achish, squatting down in front of him with a torch in one hand and his vile skin of wine in the other. He took a long draft from the leather flask and then made a sound of satisfaction, as if the stiff drink succeeded in refreshing his soul. "I don't know what your problem is. This is good stuff!"

Rucha didn't reply. He looked down at his arms and became instantly horrified at what he saw. His arms and hands were void of skin and covered in blood. He could see his own muscles flex as he moved his hand. He looked at his clothes and they had been torn to shreds. Underneath his tattered clothing was more damage. He could see layers of flesh missing and his ribs showing through his side.

His legs and feet were not much better. In some places around his knees he could see more bone peeking through.

Beginning to feel dizzy again, Rucha's mind began to go numb from shock. He closed his eyelids hard, willing himself not to pass out.

And then he noticed something.

Pain.

There was no pain.

With all the damage done to his body, why was he not writhing in agony?

After opening his eyelids, Rucha looked at Achish. "Why am I not dead? I should be dead. Right? And why can't I feel anything? With all these wounds, I should be in searing pain. There is no way I should even be able to be conscious enough to look at your ugly face."

Achish simply shrugged. "I don't know. By all rights, you *should* be dead. You're lucky I came back to get you. I am guessing your demon friend has something to do with you still breathing, because no normal man could have lived through that."

Achish took his torch and looked Rucha up and down from head to toe. "Devil's fire lad! You are an awful mess! Do you think you can get up and walk?"

"I don't know." Rucha took a deep breath and tried to stand up from his sitting position. He heard the squish and scrape of his mangled flesh rub against his revealed ribs.

Achish made a queer face upon hearing the sound. "You didn't feel that?"

Rucha shook his head no. "Help me to my feet."

Achish held out his hand and grasped the underside of Rucha's right forearm. He felt something sharp prick his hand and he immediately let go.

"What is that?" he asked.

Rucha lifted up his right arm and bent it at the elbow to get a look at its underbelly. There, sticking out right below the joint, was a bone protruding from his mangled flesh. A memory flashed in his mind of tripping in the cavern and landing hard on the cave floor. He remembered hearing a crack at the time.

Rucha raised his left arm to Achish and, with a bit of anger in his voice, he exclaimed, "Come on! Help me up!"

Achish grabbed his hand and hoisted Rucha to his feet.

At first Rucha was unsteady, so he kept his hand on Achish's shoulder for balance. Bit-by-bit, he began to feel his strength return, and soon he was able to stand on his own.

Putting his hand to his face, Rucha realized his mask was no longer there. Like the rest of his body, he felt a wet stickiness all over his face. He could feel chunks of missing flesh around his jaw and nose. At once he thought of the man in the coffin. *Does my face look like that?*

"Achish. How bad is my face?"

Achish brought his torch closer to Rucha's head and wrinkled his nose at the sight. "Well, you weren't that good looking to start with."

"What does it look like?" Rucha inquired angrily, ignoring the jab.

"You don't want to know, and I don't want to describe it to you," Achish said, stepping back a bit.

Rucha noticed pity in Achish's eyes as he stepped away from him. Rage flooded his mind. He wanted to shout, to curse, to grab Achish by the throat and rip his head off! It was Achish's fault he was down here, down in this El forsaken hole in the earth with flesh-eating flies! Curse Achish! Curse Dagon! Curse Israel! Curse everything!

What was the point of anything if he was to be a mangled walking corpse for the rest of his life?

Unable to hold it in any longer, Rucha let it all out! He screamed at the top of his lungs, a long exasperated cry of anguish, pain, anger, desperation, and hopelessness.

So great was the wail coming from Rucha's throat that Achish felt fear enter into his own soul, and he retreated back several steps, creating a good amount of space between himself and the bloodied man.

When Rucha's cry dwindled, he dropped down to the cold, damp cave floor; his bare-bone knees making a cracking noise upon impact. "Just leave me here and let me die," Rucha said, looking down at his mangled body.

It was then a rush of air blew through the tunnel. Rucha could feel the breeze and it soothed him. But then he heard something. A soft, quiet voice, whispering, *"Come. Come to me, my child."*

Rucha looked up to Achish. "What did you say?"

"I didn't say anything," Achish said in a still voice as he looked down the tunnel.

Then another gust of wind and the same voice followed, but louder this time. *"Rucha, my child, come to me and I will save you."*

Rucha was about to ask Achish where the voice was coming from, but he didn't get the chance. He began to get light headed and dizzy, as if he were about to pass out.

And then it hit him.

Utter and complete darkness consumed him. A dark feeling of dread and despair, hopelessness. It felt as though his very spirit was being crushed and cast aside, like being shoved into a small closet and the door being slammed shut and locked from the other side.

And then a different sensation.

Fear.

This was not just any feeling of fear. No, this was true fear! The fear of hell and damnation. The fear of eternal hopelessness and ultimate darkness. The fear which sparks the cold finger of evil that searches out and consumes all life and hope. This was a fear which was worse than death. This was a fear of utter imprisonment within one's own mind.

Rucha had felt this way once before. It was two years ago on the day of his demon's joining with him. At that time, the pain and the fear had been nearly unbearable. It took him weeks to recover from the joining. He had hoped he would never have to experience it ever again. And now, it was happening once more.

His demon was taking over.

Rucha began screaming as loud as he could from the recesses of his mind, shouting and pounding at the door within his soul which cut him off from the rest of his body. As he screamed he became aware that nothing was coming out of his body's throat. He could still hear through his ears, taste through his mouth, see through his so-called eyes, and feel through his fingers; but he could not speak through his voice. Again he screamed and cursed to regain control of his own body, but no sound would pass through his lips. He tried to move his arms and to stand from his kneeling position, but his body would not obey.

And then he heard it. He heard his body speak, but it was not his words. His demon was speaking through him…for him.

Rucha's mangled body swiftly stood and began to walk down the dark tunnel ahead. It walked right past Achish without looking at him and said in a deep, strained voice, "Follow me. You both have wasted enough time. Our master is waiting."

Achish knew at that point what had happened. Rucha's voice had changed and the black flames within Rucha's eyes were now blazing an almost reddish color. Rucha's demon had taken over.

Upon realizing this, Achish chose not to speak but to follow Rucha's walking corpse, giving it some distance.

After a short amount of time, the two came to a wide staircase leading down into another cavern. The steps were at least twenty cubits in width and each step was a cubit in height. This made descending the stairs a little awkward for both Achish and Rucha. Achish felt like a child, trying to find his next foothold on the overly large stone steps. His pudgy little legs made him hop down each step rather than walking down them. Annoyed, Achish swore underneath his breath.

After what seemed like an eternal descent into a dark abyss, an orange glow began to resonate ahead of them, signifying the bottom of the staircase.

Hopping off the last step, Achish looked out into the cavern and gasped at what stood before him.

The long, desperate blast of a ram's horn echoed throughout the camp. Every able-bodied soldier dropped what they were doing and headed for the direction of the blaring call to arms. Several dancing torches lunged through the night heading towards Shammah as he gave a few more long blasts from his shofar.

Dan was the first to appear before him, his arm still dangling at his side. "What is it? What is going on?" He asked breathlessly, as if he had just run a great distance.

Before Shammah could reply, Broc came sprinting out of the darkness from the opposite direction Dan had come from. Many of the other soldiers gathered in as well, openly voicing their concerns and feeling more than a little alarmed.

"What is going on?" Broc asked a little gruffly, obviously not enjoying the interruption to his rest. "There is a comfortable piece of driftwood over there with my name on it."

"I am sorry, my friend," Shammah said as he put his ram's horn back into his satchel. "But we have a big problem. Our hunt is only half done. Jordan just revealed to me that there are *two* masakhs, not just the one."

Immediately, the men began to complain and voice their concerns over the news.

"Peace!" Broc charged in a strong, yet quiet voice. "If there is another masakh, than from this point forward we must be silent! Remember, the beasts have excellent hearing."

"And since it is in the middle of the night, it also has superior sight," Dan reminded them.

The men obeyed and silence overtook the camp.

Shammah motioned for all the men to huddle closer so he could speak in a whisper and still be heard. "Men, it would be foolish for us to try and hunt this thing in the dark. In fact, it is probably nearby, waiting for us to come after it so it can take us by surprise. So, this is what we are going to do. We are going to gather all the wood we can find right here within the camp and make a giant fire. We are going to illuminate as much of this area as we can and hopefully that will deter it from attacking us. When morning comes, we finish this fight and send the beast to Gehenna."

The men nodded in agreement, many of them thankful they were not going to have to venture out into the night to hunt the masakh.

Broc took charge at this point and began whispering orders to the men, some to gather wood, some to form a perimeter, and yet others to move the wounded closer to where the fire would be built.

Shammah turned and started to head back in the direction he had come, back towards the area were Faran and Jordan where.

Dan joined him and asked, "*Who* told you there was another masakh out there?"

"Jordan did."

"Who is Jordan?"

"Jordan. The girl who ran out of the cave. The one Faran saved."

"Oh," Dan said looking a bit puzzled. "I thought she wasn't speaking."

"It is kind of a long story, but she did speak to me. She shared that she and her group were attacked by two masakh, not just one," Shammah said as they both approached Faran, who was still lying on his pallet, out cold from the medication given to him earlier. Shammah looked around and didn't see Jordan anywhere in sight.

"Jordan!" Shammah called in a loud whisper. "Jordan! Where are you?"

Shammah stilled himself to listen for a reply, but none came. He called again. "Jordan! Where did you go? You need to come with me. Quickly! Where are you?"

Shammah felt an uneasy feeling twist inside of him. Where did the girl go? He had only left her for a few moments and he had told her to stay put and watch over Faran. She had seemed more than eager to comply.

Once more, Shammah called out, and Dan joined in on the whispering call, "Jordan! This is no time to hide or run! Please come here!"

Shammah once again listened intently for any sound at all. Nothing.

The only noises he could hear were of the other men in the camp rustling to and fro, carrying out their orders. Shammah's heart pounded hard in his chest as a sense of dread consumed him. In a short amount of time he had grown fond of the girl, as if she were his granddaughter. He felt responsible for her.

"I must find her. Go and take Faran to the center of the camp and I will join you shortly," Shammah instructed.

Dan caught Shammah's arm. "Wait. It is going to take two of us to transfer him. Because of his injuries, I can't just pick him up and throw him over my shoulder. We have to move him, pallet and all. Help me, and then we will both go look for Jordan."

Looking at Dan and then at Faran, Shammah let out a deep sigh. "You are right. Let's do this quickly."

Shammah moved to the head of Faran's pallet and was about to lift up his end when he noticed Dan was going to try and pick up the opposite end with just one arm. Shammah saw that Dan's right arm was still dislocated and dangling free.

"What is the matter with you? I thought I told you to get your arm looked at!" Shammah said with a little scolding in his voice.

"I was doing just that, when someone blew a horn," Dan said with a grin.

Shammah didn't smile. He walked around the pallet, grabbed Dan's right arm by the wrist, put his other hand up near the limp arm's shoulder and in an upward and outward motion he yanked hard on Dan's arm. A loud "*pop*" echoed in the air around them.

Dan, not ready for the sudden burst of pain, grabbed his right shoulder and doubled over at the waist. He stuffed a section of his cloak into his mouth to muffle his cry. For several moments, Dan stood bent over, breathing hard, willing the pain to go away.

Giving him a few good pats on the back, Shammah walked back around to the head of Faran's pallet, ready to lift it once more. Dan took the hint and reached for his end of the stretcher, this time with both arms. They picked Faran up and made their way to the center of the camp.

In the time it took for Dan and Shammah to move Faran, Broc was able to get a large fire burning. A few of the men had found a few fallen trees and had somehow stood them erect and piled several other logs around them. The flames licked high into the night sky as if reaching out for the stars themselves. An orchestra of pops and hisses echoed throughout the camp as the wood surrendered to the invading flames. Hot red embers soon sailed in various directions as the fire grew higher and hotter.

Broc and Dan set Faran down close enough to the fire to feel the heat but far enough away to be safe from falling embers.

"Dan, come. We have to go find Jordan. I don't know why she would just—"

Before Shammah could finish his thought, an ear-splitting screech pierced the camp's silence.

At first, Shammah thought it was Jordan crying out, so he started to run in the direction he had last seen her. He halted when the horrible noise came again, this time coming from high above them.

All the men in the camp looked skyward, not knowing what to expect. The large roaring fire began to play tricks on the their eyes, casting shadows on the trees and rocks around them. Fear started to flood through them and some began to shout while others talked of fleeing.

"Stand fast, men!" Broc yelled out, no longer giving a care to silence or the unknown threat. "If we give in to fear, then our opponent will win! Check yourselves and gird your loins with strength and resolve! We have already beaten one of these beasts! I say, bring on another!"

The men drew courage from their captain's words and began to shout out, "Kavash! Kavash! Kavash!"

"Well, so much for silence," Dan said to Shammah as he continued to scan the dark sky for the source of the wail. "Do you still want to go out and look for Jordan?"

Shammah didn't reply but started to walk towards the eastern edge of the camp where the Sea of Chinnereth was lightly lapping its waves along the shore. "Wherever Jordan is, I believe she is in a safer place than we are at the moment. We will have to look for her later."

Once again, the high-pitched wail clashed against the silence of the cool night air. Shammah and Dan both threw their hands up to shield their ears from the deafening cry.

Looking up once more, Dan saw nothing but the stars in the sky, the bright full moon glaring down over the waters of the sea, and the pale yellow light of the fire, now a good distance behind them. "By El's creation, what is making that noise?"

Shammah didn't answer. His eyes were transfixed on the waves of the sea, now surging and crashing into the rocky beach before them. Each wave that came in seemed to crash louder than the one before. For some reason they were growing larger, as if something was pushing the water forward.

Then, as if Shammah had recalled a memory hidden deep within the recesses of his mind, he whispered aloud to himself, "Water! I had forgotten! They like the water. Not only can they run fast and jump high…I had forgotten! They can swim!"

In a panic, Shammah turned back towards Dan. "Dan! We have to run! It is coming! Run! We have to get back to the fire!"

Shammah took off running and Dan immediately followed after him. "Where? Where is it?" He questioned, looking up at the sky, thinking the attack was coming from above.

Shammah saw that he was looking up. "Not up, but out! The masakh is coming from the sea!"

As if the beast had heard its name, a mighty bellow swept through the air from the direction of the sea. There was so much force behind the roar, Shammah felt his chest constrict within him. Pushing his legs as fast as they could go, he began to yell out to the men around the fire to ready themselves, but he never got the chance to say the words.

An explosion of water, rock, and sand surged out from the sea behind them and overtook both Shammah and Dan. Shammah felt his body leave the ground as a massive wave of water threw him violently against a palm tree, pinning him there. He could feel thousands of shards of sand, pebbles, and rocks pelt his body. One of those rocks struck him in the head and at once the world around him began to spin and twist in all directions.

As fast as the water had lashed out, it subsided and worked its way back to the sea. Shammah slid from the side of the tree, landing on his stomach in a pile of freshly made mud. He tried to lift himself up but his body screamed out in pain. He rolled to his side and shook his head back and forth, trying to regain his bearings.

The ground began to shake, one massive tremor after another. Shammah's body bounced with each shockwave that surged through the earth.

Finally able to focus, Shammah saw two large, massively clawed, reptilian feet bound out of the sea, crushing the earth with each step. One of the beast's footfalls landed only cubits away from his limp body, the tremor tossing him once more against the hard tree.

This second blow to Shammah's body was too much for him to take. Darkness began to cloud his mind, and his last thought before passing out was that this was no masakh. This was something else, something much bigger. Something much more deadly.

CHAPTER 35

Achish felt a chill wash over his body as his bones quivered from within. The cavern looked identical to the one he had been in two years ago when he had freed Dagon from his diamond prison. The walls looked the same, the size of the room looked the same, the large pit of swirling lava in the middle of the room looked the same. Although, this time there was no giant crystal coming out of the molten rock. The last time Achish was in a room like this, he was trapped underground for days.

The door! Last time, the doorway vanished!

Achish spun around to see if his path to the surface was still there. He felt relief upon seeing the large open doorway, still present with its massive steps ascending back into the darkness of the mountain above. He let out a grateful sigh and turned back around.

Focusing on his breathing, Achish noted one big difference between this cavern and the last one he was in. This cavern was not empty. This one was full of demons. Demons he could see.

Achish watched in awe as some demons crawled around on the hard stone ground as if they were animals, growling and chasing one another. There were others clinging to the walls, hanging and watching all that was going on. There were yet others which defied the natural law of the world and floated through the air, darting this way and that, passing right through the hard stone.

Looking at the pool of molten rock, Achish stared in fascination as various kinds of shade demons emerged from the popping and hissing lava. They lazily crawled out of the pit and onto the cavern's stone floor, dripping with red-hot liquid fire. The sight made them look like terrifying lava monsters. The brimstone dripped from their dark forms, causing a high pitched hiss when it hit the cool rock floor. Steam rose from the ground with each step they took. The demons then proceeded to the far side of the cavern where a wall of smoke and ash prevented Achish from seeing further.

Achish realized he had been standing in place with his mouth agape for some time, staring at everything his eyes had not been able to see before. He was about to turn to Rucha to proclaim his wonder, but Rucha was not there. Rucha had already left his side and was walking several cubits ahead of him.

Achish was about to walk forward to catch up with Rucha, when he felt something grab his shoulder and throw him to the side, sending his body skidding across the smooth stone floor. Righting himself as quickly as his obese body would allow, Achish looked to see who his attacker was. He felt his legs grow weak as he looked up and watched two giant shade demons slowly walk by him. Both of the massive horned beasts glared down at him with bright red pupiless eyes.

Achish had not seen them before, but he instinctively knew these were the two guardians Dagon had appointed to him. As he looked up at them he felt fear grab hold of his heart, causing him to feel pain in his chest and arms. He recalled Rucha's warning, *"Do not mess with these two demons. If you don't show them respect and don't stop calling them things like 'pet', they will rip you apart, and I am guessing quite literally."*

Shrinking away from them as they continued to pass by, Achish felt their penetrating stares course through him. And then, in an instant, they vanished into a black vapor and were gone.

Looking around in every direction, Achish was relieved when they didn't reappear. He let out a deep breath and hurriedly ran to catch up with Rucha.

The two walked along the outer wall of the cavern, staying as far away from the lava pit as possible. Unbearable heat was accosting the air and Achish found it hard to breathe. He felt as though his skin was so hot and dry that it was about to crack open. His lips felt chapped and his throat was parched, but he kept pace with Rucha, hoping his journey into this hell was about over.

Soon they came to the wall of smoke and ash which Achish had spotted on the opposite side of the cavern when they had first entered. The smoke was dark and gray, heavy with toxic fumes of sulfur from unseen brimstone.

Achish began to cough and choke on the poisonous air coming up around him. Rucha, on the other hand, simply walked through the gaseous cloud without hesitation and without making a sound. He was there one minute and gone the next.

Being quick to follow, Achish walked a few paces into the gray toxic haze and once again began to choke and gasp for breath. He retraced his steps and came out of the smoke barely able to breathe. The intense heat and the fumes made him feel like he wanted to drop down to the ground and die.

Putting his hands to his knees, Achish gasped and attempted to control his breathing between fits of coughing. He began to feel a hopelessness overtake him and a fear of death consume him. He felt darkness and despair enter into him. Unnatural whispers of doubt entered into his mind, *"You will never make it out of here. There is no point in trying. There is no point in living. Ease your turmoil and cast yourself into the circle of everlasting flames. End your suffering."*

"Who is speaking to me?" Achish questioned aloud as he shook his head. "These thoughts are not my own. Why would I want to—"

Stopping in mid-sentence, Achish looked up and saw a demon with gray eyes, hanging upside down in the air above him. Its face, long and contorted, was only a handsbreadth away from Achish's face. The demon's hand was outstretched and its long snake-like fingers were inside the back of Achish's skull. The dark spirit had been playing with Achish's mind, sending thoughts of death and despair upon him.

Achish swiped his hand at the demon's intruding arm, but his meaty flesh passed right through the spirit. Achish looked around and saw several more demons coming towards him with malice in their eyes.

Panic overwhelmed Achish and he bolted for the toxic cloud once more, this time taking a deep breath before plunging in. He ran as hard as his fat little legs would allow him to go. At first he kept his eyes open, hoping to see where he was going, but he soon closed them as they began to burn from the sulfuric fumes all around him. After a few more moments, he erupted through the other side of the poisonous prison.

Achish fell to his knees, gasping and retching, desperately trying to take in clean air. It wasn't long before he got control of himself and begin to breathe normally again.

As he regained his composure he noticed something was different.

The atmosphere was cooler and a little damp, not like the dry heated misery he had just escaped from. And there was light. Not the dreary, orange glow which came from the lava pit, but true, honest light was pouring down upon him.

Pushing himself off his knees, Achish stood back up and made his way over to where Rucha was standing. As he did so, he looked upward to find the source of the light. There, hundreds of cubits high, was a large hole in the top of the mountain, allowing bright silver streams of moonlight to flood in. Never had he seen the light of the moon gleam and shine so brightly.

Achish then felt a cool breeze caress the side of his face. The darkness and despair he had felt moments ago from the oppressive demon faded away and relief took its place.

As Achish continued to take in his surroundings, he noticed this part of the cavern had life in it. Instead of the hard, cold, stone ground, he found himself in a vast meadow of short green grass, which was gently rustling about from an unknown breeze. Achish took in another deep breath and let the smell of the grass overcome his senses.

Looking further ahead, Achish noticed a immense oak tree growing at the far end of the meadow near the edge of the cavern, maybe a few hundred cubits away. Its grand boughs stretched out far and wide within the cave, casting a shadow over all of its reach, as if the tree was claiming its territory. The tree's lush green leaves rustled by the same breeze which crept along the grass.

Looking to the base of the tree, Achish saw a large throne carved into it. Sitting upon the throne was something Achish did not expect. A woman. Not just any woman, but a beautiful woman, like none Achish had ever seen. She held a commanding presence and a bold, straight posture. Her arms were resting on the sides of the royal chair, and her right leg was crossed over her left.

She was talking to three men who were clothed in long, black, hooded robes. Achish strained to see who the cloaked men were, but could not make out their faces, they were too far away.

Not really caring as to whom the men were, Achish's focus went back to the woman. He was captivated by her in every way. He couldn't get it out of his mind as to how stunningly beautiful she was. In all the years of his life he had never laid eyes on such a woman as this.

What is a lovely being like this doing here in this place? Achish thought to himself.

Rucha started to walk towards the large oak tree, towards the throne, towards the stunning creature sitting upon it. Rucha's stride was long and determined, and Achish had a hard time keeping up with him.

As they approached, the woman glanced their way and noticed them. She looked back to the three men she had been speaking to, said a few more words to them, and then with a wave of her hand, dismissed them. The men bowed, turned, and began walking away. Once they cleared the boughs of the tree, they ascended into the air and disappeared into the moonlight streaming into the cavern.

The fantastical departure of the three men startled Achish, as he had forgotten where he was. He had assumed the three figures were actually men; but of course, there would be no flesh and blood down here, only spirits and demons. He turned his gaze once more to the woman.

Who is this woman and what is she? Is she a human or is she a demon like all the others down here? Achish thought to himself.

Once the three men…or whatever they were…had departed, the woman stood and began to walk towards Rucha and Achish with calm, graceful steps.

Achish felt his mouth go dry and his breath quicken. Now that she was standing and he could see her more clearly, he became even more captivated by her beauty. The woman was tall. Very tall. She was almost twice his own height. She had long, black, flowing hair which cascaded down around her cheeks, making her face look slender and strong. Her hair also bunched around her shoulders and hung freely down to her lower back.

Her body was slender, yet strong with creamy, brown skin. She was flawless. Achish could not see a single blemish upon her.

Her body was covered in a simple black, silk cloth laced with gold along its edges. The material was loosely wrapped around her, leaving her right shoulder exposed while her left shoulder was covered with the draping material.

As the woman got closer, Achish was able to see fine jewelry upon her as well. A gold circlet with an intricate design was upon her brow, and gold bracelets decorated her wrists and ankles.

Achish looked back to her face, her eyes specifically. He could not look away from them. They were almond shaped, like the women Achish had seen from the East, but the color was a brilliant emerald green. So bright was the green in her eyes, Achish could feel her boring into his soul when she looked at him.

Upon the last few steps of her approach, a breeze swept across her, gently blowing her hair over her right eye and pushing her silk garment against her flesh, revealing the curves of her body. The sight made Achish's mouth drop open and he instantly yearned for her.

Rucha stopped, bent to his knees, and bowed to the woman as she closed in the last remaining distance between them. Achish wanted to reach out and touch her, but thought it wise to follow Rucha's example and bow. Upon doing so, Achish felt an emptiness overwhelm him in having to take his eyes off of her.

It was then, Achish heard her speak for the first time.

"You may rise."

Her voice was smooth and sweet. Gentle, as if a rose petal was being brushed against her full lips and then used to tickle Achish's ears.

They obeyed, and Achish once again filled his eyes with her beauty. The more he looked, the more he desired and lusted for her.

Rucha looked like he was about to speak, but the woman held up her hand and silenced him.

She looked to Achish and took notice of how he was looking at her, over her, his eyes desiring her. Her lips parted slightly in a grin. She looked upon Achish and her green eyes caught his, holding them captive with a playful stare.

"Do you like what you see?" She asked in a seductive voice as she stooped down to meet Achish face and to face. She reached out her hand and caressed the side of his left cheek.

Achish's face flushed red. He began to tremble at her touch and he felt his knees grow weak. Her hand was soft and smooth, feeling cool against his skin. Achish almost giggled as a child would when getting special attention. He cleared his throat and stammered out, "Y-y-yess."

The woman gave an amusing chuckle at Achish's reaction, and with her caressing hand she grabbed hold of the fat on the underside of his jaw and jerked his face closer to hers.

Now practically nose-to-nose, fear took hold of Achish as he watched the woman's eyes turn from a bright shimmering green to a haunting pale yellow with diamond shaped black pupils. Her perfect brown skin faded away to reveal blackish-green scales. A long, thick, forked tongue shot out from between her rose colored lips and danced playfully across Achish's face. Achish gasped in surprise and tried to wiggle his way out of the woman's iron grasp.

The woman laughed once more, but gone was the smooth voice which had pleased Achish only moments ago. Now her voice was low and raspy, still dripping with playful desire.

"What about now?" She rasped with a smile, now showing sharp jagged teeth. "Do you still like what you see?"

Achish howled with fright. Once more he felt his heart pound in his chest as if it was trying to break free from its fleshly prison. And then it came to him, as if the thought had been placed there in his mind. Those eyes…that voice…the scales.

"Lord Dagon?" Achish squeaked out. "Is that you?"

The now dragonesque woman threw her head back and laughed. She flung Achish down to the ground with a simple flick of her wrist. Landing on his back, he looked up at Dagon and then in fear, shielded his face with his arms.

"Please, Lord Dagon! Please don't kill me! I didn't know! I didn't know it was you!"

Dagon watched for a few moments as Achish begged and cowered on the ground, trembling. "Kill you? Why would I want to do that? You are one of the few things here which still amuses me. No, my fat little friend. You will not die today."

While Dagon was speaking, his voice changed once again and the woman's voice returned, soothing and calm. Her alluring tone instantly chased away the fear within Achish. He slowly put his arms down from his face and once again he saw the beautiful woman and not the horrifying monster.

"Come, get to your knees, son of Cain, and worship me."

Achish did so without question and prostrated himself before the woman's feet. He bent his head upwards to look upon Dagon's feminine form, but with her foot she shoved his head back down to the ground.

"Wretch! You have lost your freedom to look at me in this body," she rebuked. "When you speak to me, you may address my feet and no further. I find it fascinating that any female, human or beast, would desire to be with you. You are a disgusting bag of flesh."

"Yes master," was all Achish said as he kept his head down and stared at the ground beneath his eyes, not daring to even look at her feet.

"Although I can't really blame you," Dagon continued. "This form is quite appealing, desirable, and sensual." Dagon said, dripping each word in seduction, hoping Achish would be foolish enough to look up at her once more so she could punish his disobedience. But Achish kept his nose buried to the ground.

Disappointed, Dagon began to walk in a circle around Achish and Rucha.

"The truth is, it is not often I take on human form, as I find it degrading and limited. Although, I like manipulating and distorting the Maker's idea of his children. Did you know that the Maker originally created your kind to be perfect in every way and to live forever? Can you imagine that? Every wretched soul born into this cursed world would have lived for ever. Praise Luce he had the sense to show the Firsts the truth about the Maker."

"The Firsts, my Lord?" Achish asked with his eyes still focusing on the ground beneath him.

"The Firsts. The first man and woman the Maker stained this earth with. It is the woman's form I now take. This is what she looked like, the female, Eve. Physically flawless and perfect in every desirable way. I wear her body like a trophy, reminding me of the one who plunged the human race out of the age of innocence and into the age of truth."

Stopping in front of Rucha, Dagon looked him over more closely. Rucha's demon-possessed body stared straight ahead, expressionless, waiting for permission to speak.

"Amon. Why are you keeping this rotting corpse alive? It is obvious he didn't pass the trials," Dagon said with a disgusted look on her face as she reached out and picked off some dangling flesh from Rucha's face.

Amon, the demon within Rucha, spoke. "Master, did you not summon these two from the caverns? Your voice called to them in the caves."

The woman's eyebrows furrowed slightly as if trying to recall an old memory.

Amon continued without allowing Dagon to reply. "I would assume it to be in our best interest if you would heal this one. I believe he still has a purpose in your plan. He has the fear and respect of the men and is capable of leading your fleet of ships. If you would only mend his body, I would make sure he would serve you and carry out your commands for the sea voyage ahead."

Dagon walked over to Achish. "And what of this one, the son of Cain? Is he not capable of doing the same thing? After all, he still promotes himself as a king."

Without looking up, Achish took this opportunity to speak. "Yes, Lord. I am able to—"

Dagon kicked Achish in his side.

"Silence, whelp! I was not talking to you. The only reason you are breathing is because of my good graces."

"No, my Lord," Amon continued. "The Philistines will follow him but the rest of the men were trained by Rucha. Not only do they fear Rucha, but they have grown to honor his leadership and ability in battle. If you restore him, master, I know he will stay dedicated to you."

Dagon stood still for several moments, thinking and pondering. Finally, she relented. "Fine. Release him."

Amon's voice staggered for a moment, "M-master...if...if I release him he will suffer greatly and may not survive. I am repressing the pain and disconnecting it from his mind."

"No doubt," Dagon replied. "But I want to hear his loyalties sworn to me of his own accord and from his own lips, or rather what is left of the lips he has. Now, release him!"

CHAPTER 36

An ear piercing screech filled the night air once more as many of the Israeli soldiers pointed to the black sky, announcing they saw a white ghost flash by above them.

Broc was about to chastise the men for letting their fear get the best of them when a thunderous explosion erupted behind him from the direction of the sea. He turned in time to see a massive wall of water and debris heading straight for the camp.

"Cover!" was all Broc was able to shout before the onslaught of water knocked him to the ground. The men around him yelled and cursed as they, too, were struck to the ground by the unexpected wave.

Broc then heard something which made his heart sink. The hissing and popping sounds of flames and hot coals being extinguished by the torrent of water. Immediately, after finding his footing again, Broc ran over to the fire pit. What had been a large blazing fire, which had lit the earth for a hundred cubits in all directions, was now a heaping pile of wet wood and mud. Now, only a thin plume of smoke and steam rose from the center of the bonfire into the cloudless sky.

Looking around further, Broc found his men scampering, trying to pick up supplies which had been scattered by the unexpected wave. Some of the wounded men who had been on pallets were thrown off, now lying on the muddied ground.

Broc was about to give direction to the soldiers to forget the supplies and see to the wounded first when he felt the first tremor shake the ground. He then felt another, and another, and yet another. Each tremor grew stronger and stronger.

The warriors started to panic and fear began to once again overtake the camp.

Knowing he had to get control of his men, Broc looked to the ground and found a spear lying near him. He snatched it up and screamed, "Quiet! Silence! If you give in to fear, then we have already lost!"

The soldiers stopped running to and fro and looked to their captain.

"Quickly, men! Find a weapon and gird yourselves! It comes from the sea!"

"But captain, the fire! How are we to—"

"Forget the fire! The masakh is here!"

They all scurried to find their weapons, and after doing so they assembled into a line behind their captain, spears at the ready.

The earth continued to shake from the footsteps of an enemy they had yet to see. Puddles of water on the ground rippled and danced, giving a grave warning as to what was coming.

Broc felt his stomach tighten and a lump move up into his throat. His hands gripped even tighter around the shaft of his spear, causing his callused skin to make a rubbing sound against the hard, smooth wood. Broc had been in more battles and hunts than he could count, and each time he could easily swallow his fear and call courage up at a moment's notice. But this, this was different. What could make a wall of water rise up from the sea and travel a hundred cubits inland? What could make the earth tremble before its presence? Was the Evil One himself coming to kill them?

All at once the ground ceased to shake and silence filled the camp. A slight breeze rustled through the palm trees around them, as if coaxing the men to relax from their nervous state.

Broc strained to see through the darkness, but found it difficult with all the haze from the smoke and steam rising from their extinguished fire. The breeze swirled the smoke as it lingered lazily in the air, making a perfect cover for the danger which lied beyond them.

"Captain. Do we attack?" came a voice from behind Broc.

Without looking back, he snapped back in a whisper, "Silence! We will be as stone until we know what is coming!"

A thought came to Broc. Through all of the excitement and chaos he had not seen Shammah or Dan. He was about to whisper back to his men to ask if any of them had seen the two captains when a brisk wind swept through the camp and the smoke began to lift and move to the west.

At first, Broc didn't notice it. He was looking around at ground level, straining his eyes to see through the night. As his eyes became more accustomed to the lack of light, he saw it. Behind a cluster of palm trees was a giant shadow. Its width was massive and its height towered above the trees.

Broc felt his arms grow weak and his mouth go dry. There, at the top of the shadowy figure was a large, yellow, reptilian eye staring right at him.

The rest of the men must have seen what Broc was seeing because the soldiers began to shift and an uneasy tension consumed them.

"Steady, men. Steady. Nobody move. That is an order," Broc commanded through clenched teeth. "No... body...move."

The company became like statues and no one moved for what seemed like an eternity. It was a staring contest, the men looking up at a large yellow eye above the trees in the night sky, and the eye looking back down as if waiting for something to move so it could chase after and consume it.

The massive shadow must have grown tired of the game, because it began to shift its weight from side to side. It took a step forward. Upon doing so, its bulky frame strained against one of the palm trees it had been hiding behind. The tree bent almost to the ground and snapped at the base, causing the trunk to land only cubits away from the soldiers. Yet, even when the palm came crashing down beside them, they followed their orders and not a one of them jumped or moved out of the way.

The great shadow stepped fully into the moonlight, revealing a massive and ancient creature, like none the men had ever seen. The beast was comparable to the masakh they had killed earlier in the night, but this one was at least twice its size. Its scaly body was black, shiny, and slick, as if the creature had bathed itself in oil. Great black horns rose majestically from its head. Large bone-like spikes jutted out along its neck and back, continuing all the way down to the tip of its long tail, which was lazily swaying back and forth.

Broc couldn't help but stare at the creature's enormous head. Rows of razor-sharp teeth protruded down around its mouth. He really didn't want to see what it looked like with its jaw wide open.

Holding his breath, Broc prayed the beast would pay them no mind and leave, which would be their only chance of survival. There was no way a mere twenty to thirty men would be able to bring the monster down. It would take at least a hundred men, and with more supplies than what they currently had.

The giant reptile began to move its head, looking in one direction and then looking to another. A deep rasp came from its nostrils as its lungs contracted in and out from within its large chest cavity. Every few moments a guttural growl escaped.

It is looking for something. Broc thought to himself. And then he remembered the other masakh. It, too, had been looking for something upon coming out of the cave. *The girl! Where is the girl? Is this thing looking for her as well? And if so, why?*

After a few moments, the massive Masakh turned its head away from the men and started to walk away from them, once again shaking the earth with each step, leaving deep footprints in the mud.

The warriors watched the beast begin to leave and Broc heard some of them shift and relax. He held up a fist which was a signal for them to be ready and stand fast.

The masakh only took a few steps before it stopped. Once again, a guttural growl came from its large frame. The creature bent its head down and sniffed at the ground.

Broc could not see what it was sniffing at but he knew what was there. The corpse of the other dead masakh.

He swore to himself under his breath. *This thing is not looking for the girl, it is looking for its mate, and it has just found her dead!*

Feeling the blood in his face drain away, Broc knew what was coming next. He whispered a prayer, "El, you saved us once tonight. If you don't find it in your good graces to do so again, then we will see you soon."

CHAPTER 37

Rucha never stopped screaming.

From the point of their decent into the lava cavern to their interaction with Dagon, Rucha ravaged insults, curses and an unending torrent of profanities towards the demon who was holding him hostage within his own body. He tried repeatedly to move his arms and legs, to speak, to do anything, but all attempts ended in failure.

Then, Dagon commanded the demon to release him, to give him control of his body once more. Before doing so, his demon, Amon, spoke to him inwardly, through his mind.

"Rucha! Calm yourself!" Amon said in a stern, yet controlled voice.

"Release me, you foul creature! You have no right to—"

"Silence! If it were not for me you would have died already!" the demon declared. "Have you been listening to our conversation with Dagon?"

Rucha seethed within, picturing himself strangling the spirit with his bare hands and finding great pleasure in it.

"Have you been listening?" repeated the demon.

"Yes!" Rucha screamed in reply.

"Then you know Lord Dagon wants to hear your allegiance to him from your own lips. When I release you, massive amounts of pain are going to flood your body all at once. It will *probably* kill you. You need to prepare for it."

"What do you care whether I live or die?"

"Let's just say, I am not done with you yet."

"As far as I'm concerned, you vile poisonous succubus, you *are* done with me. Release me! Now!"

Nothing was left to be said, so the demon released him.

The invisible door which restrained Rucha to the corner of his mind vanished and his spirit filled his body once again. Rucha outwardly gasped at the pleasure he found in regaining his bodily freedom. He wanted to laugh and jump and shout out the victory of his release, but his celebration was short lived.

A wave or horrifying pain swept through his being and consumed him. Every cut, tear, scrape, break and hole on his body screamed out in painful distress. Rucha fell to his knees, in utter agony. He immediately regretted crashing down to the ground as white hot flares of pain exploded from within, convulsing through his mangled flesh. Rucha began gasping for air, now fully aware of the bruised and broken ribs squeezing around his lungs. He also felt faint, knowing he would not be able to stay conscious for very long.

He could feel his body dying.

Rucha thought of his demon once again. He now realized Amon had not only been blocking out his pain, but had been the one holding his body together and keeping it from expiring. He looked down and saw blood beginning to ooze from his wounds.

Rucha looked up to the woman who was staring down upon him. He could see the pleasure in her eyes. She was enjoying the spectacle of his death.

Another wave of sharp agonizing pain flared within him, almost causing him to pass out. He feared if he lost consciousness, he would never wake up again.

Rucha painfully raised his stripped and broken arm towards Dagon, and in barely a whisper said, "Please...help...me."

Ignoring Rucha's pathetic hand, Dagon began to walk around his disfigured body. "I am not sure I should save you. It is true. We have invested a lot of time and resources into you. Saving you from the wretched elect of El, gifting you with your own demon; who, by the way, has given you ample powers of sight, strength and speed. We have trained you, fed you, clothed you. We have granted you power and authority over men. To the average human, you are nothing short of a god. So tell me, Rucha, phantom of the seas. Why have you forsaken and betrayed me?"

The torment was getting worse by the moment. Now, hot white shards of pain began to jolt up his spine and it made Rucha's head snap back. It was hard for him to concentrate, but he could not think of a time he had betrayed Dagon.

"I have…not…betray…ed…you…" and then he gasped as if he had no more breath to give.

"No? But you have." Dagon said calmly, admiring the pain being displayed before her. "Do you even know what happened to you? Why your body looks like this?"

"…flies…" was all Rucha could find the strength to say.

"Yes, I suppose you would think they looked like flies. But, in truth, each and every single one of those little fly-like creatures was, in fact, a demon. Honestly, I think they are ugly little things. They look like tiny little scorpions with heads that look human. Their teeth are fang-like and razor-sharp. I must say, the little beasts are an abomination, but they serve their purpose. In all honesty, they are the pets of a much greater demon, although not as great as myself. The demon they obey has many names. I believe your people have called him Beelzebub or Baal. This temple was erected over a millennia ago to worship him. Well, to make a long story short, Beelzebub tried to overthrow the Lord of the Air, Luce. You can imagine how Luce responded to that. So Baal was imprisoned here within this very mountain. Actually, he was imprisoned within the very room in which you were almost destroyed.

"Now, the answer to the question which I would like to know is, why? Why were you almost eaten alive? You see, Beelzebub never attacks those who have rejected El and serve the Order of Darkness wholeheartedly; hence, the whole reason I invited you down here in the first place."

Dagon looked to Achish who still had his nose buried to the ground. "Take this fat, plump, juicy buffet-of-a-man here. If there was anyone on this island who would be a tasty morsel for Baal, it would be this wretch. But yet, he walked right through Baal's lair and there is not a scratch on him. Not one single bite. I know he is loyal because he despises El and worships us. But you, Rucha, once known as Abishai, captain and warrior of the Hebrew army—you must still carry a spark, a light of hope for El within you, or Baal would not have attacked you so."

Squatting her feminine form down in front of Rucha's kneeling corpse, Dagon firmly grabbed hold of the bottom side of his jaw. She looked intently at the graying wisps of flame coming from Rucha's eye sockets. Blood dripping from his facial wounds found its way to her hand and trailed down her arm.

The bright green eyes of the woman faded away and Dagon's reptilian eyes reemerged. In a forceful voice, she said, "Rucha, you are now a handsbreadth away from passing from this world into the black emptiness of eternity. I alone can save you. Tell me. Where do your loyalties lie?"

Rucha could barely see Dagon's face right in front of him. There was so much agony raging through him that his body was trying to shut down to find relief. Rucha only wanted the pain to stop. He faintly heard Dagon's question enter into his mind. After a few moments of collecting as much strength as he could, he answered, "…my……loyal….loyalties are to….you. It was…..light……the light you sent around me…..is why they…..attacked."

With those words Rucha felt his body go completely numb, as if the pain centers in his flesh couldn't take anymore and chose to shut down. Rucha felt his world slipping away for the second time in the last twelve hours. The last thing he remembered before giving in to death was the look on Dagon's face. A look of bewilderment, fear, and then rage filled the old demon's eyes.

CHAPTER 38

Broc and his men watched in silence as the black masakh sniffed and snorted around the head of its lifeless mate. Several times its large snout nudged the back of the dead animal's head, trying to get it to stir or move.

After a few moments, the beast gave up its efforts and stood to its full height once more. It thrust its head high into the air and let out a tremendous crushing roar, as if cursing the moon for shining its light down upon it. Broc and his men covered their ears, straining against the beast's lamenting cry. Three more times the masakh cried out, wailing for its dead mate.

One of the wounded men who had been unconscious was awoken by the roars of the beast. Startled and confused, he began to cry out at the sight of the masakh.

At once, the monster whipped its mammoth head in the direction of the soldier's panicked cry. Several men ran over to the injured man to silence him, but the commotion only made things worse.

The ancient lizard honed in on the movement and the sounds. It bent its head low, crouched its legs, and put up its tail, preparing to attack. Another massive roar resonated from the beast's open mouth, betraying row upon row of razor-sharp teeth.

Broc could feel the masakh's hot rancid breath on his face, some fifty cubits away. There was no point in being quiet any more. They had been spotted.

"Run!" was all Broc was able to get out before the agile reptile lunged itself through the air. The giant beast spanned the fifty cubits in one leap, and came crashing down on the wounded man who had been screaming. Its massive foot crushed the unfortunate soul and three other men upon its landing, causing the earth to shake violently. Every man standing lost his footing and fell to the ground.

All who were able, got back to their feet and began to run. Weapons and supplies were forgotten as the men scattered. The masakh pounced wildly in all directions, clamping its jaws around anyone close to it. The sickening sound of screaming men being crushed and ripped apart filled the night air.

A few brave men who held onto their spears tried to drive them into the animal's hide, but to no avail. The spears merely bounced off the dragon's ironclad scales. With one crushing swipe of its tale, the masakh swept the assaulting men away, flinging them into the darkness of the night.

This is insane, Broc thought to himself. *We can't fight this beast like this. We have to find a safe place to regroup and come up with a plan.* And then the answer came to him. *The cave!*

"The cave! The cave! Run to the cave!" Broc screamed, waving his left arm in a circular pattern and pointing to the cave with the spear in his right hand. Broc shouted the message over and over until the surviving members of his troop saw and understood him. Every man not severely wounded or dead now ran for all they were worth in the direction of the cave.

The masakh noticed the men fleeing and began to give chase, easily stomping out two more soldiers trailing at the back of the pack. The beast was not content with crushing them underfoot. It dug its teeth into their flesh and thrashed its head back and forth, ripping their lifeless bodies apart.

"I have to do something," Broc said to himself as he watched the carnage unfold. "Or the rest of these men will never make it to the cave."

Leading the men to safety, Broc pulled up and motioned the men to keep running. "Don't stop until you are well inside of the cave!" he instructed, urging the soldiers to run faster. "I will buy you the time you need to get there!"

With his spear in hand, Broc headed back towards the Masakh. He pushed his fear aside and let his fury consume him, finding the strength to do what needed to be done, even if that meant going to his own death. He was not going to let another one of his men die here tonight.

The last of his men ran past him. Broc took a few more steps and stopped, planted his feet fast upon the ground, and took a fighter's stance with his spear. He watched in sickening agony as the masakh chewed and swallowed its last victim.

Closing his eyes, Broc tried to regulate his breathing. He repeated the same words to himself, which he had told countless new troops over years of training. *A clear mind presents a clear kill.*

When Broc opened his eyes, he focused on the beast's mouth. An accurate throw of the spear to the back of its throat would end this hellish nightmare.

Broc felt the presence of two more men come up on either side of him. He immediately began to scold them, saying, "I thought I told you to head for the—"

"Well, last time I checked, I outrank you, so I don't have to listen to a word you say," came a familiar voice to his right.

Broc glanced over and there stood Shammah. Blood was coming down the right side of his face from a gash to his head above his ear. Shammah's stance was firm as he held a spear in each of his hands, one down by his side, ready to thrust, and the other poised over his shoulder, ready to be thrown like a javelin.

"And I don't listen to you anyway," came another familiar voice to Broc's left.

Without looking, Broc grinned at hearing Dan's voice.

"Where in the fires of Gehenna have you two been?" Broc questioned.

"Later," Shammah said bluntly. "It approaches."

The masakh took a few small steps forward, stopped, and took a giant step to the right, as if it was attempting to go around the trio.

The three warriors side-stepped back in front of it, blocking its path once more.

The masakh halted, stared at the three men, and took a step back, as if unsure of itself.

Shammah eyed the beast closely, trying to determine the cause of its strange behavior. He noticed the animal was not looking at them, but past them. Shammah followed its gaze and saw nothing behind them but darkness and the outline of some palm trees. He looked back at the masakh, and it was still staring, transfixed on something over their heads. A deep groan sounded within the beast's belly.

"What is it doing? Why isn't it attacking us?" Dan asked, beginning to feel a bit anxious.

Shammah looked behind them once more and this time he saw something. There, on top of one of the palm trees, was the faint form of a person dressed in white, tattered clothing. The moon bore enough light to give the figure away. It was Jordan. She stood there with her arms at her sides, staring down and looking straight at the masakh. Her stare seemed to keep the beast in a trance. Then, as if she was a figment of Shammah's imagination, she disappeared.

Shammah blinked his eyes, wondering if he had actually seen Jordan standing upon the tree. His attention was quickly brought back to the masakh as the animal snapped out of its trance and focused on the three men once again. The beast's groan turned into a hiss and then a growl.

The beast hunched down into an attack stance as it had done once before, and let out its mighty roar. The men could hardly stand before the force of the masakh's foul breath.

Broc grimaced when he saw parts of mangled human flesh wedged into the animal's teeth. "Here it comes!" He announced through a clenched jaw.

The mammoth beast dove straight at them with jaws wide open, ready to tear them apart as it had done to countless others.

Years of experience and training took over for all three of the seasoned warriors. Standing fast until the last possible second, all three men let their spears fly and then dodged out of the crazed animal's path.

Dan and Shammah dove to their sides while Broc took a more daring approach. After throwing his spear, he dove forward, skidding right under the beast's mouth, and then rolling furiously to the side to keep from being crushed by the underbelly of the reptile or trampled by its clumsy feet.

The masakh slammed its large open mouth into the ground right were Broc had been standing seconds ago. The beast was rewarded with a mouth full of mud and sand.

The masakh recoiled and stumbled back. It began to wail, shaking its head back and forth violently.

Broc rejoined his two friends and smiled at the sight.

There, stuck to the roof of the masakh's mouth, were Dan and Broc's spears. The animal desperately lashed out its thick forked tongue in an effort to dislodge the two projectiles. When that proved to be useless, it bent its head to the ground and began clawing savagely at the inside of its mouth with one of its massive hind legs.

It was then the men saw where Shammah's spear had planted itself. Right in the middle of the masakh's left eye. Black oily blood ran from the wound, down the side of the reptile's face and flowed in a steady stream from its jaw.

"I think this would be a good time to run," Shammah announced.

"I think you're right," said Broc. "We've given our men more than enough time to get in that cave. Let's move!"

All three turned and began to run for all they were worth.

"Wait, the cave? You mean the same cave the first masakh was hiding in when we first got here?" Dan asked as he ran to the right of Broc. "That thing will follow us right in and finish us all off!"

The masakh roared once more and all three men felt the ground beneath them shake.

It was coming after them.

"Just run!" Broc yelled.

As soon as the mouth of the cave was in sight, Shammah noticed a handful of men at the cave's entrance, waving at them and urging for them to hurry. He waved at them furiously, yelling, "Get deeper into the cave! Move back! It is right behind us!"

The warriors obeyed their commander and ran back into the darkness of the cavern.

Shammah, Broc and Dan crossed the threshold of the cave at the same time the masakh dove headfirst in after them. The rocky cavern shook from the impact of the animal's attempted entry. Because of the beast's massive horns upon its head, only its snout was able to fit through the opening.

The masakh became even more wild when it realized it was going to fail to capture its prey. Its head became a battering ram against the mouth of the cave, desperate to invade the men's safe haven. The mountain began to shake, and several men, including Broc and Dan lost their footing and fell hard to the ground.

Shammah was knocked down to the rocky floor as well, and landed only cubits away from the invading snout. The monster's jaws snapped wildly, trying to devour anything within its reach. Smelling Shammah lying close by, the beast rammed its head even harder against the cave's entrance.

Now only a body-length away from the animal's savage teeth, Shammah tried to scramble to his feet to get away, but before he could do so, something wet and strong fastened around his ankle.

Fear gripped Shammah as he looked down to see what he was caught up on. The masakh's gray, forked tongue was wrapped around his foot and it was dragging him backwards into the dragon's mouth.

Before Shammah could even cry out for help, the monster's jaws clamped down on his right leg, just below the knee. Shammah cried out, instantly feeling overwhelming pain surge through his entire body. In a fraction of an instant, Shammah could feel the beast's razor-sharp teeth tear through his flesh as a loud crunch filled his ears. The sound was his bone snapping under the pressure of the animal's immense jaws. The masakh shook its massive head from side to side, throwing Shammah hard against the cave wall and severing off his lower leg.

The masakh, claiming its new trophy, pulled its head out of the cave and could be heard devouring its freshly plucked morsel.

As soon as the beast removed itself, several men ran forward, grabbed Shammah by his limp arms, and dragged him deeper into the narrow cavern, blood trailing from what was left of his mangled leg.

Dropping down next to him, Dan immediately assessed the damage. Shammah was no longer conscious and his breathing was labored. Dan put his hand to what was left of the mangled limb and spurting blood covered his hand and arm.

The masakh once again began ramming its snout into the mouth of the cave, roaring and hissing, trying to reach another life to take, but its attempts were in vain. Everyone was now far enough back to keep clear of the animal's savage jaws.

"Galon! Galon, are you dead or are you here?" Dan shouted amongst the shadows of men standing around him.

"I am here, captain," Galon said, working his way through the men in front of him and kneeling down next to Dan. "Is he hurt badly?"

"I'd say so. His right leg is gone below the knee and he is bleeding out," Dan said in a strained voice.

Galon's eyes grew wide.

"I know you are not a healer by trade but you have had healing training. I saw you working with the wounded earlier. Can you handle this?"

Galon didn't answer the question. He didn't need to. He began barking orders to the men around him to search the cave for water, and to surrender any clean linens or wool on them. Galon stripped his own sash from his body and used it to tie a tourniquet above the wound.

"Get a torch down here so I can see better!" Galon yelled out to no one in particular.

One of the men knelt next to Galon with a torch, lighting up Shammah's injuries. Several men gasped at the mangled flesh of their commander's leg.

Galon inspected the wound and found the tourniquet was doing its job, but there was still blood oozing to the ground.

"Is he going to live?" Broc asked solemnly, cringing at the sound of the masakh as it continued to bang its head through the entrance of the cave, hissing and growling all the while.

Galon didn't answer. He didn't want to answer. He put his bloodied hand upon Shammah's chest and felt his strong lungs rapidly pushing air in and out of his body. Galon nodded in approval as he felt Shammah's heart pumping rapid and hard, but he also noticed Shammah's skin was beginning to get cold and clammy.

"We need to cover him. His body is going into shock. We have to keep him warm," Galon said.

Many of the men had already placed their outer garments on the ground next to Galon. He picked them up, several at a time, and draped them over Shammah.

"What about the bleeding?" Broc asked, taking the torch for himself. He lowered the torchlight close to Shammah's leg to get a better look at the wound.

"It has slowed, but it is still seeping. It is a lot of damage…a lot of wound to mend," Galon said with sadness in his voice. "I am sorry. I don't have enough healing knowledge or supplies to deal with this. I—" Galon swallowed hard and then sighed. "I don't know if he is going to make it."

Broc nodded. "Well, I was hoping we were not going to have to do this but it seems—"

Broc was cut off by the beast's deafening roar. It was louder and more agitated than the cries it was spewing previously. The masakh was now going mad with rage as it rammed, clawed, and smashed its head into the cave entrance, trying to find a way to finish the killing spree it had started earlier.

With each impact, dust fell from the ceiling and loose rock began to crumble away from the cavern walls.

"Hiding here will be in vain if that thing brings the mountain down upon us," Dan said, kicking away some rubble which had landed at his feet.

Anger welled up within Broc.

"That's it! I have had enough!" Broc stood, and strutted over to one of the soldiers who still had a spear in his hand. He forcefully snatched it from him, and in a determined march, headed back towards the mouth of the cave.

"You want me?" Broc screamed at the top of his lungs. "Well here I am! Take a big ol' bite out of me! Just like my friend back there!"

He stopped only cubits away from the dragon's head, which was wedged into the opening of the cave.

Holding up his torch, Broc noticed the animal had made some progress. Much of the rock had been broken and scraped away around the entrance and the masakh was now able to get most of its head inside.

Now being able to see the animal's eyes, Broc spotted Shammah's spear, which was still planted deep within its left eye.

This brought a measure of satisfaction to Broc, causing him to smile.

Broc heard someone come up behind him and felt their hand on his shoulder.

"What are you doing? Get back here, you old fool," Dan chided his superior.

Shaking Dan's hand off of his shoulder, Broc ignored him. He turned his attention back to the animal which was desperately trying to reach him...eat him...kill him.

"What's the matter? I am right here! Come and get me!" Broc taunted, lifting his torch up in his left hand and his spear in his right.

The challenge angered the masakh even more. It lashed out its long tongue, attempting to wrap it around Broc's legs, just as it had done to Shammah.

Broc was ready for the attack.

He lunged to the side, and at the same time thrust his spear down hard upon the monster's forked tongue. The sharp broad-headed iron point of the weapon plunged right through the soft flesh of the beast's appendage.

The monster immediately recoiled back, giving out a whine of pain. Upon doing so the animal clamped its jaws down on its own tongue, severing it completely off. The long appendage dropped to the ground and flopped around wildly as if it were a snake which had lost its head. An eruption of black blood came out of the masakh's mouth as it wailed and whined from its self-inflicted wound. Desperately, it writhed and wiggled its head back out of the cave and disappeared from sight, wailing and screeching as it went.

As soon as the beast removed his head from the cave, a wash of soft light peered through the opening, illuminating Broc and Dan.

Dawn had finally reached them and the night was fading away.

CHAPTER 39

Rachel lightly leaned on her bow as she stood on the palace rooftop and watched the first gleam of morning light break over the eastern horizon. Brilliant colors of red and purple glided over the sky above, tucking away the glimmering stars into the far-reaching heavens.

Closing her eyes, Rachel took in a deep breath, held it for a few seconds, and then slowly exhaled. She felt her body relax and her mind calm as the air escaped from between her lips. She kept her eyes closed for a moment longer as she listened to the sounds of the world coming to life around her. She could hear a large array of birds flying to and fro in the nearby trees, singing happily as they celebrated the birth of a new morning. She could hear the creek and crack of wagon wheels being pulled along by groaning oxen on the roads below. She could hear the murmurs of human voices and the banging of shop doors as the merchants set up their booths several blocks away. The city was coming to life and El had granted another day.

The smell of freshly baked bread stirred Rachel out of her relaxed state and she opened her eyes. She put her hand to her abdomen. Her stomach rumbled and groaned, begging her to break her fast. Rachel ignored her body's pleads of hunger and strolled to the northern edge of the rooftop. There would be time for food later when she felt a better sense of security for those beyond the wall.

Once again, Rachel looked up and took in the sun lit horizon. She smiled at the sight and began to worship El in her heart.

"Good morning, Jehovah," Rachel said in a whispered voice, knowing El could hear every prayer she delivered. "Thank you for the beautiful morning. My soul is distressed, Lord, and I yearn for the safe return of my friends who are far beyond my sight. Please protect them and bring them back to us, whole and unharmed."

Rachel felt a breeze caress the side of her face, causing a strand of hair to fall down over her left eye. She smiled, imagining that was El's way of saying, "I hear you, and good morning to you, too."

She brushed her soft, black hair back over her ear with one delicate stroke of her hand, and then lifted her eyes back over to the northern plains beyond the city. She watched as an unseen breeze swept across the wheat fields, causing them to wave from side to side, dancing a dance they had experienced many times before. Although she was too far away to hear it, she imagined the sound of the rustling heads of grain and the soothing symphony it made when the wind played over the plains. The thought relaxed and soothed her, for her soul continued to feel restless.

For the past three days, she had never felt more nervous or anxious in her life. If the pressure of her wedding was not enough, the stress of her friends and loved ones made things worse. She worried for Dan, Broc, and Shammah, along with the other brave men who had gone to hunt the beast everyone was talking about. Rumors had been going around the city that whole villages and towns had been destroyed.

She was also concerned for King Huram and her future husband, Tide. She still didn't want to get married, but she did not want to see anything ill happen to the prince or his father. They were good men and no one deserved to die within the jaws of a beast.

It was only yesterday, merchants came from Beth-Shan saying hundreds had been slaughtered and that King Huram, along with all those with him, had been killed. When the merchants were questioned and challenged for proof, they could give none. Solomon had dispatched fifty more men from his own personal guard to see if the rumors were true.

Rachel stood for some time, staring, hoping, and praying she would see a troop of men crest over the northern horizon, marching home with good news. Occasionally, a group would appear coming south on the northern road, but it always ended up being merchants or farmers, traveling to sell their fruit or wares for the day.

More time passed, and she convinced herself that looking upon the road with this kind of worry was not doing her any good. She needed to distract herself, which was why she had come up to the roof in the first place. She had come up here to practice her archery and to divert her mind from the troubles consuming her.

Placing her hunting bow over her shoulders, Rachel grabbed both ends and flexed the weapon downwards a few times like she had been taught by Captain Broc many years ago. She could still hear the old man's voice during her first archery lesson.

> *"Always flex the bow over your shoulders before you string it up. If you hear it crack under gentle strength then it will surely snap when you draw it back to fire. A broken weapon is a useless weapon, and a useless weapon will get you killed."*

Rachel smiled at the memory. She had only been a child then, maybe only eight or nine seasons old. Even at such a young age she used to follow Abaddon everywhere he went, even to his sword and archery training. As Broc tutored Abaddon, he made Rachel stand to the side and copy the techniques he was teaching, mostly to keep her out of the way. She never really had a talent for swordplay, but when it came to shooting the bow, Broc found she had a real natural ability. She did so well that Broc started training her apart from Abaddon's lessons. After years of practice, she became better than any archer in the military or in the king's guard. She could hit any marker or target dead on from fifty cubits.

Over the last few years, she had also mastered shooting her bow from horseback and was now able to accurately shoot two or three arrows at a time.

Broc had mentioned to her more than once, *"Too bad you're not a man. Your skill would be a huge asset on the battlefield."*

Rachel smiled to herself as the thoughts kept flowing through her mind. She bent her bow a few more times, satisfied she heard no cracks in the wooden weapon. She looped her ox-gut string around the bottom end of the bow, used her foot to bend the bow back, and then tied off the string to the other end. Within moments she was ready to shoot.

Rachel had brought thirty arrows up with her and had set up three straw mannequins to use as targets. Each mannequin had painted marks on it, identifying strike points on the human body. Each mark represented a kill shot or a terminal wound.

In less than a minute Rachel had shot all thirty arrows, each one finding its target.

She was about to move towards the lifeless dummies to retrieve her arrows when a loud noise came from a shofar, a ram's horn, from the northern gate. Rachel dropped her bow and ran to the northern side of the roof, just in time to see one of the guards on the northern tower blow his shofar once again. The trumpet blast was long and clear as it resounded throughout the hillside.

Looking north to the horizon, Rachel saw a great mass of men, horses, and carriages come into view. Even though the site was some distance away, she could tell it was Benaiah and the royal guard returning. She smiled when she saw King Huram, Prince Tide, and their vast accompaniment traveling amongst Benaiah's troops. The rumors were false! The king was alive!

The guard on the tower blew a third long blast on his shofar.

One of Benaiah's men responded with three long horn blasts of their own, signaling the troop approaching was friend and not foe.

Upon hearing the trumpeted response, the guard atop the tower blew one more blast, although this time it was higher pitched and in varied notes, signifying a welcome call.

For the next hour, Rachel watched with curiosity and fascination as King Huram's company entered the city. She guessed there must have been more than a thousand men accompanying the king and the prince, which didn't include the many women, children, and servants trailing behind them.

The whole sight made her smile and joy consumed her. El had answered her prayers for protection. Then, as she thought a bit, her stomach began to flutter and well up into her throat. A sense of panic and anxiety came over her. Sure, she was glad the king and the prince were safe; but now, seeing her future husband arrive…made her marriage arrangement feel even more real. It was no longer idle talk about a man from a distant land, coming to marry her. It was now a reality, and the man *himself* was here, in this very city. In a week's time she would be saying good-bye to all she knew and loved and moving to a different kingdom to live with a people she knew nothing about. She would be married to a man she did not know, did not love, and felt no respect for. This was happening, and she felt powerless to do anything about it. She wanted to run. She didn't care where, she just wanted to run away and leave it all behind.

Her emotions were getting the best of her and she felt a tear of frustration and self-pity escape down her cheek. She looked back to the northern horizon, hoping…willing one more person to come trailing into view.

"Abaddon. Where are you? Please come home. I need you," Rachel said in a whisper…in a prayer.

CHAPTER 40

"Can he be moved?" Broc asked, returning to the interior of the cave where Galon was attending to Shammah.

Galon shook his head. "I wouldn't recommend it. He is still oozing blood and it is starting to turn black. If we don't do something soon, I fear blood poisoning is going to take him before the actual injury will."

Broc swore under his breath. "I was able to wound the masakh and it has left for now, but I am afraid it will return. We have a small window of escape."

Galon nodded, knowing the choice Broc needed to make. "Go. Take the men and make a run for it. I will stay here with Shammah and try to keep him alive until you can come back with more men to extract us."

"That could take days," Dan pointed out. "We all know he won't make it that long. Plus, I am willing to bet that some of our men are still alive out there. Some of them may just be wounded, and if so, they need our help. I don't feel right about turning tail and running."

A weak voice escaped from Shammah's lips, "Go. Get the…..the men to…safety. Don't let them die….here. Get them…" Shammah's face twisted in pain and his eyes rolled to the back of his head.

Squatting next to him, Broc put a gentle hand to his shoulder. "You focus on staying alive, my friend, and you let me worry about getting these men home."

Standing back up, Broc looked at his men. He then realized just how few of them were present. *How many have we lost to this beast?*

Dan must have known what Broc was thinking. "Eighteen," he said with a bit of pain in his voice. "Out of fifty men, we only have eighteen left."

Thirty-two dead men were lying slaughtered or severely injured outside of the cave. The realization made Broc queasy. He took a deep breath and pushed the thought aside.

Looking to the remnant around him, Broc said, "Men, I know you are tired, weary, and hungry. We have been beaten up and knocked down, but we who remain alive still have a job to do. We set out three days ago to hunt down a beast and send it back to Gehenna where it came from! We accomplished that feat. But then, we found out the enemy has plagued us with another abomination. One bigger, faster, and deadlier than the first. But mark my words, men: This beast will also be struck down and killed!"

Broc looked to his fellow captain, "Dan?"

Dan held up the masakh's severed tongue, measuring almost four cubits in length, lying limp and lifeless in his large hand.

The men began to murmur and voice their approval, feeling the pride of war well up within them once again.

Snatching the tongue from Dan's hand, Broc raised it high into the air. "We will beat this thing and that monster will fall, even if we have to do it one piece at a time!"

The men shouted, chanting over and over, "Harag! Harag! Harag…Kill! Kill! Kill!"

The sound of the men's charged voices echoed loudly throughout the cave. Not far away, the masakh heard the war cry and responded with a roar of its own, just to let the men know it was not afraid and was waiting for them.

Looking to the faces of his men, Broc saw confidence and strength, where moments ago, their eyes had betrayed weariness and self-doubt.

One of the men spoke up. "Captain. What now? What is the plan? Between all of us, we only have three spears. We can't launch much of an attack with that."

"Fear not, men," Broc reassured. "First things, first. We keep Shammah from dying, and to do that we are going to need a fire. A really hot fire. We are going to have to scorch his flesh over the wound, which will close up the blood vessels and prevent him from bleeding out. And to do that, we need wood."

The men glanced around the cave. It was clear that there was no wood to be had inside of the rocky cavern.

The same soldier who had spoken up earlier did so again. "Ah, sir? We have no wood to burn except the shafts of our three spears. Do you want us to break them down?"

"Save the pig stickers, boys," Broc said, and then looked to Dan. "Feel like getting some sunshine?"

Dan smiled. "I thought you would never ask. I need two volunteers. Just outside the mouth of the cave on the right hand side is a large downed oak branch. We need to run out, grab it, and bring it back inside. Who is with me?"

Seventeen men raised their hands, all save Galon, whose hands were busy keeping pressure on Shammah's wound, though his eyes said he was willing to go.

Dan felt humbled by the show of dedication from his soldiers. He looked to two of the larger men and pointed at them to come along with him. Not knowing how heavy the tree limb was, he wanted to make sure they had enough muscle to move it quickly.

The two men asked for the available spears, but Dan interjected. "Forget the weapons. You are going to need both hands to drag that branch. It's a pretty good size."

"Then how will we defend ourselves?" one of the men asked.

"We're not," Dan stated. "A couple of spears is not going to matter if that thing is waiting for us. We just have to get out there, get the branch, and get back into this cave as fast as we possibly can. Hopefully we can do this without the masakh even seeing us."

Leaving the torches behind with the rest of the men, the three warriors traveled through the darkness of the cave until streams of sunlight revealed the opening to the outside world. The transition from darkness to light was hard on their eyes. They took a moment to let their eyes adjust, and then they slowly brought themselves to the edge of the entrance. Dan motioned for the two other men to stay close to the cave's inner wall to avoid standing out in the open.

Looking out at the large area outside of the cave, Dan took in the damage and chaos of the previous night's massacre. What had once been a grassy area with palm and oak trees littering the field was now a trampled mess of beaten grass mixed with mud and blood. Trees were broken and splintered as if a great storm had passed through and decimated the land.

Worse yet, Dan could see the bodies of his fallen brothers cluttering the ground. Many of them were dismembered and savagely torn apart. The sight made Dan queasy and furious at the same time. "These men deserved better than this!" Dan said to himself.

As they moved further out, the group of men heard a low growling accompanied by crunching and gnawing sounds. In slow, deliberate steps, Dan exited on the right side of the cave's entrance while keeping his back against the rock wall. Looking around, he saw the source of the grotesque noises.

About one hundred cubits to the left of the cave stood the masakh with its back towards the men. Its large legs were bent down and its massive head was greedily eating something on the ground in front of it. It didn't take long for Dan to realize what it was devouring. The black beast was consuming its mate, the other masakh they had killed earlier. It was eating its own.

Dan stared at the scene in disgust, as did the two other men with him, but then thanked El for their good fortune. The creature was distracted, which gave them a chance to do what they needed to do.

Turning his eyes away from the beast's feast, Dan looked to his right where the large oak branch sat, no more than ten cubits from where they were standing.

Motioning for the men to follow him, Dan hunched over into a hunter's crouch and silently moved to the fallen tree limb.

Dan glanced back to the masakh, relieved to find it oblivious to their presence and enjoying its meal.

Once the men had a firm hold of the branch's base, Dan mouthed the word, *Slowly,* to his crew.

The men nodded, and as one they carefully began to turn the massive branch towards the entrance of the cave. Dan felt the heft of the tree limb and every muscle in his body groaned against the strain. The oak branch was heavier than he had anticipated. The group had a difficult time stifling their grunts and groans as they moved the branch closer to the cave.

And then it happened.

A twig from under the branch snapped, loud and clear. Immediately, all three of them dropped into a crouch, hoping to blend in with the green foliage sticking out around the branch. They felt their pulses quicken and their faces drained of blood as they hoped and prayed the beast didn't hear their mistake.

The masakh stopped eating and held its head high up into the air. It had obviously heard the noise, for it stood motionless for a moment and then turned its large head towards the cave.

The animal's snout was covered in black, oily blood, and chunks of flesh were hanging off of its razor-sharp teeth. Dan held his breath, daring not to breathe, willing himself to be as stone.

After what seemed like an eternity, the beast finally broke its stare away from the cave and went back to devouring its mate.

Dan slowly breathed out and closed his eyes to calm his nerves. He re-opened his eyes with a determination to get the job done. With great care, he rose back to a standing position, as did the other two men. Once again they hefted the enormous branch and it began to move behind the men's pull.

They had gained about two cubits worth of distance when a loud screech rang out in the sky high above them. Dan instinctively looked up to see a large, white bird flying in a wide circular pattern around the decimated camp. He recognized the shrill cry of the fowl from the previous night's attack. Before the masakh had emerged from the sea, it had been these same cries which had terrorized the camp.

As the bird continued its horrid cries, Dan looked to the masakh and noticed the beast had stopped eating and was now looking straight at him and his men. The trio stood there, unmoving, staring back into the dragon's yellow eyes. Dan made a mental note that Shammah's spear was still lodged firmly into the beast's left eye.

"Don't move!" Dan said sternly to his men under his breath. "Don't crouch, don't breathe, don't do anything! I am not sure he can see us very well in the sunlight, and with only one good eye at that."

The masakh stood still, staring but not advancing, knowing something was there, but not certain of it.

The large, white bird screeched even louder, causing the men to wince upon hearing the high-pitched wail. But then, unexpectedly, the bird dove down and attacked the masakh. It came down hard on the beast's right eye and savagely began to claw at it. Again and again, the bird soared high into the air only to come diving down again to assault the Masakh's eye.

The monster forgot about the men and focused on the aerial attacker, snapping at it with its powerful jaws, each time missing its target.

"This is our chance! Move!" Dan said. The men put all the strength they had into picking up the large piece of wood and moving it forward. No longer caring about silence or stealth, they were able to drag the branch surprisingly fast. They passed through the entrance of the cave, and none too soon. As they scrambled across the threshold, the beast came skidding over the ground behind them, snapping its jaws, desiring one more morsel of human flesh.

The rest of the men in the cave had heard the commotion and came running to the cave's entrance, helping the three brave souls drag the large branch further into the mountain.

The masakh bent its head low to the ground and roared upon seeing all the men outside of its grasp. It appeared as though it was about to ram its head into the cave as it had before, but then halted, as if remembering what happened the last time it attempted such a feat.

The angry animal began to pace back and forth, causing the earth to tremble with each step it took. Its roar was a clear sign of anger, losing its patience, desiring to end this long, drawn-out game.

The pacing stopped as the beast stared at the group of men for a moment. The warriors stirred a bit, feeling death radiate from the creature's unnerving glare.

"If I didn't know better, I'd say that thing is thinking and plotting on how to kill us," Dan said.

"That is nonsense—" Broc replied, coming up beside him, his voice trailing off as the masakh backed up, taking one giant step at a time.

"Have you ever seen an animal walk backwards like that before?" Dan asked, eyes glued on the large reptile. Once the masakh had backed up to about fifty cubits, it stopped, roared out a menacing cry, and ran forward at full speed.

"No…never have I—" Broc began to say, not believing what he was seeing.

Curiosity turned to horror as Broc saw the charging beast. The men had little time to react as the creature reached the cave with a few giant leaps of its massive feet.

Broc thought for sure the beast was going to dive in and try to snatch as many of them as possible, but he was wrong. Instead, the masakh slammed its head into the rock above the cave's entrance and the whole mountain above them shook.

Immediately dust and rock jolted loose from the ceiling of the cavern and came crashing down upon the men. Several of the soldiers, including both captains, were knocked to the ground by the falling debris. Dust filled the air, causing the men to choke and gag with each breath they took.

"We have to get out of here," one man coughed out. "I can't breathe."

"Nobody leave!" Dan ordered as he made his way back onto his feet, coughing as well. "That is what it wants! It wants us to go running out! Quick! Tie your sashes around your mouths to filter out the dust!"

As the men complied, Dan reached down and helped Broc get up. Broc winced as he felt pain shoot through his body. He inspected his shoulder and noted a bloody gash on his left arm.

"You're hurt." Dan said, noticing the wound.

"It is just a scratch. Anyway, that is the least of our worries. Look."

Dan looked up and took a few steps towards the mouth of the cave. About a cubit of fallen rock from the hillside above had come down to cover the entrance.

And then, all of a sudden, just as the dust was clearing, Dan saw the giant beast slam its head again above the cave, causing more rock to tumble down around them.

"He is trying to bury us alive!" Dan shouted, noting that the way out was now half covered in fallen rock. "We have to flee or die!"

"What about Shammah?" one of the men asked urgently. "We can't leave him!"

"I've got him!" came a voice from the back of the cavern.

The men looked back and there stood Galon with Shammah draped over his right shoulder. "We are not going back that way!" Galon shouted through a piece of cloth wrapped around his head. "The whole back end of the cave is coming down. We barely got out of there!"

Broc and Dan looked forward again and dread filled their hearts as they watched the masakh prepare itself for another crushing charge.

"If it hits the mountain one more time, we will all be buried alive." Broc announced, feeling his hope draining away.

"And if we make a run for it, we will be torn apart and slaughtered." Dan said, giving in to the same despair.

"Either way…we're dead."

CHAPTER 41

Rucha felt himself floating in a sea of black, a dark formless void which toyed with his mind and thoughts. He felt as if his body was numb and weightless, bobbing along some eternal river of lifelessness. Time and again, he would desperately call out, but he found there was no one there to receive his cries. The eeriness of the darkness began to strain against his soul and the fear of loneliness and abandonment consumed him.

Is this death? Is this what life will be like past the doors of the living? Alone...dark...empty?

Rucha recalled these thoughts over and over until what seemed like an eternity had passed. Floating, formless, and in total despair, Rucha desired death all over again and wanted no part of the great abyss he found himself in.

But then...there *was* something.

Something gleamed in the distance. It was small. A pinprick of hope in the darkness.

What is that? Does it bring pain or does it bring life? Rucha desired to know.

Rucha closed his eyes, or at least he thought he closed his eyes. It was so dark and he had been there for so long, he could no longer tell the difference. And then he remembered something. He had no eyes. They were taken from him. Gone. Just like his life.

But yet, there it was. A pinprick, a gleam, a radiance of life in the void.

It was light.

Rucha attempted to move toward it, but there was no ground to walk upon, no footholds to grasp with his hands and feet. He tried calling out but his voice was distant and strange, as if the darkness craved his silence.

But then he noticed something. The light was coming to him. Fraction by fraction, breath by breath, the pinprick of hope was getting closer. Or was it growing bigger? He could not tell. All he knew was this thing was giving him hope anew. He could feel the darkness around him straining and fighting to keep its place, to keep its hold on him, willing him to stay in his isolated coffin of death.

But death would not have its reign, not in this moment. Rucha wanted to feel life again, to feel freedom apart from the gloom and darkness which was consuming him.

As the light continued to grow, the black around him grew grayer and the void suffocating him gave way to a voice. A soft, kind voice. A voice which drew Rucha up from the depths and ignited a small spark of warmth within him. The voice gave no hint of male or female, but provided calming tones, like gentle waves lapping upon a lazy shore.

The voice stirred deep within his soul, *"Abishai, son of Zeruiah. It is time to come home."*

When Rucha heard his Hebrew name, he felt the light recede from him and the shadow of darkness pushed back in around him, through him. A strain of anger and mockery twisted in his gut.

"Abishai is no longer here, but only Rucha remains," Rucha spat. "I am Rucha! The Phantom of the Seas, the Ghost who terrifies the souls of men!"

> *"A ghost…yes. Formless and without substance you have become. In this your name is rightly given. But can a soul know purpose, peace, or fulfillment without a heart to contain it, without love to seal it? Aren't you tired of floating aimlessly, not knowing, not caring, not believing?"*

The words coursed through him and he felt desire with every word he heard. The voice brought with it hope and yearning, something he had not felt in a very long time. The voice's last words hung upon him like a great weight, a burden too big for him to carry.

"Believing." Rucha mumbled. He thought for a moment, and then shouted, "Belief in what? What is there to believe in? What is there to have faith in? How can one have hope in such a place as this?"

Rucha stared into the small gleam of distant light, waiting, desiring an answer which would make sense. When no reply came, a new force of frustration erupted within him.

"How can I know this faith or hope, or even love, if all I have ever known has deserted me? Turned its back on me! Betrayed me! Shall I love deception and those who have abandoned me?"

Again, Rucha listened intently for the voice's reply, but all was silent. He noticed the small speck of light was now growing smaller and was moving away.

"Wait! No, don't leave!" Rucha cried out, fearing the thought of being alone and encased in darkness again. "I am sorry! My rage is only out of frustration. I still seek your counsel!"

The voice spoke once more, although now it was quieter and distant.

> *"Do you not know the meaning of your true name?
> Abishai, gift from El. Remember and know your name. El
> still loves you. He desires you to come home. Return to Him
> and all will be forgiven; all will be made right again. Come
> home, Abishai, come home."*

And with those few words the voice faded away completely.

Rucha watched with inner turmoil as the pinprick of light grew dimmer and dimmer until utter darkness consumed him once again.

But something was different than it was before. He no longer felt weightless or disoriented. He could now sense pressure on his back, under his legs and on the back of his head. The sense of emptiness was going away and he began to feel his body again.

He didn't feel like he was standing up, but possibly lying down on the ground. One by one, his senses began returning to him. His ears were the first to respond. He could hear the calling of birds around him…gulls, if he wasn't mistaken. And there was something else…a roaring sound…or was it lapping? It was definitely water, possibly from the waves of the sea hitting a sandy beach.

Next, his sense of smell rushed in upon him as if someone had flipped a switch inside of his mind. He could smell fresh air and the aroma of the salty sea. He also took in the scent of wet earth and sand all around him.

And then the greatest pleasure of all made him gasp. A warm wind caressed his face and tickled his skin, sending goose-flesh rippling all throughout his body.

Becoming overwhelmed with the return of his senses, Rucha began to laugh and cry out his good fortune. "I cannot be dead, for a dead man could not feel such things!"

He calmed himself, for something was not completely right yet. He still could not see. He knew he had no eyes, but before, he had a sight beyond sight.

Is that gone now? Never to return?

These thoughts brought another thought to mind. He had once held a demon within which granted him special abilities. Was the demon gone along with those gifts, and if so, what kind of man would he be now? Without the ability to see, he would be no better than the old blind beggars who scrapped for food outside the city gates.

As Rucha pondered these things, a great flash of light erupted before him, sending a jolt of pain shooting through his skull. His body felt as though a living fire was consuming him, ravaging him and eating away at his flesh.

He heard a voice call out from within him. Not the tender sweet voice of peace he had experienced earlier, but a raspy voice, one he had heard before. The demon, Amon, was once again possessing him, making its claim upon his soul.

"Peace, human. Relax and let it happen. The pain is less if you just let go," the demon coaxed.

Rucha couldn't help but to scream out in agony as the demon settled in. And then, it was over. The pain faded away and Rucha worked to calm himself and regulate his breathing.

And then, as if someone had sparked a candle, his vision returned to him. Not his original eyesight in which he could witness the world in vibrant color, but the sight of the spirit world in which all was gray and void of life.

"Do I not give you what you desire?" the demon voiced in a hissing tone. "Do you not need what I can give you?"

Rucha gave no reply and the spirit needed none as it went silent, sealing its lips once more.

For the longest time, Rucha laid there on the beach and enjoyed the senses of life. He took in the sound of the crashing waves from the sea, only cubits away from him. He breathed in the salty air, enjoying every breath he consumed. He even found pleasure in the coarse wet sand beneath him.

Within a short amount of time, Rucha's memories fully came back to him and he remembered the horror which brought him to this point. The memory of thousands of flies...no, wait. Dagon had said they were demons. Tiny demons who did the bidding of their master, Beelzebub. They had eaten his flesh and nearly killed him. He had gone to Dagon to save his life, which was the last thing he remembered before waking up in the darkness...in the void.

The memories made him sit up straight so he could look over his body. The first thing he noticed was his lack of clothing. There he lay, naked and exposed for all the world to see. In embarrassment, Rucha looked all around, but found he was alone and no one was there to see him in such a state.

He took a closer look at his body and was relieved to find no open wounds, no bones sticking out, and his skin was once again whole. That was the good news. The bad news was, his body was now covered in scars and dark blemishes.

Rucha felt a sense of dread well up within him as he realized how many scars decorated his body. He dragged his fingers lightly over his arms, chest and legs and despaired at how thick and angry each scar was. He had seen marks like these before, on men from battle whose wounds had been sealed up by heated iron. The skin would welt and eventually, when the wound healed, the scar would be thick and protruding from the body. Rucha's body was now covered with hundreds of these grotesque scars.

His dread turned to numbness as Rucha reached up to touch his face. He felt two long, thick, scars. One ran from his right temple down to the corner of his mouth, and the other went from the center of his forehead, down between his eyes, over his nose, and then turned to go over his left cheek and down to his neck.

Rucha felt his hands begin to tremble as fury surged up within him. "Is this what it means to be healed?" He screamed out at the top of his lungs. "Is this the work of the great and mighty Dagon? To sear up my flesh with fire and leave me as a living monster?"

Rucha half expected his demon to voice itself and chastise him for his words, but all was silent.

In his anger, Rucha had managed to get to his feet, but found his legs to be weak and fell back down to the sandy ground. This only fueled his rage even more and he screamed out violent curses as he worked himself up again.

After spewing every curse he could think of, Rucha reached up with both hands and grabbed fistfuls of his own hair. He pulled hard until he could feel severe pain in his scalp. And then, he began to laugh. He didn't know why. He just started laughing as if he didn't care any longer. Maybe it would be better to be dead than to live looking like this.

Rucha realized he had been stumbling forward and now found himself knee deep in the sea. Cool water gently lapped up against his thighs. He let go of the hair on his head and looked out upon the vastness of the Great Sea lying before him.

All I have to do is start walking and I can let the sea take me. A man who looks like this deserves death, Rucha thought to himself.

Rucha took a step forward, seriously considering the watery fate, but stopped and took two steps back. The thought of the void, the darkness, and the loneliness he had experienced earlier came rushing back to him.

Is that what I really want?

"Hey! You're awake!" came a voice, loud and boisterous from behind Rucha.

Dropping his head to his chest, Rucha let out an agitated sigh. There was no point in turning around to see who it was. The irritating tone was unmistakable. "Maybe I should kill myself, just to be rid of Achish's nagging presence," Rucha uttered to himself.

He was about to turn around and walk back to the shore, when a large black cloth landed on top of his head.

"Put that cloak on!" Achish yelled. "I am tired of looking at your naked body and seeing all those nasty looking scars. I tell you, it was no pleasure watching Dagon work on your body. After you passed out, he turned back into his dragon form, and boy, was he mad! I don't know what you said to him before you blacked out, but he went completely insane. He spewed fire everywhere! That ancient tree we saw? Gone. He lit that thing up like the sun itself had come down to earth. When he finally calmed down, he ripped out one of his teeth. He breathed on the tooth and it ignited into a white hot flame. Then he went to work on you, burning and searing your flesh to close up your wounds."

As Achish continued speaking, Rucha slowly put on the cloak and wearily made his way back to the sandy shore. Achish's voice sounded like a buzzing in his mind. A buzzing he wanted to stop.

"Shut up, Achish! I don't want to hear it," Rucha said, putting his hands to his temples.

"It was the most amazing and yet gruesome thing I have ever seen. And I can still smell it. The smell of your flesh as it melted under the intense heat of Dagon's tooth."

"I said, shut up!" Rucha said louder, now covering his ears, not wanting to hear how Dagon had made him into such a monster.

Achish continued, not even bothering to acknowledge Rucha. "Man, it was a good thing you were out cold because the whole thing looked extremely painful. It was like I could feel your pain, just by watching it."

"You could feel my pain?" Rucha screamed. "You don't know what pain is!"

Quickly closing the gap between himself and Achish, Rucha punched him in the face as hard as he could.

Blood exploded from Achish's nose and the fat king went flying backwards to the ground, landing squarely on his back. Rucha was about to jump on top of him to deliver several more blows, but stopped short when he saw both of Achish's bodyguards appear twenty cubits to his right.

Clenching his fists, Rucha shrilled out, "What do you know of pain, you fat sow? All you have ever known is pleasure, with your wine and women and all your many servants. You are weak, Achish! Weak and foul! Why you were ever picked to lead Dagon's army is beyond me!"

Achish rolled to his side and quickly stood back up. "Goats blood!" He cursed, holding his hands over his face. "You broke my nose, you little whelp! And after all I have done for you!"

Rucha watched Achish turn from his light-hearted self to a crazed animal. His eyes grew wide and bulged slightly outwards. Malice filled his face as he licked at the blood running from his nose down over his lips.

Lunging forward, Achish threw a crushing blow to Rucha's jaw. Rucha felt something crack in his mouth and his body violently whipped around as he fell to the ground. He then felt an even greater blow to his back. Achish's knee came down hard between his shoulder blades as the king grabbed a fistful of Rucha's hair and wrenched his head backwards.

"Now you listen to me, you Hebrew puke!" Achish said angrily, leaning in close to Rucha's ear. "Do not forget why I am the king of this army. I...*hate*...Hebrews! I want everyone of your kind dead and impaled on poles, littered all throughout the land of Israel. And I want all the world to know that it was I, King Achish, who slaughtered them all! And know this, you little worm, if you are not with me, you are against me! I have no problem ramming a pole down your gullet and staking your corpse right beside your kindred! Am I clear?"

Rucha's anger burned within him as he listened to Achish spit his words into his ear. No matter how hard he tried, Rucha couldn't budge underneath Achish's weight and strength. Even with the power of his demon, he could not move.

Achish continued speaking, but the crazed anger seemed to drain away from his voice. "I know this has been tough on you, and what happened to you down in that cave would have been hard for any man to take, but you have been given a second chance. You joined me of your own free will because you wanted revenge on those who betrayed you. Don't lose your focus! We have to work together to destroy Israel."

Achish released Rucha and took several steps back, preparing himself in case Rucha tried to attack him again.

Feeling the pressure leave his shoulders, Rucha jumped to his feet and turned towards Achish, ready to fight…ready to kill!

"I know you are having a hard time dealing with the way you look," Achish said, holding up his hands to deter Rucha from charging again. "Trust me, I know. Look at me. Do you think I enjoy looking the way I do? Being this fat? I see how people look at me and how disgusted they are by my appearance. I know what it means to care about your vanity, but you have to realize there is another side to the coin. Your scars, your blemishes, your eyes, they now strike fear into all who see them. Men fear all things which are different from them. They fear things they don't understand. Use the tainted body Dagon has given you to ignite that fear into those who serve you *and* oppose you!"

Rucha felt his body relax as he found truth in Achish's words. He knew his men already feared him, but now…now they would be terrified of him. Achish was right. Instead of mourning what he had lost, he should be taking advantage of what he had gained.

"Are we good?" Achish asked as he wiped his arm across his bloodied nose.

Rucha glared at Achish and still felt a strong desire to leap forward and strangle the life out of him. He noted Achish's two shade demons were gone, but probably not far away.

"I said, are we good?" Achish repeated in a loud, stern voice.

"Yes! We're good!" Rucha shouted back. *For now.*

"Good," Achish said, lowering his arms back to his sides. "Now that we are done with this foolishness, we have a lot to discuss. Dagon has revealed to me the next stage of his plan."

CHAPTER 42

Broc and Dan watched hopelessly as the masakh bent its head low to the ground and began to flex its hind legs, preparing to make one more deadly charge for the cave.

"Forget this!" Dan said loudly for all his men to hear. "I am not dying this way! I would rather die fighting than to be helplessly buried alive! Who is with me?"

The men gave a loud shout in agreement.

As one, the group sprinted forward, Dan and Broc leading the charge. They came to an abrupt halt when they met the waist high pile of rocks which had fallen at the cave's entrance.

An ear-piercing screech filled the air. The masakh lifted its head skyward towards the irritating sound.

The men watched in amazement as they witnessed a large white bird descend and attack the beast's face. The bird's sharp talons repeatedly clawed and tore at the masakh's eyes, all the while screeching its ear-piercing war cry.

"This is our chance," yelled Broc. "Let's get out of here!"

The men started to make their way over the pile of rocks in front of them when something black fell from the mountainside high above them and landed with a loud thud upon the ground between them and the masakh.

At first glance, Broc thought it was a black lioness, coming down from the northern hills to take part in the feast of dead flesh which was scattered around the camp. He realized he was wrong when the dark figure slowly stood from its crouched position.

It was no animal at all. It was a man. A man covered from head to toe in a black hooded cloak. Except for the man's hands, not a hint of skin could be seen on the stranger's entire body.

"Who in thunder is that?" Dan asked out loud.

Broc didn't answer but simply watched.

The man dressed in black turned his head to the side, but did not look back at the men in the cave. His facial profile revealed nothing but a large hood overshadowing his face. A low, calm voice came from the mysterious man.

"Stay in the cave and don't come out until this is over."

Without waiting for a response, the stranger withdrew a sword from within his cloak and calmly began to walk towards the wild beast, which was still savagely snapping its jaws at the large bird.

When the man was no more than twenty cubits from the masakh, he called out in a loud voice, "Leirba! Retrieve the spear!"

Upon hearing the command, the white bird flew high into the air, hovered for a moment, and then, with great speed, dove down towards the masakh again. The giant reptile saw the bird coming and opened its jaws wide to devour its attacker.

Right at the last moment, the bird broke to the right and firmly grasped the wooden shaft of the spear sticking out of the masakh's left eye. Using its searing speed and the heft of its powerful wings, the bird ripped the weapon from the beast's eye socket, along with its eyeball. The great bird lifted the spear away in its large talons and disappeared over the surrounding trees.

The masakh roared out in pain and whipped its head back and forth, clawing at its own empty eye socket, as if it could fix what it had just lost.

Without giving it time to adjust, the man in black took a few more steps forward and jeered, "Demon! Finish what you have started! Come and get me, you foul beast!"

The masakh stopped shaking his head and wailing in pain as it let out a massive snort from its nose, spraying bile and black blood all over the ground in front of it. The dragon tilted its head to the side and glared at the man with its one good eye. The masakh's eye grew large and wide as if it recognized the hooded man. The animal reared its head back and hissed a great guttural hiss, which shook the earth and made the flesh on the man's bones vibrate.

With a speed greater than a creature of its size should have, the masakh pounced forward, jaws open wide, ready to devour the man.

Even though the monster's speed was impressive, the man's reaction was even more so. The stranger bolted to his right, rolled once, and leapt high into the air, grabbing hold of the beast's protruding horn on the side of its head. Before the masakh could respond to what was happening, the stranger thrust his sword deep into the monster's empty eye socket.

The beast threw its head back and roared for all it was worth. With an iron grip, the man held firm to the animal's horn with one hand and the hilt of his planted sword with the other. The masakh tried to swat away the intruder with its front claws, but the warrior simply kicked them away.

When the moment was right and the masakh stopped moving its head, the cloaked warrior forced his weapon in deeper, giving the blade a mighty twist, grinding the blade into the base of the monster's skull.

As if El had taken its very soul away, the animal stopped roaring, its claws stopped flailing, and it became like a stone statue towering over the clearing. Dark black streams of blood began to run freely from the beast's mouth and eye socket.

Like the falling of a freshly cut cedar tree, the great and terrible masakh came crashing down to the ground, dead and lifeless.

The earth shook from the impact of its landing.

The stranger jumped clear of the falling beast before it hit the ground, and rolled several times before gaining his balance. After he stood back up, the Israelite warriors watched the hooded man walk back to the dead dragon. He stood there for a long moment, looking at the lifeless animal. He held up his hands, saw they were covered in the dark, black blood of the beast and shook his head in disgust. He then looked up into the sky above and spoke some words which the men in the cave could not hear. Broc thought it may have been a prayer.

They all watched the stranger reach down and put his hand into the masakh's eye socket, and with a mighty heft, he retrieved his sword. Without cleaning the blade, the mysterious man sheathed his weapon beneath his cloak and began to walk away in the opposite direction of the cave.

"Wait!" called out Broc as he scrambled his way over the mound of rocks in front of him. "Wait! Don't leave! Let us thank you for your help!" Broc said as he ran to catch up with the man in black.

Without turning around, the stranger moved his head to the side and put his hand inside of his cloak as if reaching for his sword.

Seeing the gesture, Broc stopped. "Listen. I mean you no harm. We are no threat to you. We would like to thank you. Have you broken your fast yet this morning? We can offer you food if you are willing to stay a bit while my men go and hunt some game. It is our custom to share a meal with those who help one another, and you have certainly helped us out today. Not only us, but all of Israel!"

Broc noticed Dan and the rest of the men were standing around him, staring at their unknown champion and waiting for a response.

The man in black looked forward again, away from the men, and bowed his head to his chest, as if considering the proposition. But then, without a word, he began to walk away once more.

"Wait!" Broc called out one more time. "At least give us your name."

The man stopped. He stayed quiet for a moment as if the simple question had stumped him. "Just call me...The Stranger. Oh, and captain, you have five wounded men who are still alive. They are half a league west of here within the grove of oak trees. There is also a woman with them."

And with that, the man ran off, disappearing into the vast realm of palm trees which grew along the shore of the sea.

As the last glimpse of the stranger disappeared, a loud *thud* came from the ground, only cubits away from Dan's right foot. All looked to see a spear planted firmly into the ground with the masakh's eye still lodged onto it. It had fallen from the sky.

The men looked upward to see if they could spot the amazing bird that had ripped the spear from the masakh, but it was nowhere in sight.

"Who *was* that?" Dan asked, walking past the dead masakh and staring south, hoping to see one more glimpse of the dragon slayer.

"Didn't you hear him?" Broc replied. "That was…The Stranger."

CHAPTER 43

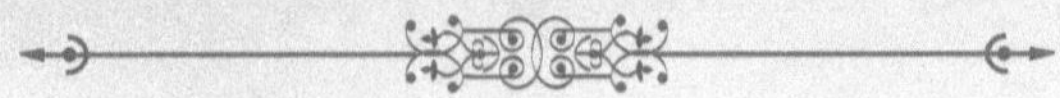

Solomon walked slowly between two rows of grape vines within his own personal vineyard. He reached his hand out to a cluster of grapes and was amazed at the fruit's size. Each grape was no smaller than a quail egg, ripe and lush for the picking.

After breaking the cluster from the vine, Solomon held it along his arm and cradled it to his chest in the same way a parent would with an infant child. He pulled off a single grape from the bundle and popped the whole thing into his mouth. The king was rewarded with a mouthful of nectar as he bit down, cool and sweet to the taste. As he chewed the fruit, he closed his eyes and tilted his face skyward, soaking in the rays from the mid-afternoon sun.

After swallowing the fruit, he let out a deep sigh, willing his body to relax. The last twenty-four hours had been strenuous and nerve racking.

Yesterday morning Benaiah had returned with King Huram and Prince Tide. After they had settled in, the King of Tyre was shocked to hear about his men who had been slaughtered by the masakh. His own trip had been calm, peaceful and without incident, so it was hard for him to believe such a travesty had happened to his men.

King Huram had insisted a company of his own men be sent to Hazor to retrieve the bodies of his fallen soldiers. Solomon had done all he could to reassure the king that he had already dispatched men to Hazor and they would bring back the slain men so they could be honored in a proper burial. After some further reassurances, Huram relented to let Solomon handle the matter.

Later, soon after midday, Jacob had come back with about a fourth of the men he had left with. He reported the massacre in Hazor had been highly exaggerated. There were many casualties, but the majority of the city was alive and well. It was the farmers and the shepherds north of Hazor who were not so lucky. Several farms were decimated and whole flocks of sheep and herds of cattle were slaughtered and devoured.

"The strange part, there were no bodies. We found plenty of animal carcasses, but no human remains," Jacob had reported.

That was the reason he had come back with so few men. He had left the rest of his regiment there in Hazor to look for the missing people, to find out whether they were dead or alive.

It was then, King Huram insisted on sending aid, and sent fifty of his own men to help with the search. This time Solomon did not argue, but simply thanked him for his assistance.

Later that night Solomon was awoken by his servant, Aaron, reporting four riders had arrived from Shammah's hunting party. Without delay, the king met with them and received the news that they had killed the masakh. They also reported that there were casualties and wounded, so the company had set up camp for the night and would be back on the morrow. Solomon was grateful to hear the report, but an uneasiness still stirred within him.

Thanking the four men for their faithful service, Solomon dismissed them to go get a hot meal and to go home to their families and rest. All four of them declined the offer and asked for fifty more men to go back and help the rest of their troop get home safely.

Looking at them closely, Solomon noted the weariness in their eyes and faces. He knew it was useless to deny the request. When warriors made a bond with one another, it was a bond for life. Solomon granted them leave and in less than an hour the four men, along with fifty additional riders, were heading back through the northern gate of the city.

Plagued with an anxious heart, Solomon stayed up the rest of the night pacing on the rooftop and praying for Shammah and his men. Before he knew it, dawn had broken over the horizon and the night had gone. He had returned to his quarters and dressed for a new day, wishing he had returned a bit earlier to try and get a few hours of sleep.

Solomon's morning had been filled with entertaining King Huram and getting to know his future son-in-law, Tide. Solomon discovered they had little in common. The king and his son were sporting men and loved all things of the sea: fishing, whaling, sailing, crafting ships, hunting, and so on and so forth. Solomon had done some fishing when he was a kid but found no joy in it. He enjoyed more personal things, such as reading, painting, writing, and teaching. Clearly, the kings were from two different worlds. Although, there was one thing they did have in common. They both loved Jehovah and enjoyed worshiping the one true El. They had talked at length about the temple Solomon was planning to build, and the voyage ahead to Ophir.

As they communed, Solomon had made it a point to boast upon the ships which Huram and his men had built for the venture. This made Huram swell with pride, which caused him to go on and on as to how the vessels were constructed and how they were the best seafaring crafts he had ever made.

By noon-day meal, Solomon had really wished he had gotten a few hours of sleep the night before. But what was worse than his weariness was the constant anxiety stirring within him. He couldn't help but feel great concern for the hunting party. An overwhelming desire to pray kept washing over his soul and the short silent prayers he had been offering all day was not enough to ease away the worry.

After he had eaten with his guests, Solomon took his leave, explaining he had matters of state to tend to. They would reconvene for the evening meal after sundown, and they would then go over the finer points of the wedding ceremony. This seemed to please King Huram and Prince Tide.

After leaving the banquet hall, Solomon had come straight to the vineyard. This was a place he had come to know well, as he came here whenever he needed to be alone with the Lord. It was not uncommon for him to walk every row within the field, and there were many. On days when he was especially troubled, like today, he would walk the vineyard twice, even three times if need be.

Looking up to the sky, Solomon sighed deeply. The sun was already setting.

Have I really been out here all afternoon? Solomon thought to himself. *Where did the time go? And still no word from Shammah.*

The king found he was on the far side of the vineyard and had a good walk ahead of him to get back to the palace. He figured he still had enough time to return and clean up a bit before meeting King Huram to sup.

As he started his trek home, he heard the voice of someone shouting for him off in the distance.

"My king! Is that you?"

Solomon stopped and strained his eyes to see who was calling out to him. He couldn't make out the man's face, but he did recognize the stature. There was also another man with him. Both men were walking quickly towards Solomon.

Cutting through a few rows of vines, Solomon walked out into the clearing. Eager to see the men, he ran to meet them.

"Broc! Dan! It is good to see you!" the king exclaimed as he approached them, a little out of breath. Solomon embraced them both and kissed their cheeks. "You are well? How fares your company?"

Broc and Dan looked at each other, a little unsure as to how to answer the question.

Dan looked like he was about to say something but closed his mouth and looked to the ground.

Solomon noted the weariness on their faces and the distant look in their eyes. He had seen that look on many men before. It was the look men held when they were not able to talk about the horrors of what they had experienced.

"How many?" Solomon asked.

"Out of fifty men, we only came back with twenty-three. Five of those are severely wounded. And then there is—" Broc found it hard to finish the sentence.

"Then there is what?" Solomon asked.

Dan spoke for him. "It is Shammah, sir."

"What about Shammah?" Solomon pried. "Is he—"

"No. No." Broc was quick to say. "But he is badly wounded. He lost the lower part of his right leg and he lost a lot of blood. We were able to close the wound by burning the flesh, but by the time we got back here, he was barely alive. His wound had turned black and we feared his blood had been tainted. It was a good thing you sent more men, because our travel was slow and our resources were all but gone. Because of the new men, we were able to hurry ahead with the wounded. Shammah is now with the healers."

Solomon felt sick to his stomach. He now knew why El had been burdening his heart so deeply for Shammah and his men. His first thought was to run inside and see what more could be done for his friend, but he knew there was nothing he could do which the healers were not already doing.

Solomon gave a quick, silent prayer and then asked the men for a full report.

Broc and Dan told Solomon everything which had happened to them from the last two days. They told him about tracking the beast and all the carnage they had found before getting to the masakh's cave. They shared the part about the unnatural weather and how they had almost frozen to death, and how after praying to El, a great battle of lights had taken place in the sky. They told him about Jordan and the massacre of her family and how she had been the sole survivor. They walked through their battles against, not just one masakh, but two.

Solomon continued to listen to the brave men's story and found much of it unbelievable. If these had not been two of his own captains telling the tale, he would not have believed it.

They ended their narrative with the stranger who had saved them from being buried alive.

"Do we know who he is?" Solomon asked.

"No, sir," Broc answered. "But the men have their suspicions. Many of them said it was a warrior angel, sent by El to save us."

"What do you think?"

"I think it was just a man. His clothes were black and tattered, well worn. He looked more like a highwayman...a thief. He kept himself covered and wasn't willing to reveal himself, as if he was wanted for a crime. Why else would the man keep his identity a secret?"

Dan disagreed. "I don't see it. That was no average man. The way he moved and the speed in which he took down that masakh… well, it was impressive. It was as if he had been hunting those things all his life."

"Either way, El used this…what did you call him?" Solomon asked.

"Stranger. He just called himself 'The Stranger'."

"Right. It is clear El purposed this… *Stranger,* to come along at the right time and to be in the right place when he was needed the most."

Beginning to walk towards the palace, Solomon motioned the two men to walk with him. "Come, it is getting late. Let us go and check on Shammah and then you both will join me to sup. I believe King Huram would like to hear your tale as well. He will like to know the beasts which killed his men have been dealt with."

"There is one more thing we need to talk to you about, my king," Broc said as he kept pace with Solomon. "After both of the animals had been killed, the blood which flowed from their wounds was not red like the rest of El's creation. It was black. It was as if the dark oil of the earth itself ran through their veins. Shammah said he had never seen anything like it in all his years of hunting and war."

Solomon said nothing, but continued to listen, his eyes betraying a sense of worry.

"I feel this whole conflict was much more than just an animal attack," Broc said. "This was something greater. Almost as if something evil and sinister is happening behind the veil of this world."

"I agree," Dan spoke up, walking on the other side of the king. "Too many weird things happened. The size of those creatures alone was not normal. And the drastic cold weather and the battle of lights in the sky, I have never seen such a thing."

Broc cut in again. "Solomon, we could feel it. We could feel the evil all around us, as if it was trying to reach out and destroy the very souls within us."

Solomon felt the weight and worry in their words. He prayed as the two men spoke and voiced their concerns. He prayed for El to give him greater wisdom to understand the evil he was hearing about.

When Broc and Dan had stopped talking, Solomon put his arms around their shoulders and tried to comfort them. "Men, I don't have the answers you seek, and it does indeed sound as if the Evil One is at work. The truth is, the Evil One is *always* at work. Moving this way and that, searching out those he can fool and destroy. We will thank El for your safety and for the lives of those men who survived. We will also pray that El will reveal to us this evil so no further harm comes against our people."

Solomon stopped walking and looked to each man. "Trust in El."

Both men, having heard the challenge many times, replied with the same familiar words. "Trust in El."

Smiling, Solomon began to walk forward again. For a short time, the three men journeyed in silence until Dan raised a question to Solomon, changing the subject.

"So, how is Rachel doing? It is no secret she has not been looking forward to the wedding."

Broc looked over to Dan and gave him a stare which communicated, *That is none of our business!*

Solomon saw the exchange and smiled. He knew Dan and Rachel were friends and he also knew that Dan cared and looked after her as a brother would. "I believe Rachel is doing well. We had a good talk a few days ago and I think she has come around."

"How did she do, meeting the prince?" Broc asked.

Solomon smiled again and shook his head. "You guys know how these weddings work. The groom doesn't get to meet the bride until the time of the ceremony, and even then, the bride is veiled until their wedding night."

"I always thought that was a silly tradition. What if the woman is ugly?" Broc said with a light chuckle.

Dan glared at Broc. It was his turn to give a disapproving stare.

"Well, in a state wedding, looks don't matter," Solomon continued. "The marriage is more of a contract between two kingdoms to keep a peace."

Dan nodded, having been the guest to more than one state wedding in his lifetime. The thought of the whole ceremony made him feel sad for Rachel. More than once she had poured her heart out to him, sharing her wishes to be with Abaddon. Love was important to Rachel, and being loved was even more so. Dan had to ask the question. "What about love? Does not love factor into Rachel's marriage?"

"Of course it does. Are we not commanded by El to love our spouses after we are wed? It is just not a prerequisite," Solomon said, noting Dan's concern in his voice. "Besides, I believe Rachel is looking forward to her wedding."

CHAPTER 44

It took Rucha and Achish a full day to return to the shipyard and camp. They found themselves on the north end of the island when they needed to be on the southern end. Rucha had asked Achish how they ended up on the wrong side of the island and Achish had explained how his demon guards had carried both of them up through the center of the mountain after Dagon was done with them.

"And they didn't think to set us closer to our destination?" Rucha sneered at Achish.

Achish said nothing and continued to walk along the beach, heading south.

After several hours of walking in silence, Rucha began to feel weary and hungry. He realized he had not eaten anything for over a day. He looked to Achish waddling ahead of him and wondered if he, too, was hungry and beginning to tire. The large king was at least twenty years Rucha's senior and yet he never seemed to run out of energy and strength.

Rucha wanted to stop and rest and find something to eat but he didn't want to appear weak to Achish; although, if he didn't get food soon, he wasn't sure how much farther he could walk.

Finally, Rucha decided he couldn't go any further. Between the heat and the hunger pains, he had to rest for a bit. Rucha spotted a large piece a driftwood on the beach to his left. He made his way to it and sat down in front of it, using the log to lean his back up against.

Achish looked back and seemed to understand the need for a break, but instead of coming over to join Rucha, he turned and walked out into the sea until the cool salt water came up to his waist.

Rucha watched the Philistine stand there, letting the water lap against his large frame. Achish stared into the water as if he had never seen his reflection before.

Rucha imagined the fat king walking out into the depths of the sea and disappearing altogether. He smiled at the thought. His smile got even bigger when he thought of Achish drowning and flailing his stubby arms and legs drastically, trying to reach the surface, but never *quite* getting there. Rucha snapped out of his daydream when he heard a splash, and then another splash. He looked to Achish again and the man was walking back to the beach with two large, red dart fish, one in each hand.

Did he just catch two fish with his bare hands? Rucha thought to himself, amazed.

The king walked up to where Rucha was sitting and plopped down on the ground next to him. Without a word, he tossed one of the fish onto Rucha's lap. Still very much alive, the fish flopped and jumped desperately to try and find its way back to the safety of the sea.

Rucha grabbed hold of the fish to prevent it from moving.

"So, should we start a fire so we can—" before Rucha could finish his sentence, he heard a loud crack.

Achish had taken his fish and snapped off its head with his bare hands. He proceeded to stick two of his fingers down inside of the fish and in one quick motion he ripped out the animal's guts and threw them aside. He lifted the gutted carcass to his nose, took a deep whiff, and bit into the soft flesh of the fish. After his first bite, Achish looked to Rucha, who was staring at him with his mouth partially open.

"What?" Achish asked, taking another bite of his fish. "Is dart fish not to your liking? You are welcome to walk out and get your own fish if you like."

Rucha looked down at his fish. He had never eaten raw fish before. He preferred the flesh of land animals over fish, and the few times he *had* eaten fish, he had cooked it. In the end, his hunger won over his disgust. He copied Achish's approach and removed the head and gutted the fish.

His first bite into the dart was one of the worst tastes he had ever experienced. Out of the corner of his eye he could see Achish smiling at his displeasure. But, with each bite, Rucha was able to stomach the taste a bit easier.

"So what's the plan?" Rucha asked quietly as he flicked a few grains of sand off his fish. He looked over to Achish to find the king almost done eating as he was sucking at the animal's flexible bones.

"Well," came Achish's reply. "I was hoping we would get back to our camp by nightfall."

Idiot, thought Rucha. "Not that plan. I mean *the* plan. What did Dagon tell you our next move would be?"

Tossing the spent fish bones behind him, Achish picked up the fish's head and bit into it. "Well, it is simple really. We are to split up. I am to take the majority of the fleet with me and we are to head south down along the coast of the Great Continent and pillage and burn every town and city we come across. Dagon wants us to cause as much fear and chaos as possible."

Achish took another bite of the fish's head and noisily chewed on the animal's skull. When Achish didn't continue, Rucha spurred him on.

"And then—"

"And then, what?" Achish asked.

From the fires of heaven! It is like talking to a child! Rucha screamed inside of his mind. "And then what do *I* do, if you are to go burning and pillaging down the coastline?"

"You are to stay here."

Achish saw the puzzled look on Rucha's face and the surge of questions about ready to come out of the younger man's mouth. He put up his hand to silence him.

"Before you get all bent out of shape, let me tell you *why* you are staying here. Dagon has received word that King Solomon is launching his ships, twelve in total, tomorrow at midday from Ezion-

Geber. It is supposed to be a part of some wedding celebration. From there it will take the fleet a few days to get through the Red Sea and out into the Great Sea. At which point Dagon has a little surprise for them. And, if all goes right, some of their ships will be in need of repairs."

Rucha was about to ask a question, but Achish already knew what he was going to ask and waved him off.

"I don't know what or how Dagon is going to disable their ships, but it is going to happen. Now, we have it on good authority that most of the Israeli vessels will continue on their voyage towards Ophir. The few of their ships that get damaged will go to the nearest port for repairs, which is—"

Rucha smiled faintly. "Which is here."

Taanug was one of the best ports in the area for making masts. The island was full of tall strong cedar trees, perfect material for fixing masts and deck boards. The prior inhabitants were quite successful in the trade until he and Achish raided the island to make it their home base of operation.

"So Dagon wants me to kill those who come here and destroy their ships."

"Yes, and no," Achish replied. "He does want you to kill all the men on the Israeli ships, but the ships themselves he wants untouched. In fact he commands you to finish their repairs."

"What? Why would Dagon want me to fix the boats? That makes no sense. I thought our objective was to *prevent* Solomon's ships from completing their mission, to keep them from Ophir, which would prevent the temple from being built. Destroying the vessels is the logical course of action."

Achish shook his head. "You are thinking to small, Rucha. The goal is not to prevent the temple from being built. The goal is to completely wipe out Israel. That starts with us taking all their ships, filling them with our own men, and sailing right back into the heart of their land and crushing them. When they see their own ships returning home, they will never expect them to be filled with enemy soldiers."

Rucha stared out over the sea while Achish spoke. He thought about the plan and it was unsettling to him.

"It doesn't make sense," Rucha said after Achish stopped talking. "If that is our plan, then why is Dagon sending you away to the South. Why not stay here as a group and take the fleet by surprise when they pass by here? We outnumber them at least three to one. We could take their ships here, instead of sailing all over creation."

"I thought the same thing," Achish said, grabbing Rucha's half eaten fish out of his hands and then proceeding to eat it himself. "But I didn't ask. Dagon wasn't in the best mood last we saw him. I didn't feel like being roasted alive for questioning his directives, but I did get the feeling he wanted the Hebrews to get to Ophir. Why? I don't know, and I don't care. As long as they are all dead in the end."

Both men sat there for a bit longer, silent and pondering upon the task which was ahead of them. Finally Rucha looked skyward and took note of the time of day. "If we want to get back by nightfall, we had better keep moving. I am not spending the night out here with you, and I am not having another one of your fish dinners."

Achish nodded his head in agreement and hopped to his feet as if he were a mere lad.

The two men began their trek again, and after they had reached a few hundred cubits Rucha stopped. "What are we doing? Why are we following the beach around? If we cut through the jungle and go across the island we can take a few hours off our walk."

"Nope," Achish said as he continued forward.

"What do you mean, nope?" Rucha called out as he resumed his walking, going a little faster to catch up with Achish. "Why not? It is not like we haven't traveled through there before."

Rucha looked at Achish and he saw fear in the old king's eyes.

Achish stopped walking and glared at the tree line. "Look into the jungle and tell me what you see."

Rucha complied and he saw many of the trees moving. As he looked closer, he realized there were shadows and shades dashing around in all directions. He hadn't noticed it before, but hundreds, maybe thousands of demons were traipsing through the jungle.

"Can you see them?" Achish asked, looking in the same direction as Rucha.

"Yes. Can you?"

"No. Not now. I could while I was in the temple, and I don't care to see them again. One of them actually put its hand inside of my head and tried to control my thoughts. I have had enough of demons for one day." Achish turned and continued walking down the beach.

For once, Rucha agreed with Achish.

After four hours of trudging through the sand, Rucha and Achish rounded a bend and finally caught sight of the southern bay. They could see many of their ships in the distance, lazily floating in the calm waters, anchored and ready to go when called upon. Achish guessed they were no more than an hour away.

Trudging along beside Achish, Rucha wiggled his toes as he walked, now feeling the weariness of the day's hike. He really wished he had sandals. Rucha felt blisters forming on the soles of his feet, and each step was beginning to feel like nails biting into his skin. To get his mind off the discomfort, Rucha decided to ask Achish a few more questions, questions which had been nagging on him all day.

"I've been thinking. You told me earlier, Dagon knew how many ships were departing from Ezion-Geber and when they were leaving."

"Yeah, so?" Achish replied with a hint of exhaustion in his voice.

"How does he know how many ships there are? And how does he know that when the Israeli fleet is attacked, the rest of them will leave the damaged vessels behind for repairs and keep heading south?"

Achish nodded, understanding Rucha's train of thought. "Hmmm. Dagon did not tell me this directly but I did overhear one of his demon messengers. After Dagon was done healing you and before he talked to me about our plans, a bat-like creature flew into the cavern. It told Dagon that the beasts they had released into Israel had finished their tasks and their spies were now in place. The bat also reported the information about the ships and about some royal wedding taking place tomorrow."

"Royal wedding? Is Solomon getting married?"

"Don't know? The bat didn't say, and since they didn't know I was listening, I didn't think it wise to ask."

"Well, that's not helpful," Rucha commented. "That actually creates more questions than answers. What are these beasts they were talking about and what exactly was their purpose? Who are the spies? How many spies are there? Are they going to give us more information; and if so, how are they going to get it to us?"

Achish stopped walking and put his hand to Rucha's chest to halt him.

"I can see you are the type of guy who likes to know every little detail of the plan, but need I remind you, you don't *need* to know every, little, detail! Your role is to pirate the ships that land here, load them with your men, and then follow us south. That is all you need to know. Don't burden yourself with all the other details. That is for Dagon to worry about. Right?"

Giving Rucha a hearty slap on the back, Achish began walking forward again.

"You're too trusting, Achish. Knowledge is power, and neither one of us have enough of it. It has been my experience, the less you know, the more dispensable you are. If we are not careful, Dagon will throw us away like used rags at the end of all this."

"You worry too much! I trust Dagon. If you put your trust in him, then he will always take care of you. That is how it works. Have a little faith, Hebrew."

"I guess that's part of the problem. I don't trust him."

As soon as Rucha said the words, a sharp pain welled up in his belly. He knew his demon was not liking the direction of this conversation. Rucha chose to change the topic.

"Another question."

Achish sighed, obviously getting a little annoyed with Rucha's inquiries. "Goat's blood, lad! We traveled all the way across this island and you hardly said a word, and now that home is in sight I can't get you to shut up! Yes, yes! Ask your question!"

"You said earlier, Dagon got angry and almost torched the whole place down. What happened? What set him off?"

Again, Achish stopped walking, turned and faced Rucha. The large king stared straight into Rucha's black flaming eyes for a few moments, long enough to make Rucha feel uncomfortable. "I don't know. You tell me why he got so angry?"

"How would I know? I passed out, remember?"

"Hmmmm, yes. But right before you collapsed to the ground, you said something. Something Dagon did not like. You said it so quietly, I actually didn't hear what you said. So. You tell me. What did you say? Because whatever it was, it really set him off."

Without waiting for an answer, Achish turned around and walked away, leaving Rucha there to ponder his thoughts.

"What did I say?" Rucha said to himself aloud.

In all honesty, he couldn't remember. His most vivid memory before he lost consciousness was the way he had physically felt, not the words he had said. All he could recall was the extreme pain he had been in.

Dagon had asked him something…something about his loyalty and whether he was for or against him…or something like that.

Rucha put his hands to his head and pushed his fingers through his tangled hair, as if doing so would bring his memories to life. He shook his head. Nothing was coming to him.

Rucha looked up and saw Achish was now far down the beach. He looked skyward to the horizon and noted the setting sun. Although he could not see the color, he could tell the shade of the sky was changing and stretching across the heavens.

A memory immediately came to mind of when he was a child, maybe ten or eleven seasons old. He and his older brother, Joab, had sneaked onto the city wall in Jerusalem to throw pebbles off the guard tower. They would then compete to see who could throw the furthest. That evening, they had witnessed the most colorful sunset they had ever seen.

Rucha felt a pain in his heart thinking about Joab and all the good times he used to have with him. He wished his brother was here now.

He broke his stare away from the sky, but as he did so, a bright glint of light flashed just above the setting sun. In that fraction of a moment, Rucha's gray-tinted world erupted into color. In the time it took a person to blink, Rucha saw a rich blue sky scattered with long white reaching clouds which were painted in gold, red and purple. The sky was an artist's work of wonder, giving hope to a bleak day. The flash of light winked out, and so did all the colors it had brought with it.

Before Rucha even had a chance to comprehend what had happened, a soft gentle voice whispered into his ears.

"Remember, Abishai, it is never too late to go home. You are still loved."

Upon hearing the voice, a floodgate of memories erupted within him. Immediately his thoughts went back to the void, to the darkness he had found himself in before waking on the beach. Rucha thought he had been simply dreaming about that horrible place, but now, hearing that voice again—

"Who is there?" Rucha said aloud.

He looked around, wondering if another demon was playing tricks on him, but as he scanned the area there was nothing in sight.

Rucha called out again but this time louder.

"I said, who is there?"

Again, silence.

I think I am going crazy, he thought to himself. *First I see bright lights and colors in the sky and now I am hearing voices. What is happening to me?*

"Wait, that's it!" Rucha said aloud. "The light! I remember now! I told Dagon the reason Beelzebub attacked me was because of the light around me, the light I *thought* Dagon had provided to guide Achish and I through the tunnels!"

Rucha remembered the look on Dagon's face when he told him about the light. There had been confusion in his eyes. Now it made sense. Dagon hadn't known anything about the light because he hadn't provided it.

Now it was Rucha's turn to be puzzled. "If Dagon didn't provide the light, then who did? And why?"

An old memory came to the surface of his mind, a memory of an old Jewish teacher from his youth.

"Only El can create light and hope in your life."

Rucha looked again to the horizon, the sun now all but set. Once more, the memory of the voice's words echoed in his head.

"Remember, Abishai, it is never too late to go home. You are still loved."

CHAPTER 45

"I am *not* looking forward to this wedding!" Rachel said in a frustrated tone as she paced back in forth in her room. "I can't believe this is happening! I can't even leave my own room, or move about in my own home, because of the off chance I may run into the prince! Heaven forbid we might actually *meet* before the ceremony. I hate these stupid traditions!"

Rachel stopped pacing and looked at Hinda. "Are you even listening to me?"

Hinda was in the corner of the room, mesmerized by the craftsmanship and beauty of the wedding gown hanging before her. It was a dress like none other. Never, in the history of Israel, had such a garment ever been crafted.

It was made with two separate layers. The first layer was pure white silk, sewn together with gold thread. Flecks of emerald stones were embroidered along the neck line and the cuff of the sleeves. The length of the inner gown was a good cubit longer than Rachel's actual height. She had complained during the fitting about not being able to walk without stepping on the slick fabric. The seamstresses had taught her how to take small steps when she walked to prevent that from happening.

The second layer for the gown was thick and heavy. The upper torso and sleeves were made of badger fur, bleached completely white. Within the fur, thousands of tiny gold and silver chords had been sewn in. Fastened within the chords were green emeralds and bright blue sapphires. Down both sleeves, across the neck line and around the waist was a detailed embroidery of green vines with gold leaves. To highlight the stalk of the vines, there were crushed emeralds glued into the fabric. Gold dust was used to enhance the color of the vine's leaves. From the waist down, the gown was made of several layers of fine linen dyed white and gold. Thousands of gold and silver studs and rings were woven into the material. Gold for the sections in white and silver for the material dyed in gold.

To complete the ensemble, the headdress and veil were the most elaborate of all. The top of the head piece was cone shaped, about a cubit in height. It was made in such a way as to fit all of Rachel's hair inside of it. An embroidery of gold and white flowers decorated the front and several white, honey flowers were attached all around the edge. Small, shiny, golden plates were strung together in long rows along the sides and back of the headpiece. They were designed to hang down to the shoulders, covering the back of the wearer's neck and ears. The veil itself was attached to the front, hung to fit just above the brow. It was made from hundreds of tiny pearls strung onto pure gold thread. When it was time for the bride's face to be revealed, the pearl veil was made to part in the middle and fasten to both sides of the headdress above the ears.

Hinda had been spending the last hour preening and examining every inch of the beautiful ensemble. More than once Rachel had heard her servant say, "This is gorgeous!" and "This work is amazing!" or "You are so blessed!"

Ignoring the comments, Rachel continued to vent her frustrations.

"Hinda, I asked if you were listening to me." Rachel said again, plopping herself down on her soft feathered pallet. "I am in real trouble here! How am I going to get out of this?"

Sighing deeply, Hinda turned around to face the impetuous princess. "You should be ashamed of yourself. Do you know how lucky you are? Do you know how every single woman in this kingdom would trade places with you in an instant? It is every woman's dream to be so well taken care of, to be lavished on by such beautiful things, and to live a life of royalty as a queen!"

"Then let them have it!" Rachel voiced out, standing up from her bed and marching over to the open window. She leaned over the sill and shouted, "All those who are willing to become the future queen of Tyre, please step forward!"

Running over to Rachel, Hinda grabbed her by her thin waist, and pulled her back into the room. She then grabbed the shutters to the window and slammed them shut.

"What is the matter with you?" Hinda snapped sharply as she dragged Rachel back to her pallet and forced her to sit down. "I swear! If your mother were here, she would be furious with you, acting so childishly! It is time to grow up and stop living your life in such a selfish manner. This wedding is going to happen, and it is better for you to find joy in it rather than grief and misery." Hinda was about to continue on her rant until she looked down and saw Rachel's face, buried in her hands as she began to weep.

In a mere instant, Hinda's heart broke. She often forgot what Rachel had been through in the past few seasons, and how difficult it was for her to stay positive. Hinda swallowed hard, took a calming breath, and sat down next to her.

"I am sorry, child," Hinda said, taking Rachel's hand in hers. "I wasn't thinking. I shouldn't have brought your mother into this."

"I miss her. I really wish she were here now," Rachel said in a quivering voice, trying to calm her breathing and control her tears. "It is just…this is not the way I envisioned my wedding day. None of this is what I wanted. In fact, not once has anyone even asked me what *I* wanted for this wedding."

Reaching into her sleeve, Hinda pulled out a small white cloth and handed it to Rachel. "For your tears, dear."

Hinda waited for a moment while Rachel calmed herself and dried her eyes, and then gently asked, "So, tell me. What is your perfect wedding?"

Rachel looked down at her hands and at the tear stained cloth she was holding. She was about to speak, but then shook her head. "It doesn't matter. I'll never see it."

"Come on," Hinda urged, giving Rachel a gentle nudge with her elbow. "I want to know. Every girl dreams of her wedding. Tell me yours."

Rachel stayed silent for a moment longer, but a smile slowly crept across her lips. "I want it simple, plain, yet beautiful. I want it outdoors under the warm sun, with a cool breeze gently blowing through the air, just enough to rustle my hair. I want it to be in the woods during the color season, when all the trees are yellow, gold, orange and red. I imagine leaves gracefully falling from the branches above as if they are small blessings from El coming down from heaven." Rachel's smile grew ever wider. "I don't want the whole kingdom to be there, only a few people, the people I care about the most. I want my mother to be there, smiling the way she would whenever she was proud of me. And the man standing next to me, ready to be my husband forever, will love me, and I will love him."

Hinda now felt as if she were going to cry. She let go of Rachel's hand and put her arm around the young woman and squeezed. "I know I am not your mother, but I will *always* be there for you. I am so proud of you and I know your mother is proud of you, too."

Leaning her head on Hinda's shoulder, Rachel gave a deep sigh. "I know. I wish things were different."

"Me, too, my sweet one. Me, too."

The two women sat for some time without speaking, and Rachel enjoyed the feeling of being held by her friend.

After a while, Hinda heard Rachel's breathing change and she knew the bride-to-be had fallen asleep.

Hinda removed her arm from Rachel's shoulders and slowly stood. Rachel, now with her eyes closed, moaned a bit at the disturbance of her comfort. Hinda took her by both of her hands and urged her to stand as well. "Come on my dear. Let's get you into bed so you can rest. It is getting late and we have a big day tomorrow."

Rachel reluctantly got up with Hinda's help. Hinda pulled back the soft covers and tucked them back in around Rachel after she had crawled into the bed.

Hinda was turning to leave the room when Rachel quietly called her back. "Hinda, tell me again the plans for tomorrow."

"We have been through this, my love, now go to sleep."

"Just go over it again with me. *Please.* I am nervous."

Hinda smiled and gave out a small sigh. She came back to the pallet and sat down next to Rachel. "Alright, dear. We will go through it one more time. We will be getting up a few hours before first light to start your wedding preparations: bathing and scenting. That will take a few hours, and then we will begin dressing you in your pre-wedding attire. We will then take a caravan accompanied by bodyguards to Ezion-Geber and set up in the king's southern palace. The trip there should take about six hours, eight if we take our time. You will rest for the night and then we will be up bright and early the next morning to dress for your wedding. The ceremony will be at midday and then, finally, you will get to see your handsome prince."

The princess glanced over to her gown and asked, "And how long will it take to put that thing on, along with the makeup and jewelry?"

"If everyone is efficient, about six hours. Don't worry. The wedding is at midday and we will have you looking beautiful and ready to go before then."

Rachel didn't feel worried, but more exasperated. Six whole hours of poking and prodding with yanking and pulling to make sure everything was perfect.

To keep up a positive appearance, Rachel gave up a weak smile and decided to change the subject. "And what of the ships? When are they supposed to launch?"

"I believe Captain Broc mentioned they are to depart mid-morning on the morrow, about the time we will be traveling. Something about the tidal waters being just right at that time."

With a concerned look on her face, Rachel sat up a bit, propping her weight on her left elbow. "Wait. You mean we won't even be there for the launching of the boats? Wasn't that supposed to be a big part of the wedding? And I can't even be there for it?"

"I am sorry, dear, but that is just the way it is," Hinda said in a soothing voice, tucking Rachel back under the covers. "I guess that is the price you have to pay as the bride. It takes longer for you to prepare."

"Well we could skip the bathing and prepping in the morning. We could leave right away and be there for the festivities and the departure of the ships."

Hinda laughed. "Oh yes! Let's skip the bathing. I am sure your husband-to-be will be thrilled with that decision, especially on the first day he meets you."

Frowning, Rachel pulled the covers over her head. "Fine! So we will do it your way! Good night," came her muffled voice under the mass of linens.

Hinda patted Rachel's leg, "All you need is a good night's rest and you will see things differently in the morning." She stood, said good night, blew out the two candles on either side of the doorpost, and left the room.

As soon as Rachel heard the door close she slid the covers down off her face and listened to Hinda walk away. When the sound of footsteps had disappeared, she held her breath and strained to see if she could hear anything else. Her heart was beginning to race and all she could hear was her own blood pumping though her ears.

"Am I really going to do this?" she asked herself. "You can do this, Rachel. Every journey starts with a single step."

Moving her covers to the side, Rachel silently slid off her pallet. She put her feet to the floor and without making a sound she walked over to her armoire and gently opened its doors. One of the wooden hinges creaked and her heart almost jumped out of her chest. She stood perfectly still for several long moments, half expecting the guard down the hall to check on the noise which so rudely interrupted the silence of the night. When no footsteps came, she let out a deep breath.

I have to be more careful. Rachel thought to herself.

She reached down to a cloth bundle at the base of the armoire, lifted it up, and brought it over to her pallet. She opened up the bundle and with care, took out its contents: a small cloth sack filled with nuts and dried dates, two skins of water and wine, and a stale loaf of bread. She placed the items aside and held up the material they were wrapped in. It was a tattered and dirty cloak, comparable to the ones beggars wore. She felt the fabric and it was coarse like goat hair. She brought her nose close to it and the smell almost made her eyes water. Not only did it feel like goat's hair, it also smelled like goat hair.

Quickly and quietly, Rachel removed her bed clothes and put on the beggar's clothes. Inside the bundle was also a simple black headdress made of cotton. She tied her hair up into a bun and expertly wrapped the headdress around her head. She reached down and pulled out a leather satchel from underneath her pallet, in which she proceeded to place the skins and food.

Ok, what is next? Rachel thought to herself, feeling her heart pound uncontrollably.

The pillows.

Tiptoeing over to her window, Rachel picked up several of the pillows gathered on the floor. She took the pillows back to her pallet, carefully arranged them into the shape of her body, and gently tucked the covers in around the decoy. Rachel took a step back and looked at her lifeless double lying in her bed. She nodded her head in approval.

One more thing to do. Rachel thought as she silently walked over to the wedding gown in the corner of the room.

Choosing not to look at the dress, Rachel focused on the small table sitting next to it. Upon the table were dozens of small jewels: pearls, diamonds and rubies, along with thin gold coins. The precious stones were supposed to be used as jewelry which would be glued to the skin of her hands, face, and neck, to complete the look of a wedding bride.

Carefully picking up the precious stones and coins, Rachel dropped them into her satchel. She then pulled a piece of parchment out from under the table. She had hidden it there earlier in the day and had written a note to Solomon on it. She placed the note where the jewels had been and froze in place after doing so.

She realized this was the point of no return. If she wanted to, she could undo everything she had already done and simply go back to bed and no one would be the wiser.

Closing her eyes, Rachel willed her heart to calm itself. She could feel the rush of fear, excitement, and worry pounding through her. The feeling was exhilarating and yet completely frightening. She wondered if this was what the *fury* felt like. She had heard Abaddon describe it many times, but she herself had never experienced it.

Now standing in the middle of her room, she stared up into the dark ceiling and offered up a quiet prayer to El.

"Jehovah. You know my heart's desire. I believe you would want me to live free and have the ability to choose for myself. El, if you don't want me to go through with this, prevent me from leaving. If you find no fault in my actions, I pray you will clear the way ahead of me."

Rachel moved silently back across the room to her window, her escape route to freedom. She reached the window and realized Hinda had closed the shutters earlier. She let out a frustrated sigh. It wasn't that she couldn't open the shutters, that was no problem. The problem was the hinges to the shutters made a terrible creaking noise when they were opened.

Carefully unhooking the latch in the center, Rachel very slowly parted the thick wooden slats. As she feared, a loud screech came from the small door's hinge. The princess froze in place and held her breath.

Please, oh please, oh please, nobody come down the hall, please!

After a moment of intense listening, Rachel could hear no one approaching her room. She looked back to the window and cringed at how she had only opened the shutters a handsbreadth. She had to open it more.

Maybe if I do it fast, it won't be so bad, she thought.

In one quick motion she yanked both shutters upon wide and once again the sound of whining hinges filled the air, and once again Rachel stood like a statue, hoping her deed had gone unnoticed. She waited several moments and when she had heard nothing, she felt her body relax and relief wash over her.

Looking out the window, Rachel found a full moon staring back at her, taunting her, threatening to expose her with its bright silver rays of light. She poked her head out and looked down, and then to the right and then to the left.

No guards in sight.

She looked straight down once more and noted how high up she was, maybe thirty or forty cubits. Her plan was to climb down the stone wall and simply walk out of the city as a poor old beggar. Once she was free and clear, she would begin her journey to go and find Abaddon.

Rachel was about to step out on the window sill when suddenly she heard something. Out in the hall there were footsteps coming.

The hall guard stood from his sitting position on the bench at the end of the corridor. He had heard a noise, but after listening for a bit he brushed it off, thinking his mind was playing tricks on him. While working the night shift, the guard was used to hearing various sounds and the settling of the wood and stone within the palace. He was about to sit back down when the noise came again, although this time it was much louder, as if someone was opening an old rusted door.

The guard drew his sword and stood motionless for a time, listening and hoping to hear the sound again so he could find a better direction as to where it was coming from. When no other sound came, the guard convinced himself it was probably nothing and sheathed his weapon. He attempted once more to sit back down, but an uneasy feeling came over him. What if there was something wrong and he did nothing to investigate?

The guard grabbed the burning torch which was attached to the wall next to him and began his walk down the long hall. There were only two rooms in this section of the palace, the one on the right was the princess' room, and at the very far end of the corridor on the left was the servant Hinda's room.

The guard came to Rachel's room first and was about to knock on the door, but he paused.

Maybe I should go and get Hinda first. It wouldn't look right to have a man enter into the princess' room in the middle of the night. The man thought to himself.

He was about to continue down the hall to do just that when he heard the noise again, but this time it was much louder and it was followed by a loud bang.

The sound definitely came from the princess' room!

Upon hearing the commotion, the guard threw his reservations aside, knocked on the door, and announced he was coming in.

The door opened easily and he carefully came into Rachel's room; cautious, just in case the noise he heard was an intruder. The room was dark and quiet except for the crackling of the torch in his hand. The guard looked to Rachel's pallet and saw her form completely covered by her thick linens. He took a few more steps, moving his light around, straining to see the rest of the room. It was then, he noticed the shutters on the window were open. One of the shutters slightly moved and it made the sound which he had heard. The guard smiled and gave a silent sigh of relief. What he must have heard was the wind blowing open the shutters.

The guard walked up to the window, took a moment to look out into the night, and then closed the wooden slats. Upon doing so, the hinges creaked aloud once more. The guard cringed at the sound and looked to see if he had woken the princess. Her form had not moved. The man let out a sigh and was grateful. He really didn't want to have to explain himself if she woke up and caught him in her room, especially a few days before her wedding.

The guard latched the shutters closed so they would not blow open again and silently exited the room.

Rachel thought the guard was never going to leave.

She had heard the guard announce himself and she had leapt out of the window, grabbing hold of the edge of the outside sill. There she hung, her body dangling against the outer stone wall. Her heart was pounding through her ears as she desperately held on by her fingertips. Every few seconds, she felt her sweaty hands slowly slipping off the cool, smooth stone of the sill. She would then have to shift her weight and readjust her grip. Finally Rachel found a crack in the wall beneath her and she wedged her foot into it, helping to ease some of the pressure off her hands.

Rachel thought she was caught for sure when the guard came to the window. She could see his torchlight right above her. All he had to do was look down and she was done for.

Please don't look down! Please, oh please, don't look down. Rachel prayed.

The guard seemed to linger there at the window for a time. Finally the light moved back and the shutters creaked shut, and then she heard the guard latch the wooden slats closed.

Letting out a long sigh of relief, Rachel rested her forehead on the cool, stone wall in front of her. She waited for a moment, long enough to hear the guard leave her room, and then continued her descent, one careful step at a time. Within moments she was on the ground.

Rachel took one more look around her and found she was still alone. She straightened her ragged clothes, made sure her face was covered with her headdress, and walked off into the night.

CHAPTER 46

Rucha stood on top of the cabin of his new command ship, overlooking his crew below. He was dressed in his battle uniform, a black breastplate with a black leather lappet around his waist. Underneath his armor he had on a black robe with black trousers. Even his sandals were stained black. A dark red sash was tied neatly over the top of his lappet, keeping the sword at his hip in place. Rucha also had at least a dozen throwing knives strapped to his midsection, two Sicarrii daggers sheathed at his lower back, and a long sickle sword fastened to his upper back.

The hood from Rucha's robe covered his head and a new Sicarrii mask covered his face. This mask was not white like his previous one. This one was blood red with tiny slits at the eyes. The black flames from Rucha's eye sockets swirled within the slits, enhancing a demonic appearance.

The only flesh which could be seen on Rucha was on his blemished hands. A few of the crew had pointed out Rucha's scarred hands earlier that morning. They were now headless and hanging by their feet from the yardarm of the center mast. Needless to say, no one else had anything to say about Rucha's scars.

Rucha slowly paced back and forth atop his cabin as he continued to look down upon the few hundred men standing on the ship's deck. He looked to his right and then to his left. There were a dozen more ships on each side of him, anchored and ready to sail whenever the command was given. There were twenty-six vessels in all. Every ship was different, varying in size and shape, holding crews anywhere from fifty to two-hundred men, totaling almost three thousand warriors in all.

Every man on every vessel now stood at attention, looking towards Rucha and his ship. Today was the day they would finally set sail and begin their voyage of plunder and mayhem. Rucha hated the idea that he would not be going with them, even though the plan was to join them when his work on the island was done.

Rucha noted that not only were his men looking to him, but thousands of demons had also come into the cove to witness the great departure.

Looking back and to his left, Rucha nodded to Achish standing off to the side. They had agreed that he would be the one to talk to the men and instruct them before they set sail.

Achish, also dressed for battle, nodded to Rucha, signaling he was ready for the speech to commence.

Rucha held up his hands and the mumbling and murmurs of the men quieted, all eyes and ears fell upon him, the Ghost of Souls. Even the demons hovering above the ships and clinging to the rock walls all around the cove seemed to settle and silence themselves, waiting to hear the words of the mortal man standing before them.

"Enemies of El and Israel, welcome!" Rucha shouted at the top of his lungs.

A deafening roar of men and demons filled the cove. A loud racket of swords clamoring against shields engulfed the enclosed bay and echoed off the surrounding rocks.

Rucha let the men shout their taunts and express their rage for a few moments before putting his arms up into the air, a sign calling for silence.

When he could be heard once again, Rucha continued.

"Some of you are here today because you desire wealth, gold, silver, and jewels beyond your imagination. Well, today is the day you will begin to claim it!"

A wave of cheers and shouts erupted once more.

"Some of you are here because you were once slaves, bound to the duties of men who cared nothing for you. Today, you are slaves no longer! Today you are free men! Free to return to those who had enslaved you. Free to throw your old masters to the whipping posts and beat *them* until they are at *your* mercy! Free to take their women and their children as your own slaves, and burn *them* out of their homes!"

Wild chants of anger and fury erupted from the men on every ship. Loud cries of savage agreement filled the air.

"There is another breed of men standing here amongst us. There are those of you who care nothing for wealth or treasure! There are those of you who have grown too wild for the chains of slavery. These men can hardly be called men at all, because they were born and bred for a single purpose. To kill! Are there any killers amongst us today?"

This time the warriors lost all control. Deafening shouts and chants of, "Kill! Kill! Kill!" filled the cove. Not only had the men become crazed, but the demons had as well. Rucha witnessed many of the dark spirits diving into the crowds of men and possessing their bodies. Once possessed, the men would start fights, punching and clawing at anyone around them.

Rucha smiled at the chaos which had erupted all around him.

Dagon, you wanted a bloodthirsty army. Well, you have one.

Rucha held up his arms again and after a few moments the wild mob brought their attention back to him. When it was quiet enough for him to speak, he continued.

"You are no longer individuals. You are no longer alone in this soulless world which El has created. You are now a part of a legion created by Dagon himself. A legion of death! Today, a dawn of darkness rises upon the whole earth!"

Cheers exploded once more.

"Unfortunately, I regret to inform you that there are those who don't agree with our vision, who don't agree with the world which our god Dagon is trying to make. Some of those cowardly men walk amongst us!"

As Rucha continued to speak, Achish brought a man forward who was bound and gagged. He threw the poor wretch to his knees right beside Rucha.

The crazed men began to quiet upon seeing the bound man. As the men looked around, they realized there was a chained prisoner being presented on each of their ships.

"These men you see bound before you are traitors!" Rucha announced as he walked over to the helpless soul. He grabbed a fistful of the captive's hair and yanked the man's head up and forward for all to see his face.

"These men were caught trying to escape the island last night, trying to leave the fold of Dagon! There is only one way to leave the Legion!"

Without being prompted, over three thousand men shouted out, "Death! Death is our only release!" Then, in an angry torrent, the men hollered out once more, "Kill! Kill! Kill!"

Rucha raised his free hand and the chanting slowed and quieted.

"Death is our only release and death these men will have!"

Upon hearing these words, the man beneath Rucha's grasp began to squirm and attempted to get to his feet to flee. Rucha held firm to his hair and Achish came up from behind and slammed his foot down on the prisoner's ankle, snapping it to the side.

A muffled cry of pain came from the gagged man.

Rucha continued as if nothing had happened.

"These men will have a special death, one that will not just punish them for their treachery, but will also honor us as a sacrifice. These traitors will become a blood offering to our lord and master, Prince Dagon!"

Wild cheers and taunts of bloodthirsty men and demons exploded over the whole cove. So loud were the men, the noise became crushing, bringing a ringing sound to Rucha's ears.

Without another word, Rucha dragged the bound man by his hair over to the side of the ship, withdrew one of his daggers, and slit the man's throat, allowing the blood to drain directly into the clear blue waters below. Likewise, the captains on all the other ships executed their prisoners as well.

Rucha then cut the traitor's head from his body. With his foot, he pushed the decapitated corpse off the deck and watched as it plunged into the sea below. The sound of similar splashes could be heard all around the cove from the other ships disposing of their sacrifices.

Still grasping tightly to the hair on the traitor's head, he lifted up his prize for all to see. If it was possible, the crew's howling screams of depraved pleasure grew even louder. Rucha threw the ghastly head into the mob and the men began to fight over it as if they were a pack of dogs trying to claim a prized piece of meat.

One of the crew members broke away with the head tucked securely under his arm. He proceeded to scale the center mast, climbing it clear to the top rung. Once there, he plunged his trophy upon a pole, a pole normally used for hanging lanterns. The head was now the highest part of the ship.

Rucha smiled at the sight before speaking further.

"The sacrifice is not yet over! There are still traitors amongst us! Look to the men around you! If you have ever heard a man speak ill of our god Dagon, or know of a man who has shared his wishes to leave, take your sword and kill him now!"

In an instant, thousands of swords rang out from their scabbards. The cheers of wild men became the roars of maddened warriors, followed by the screams of dying men.

For a good length of time, blades clashed and men died. Rucha and Achish watched in mild amusement as their hard-trained warriors slaughtered one another, body after body falling from the decks of the ships and plunging into the sea around them.

Rucha was about to call out to the men to cease their fighting when he felt something slam into the bottom of his ship, causing the vessel to pitch back and forth. He looked to the other ships and noticed that they too were bucking against something moving under the water.

All the warriors ceased fighting and reached out to grab hold of something, for fear of being tossed overboard.

Once again, something slammed into the ships from below, tossing them around violently.

"There is something in the water!" came a random voice from one of the men.

All eyes peered into the blood stained waters. Hundreds of lifeless bodies bobbed around the ship's hulls. Then, one by one, the bodies began disappearing.

Rucha watched in fascination as the floating corpses were yanked down into the depths of the sea by some unknown force. He noticed something else as well. Not only were the bodies disappearing, but the water within the cove had begun to turn and move in a large circular motion.

Because of the closeness of the ships, the vessels began to collide, grinding and scraping their wooden hulls together.

Panic washed over the men and several of them started to shout and beg their captains to weigh anchor and leave the cove, but Rucha and Achish, along with all the other ship's captains, stood fast, ignoring their men.

And then it happened.

An explosion erupted from the middle of the cove, spewing the reddened waters in all directions. From the explosion came forth Dagon in his dragonesque form, roaring as if the bowels of the sea itself had given birth to him. Within his jowls were the bodies of the dead.

The legion watched in fear and awe as Dagon spread out his massive wings and smoothly flapped them up and down, causing him to hover in place above them. They stood transfixed as the ancient demon consumed their sacrifice of flesh.

Another explosion came from the depths of the water. This time thousands of demons shot up out of the sea and began to fill the sky above. There were so many demons pouring forth, they blocked out the light of the rising sun.

Looking at the torrent of dark spirits flooding the heavens, Rucha found himself, for the first time in a long time, feeling fear. Even when he had been dying in the depths of the temple and had seen demons all around him, he had not felt this kind of fear. This was different. These demons were different. These demons were the embodiment of darkness itself, void of all light and hope. It was pure evil, rising to destroy the living world.

As the hellish black demons rose high into the sky, a blanket of shadow consumed the heavens as far as the eye could see.

Dagon, still hovering above the ships, finished his meal of the dead. He then spoke in a deep dark voice.

"I accept your sacrifice and I will be your god. Now let me give you a gift in return. And you will truly be a legion to contend with!"

Dagon then let out another mighty roar. As he did so, the thousands of demons which had been clinging to the rock walls around the cove descended upon the ships. Every man still alive was thrown down to the hard wooden floors of their vessels and possessed. Men screamed and hollered in pain as their bodies were consumed with pure evil and their souls were cast aside for the invading demons.

Rucha looked away, not because he felt pity or sympathy for the men, but because he had felt that pain and didn't care to be reminded of it.

Rucha stood on the beach of the cove with fifty newly possessed men, and watched his fleet sail away. He watched Dagon flap his mighty wings and soar high above them, leading them to their first of many destinations of destruction. Darkness continued to plague the sky and seemed to stretch out further and further, snuffing out the light of day ahead of the ships.

One thought filled Rucha's mind as he watched his legion sail away.

The Shadow of Death has come, and Israel will finally *burn!*

EPILOGUE

Before the dawning of the day and just as the night was giving up its darkness, the Stranger calmly walked through the northern gate of Ezion-Geber. The guards had just opened the massive doors to the city and vendors from all over Israel were beginning to pour in to set up their wares for the day. The Stranger, dressed in a dirty, ragged, old traveler's cloak with a cowl draped over his head, walked in amongst the crowd. No one seemed to pay him any mind.

The mysterious man walked casually but purposefully with his hands joined together within the sleeves of his robe, giving him the appearance of one of the old priests from the city of Hebron.

Once inside the gates, the merchants continued towards the market square to set up their stands, whereas the hooded Stranger broke away from the group and made his way to the back alley streets which eventually lead down to the harbor.

As the man walked, he listened and watched intently to all the things around him. The creek of a door sounded ahead of him and a large man came stumbling out. The man wobbled a few steps and fell to his knees and retched upon the ground. The Stranger picked up the scent of strong ale and vomit. The drunken man tried to get up but failed in his attempt and landed face down in his own bile. The Stranger kept pace and stepped over him.

The Stranger heard a rustling sound to his right, accompanied by high pitched screeching. The man didn't need to even turn his head to know what that was. Rats rummaging in a trash heap.

After a few more steps, the Stranger noted the deep caws of a flock of crows call out in the distance, looking for their first meal for the day.

With each step the Stranger took, the shadows of night began to betray him more and more, and the exposure of the rising sun came closer and closer. He quickened his pace, hoping to reach his destination before the first rays of light broke over the horizon.

The Stranger noted that more and more of the sounds he heard were those of people. Folks were starting to come out of their homes to make their way to the local well or market for their day's food. The smell of freshly baked bread and cooked fish was beginning to waft through the air, reminding the Stranger he had not eaten for a few days now. He pushed the hunger pains aside as he knew there would be plenty of time for eating later.

After walking some distance at a quickened pace, the man was relieved to finally see the harbor at the southern end of the city. Although he had been there many times before, he had to stop and take in the view. The great waters of the Red Sea stretched out before him and the salty sea air made him breathe deep. Tall, thick palm trees littered the shores of the sea in all directions for leagues and leagues. There in the harbor were hundreds of small fishing boats docked around the east and west sides of the bay. On the northern end of the harbor, were the twelve majestic ships which would later in the day sail for Ophir, the land of gold.

The stranger scanned the vessels and noted the largest ship was the one in the middle. That would be the command ship, which was the Stranger's destination.

The cloaked man stealthily made his way to the shipping docks by staying to the waning shadows, making sure he was not seen. It was vital to him and his mission that no one see him boarding the boat.

Upon approaching the large vessel, the Stranger heard voices on the deck of the ship. He quickly hid behind some sacks of grain which were waiting to be loaded into the ship's cargo hold.

From the shadows of his hiding spot, the Stranger watched three armed men come down the ship's gangplank onto the dock. They were laughing and speaking in Phoenician. This caught the Stranger off guard for a moment, as he was not expecting to hear the foreign language in a Hebrew port. But then he remembered, it was King Huram's men who had built the ships. It only made sense, it would be some of King Huram's men to help sail them was well.

The Stranger waited for the men to leave, but after a short amount of time it became clear the Phoenicians were there to stay. The three men kept talking and laughing. The cloaked man sighed and shook his head. He was hoping he wouldn't have to use any violence to get on board. He really didn't want to draw any attention to himself or his mission, but, if there was no other way.

The Stranger was about to stand and draw his sword when a loud screech filled the air. He looked over to the far end of the dock and saw a large, white bird soaring in circles.

The man smiled and whispered to himself, "Clever bird."

The three guards looked up into the sky as the bird called out. Seeing the white object fly around in the darkened sky, they became curious and began to walk down the pier to get a better look. As the Phoenicians walked away, the Stranger stood and soundlessly walked to the gangplank and up onto the ship. He made his way to an open floor hatch which led to the cargo hold below.

The Stranger was about to drop down into the hold when the morning sun broke over the eastern horizon. The cloaked man immediately felt the heat of the sun flood into his cowl and bring warmth to his face. The sensation made him pause and it brought him a small sense of joy, a feeling he had not had for a long time. He closed his eyes and suddenly felt the urge to pull back his hood to feel the sun fully on his face and skin, but reason convinced him otherwise.

Once again, the Stranger was about to drop down into the hold below when something stopped him for a second time. It was something he heard, and it puzzled him.

In the distance, from the north end of the city, was the sound of a shofar, and not just one, but many. Hundreds of them. The Stranger listened intently to the tones they made. He raised an eyebrow when he deciphered the shofar's blasts. It was to announce the celebration of a wedding.

Who is getting married? Has the King of Israel taken a wife?

An emptiness flooded into the Stranger's heart.

He shook the feeling off as it reminded him of a past life. He took one more look at the rising sun, and then jumped down into the darkness of the hold.

Coming Soon

Book II

The Shadow of Death

GLOSSARY

Arnavon:	Large rabbit like creature
Bath:	9 gallons
Cubit:	Roughly 18 inches/1.5 feet, commonly measured from one's elbow to the tip of their middle finger.
El:	The one true God of all creation
Ezion-Geber:	A town that sits on the North tip of the Red Sea, place of Rachel's wedding and the departing point for the Ophir voyage.
Gehenna:	Israelites use this word to describe the eternal hell.
Handsbreadth:	3-6 inches
Harag:	Hebrew word for "kill"
Hazor:	A city north of Jerusalem, attacked by the masakh
Jehovah:	God
Kavash:	Hebrew word "to conquer"
Kor:	6.25 Bushels of dry material – 58 gallons of liquid
League:	3.5 miles
Maavac Krav:	Martial arts created by Aabaddon's father, Josheb.
Malakh:	Angel
Masakh:	Literal translation - monster

Pallet: Bed with a stuffed mattress of straw, grain or goose feathers.

Rhuse: Pain medicine made from the stalk of a poisonous plant

Season: Year

Sheol: Literal translation - grave. Term also used for the underworld or the place of the dead.

Shofar: Trumpet made from a ram's horn

Sicarrii: Personal guard and assassins to King Achish

Taanug: Name of the island Dagon used to build his army. Literal translation – pleasure.

Tsipor: Bird native to Israel

Yahweh: God, literally from "I AM" or the self-existing one